THREE KINGDOMS

Vol.
01

Three Kingdoms

Many centuries ago, China was made up of several provinces that frequently waged war with one another for regional supremacy. In 221 BC, the Qin Dynasty succeeded in uniting the warring provinces under a single banner, but the unity was short-lived, only lasting fifteen years. After the collapse of the Qin Dynasty, the Han Dynasty was established in 206 BC, and unity was restored. The Han Dynasty would last for hundreds of years, until the Post-Han Era, when the unified nation once again began to unravel. As rebellion and chaos gripped the land, three men came forward to take control of the nation: Bei Liu, Cao Cao, and Ce Sun. The three men each established separate kingdoms, Shu, Wei, and Wu, and for a century they contended for supremacy. This was known as the Age of the Three Kingdoms.

Written more than six hundred years ago, *Three Kingdoms* is one of the oldest and most seminal works in all of Eastern literature. An epic story spanning decades and featuring hundreds of characters, it remains a definitive tale of desperate heroism, political treachery, and the bonds of brotherhood.

Wei Dong Chen and Xiao Long Liang have chosen to draw this adaptation of *Three Kingdoms* in a manner reminiscent of the ancient Chinese printing technique. It is our hope that the historical look of *Three Kingdoms* will amplify the timelessness of its themes, which are just as relevant today as they were thousands of years ago.

THREE KINGDOMS
Vol. 01

Heroes and Chaos

Created by WEI DONG CHEN

Wei Dong Chen, a highly acclaimed and beloved artist, and an influential leader in the "New Chinese Cartoon" trend, is the founder of Creator World in Tianjin, the largest comics studio in China. Recently the Chinese government entrusted him with the role of general manager of the Beijing Book Fair, and his reputation as a pillar of Chinese comics has brought him many students. He has published more than three hundred cartoons, which have been recognized for their strong literary value not only in Korea, but in Europe and Japan, as well. Free spirited and energetic, Wei Dong Chen's positivist philosophy is reflected in the wisdom of his work. He is published serially in numerous publications while continuing to conceive projects that explore new dimensions of the form.

Illustrated by XIAO LONG LIANG

XiaoLong Liang is considered one of Wei Dong Chen's greatest students. One of the most highly regarded cartoonists in China today, XiaoLong's fantastic technique and expression of Chinese culture have won him the acclaim of cartoon lovers throughout China. His other works include "Outlaws of the Marsh" and w003"A Story on the Motorbike".

Original Story
"The Romance of the Three Kingdoms" by Luo, GuanZhong

Editing & Designing
Design Hongs, Jonathan Evans, KH Lee, YK Kim,
HJ Lee, JS Kim, Lampin, Qing Shao, Xiao Nan Li, Ke Hu

Original Chinese edition published by Anhui Fine Arts Publishing House.

Characters

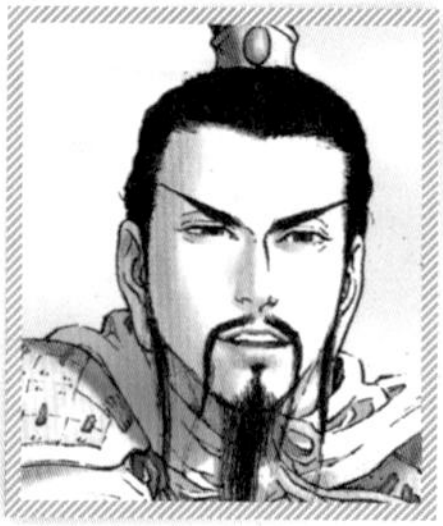

BEI LIU

Bei Liu is one of the main characters of *Three Kingdoms*. Although a descendant of the Han Dynasty, Bei Liu had lived a simple life selling shoes and mats in his rural homeland before swearing a blood oath to restore his nation. In 184 AD, Bei Liu helped Zhuo Dong defeat the Yellow Scarves, whose rebellion had torn the country apart. But Zhuo Dong dismissed Bei Liu and his brothers as simple peasants, and cast them out. Years later, when Zhuo Dong seizes power, Bei Liu joins the coalition army formed by 18 feudal lords to defeat Zhuo Dong. Bei Liu acts with tremendous valor during the struggle, and in 219 AD he becomes emperor of the Shu Kingdom.

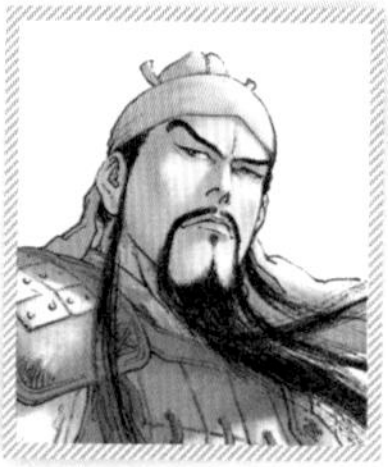

YU GUAN

Little is known of Yu Guan's birth. What is known is that he was forced to flee his hometown after killing a local tyrant. While wandering the countryside, he received word of Bei Liu's efforts to raise an army. He joined the effort, and swore a blood oath of brotherhood with Bei Liu and Fei Zhang. A tall man with a long beard and a legendary sword, Yu Guan is considered the embodiment of loyalty and fidelity, and is deified in Chinese culture.

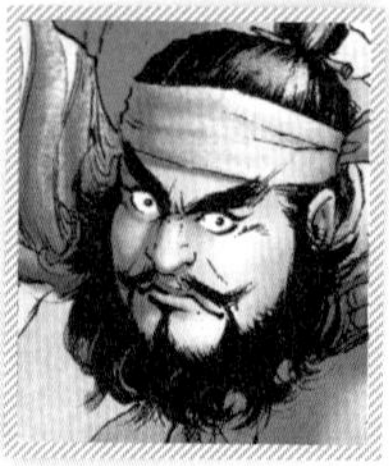

FEI ZHANG

Fei Zhang is the youngest and most volatile of the three blood brothers. He enjoys eating, drinking, and fighting. Despite his temperament, Fei Zhang is a valuable ally who can take on an army single-handedly.

ZHUO DONG

Zhuo Dong began his career as a regional general in the military of the Han Dynasty, but he was able to expand and consolidate his power during the long years of battle against the Yellow Scarves. In AD 189, Zhuo Dong was summoned to the capital city of LuoYang and asked to rid the city of eunuchs. Along the way he encountered the emperor and his younger brother, who had fled the city. Upon entering the city with the two members of the royal family, Zhuo Dong ordered the emperor killed and the crown given to the weak sibling. This allowed Zhuo Dong to assume total control of the kingdom.

BU LU

Bu Lu was the greatest and most feared warrior in ancient China. Though he has sworn his allegiance to Zhuo Dong, Bu Lu is known to be loyal only to himself, and it is believed that he has killed two father figures in his life. Sure enough, Bu Lu is soon caught up in the race to usurp Zhuo Dong's power, a choice that will have severe consequences.

RU LI

Ru Li is Zhuo Dong's son-in-law, and serves as his most trusted advisor. Ru Li's counsel often prevents Zhuo Dong from succumbing to his destructive impulses. As a result, Zhuo Dong is able to retain his power for far longer than expected.

SHAO YUAN

Shao Yuan was born into nobility during the Han Dynasty, and his ambition matches his pedigree. After working with the royal family to battle the eunuchs during the Yellow Scarf Rebellion, he fled LuoYang just before Zhuo Dong seized control. He assumes leadership of the coalition army formed by the 18 feudal lords, but soon the unity is shattered, and Shao Yuan sets out to conquer Ji Province.

SHU YUAN

Shu Yuan is Shao Yuan's younger brother. Although he does not command the coalition army, he is often maligned by the other commanders for failing to send adequate supplies to the soldiers in the field. Though his allegiance is to his older brother, Shu Yuan harbors his own ambitions, which may one day put the two at odds.

JIAN SUN

Jian Sun is one of the 18 feudal lords who form the coalition army. He led the coalition forces in the first battle against Zhuo Dong's army, but was defeated when much-needed supplies for his men never arrived. After Zhuo Dong aban-dons LuoYang and sets fire to the capital, Jian Sun leads the effort to save the city, which leads to his discovery of a precious item that will change his fate.

ZAN GONGSUN

Zan GongSun is another of the 18 feudal lords who helped to form the coalition army. He and Bei Liu shared a mentor, and the two consider each other brothers. After the coalition army falls apart, Zan GongSun does battle with Shao Yuan over the Ji Province. When the battle turns against him, Zan GongSun reaches out to Bei Liu for help.

CAO CAO

Cao Cao is one of the main characters of *Three Kingdoms*. Cao Cao was a highly decorated commander during the Yellow Scarf Rebellion, and after Zhuo Dong seized power, he joined forces with 17 other feudal lords to form the coalition army. When the alliance begins to crumble, Cao Cao takes it upon himself to chase down Zhuo Dong, which leads to a confrontation with Bu Lu.

Chapter 1

A World of Chaos
and the Oath of the Peach Garden AD 184–189

Summary

For centuries, China was divided into many kingdoms. These kingdoms fought often for supremacy of land and resources, which meant that various rulers gained and lost power with alarming frequency. It wasn't until 221 BC that the imperial reign of the Qin Dynasty brought together the various warring territories under the banner of a unified nation. But the Qin Dynasty lasted a mere fifteen years before collapsing, after which Bang Liu established the Han Dynasty.

Our story begins toward the end of the Han Dynasty, when centuries of rule has given rise to corruption, greed, and cruelty. After years of enduring poverty, drought, and famine, the people of the Han Dynasty begin revolting throughout the land. The most powerful of these rebellions is led by the Yellow Scarves, who provoke the masses into attacking the royal forces, leading to a series of defeats for the empire.

During this time, Bei Liu, Yu Guan, and Fei Zhang, three men without official rank or title who are nonetheless brilliant fighters, take a blood oath in a peach garden, swearing fidelity to one another and pledging to restore the greatness of their nation. They come to the rescue of General Zhuo Dong, who is being ambushed by Yellow Scarves. The general treats the three brothers like peasants, and they leave. Afterward, Zhuo Dong becomes more powerful until one day he enters the city of LuoYang with an army of 200,000, executes the emperor, and installs a new, weaker emperor. This makes Zhuo Dong the most powerful man in the world.

Zhuo
B
XiLiang
ChangShan
A
BeiHai
PuYang
XiaoPei
HuLuo
ChangAn
LuoYang
GuanDu
XiaPi
XuChang
XuZhou
HanZhong
NanYang
ShouChun
HeFei
XiangYang
ChengDu
CHINA

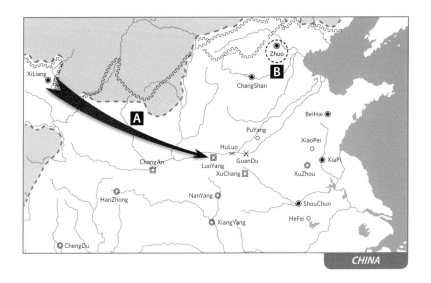

A Zhuo Dong Enters LuoYang

Zhuo Dong, a regional general of the Han Dynasty, gains power until he becomes the most powerful man in the northwest region. He is summoned to the city of LuoYang and asked to drive the eunuchs from the city. Instead he kills the emperor, installs a new one, and takes control of the kingdom.

***Eunuch**: low-level servants to the royal court who often form close relationships with the emperor and various officials, and take bribery for the influence. Their influence leads to the widespread corruption that causes the rebellion.

B Bei Liu Appears

Bei Liu is a common, but ambitious, citizen who sells shoes and mats for a living. When the Yellow Scarf Rebellion breaks out, he tries to raise a volunteer army that will bring an end to the war.

Bei Liu pledges his brotherhood to Yu Guan and Fei Zhang by taking a blood oath of fidelity in which the three men commit themselves to one another and the cause of fighting for their nation. This comes to be known as the Oath of the Peach Garden, one of the earliest and most legendary blood oaths ever taken.

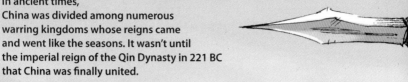

In ancient times,
China was divided among numerous warring kingdoms whose reigns came and went like the seasons. It wasn't until the imperial reign of the Qin Dynasty in 221 BC that China was finally united.

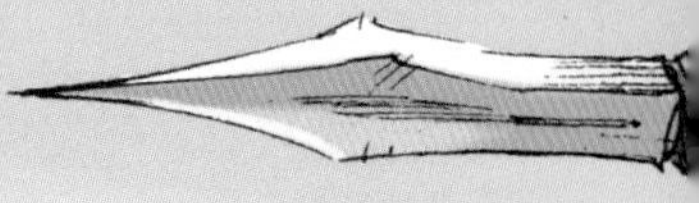

But time erodes everything, and despite numerous achievements, the Qin Dynasty lost control of the land and gave way to the Han Dynasty, led by Bang Liu, in 206 BC. Thus, a mere fifteen years after the Qin Dynasty first came to power, China was once again united under a single banner.

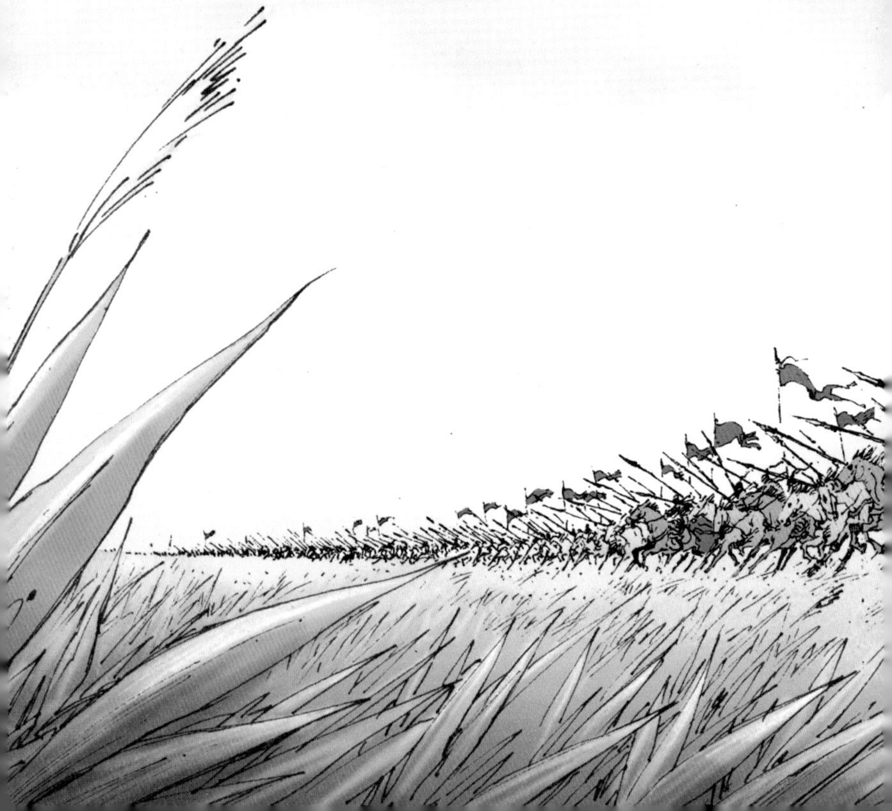

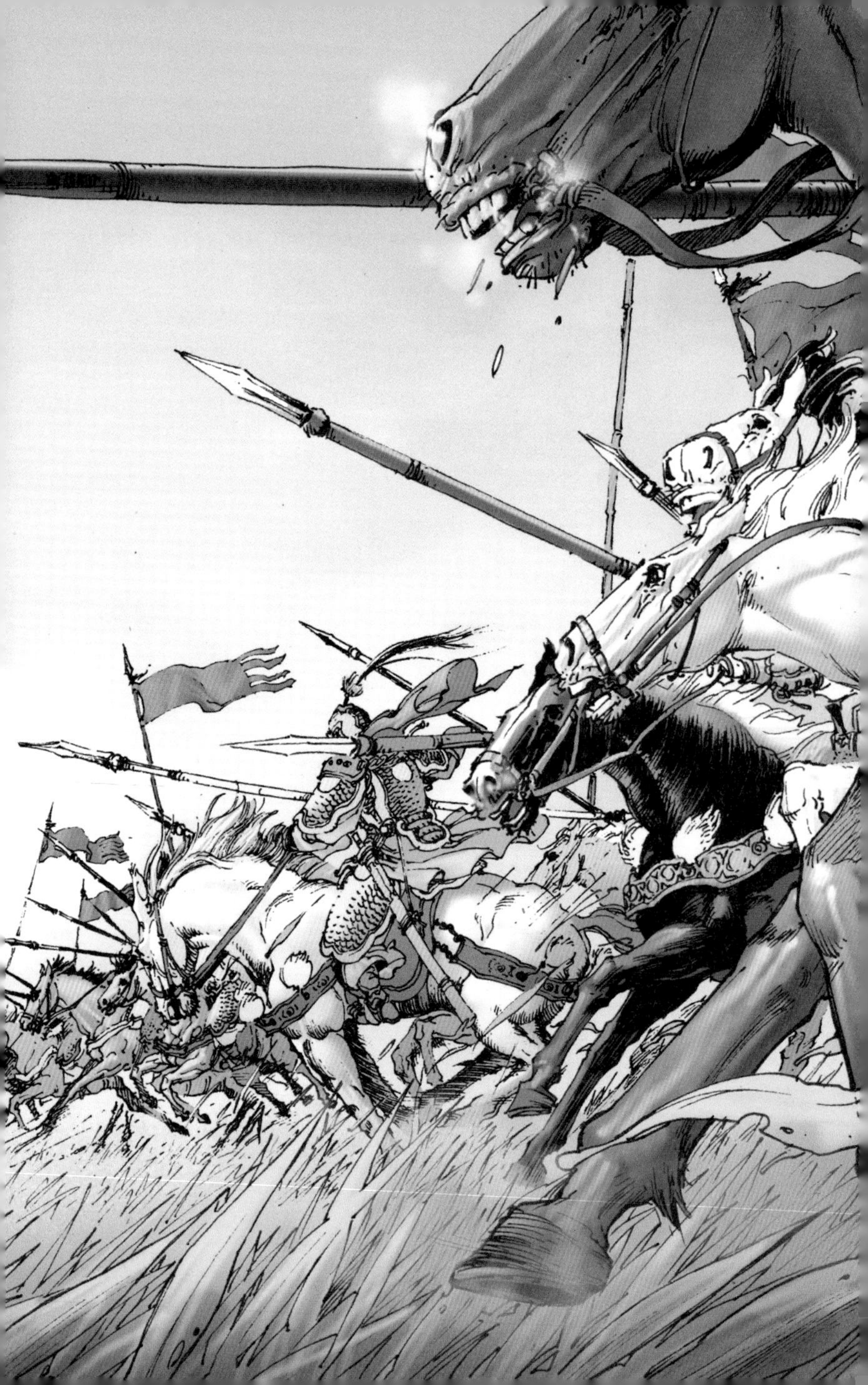

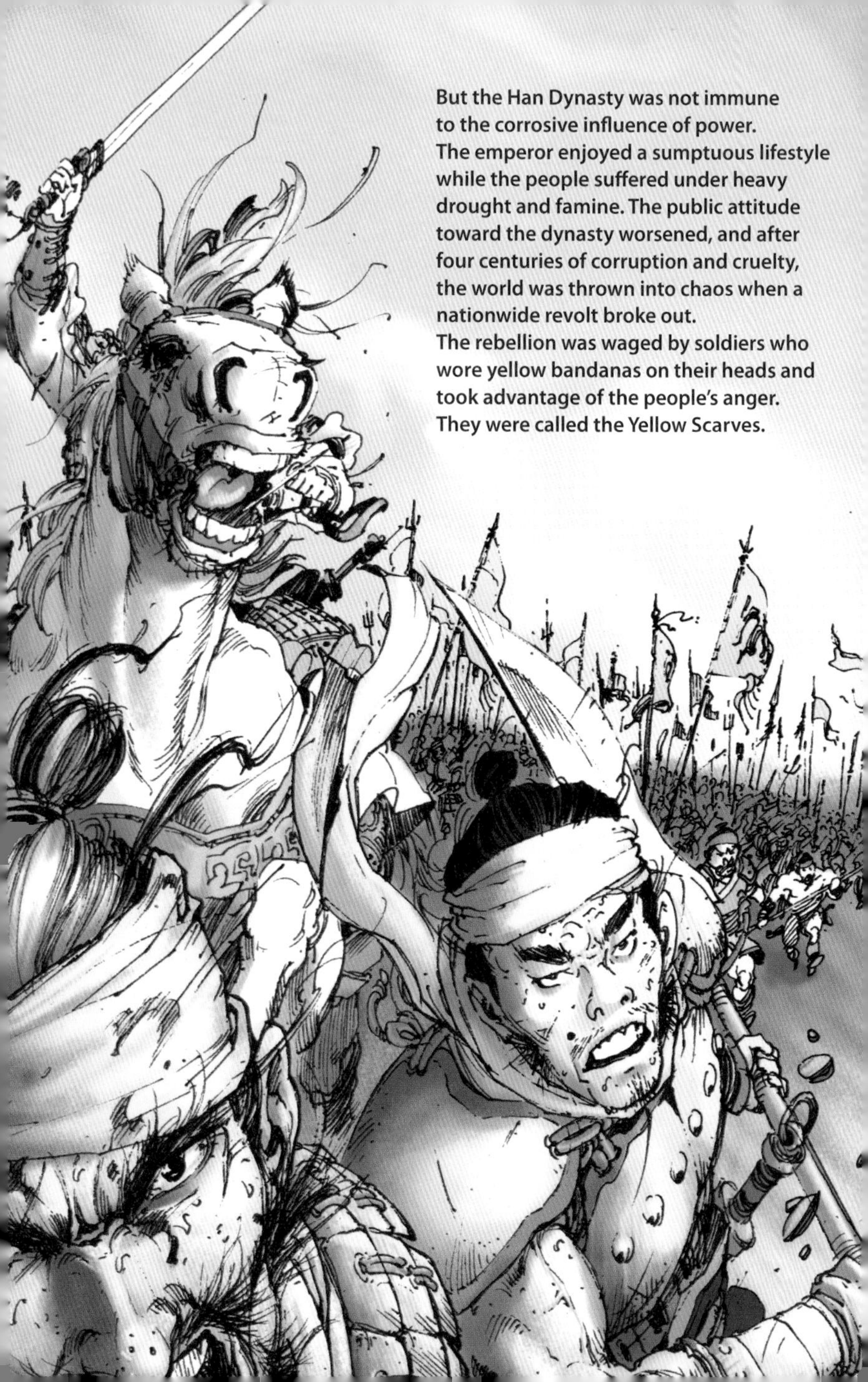
But the Han Dynasty was not immune
to the corrosive influence of power.
The emperor enjoyed a sumptuous lifestyle
while the people suffered under heavy
drought and famine. The public attitude
toward the dynasty worsened, and after
four centuries of corruption and cruelty,
the world was thrown into chaos when a
nationwide revolt broke out.
The rebellion was waged by soldiers who
wore yellow bandanas on their heads and
took advantage of the people's anger.
They were called the Yellow Scarves.

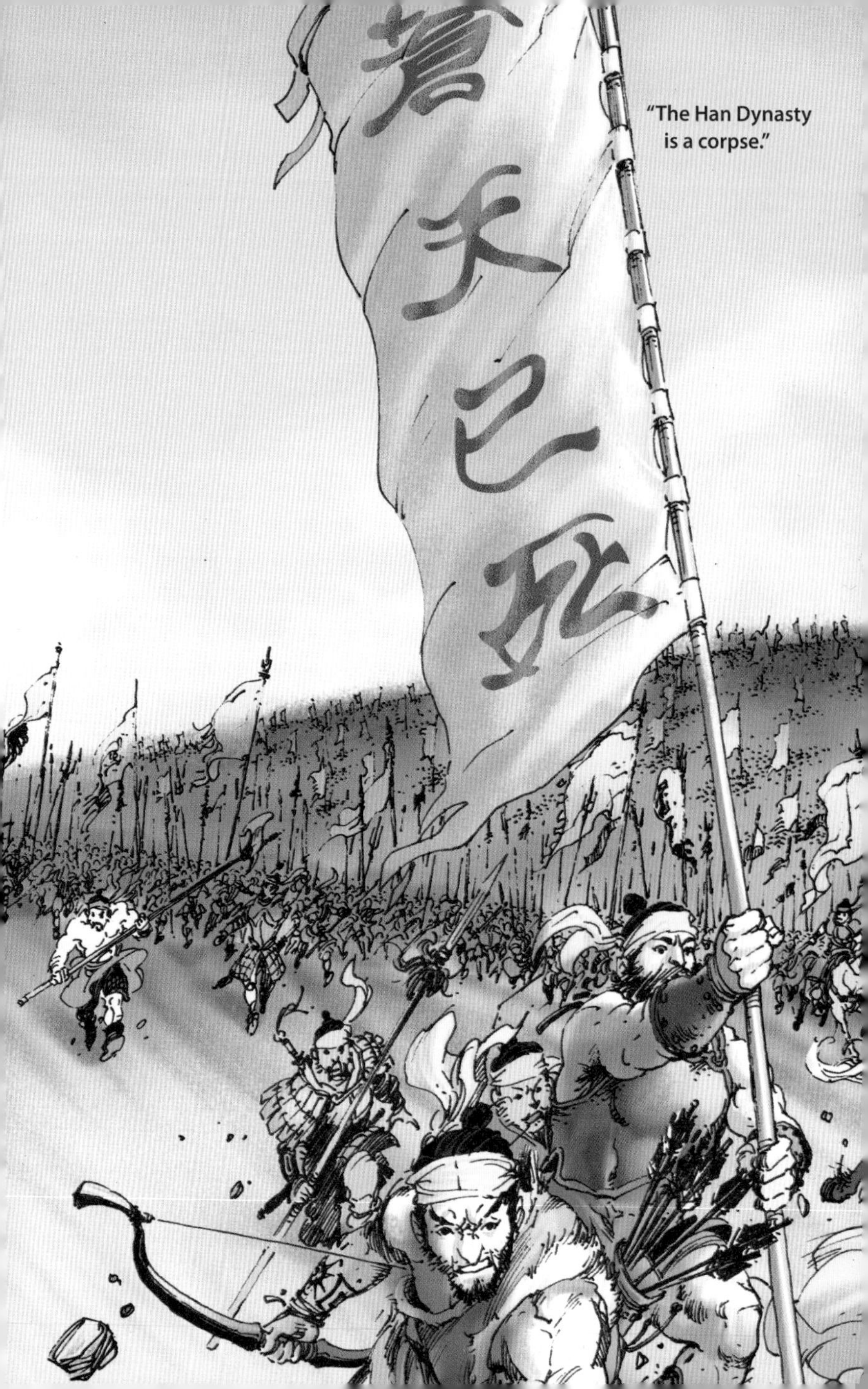
蒼天已死
"The Han Dynasty is a corpse."

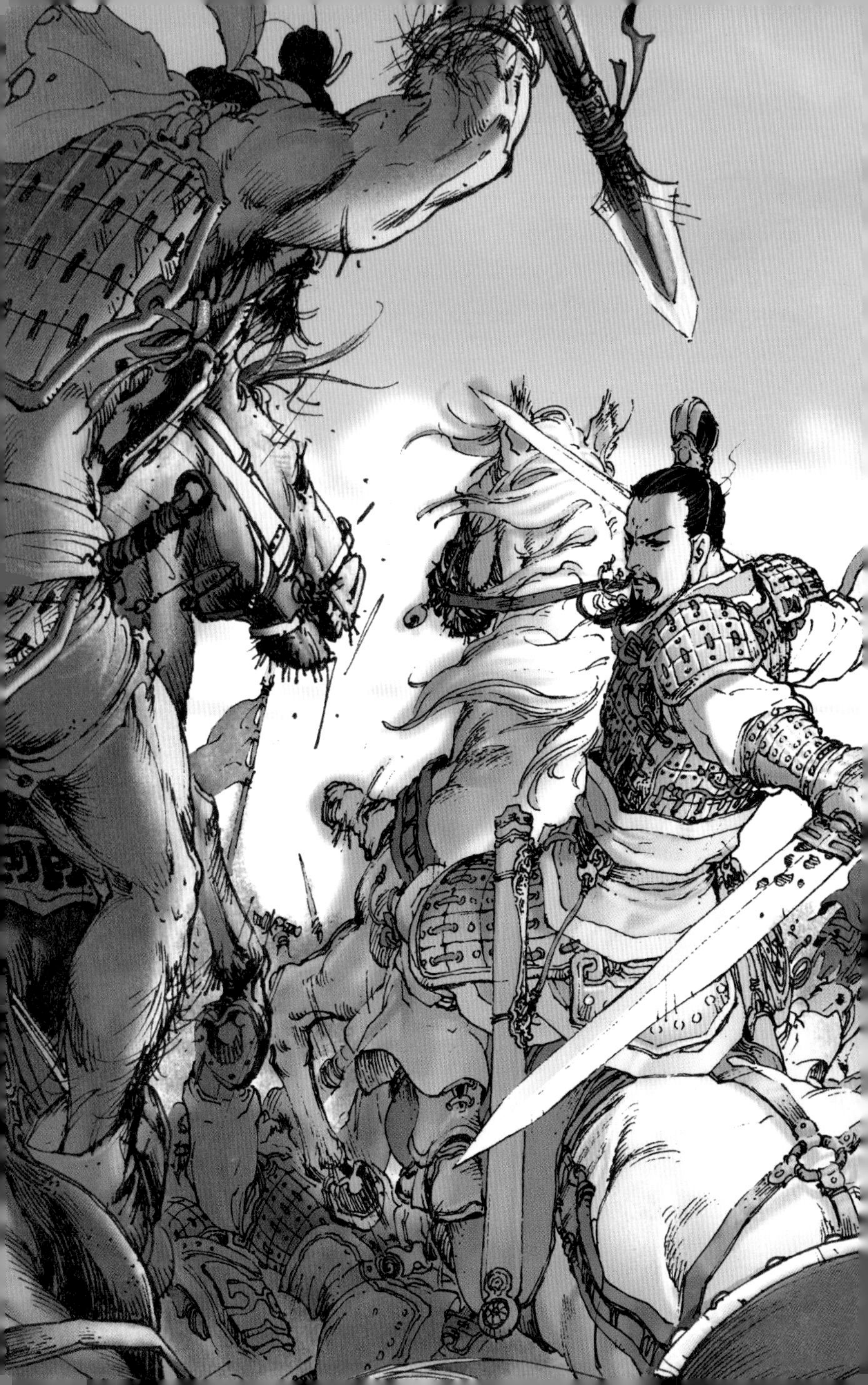

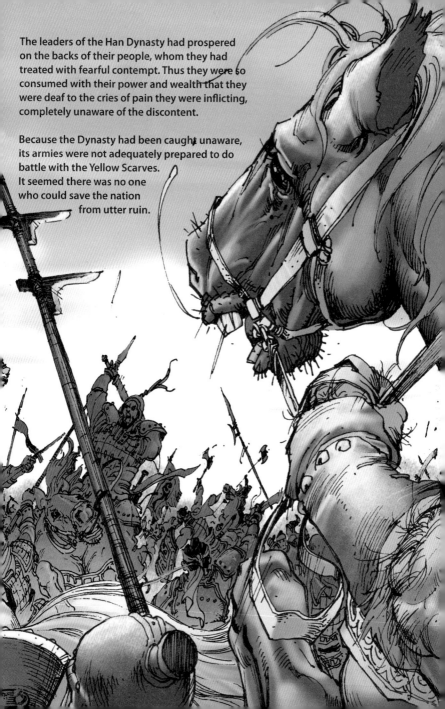

The leaders of the Han Dynasty had prospered on the backs of their people, whom they had treated with fearful contempt. Thus they were so consumed with their power and wealth that they were deaf to the cries of pain they were inflicting, completely unaware of the discontent.

Because the Dynasty had been caught unaware, its armies were not adequately prepared to do battle with the Yellow Scarves. It seemed there was no one who could save the nation from utter ruin.

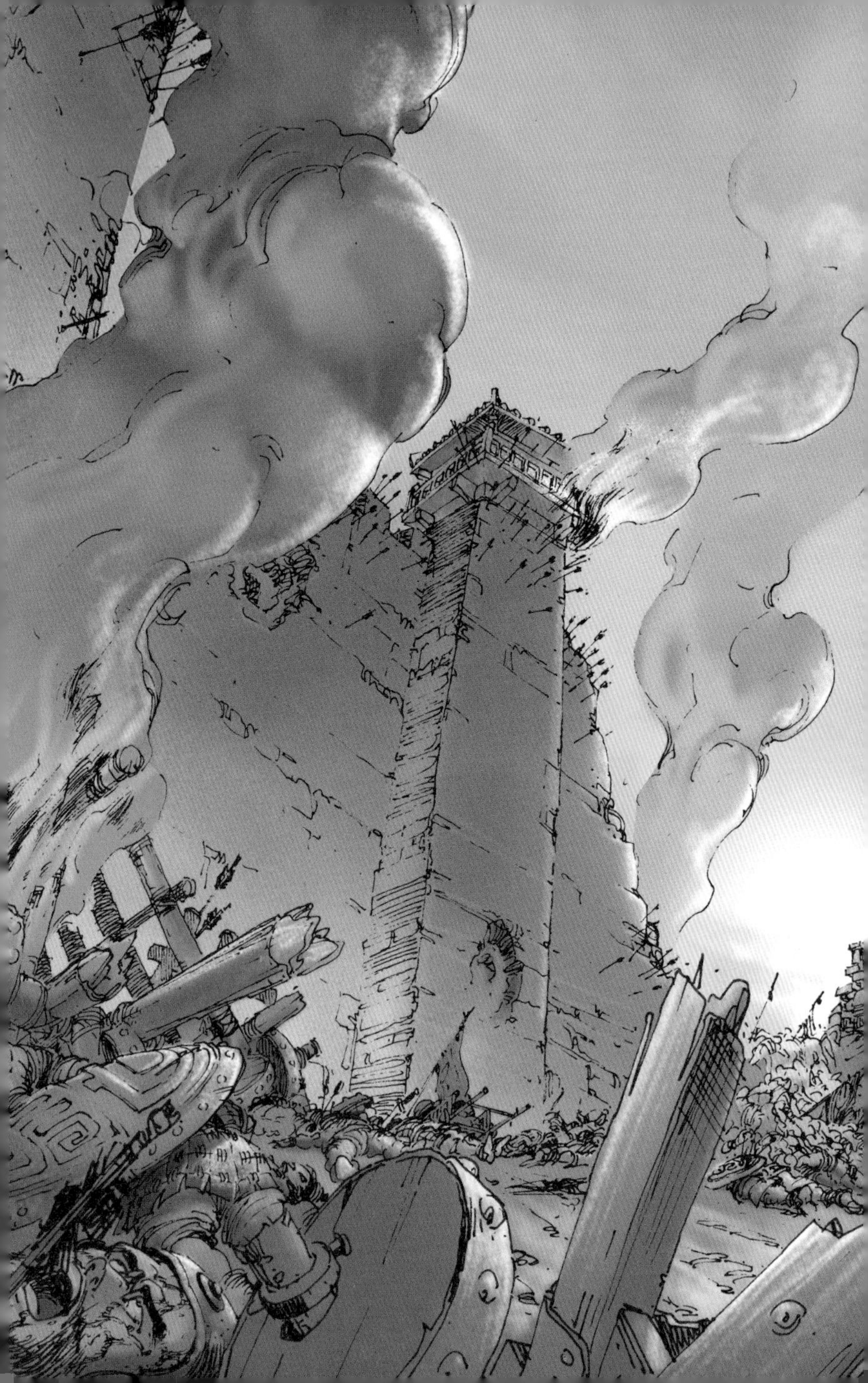

Palaces were reduced to rubble and the landscape was strewn with bodies. The rivers ran red with blood and the world was filled with sights so horrible they have never been put into words.

But from the depths of this abyss, three heroes would rise. Their names were Bei Liu, Yu Guan, and Fei Zhang. They pledged to bring an end to the discord and restore their nation to its former glory.

The three men became blood brothers, then went about the business of saving the world.

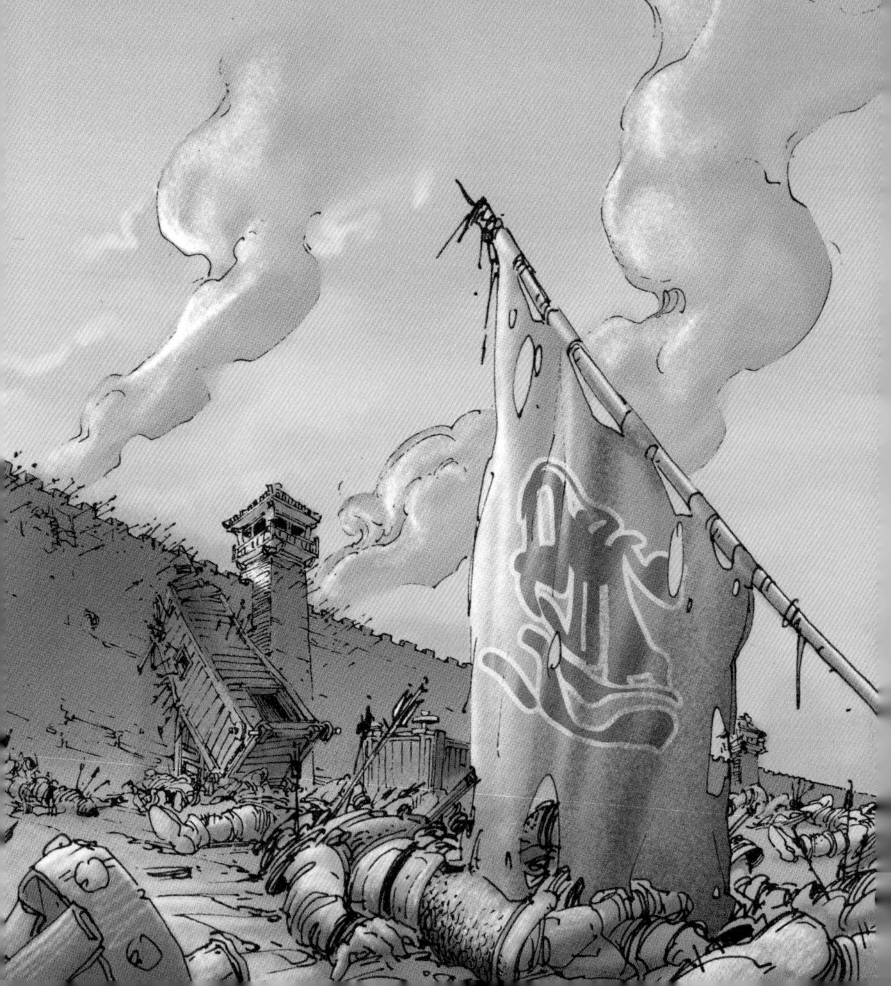

THE OATH OF THE PEACH GARDEN (AD 184)

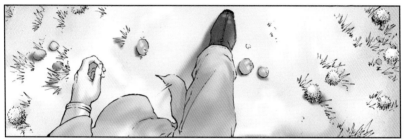

HA HA!

HURRY UP, SLOW POKE!

YOU'LL NEVER MAKE IT!

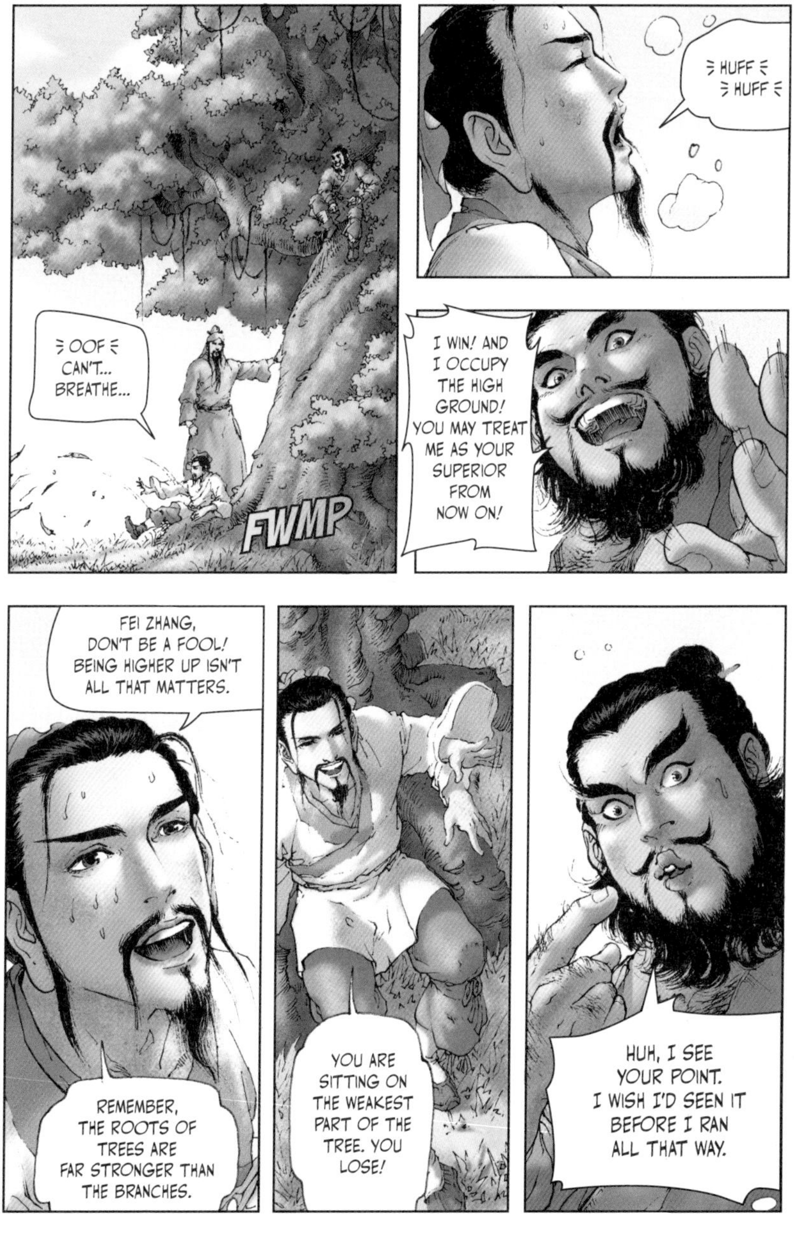
≡ OOF ≡ CAN'T... BREATHE...
FWMP
≡ HUFF ≡ ≡ HUFF ≡
I WIN! AND I OCCUPY THE HIGH GROUND! YOU MAY TREAT ME AS YOUR SUPERIOR FROM NOW ON!
FEI ZHANG, DON'T BE A FOOL! BEING HIGHER UP ISN'T ALL THAT MATTERS.
REMEMBER, THE ROOTS OF TREES ARE FAR STRONGER THAN THE BRANCHES.
YOU ARE SITTING ON THE WEAKEST PART OF THE TREE. YOU LOSE!
HUH, I SEE YOUR POINT. I WISH I'D SEEN IT BEFORE I RAN ALL THAT WAY.

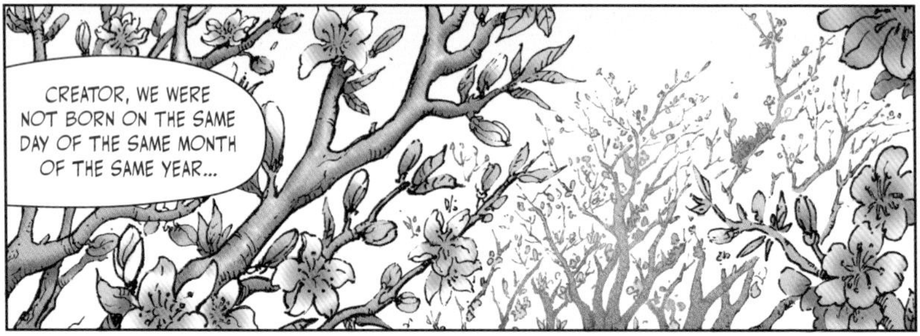
CREATOR, WE WERE NOT BORN ON THE SAME DAY OF THE SAME MONTH OF THE SAME YEAR...

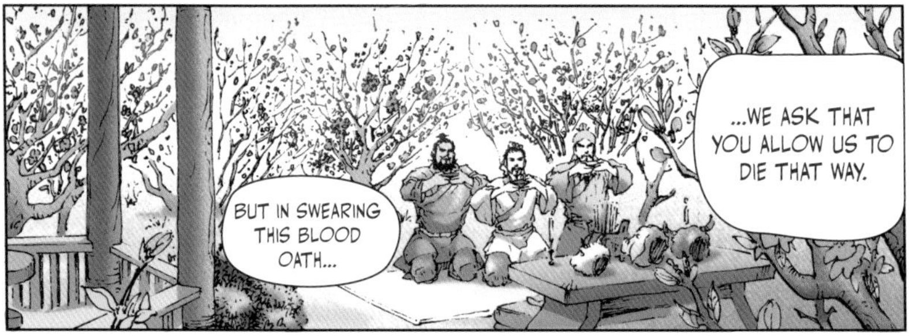
BUT IN SWEARING THIS BLOOD OATH...
...WE ASK THAT YOU ALLOW US TO DIE THAT WAY.

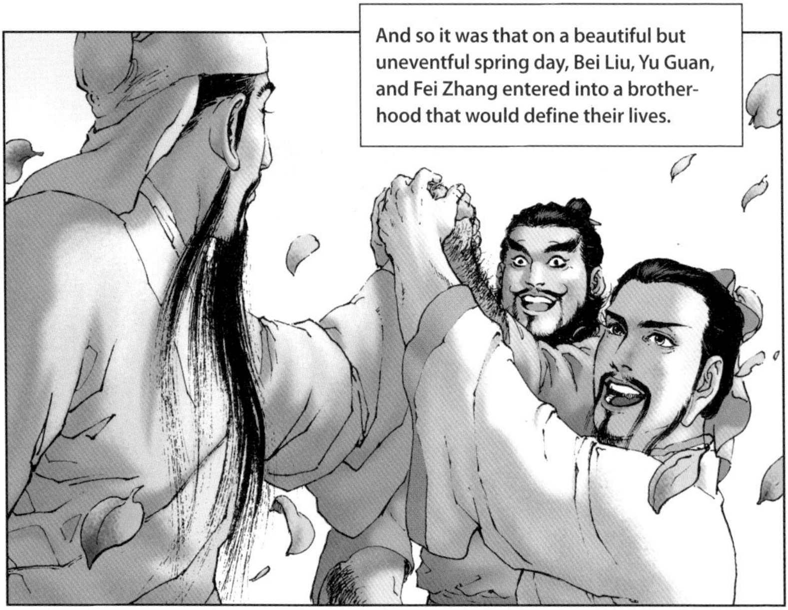
And so it was that on a beautiful but uneventful spring day, Bei Liu, Yu Guan, and Fei Zhang entered into a brotherhood that would define their lives.

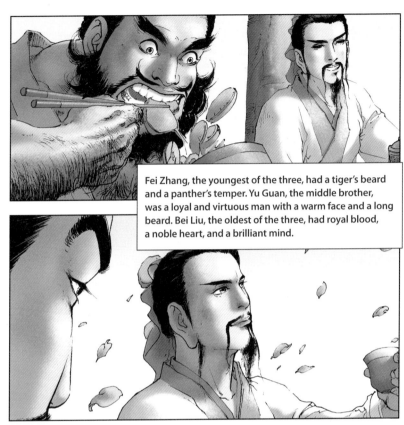

Fei Zhang, the youngest of the three, had a tiger's beard and a panther's temper. Yu Guan, the middle brother, was a loyal and virtuous man with a warm face and a long beard. Bei Liu, the oldest of the three, had royal blood, a noble heart, and a brilliant mind.

Not every band of brothers forms in the furnace of war. For three of history's greatest warriors, the path to glory began with a sacred oath taken in a peach garden.

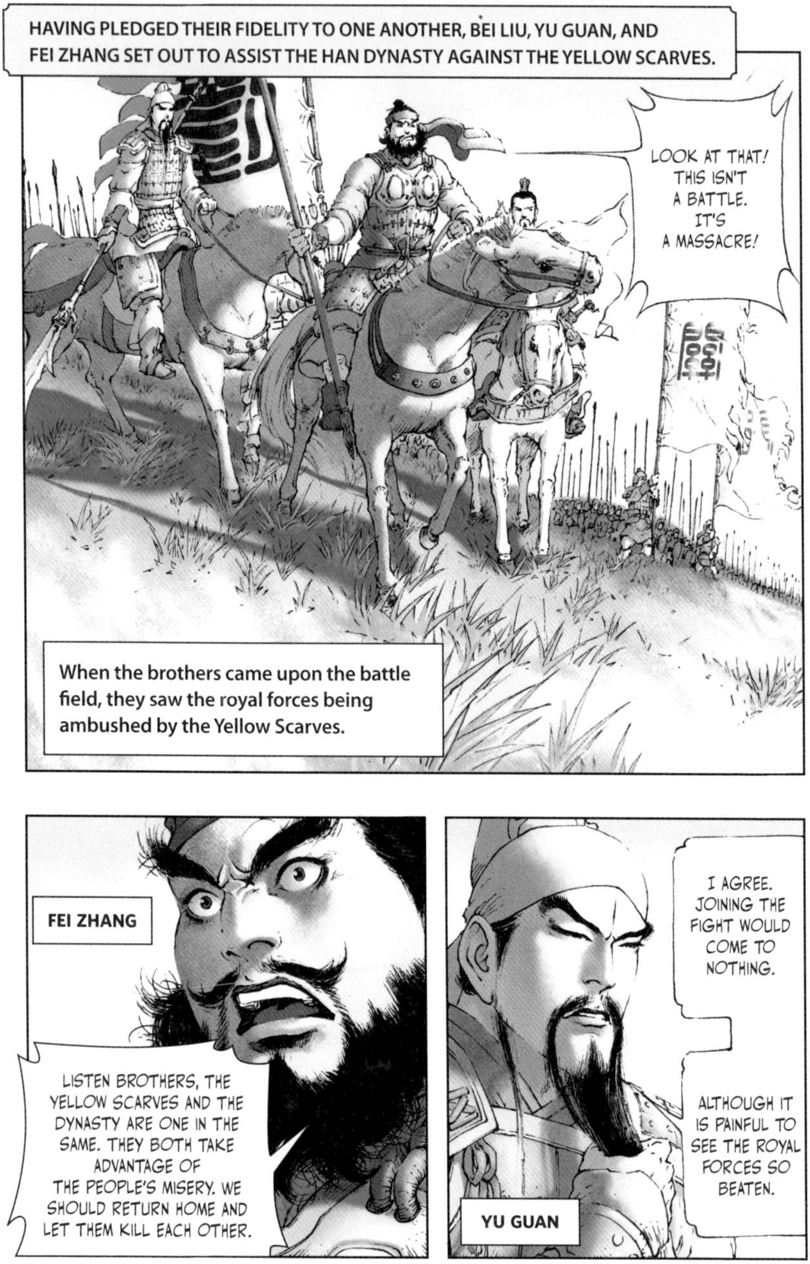
HAVING PLEDGED THEIR FIDELITY TO ONE ANOTHER, BEI LIU, YU GUAN, AND FEI ZHANG SET OUT TO ASSIST THE HAN DYNASTY AGAINST THE YELLOW SCARVES.
LOOK AT THAT! THIS ISN'T A BATTLE. IT'S A MASSACRE!
When the brothers came upon the battle field, they saw the royal forces being ambushed by the Yellow Scarves.
FEI ZHANG
LISTEN BROTHERS, THE YELLOW SCARVES AND THE DYNASTY ARE ONE IN THE SAME. THEY BOTH TAKE ADVANTAGE OF THE PEOPLE'S MISERY. WE SHOULD RETURN HOME AND LET THEM KILL EACH OTHER.
I AGREE. JOINING THE FIGHT WOULD COME TO NOTHING.
ALTHOUGH IT IS PAINFUL TO SEE THE ROYAL FORCES SO BEATEN.
YU GUAN

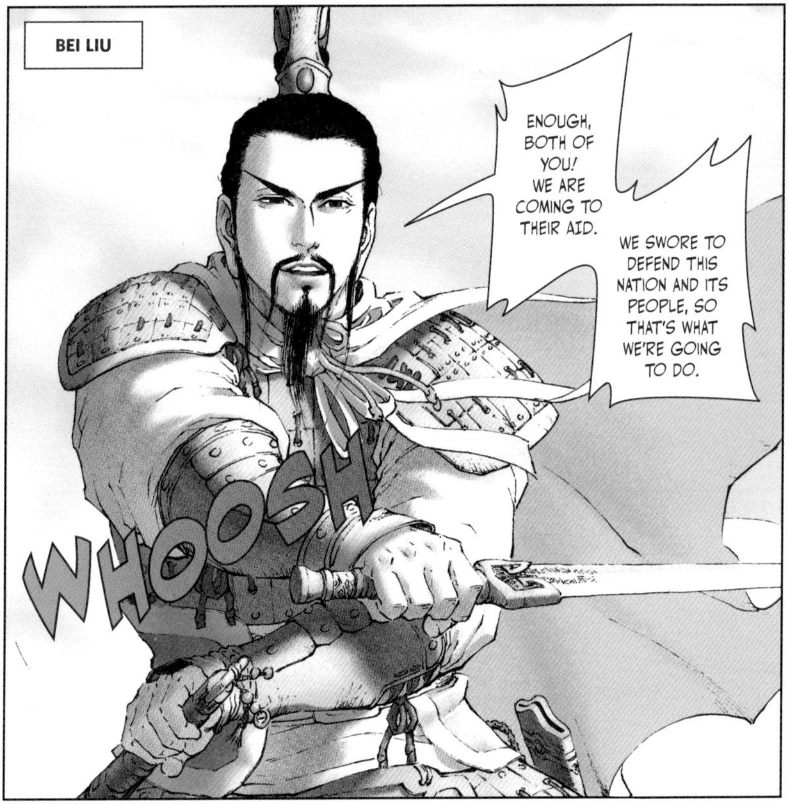
BEI LIU
ENOUGH, BOTH OF YOU! WE ARE COMING TO THEIR AID.
WE SWORE TO DEFEND THIS NATION AND ITS PEOPLE, SO THAT'S WHAT WE'RE GOING TO DO.
WHOOSH

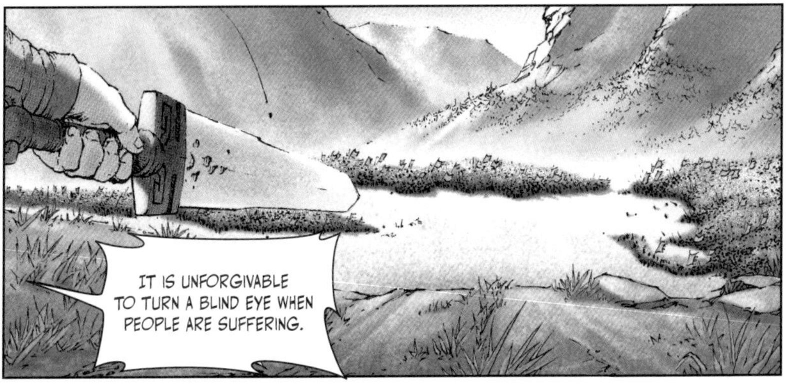
IT IS UNFORGIVABLE TO TURN A BLIND EYE WHEN PEOPLE ARE SUFFERING.

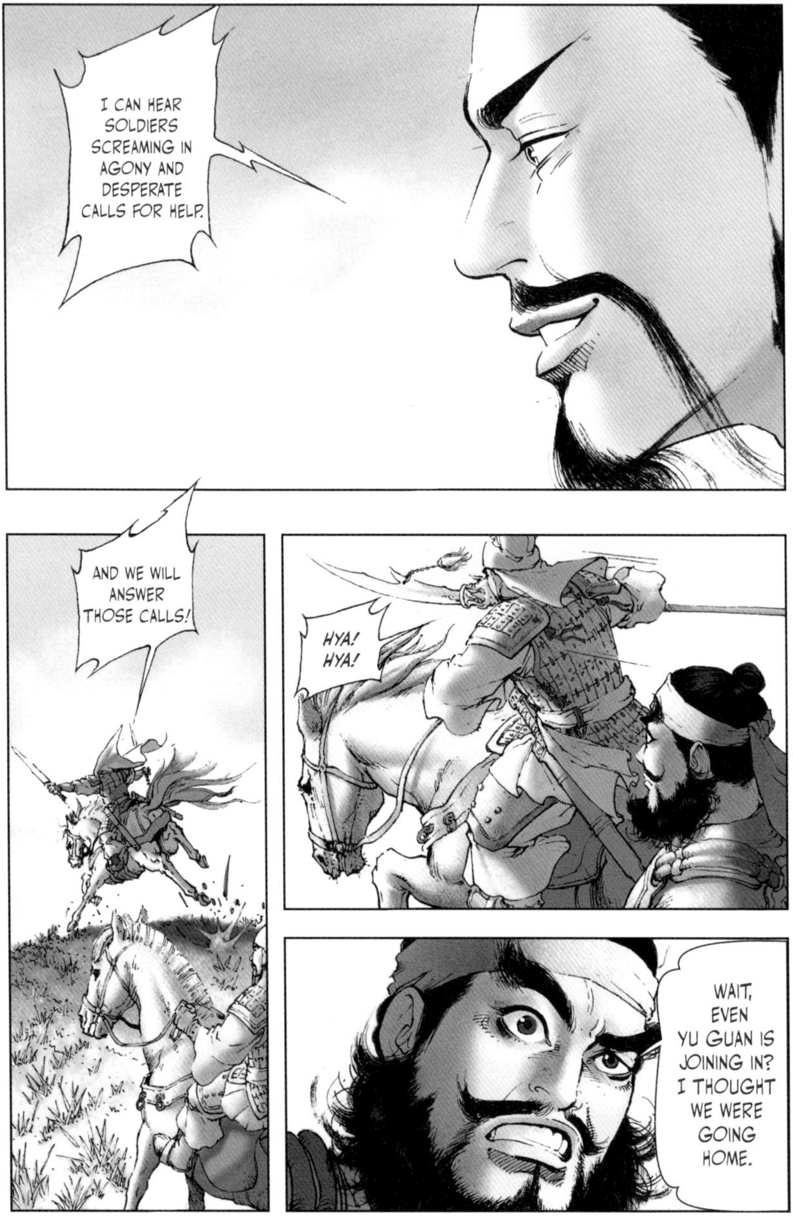
I CAN HEAR SOLDIERS SCREAMING IN AGONY AND DESPERATE CALLS FOR HELP.
AND WE WILL ANSWER THOSE CALLS!
HYA! HYA!
WAIT, EVEN YU GUAN IS JOINING IN? I THOUGHT WE WERE GOING HOME.

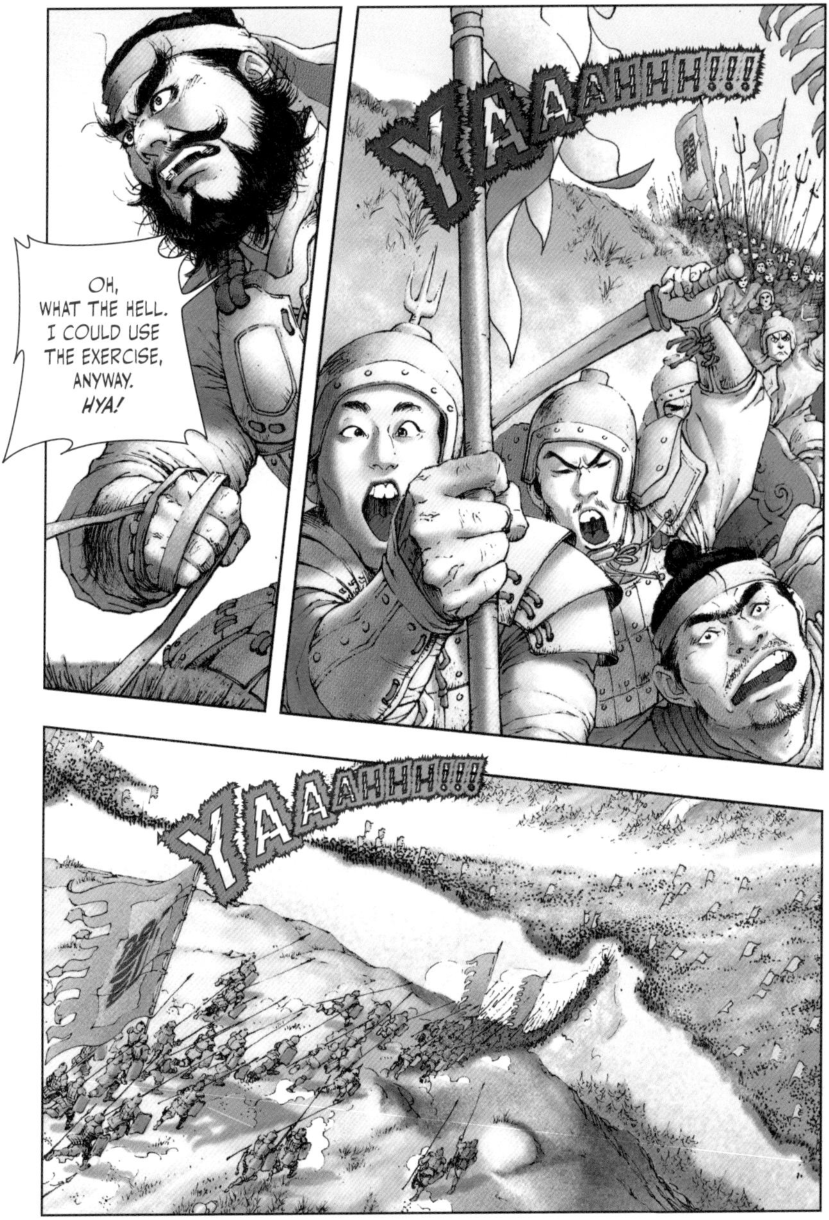
OH, WHAT THE HELL. I COULD USE THE EXERCISE, ANYWAY. *HYA!*
YAAAHHH!!!
YAAAHHH!!!

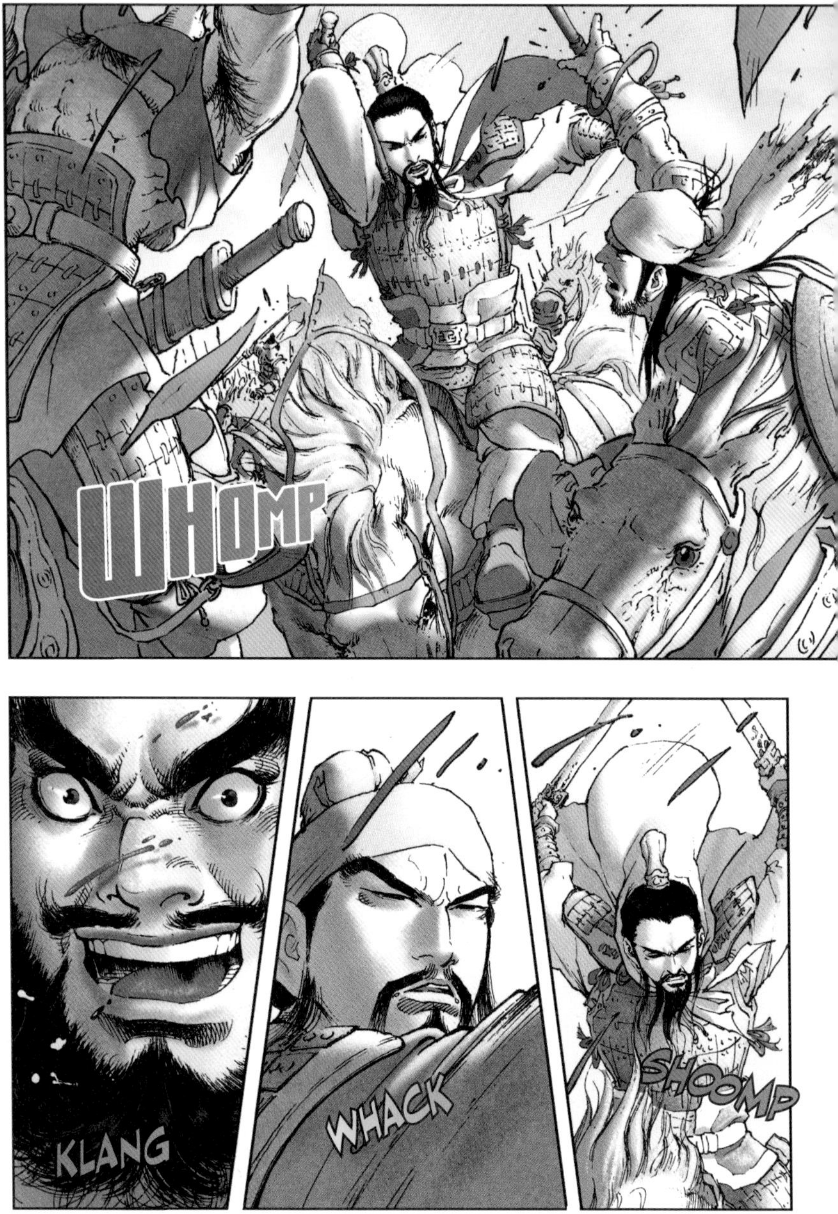
WHOMP
KLANG
WHACK
SHOOMP

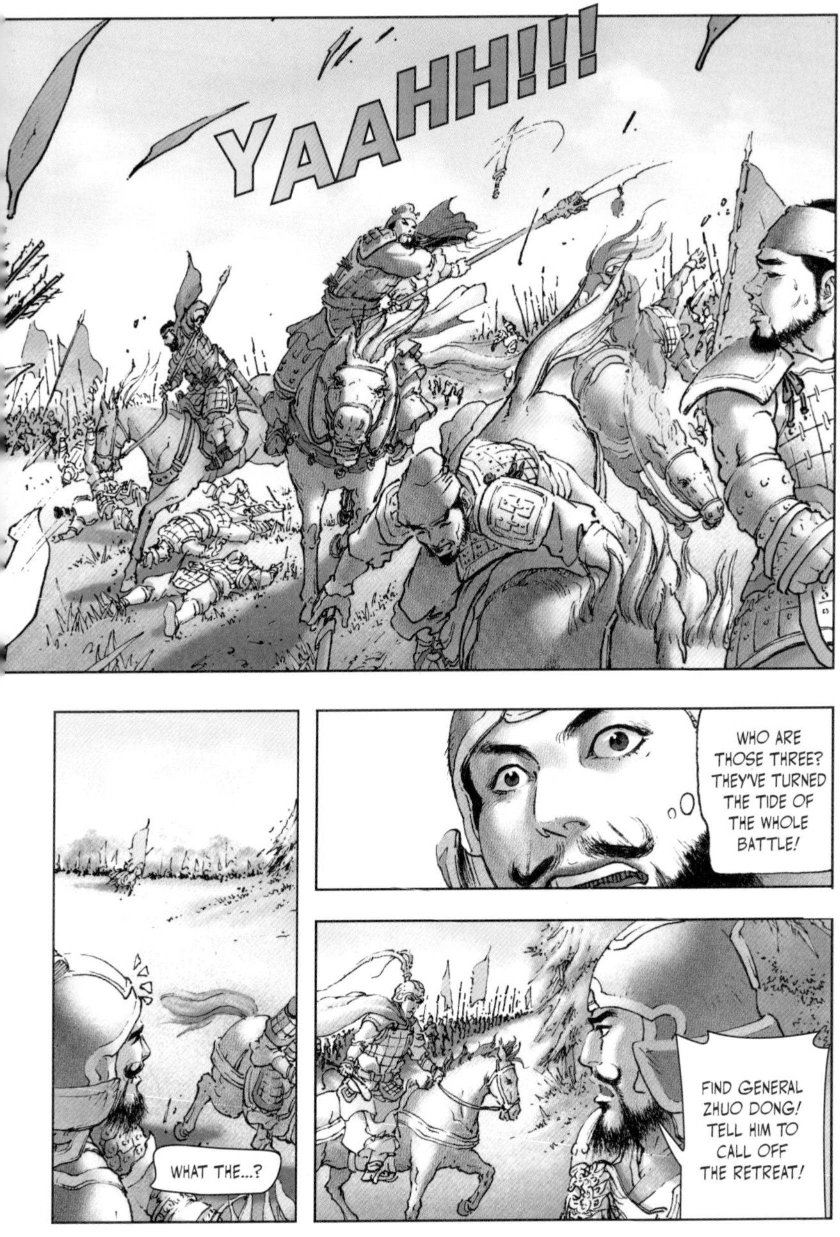
YAAHH!!!
WHO ARE THOSE THREE? THEY'VE TURNED THE TIDE OF THE WHOLE BATTLE!
WHAT THE...?
FIND GENERAL ZHUO DONG! TELL HIM TO CALL OFF THE RETREAT!

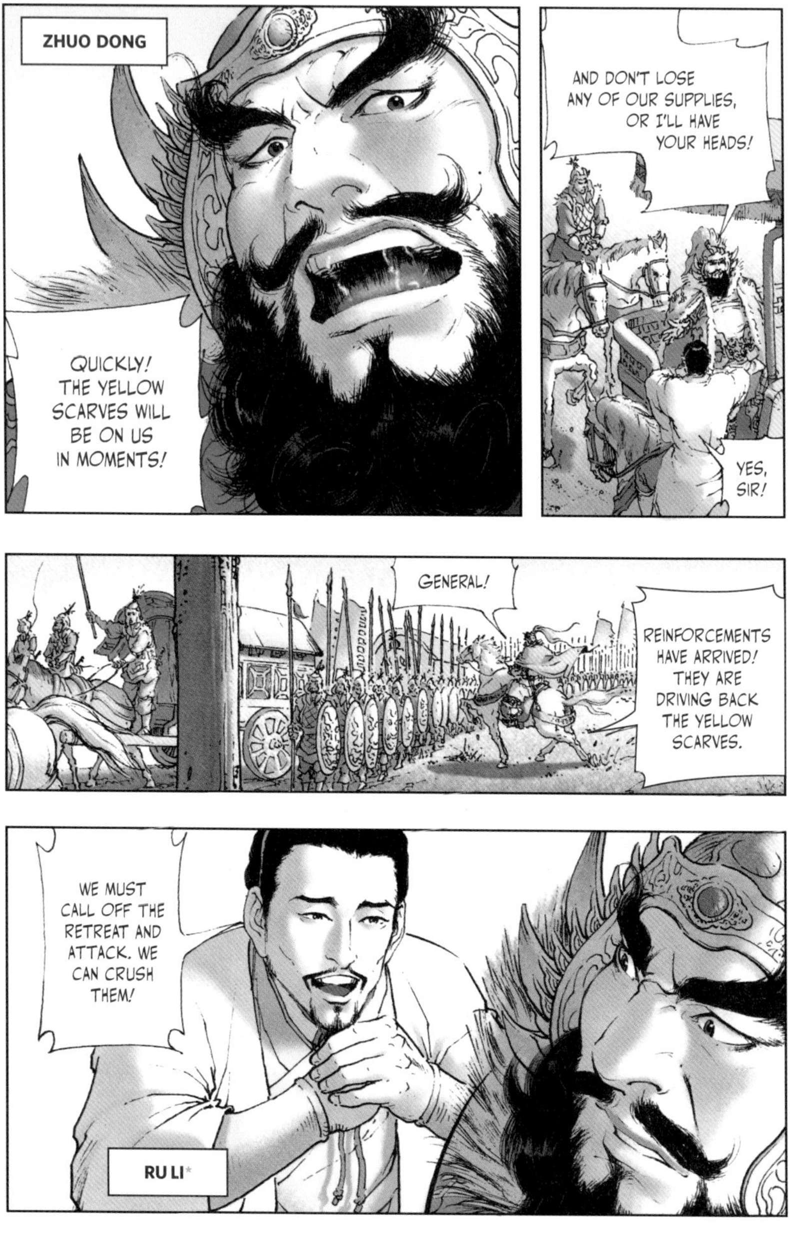
ZHUO DONG
QUICKLY! THE YELLOW SCARVES WILL BE ON US IN MOMENTS!
AND DON'T LOSE ANY OF OUR SUPPLIES, OR I'LL HAVE YOUR HEADS!
YES, SIR!
GENERAL!
REINFORCEMENTS HAVE ARRIVED! THEY ARE DRIVING BACK THE YELLOW SCARVES.
WE MUST CALL OFF THE RETREAT AND ATTACK. WE CAN CRUSH THEM!
RU LI*

* Zhuo Dong's son-in-law and a military strategist

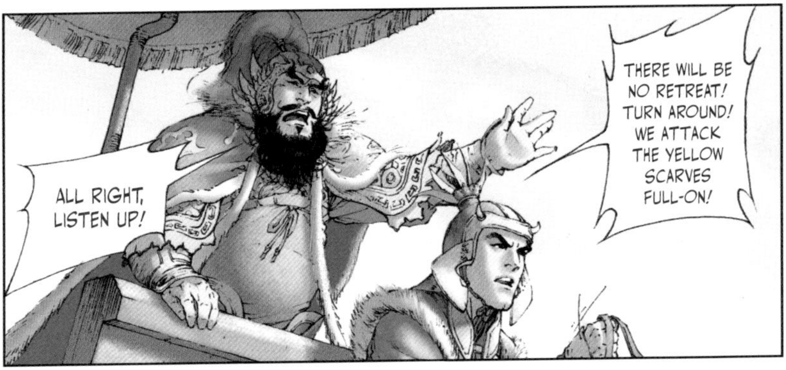
ALL RIGHT, LISTEN UP!
THERE WILL BE NO RETREAT! TURN AROUND! WE ATTACK THE YELLOW SCARVES FULL-ON!

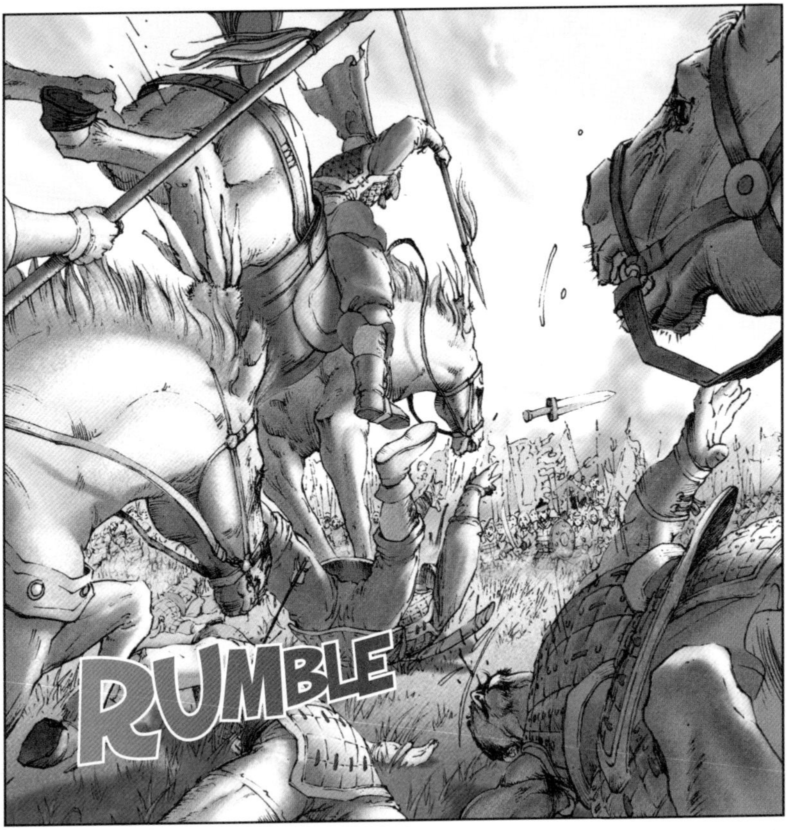
RUMBLE

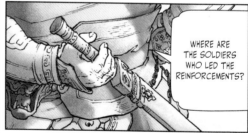

WHERE ARE THE SOLDIERS WHO LED THE REINFORCEMENTS?

AH... IT'S BEEN A WHILE SINCE I'VE SWUNG MY SWORD. VERY SATISFYING!

SHOONK

I SAW THEM ATTACKING FROM THE LEFT FLANK BEFORE WITHDRAWING.

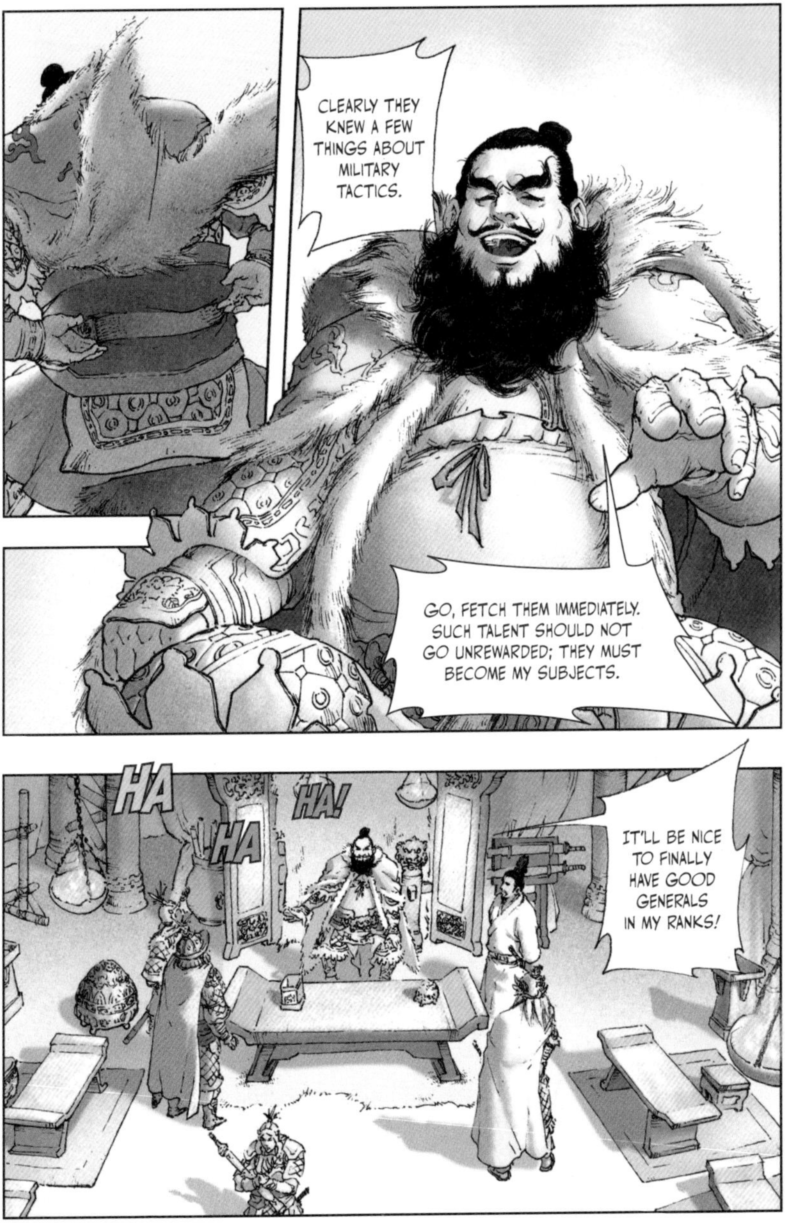
CLEARLY THEY KNEW A FEW THINGS ABOUT MILITARY TACTICS.
GO, FETCH THEM IMMEDIATELY. SUCH TALENT SHOULD NOT GO UNREWARDED; THEY MUST BECOME MY SUBJECTS.
HA
HA
HA!
IT'LL BE NICE TO FINALLY HAVE GOOD GENERALS IN MY RANKS!

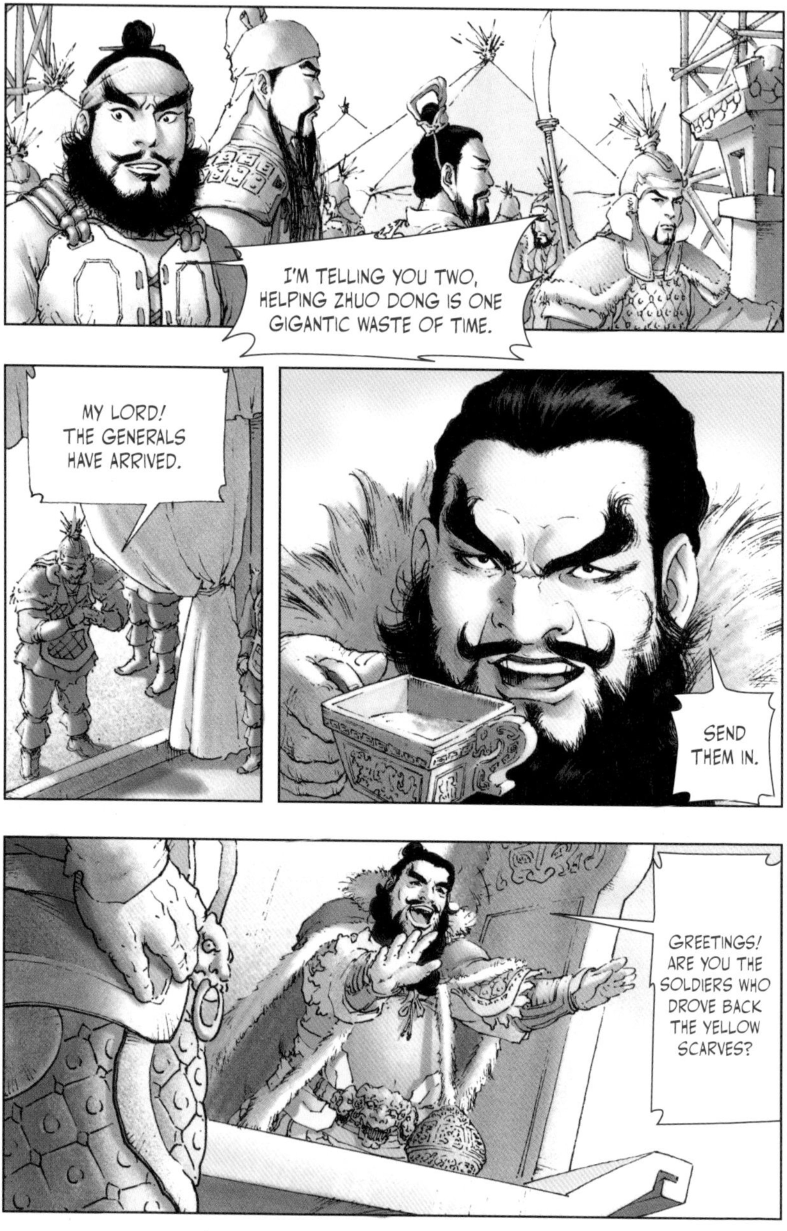
I'M TELLING YOU TWO, HELPING ZHUO DONG IS ONE GIGANTIC WASTE OF TIME.
MY LORD! THE GENERALS HAVE ARRIVED.
SEND THEM IN.
GREETINGS! ARE YOU THE SOLDIERS WHO DROVE BACK THE YELLOW SCARVES?

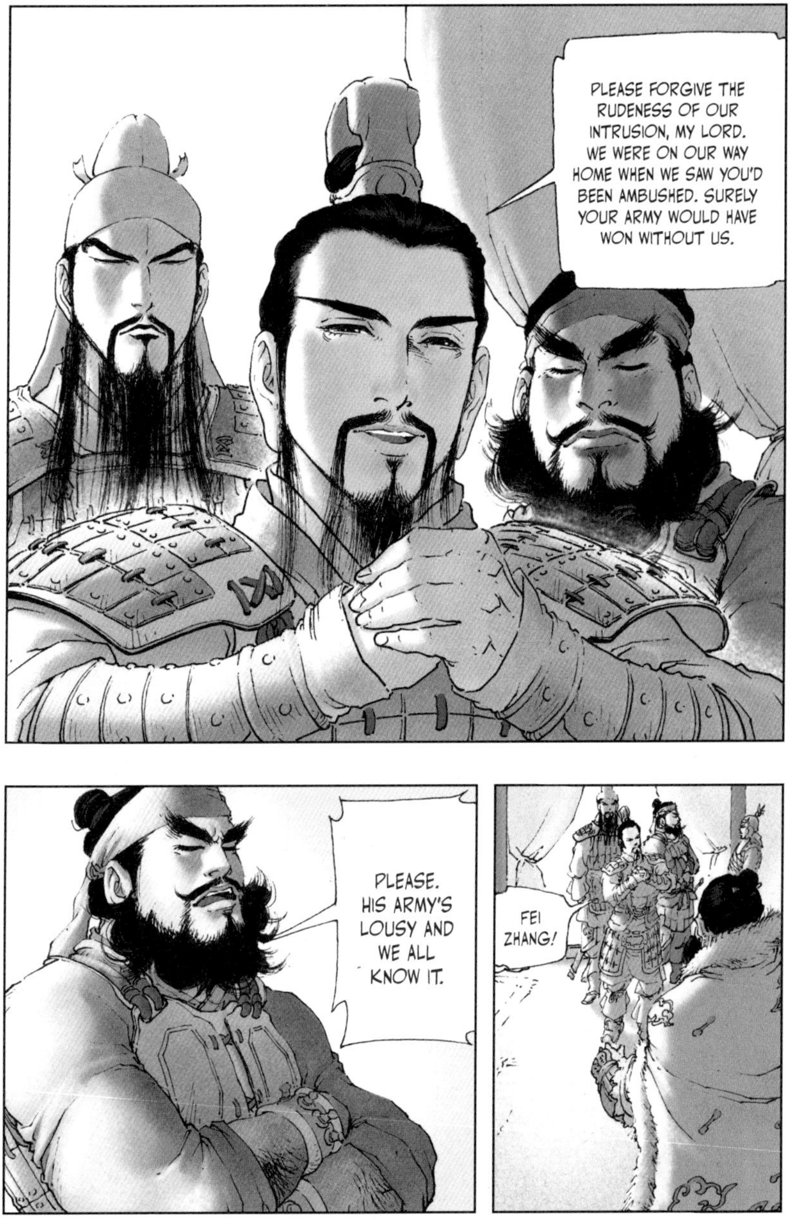
PLEASE FORGIVE THE RUDENESS OF OUR INTRUSION, MY LORD. WE WERE ON OUR WAY HOME WHEN WE SAW YOU'D BEEN AMBUSHED. SURELY YOUR ARMY WOULD HAVE WON WITHOUT US.
PLEASE. HIS ARMY'S LOUSY AND WE ALL KNOW IT.
FEI ZHANG!

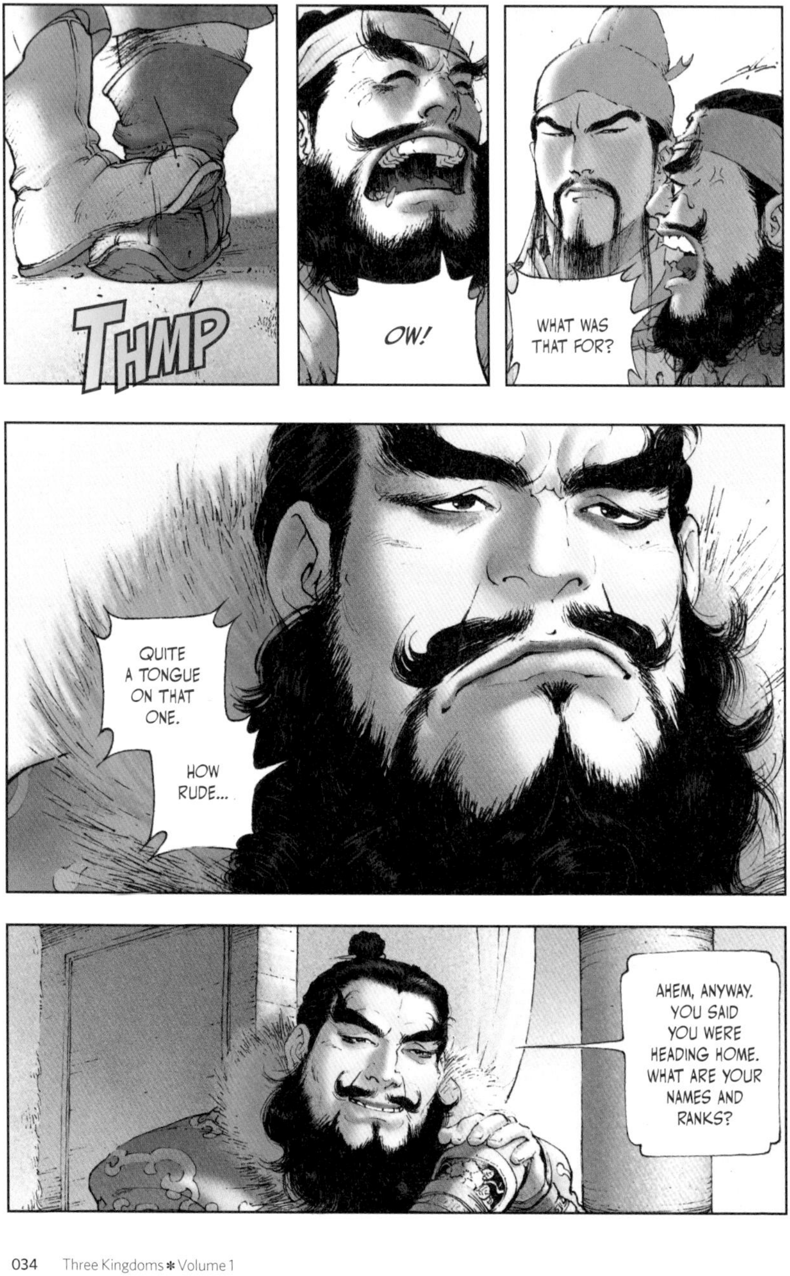
THMP
OW!
WHAT WAS THAT FOR?
QUITE A TONGUE ON THAT ONE.
HOW RUDE...
AHEM, ANYWAY. YOU SAID YOU WERE HEADING HOME. WHAT ARE YOUR NAMES AND RANKS?

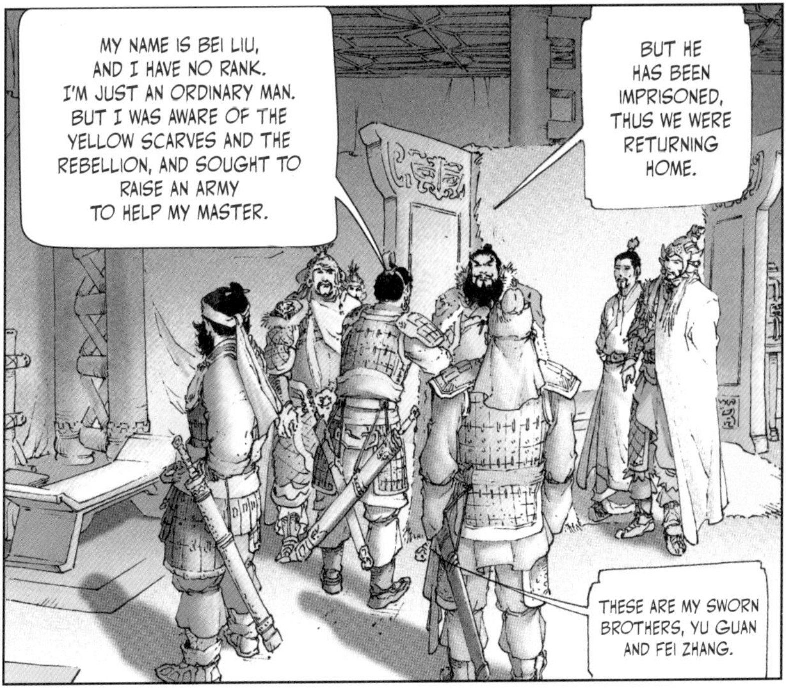
MY NAME IS BEI LIU, AND I HAVE NO RANK. I'M JUST AN ORDINARY MAN. BUT I WAS AWARE OF THE YELLOW SCARVES AND THE REBELLION, AND SOUGHT TO RAISE AN ARMY TO HELP MY MASTER.
BUT HE HAS BEEN IMPRISONED, THUS WE WERE RETURNING HOME.
THESE ARE MY SWORN BROTHERS, YU GUAN AND FEI ZHANG.

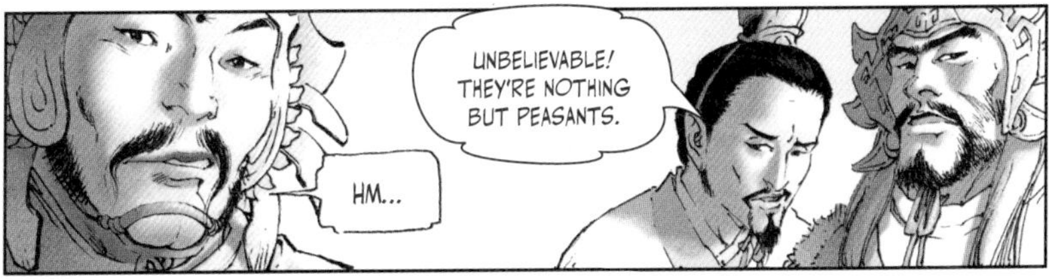
UNBELIEVABLE! THEY'RE NOTHING BUT PEASANTS.
HM...

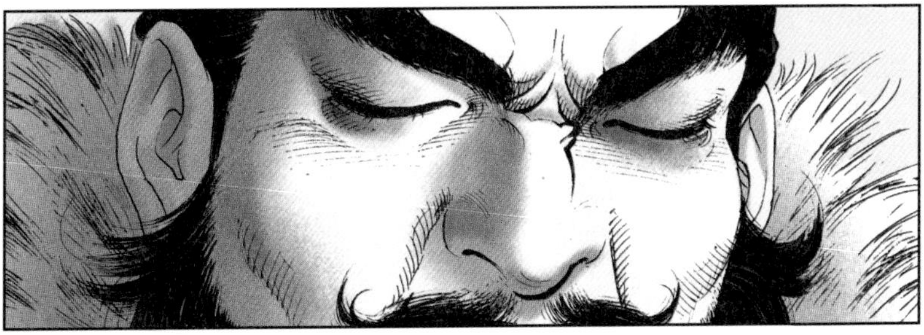

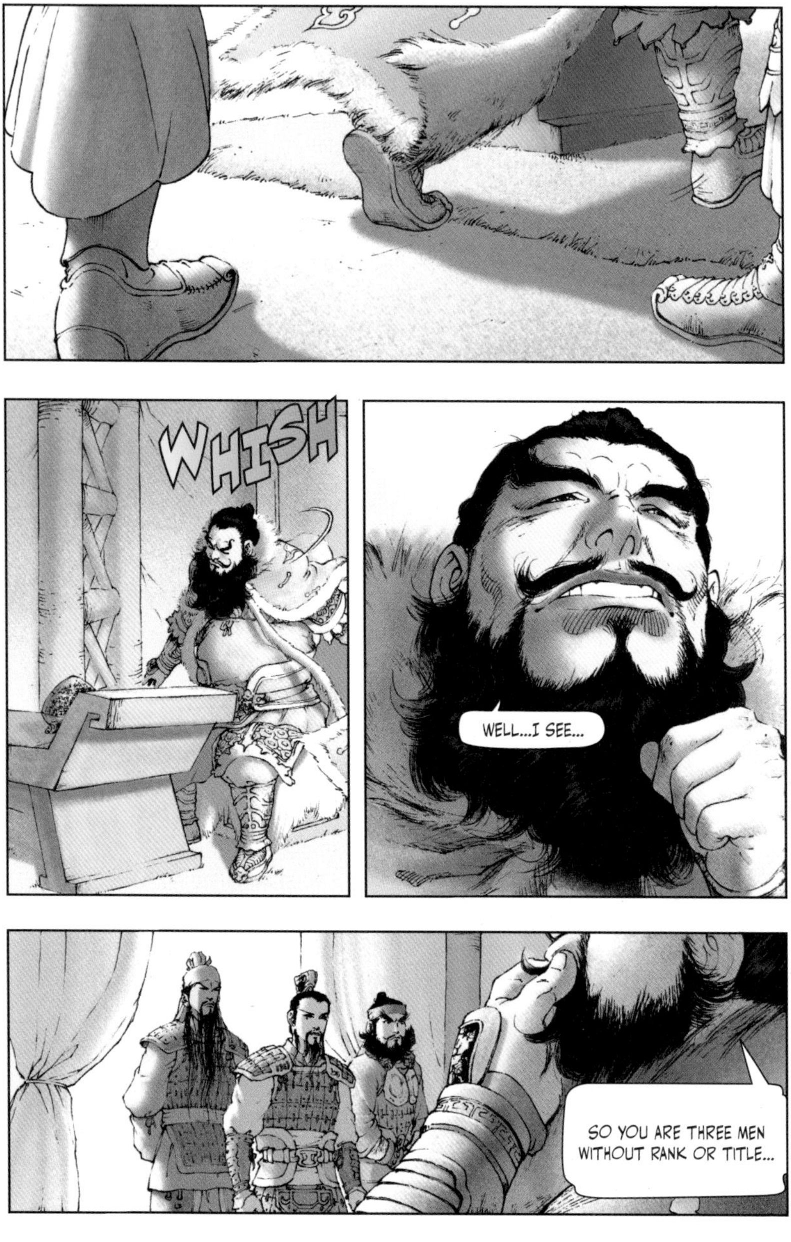
WHISH
WELL...I SEE...
SO YOU ARE THREE MEN WITHOUT RANK OR TITLE...

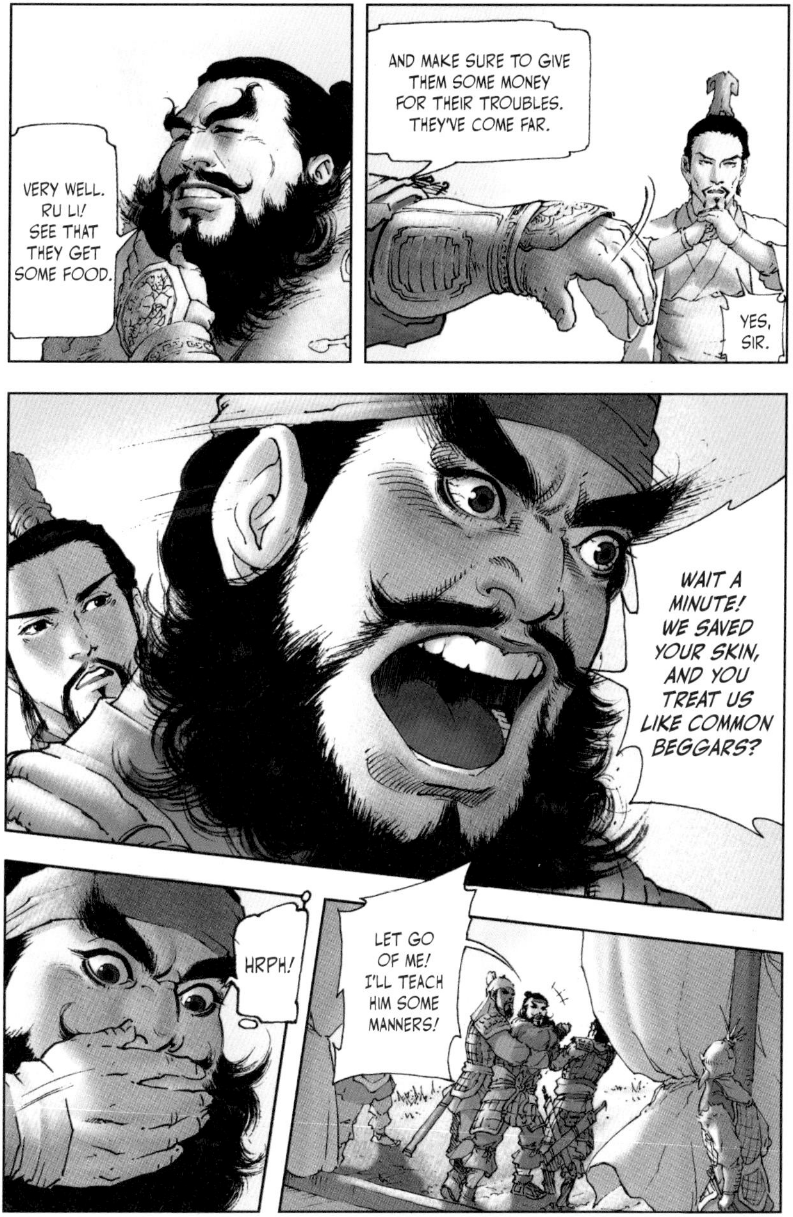
VERY WELL. RU LI! SEE THAT THEY GET SOME FOOD.
AND MAKE SURE TO GIVE THEM SOME MONEY FOR THEIR TROUBLES. THEY'VE COME FAR.
YES, SIR.
WAIT A MINUTE! WE SAVED YOUR SKIN, AND YOU TREAT US LIKE COMMON BEGGARS?
HRPH!
LET GO OF ME! I'LL TEACH HIM SOME MANNERS!

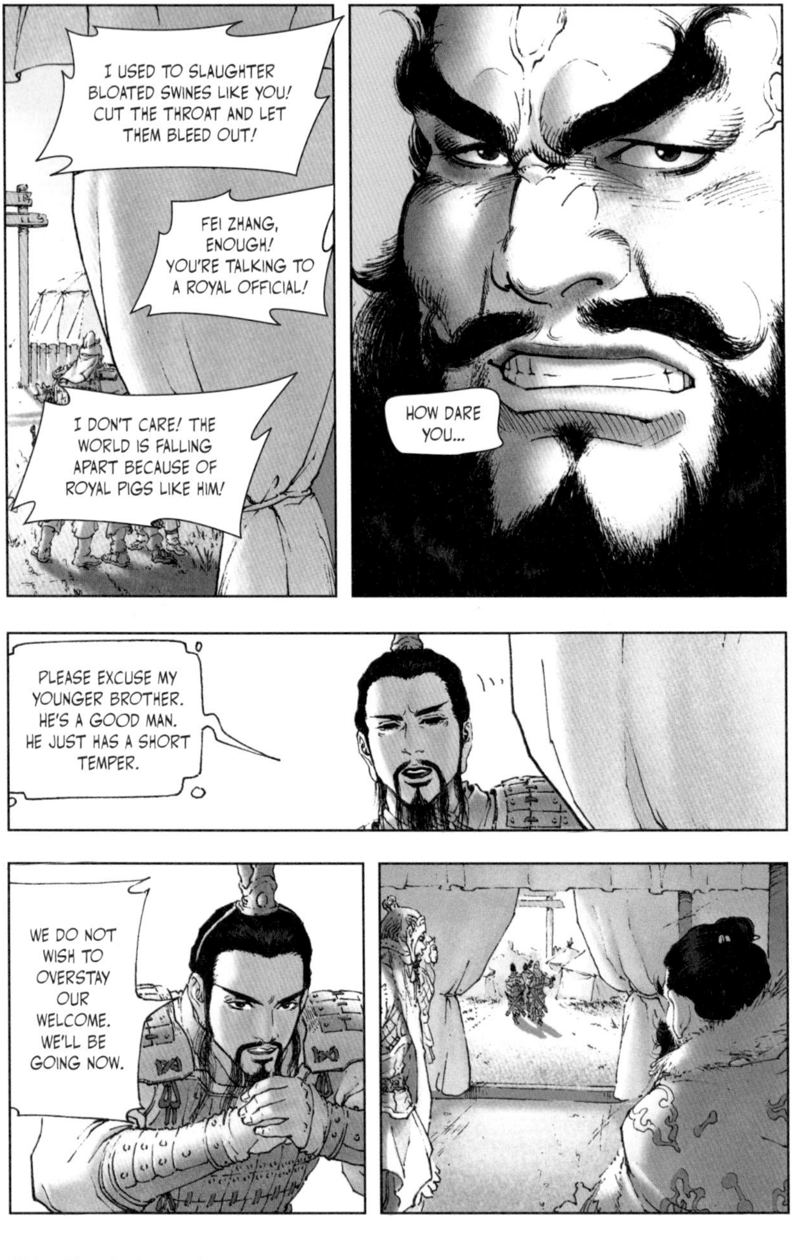
I USED TO SLAUGHTER BLOATED SWINES LIKE YOU! CUT THE THROAT AND LET THEM BLEED OUT!
FEI ZHANG, ENOUGH! YOU'RE TALKING TO A ROYAL OFFICIAL!
I DON'T CARE! THE WORLD IS FALLING APART BECAUSE OF ROYAL PIGS LIKE HIM!
HOW DARE YOU...
PLEASE EXCUSE MY YOUNGER BROTHER. HE'S A GOOD MAN. HE JUST HAS A SHORT TEMPER.
WE DO NOT WISH TO OVERSTAY OUR WELCOME. WE'LL BE GOING NOW.

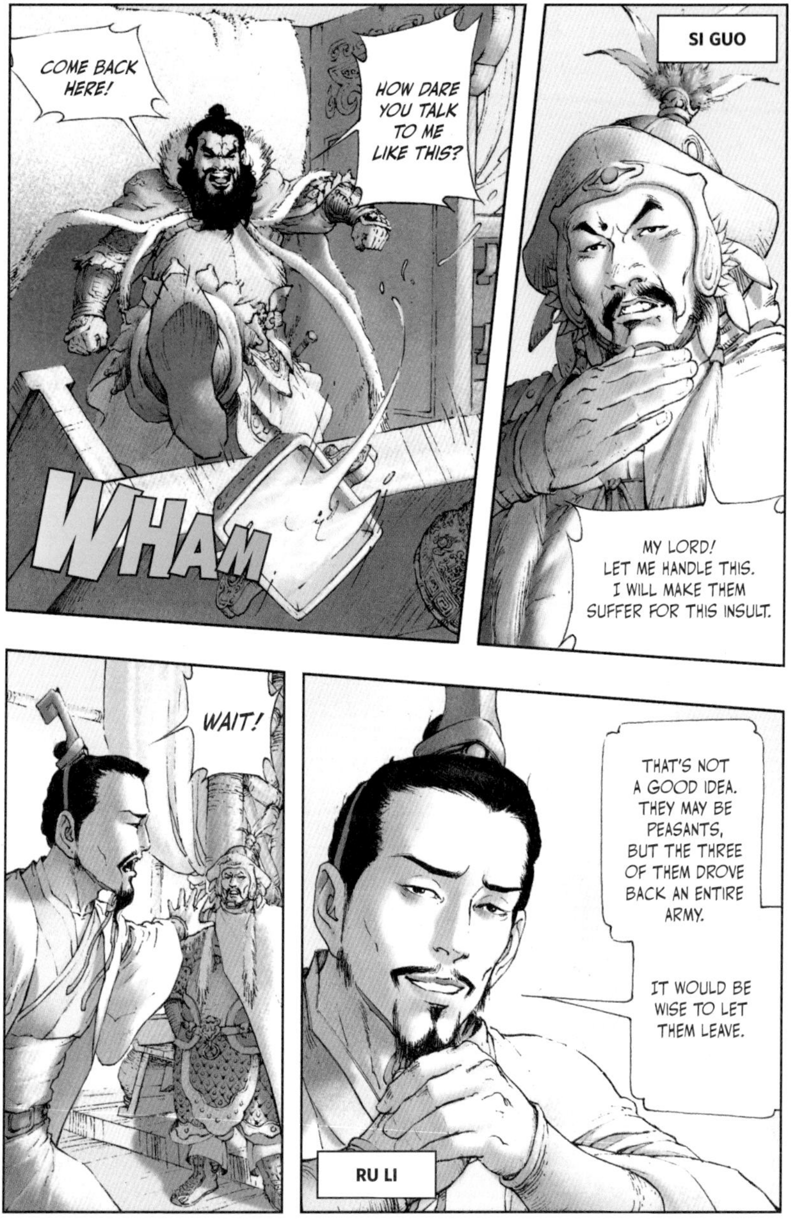
COME BACK HERE!
HOW DARE YOU TALK TO ME LIKE THIS?
WHAM
SI GUO
MY LORD! LET ME HANDLE THIS. I WILL MAKE THEM SUFFER FOR THIS INSULT.
WAIT!
THAT'S NOT A GOOD IDEA. THEY MAY BE PEASANTS, BUT THE THREE OF THEM DROVE BACK AN ENTIRE ARMY.
IT WOULD BE WISE TO LET THEM LEAVE.
RU LI

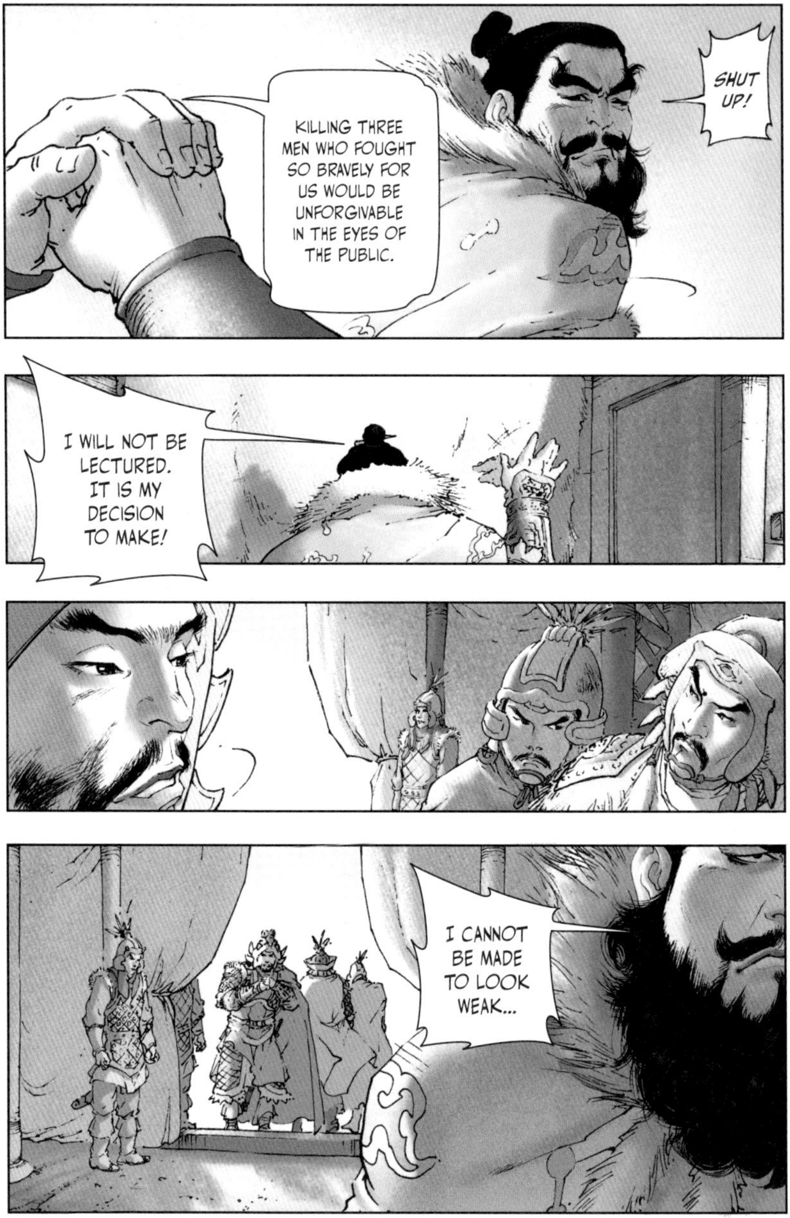
SHUT UP!
KILLING THREE MEN WHO FOUGHT SO BRAVELY FOR US WOULD BE UNFORGIVABLE IN THE EYES OF THE PUBLIC.
I WILL NOT BE LECTURED. IT IS MY DECISION TO MAKE!
I CANNOT BE MADE TO LOOK WEAK...

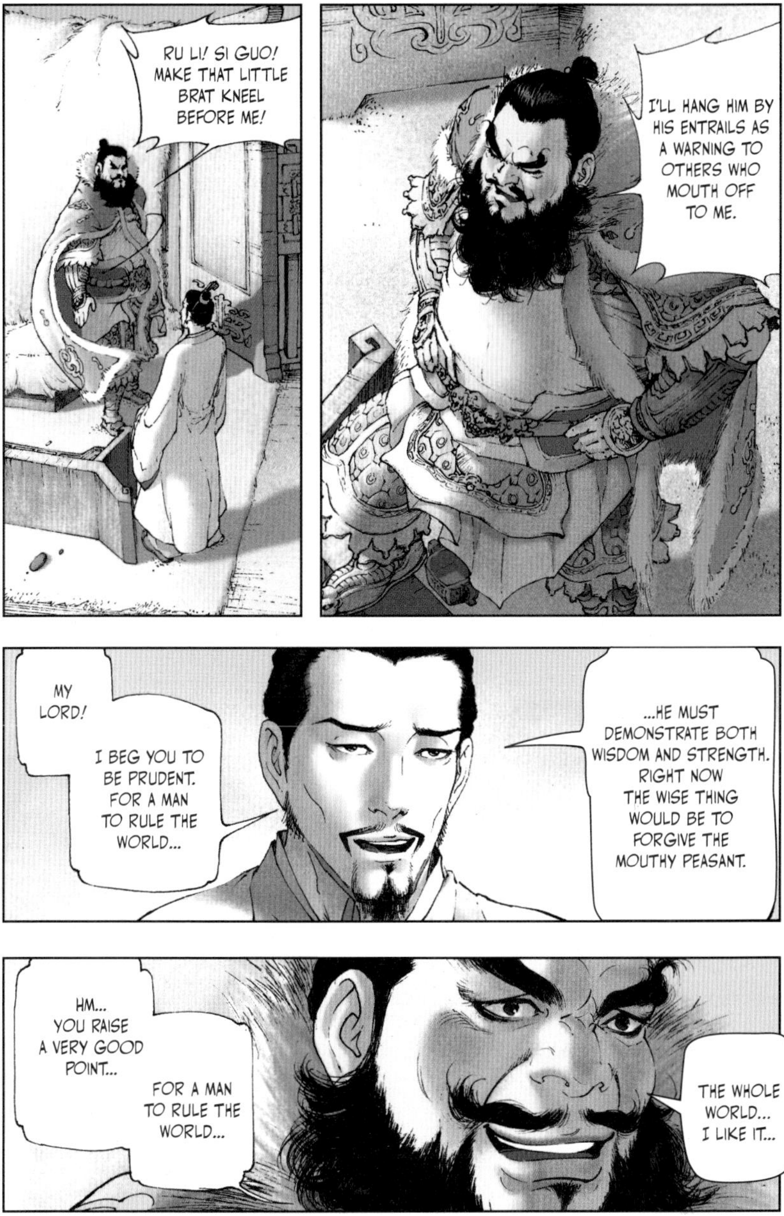
RU LI! SI GUO! MAKE THAT LITTLE BRAT KNEEL BEFORE ME!
I'LL HANG HIM BY HIS ENTRAILS AS A WARNING TO OTHERS WHO MOUTH OFF TO ME.
MY LORD!
I BEG YOU TO BE PRUDENT. FOR A MAN TO RULE THE WORLD...
...HE MUST DEMONSTRATE BOTH WISDOM AND STRENGTH. RIGHT NOW THE WISE THING WOULD BE TO FORGIVE THE MOUTHY PEASANT.
HM... YOU RAISE A VERY GOOD POINT...
FOR A MAN TO RULE THE WORLD...
THE WHOLE WORLD... I LIKE IT...

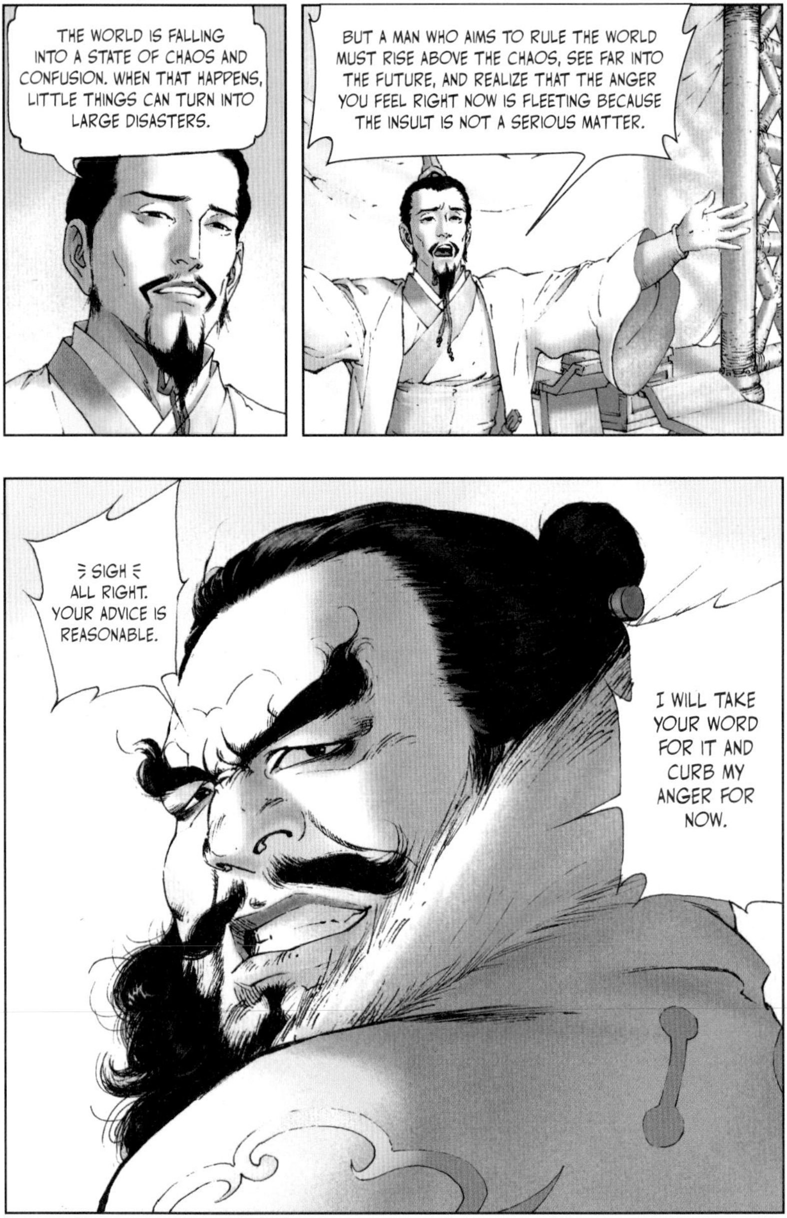
THE WORLD IS FALLING INTO A STATE OF CHAOS AND CONFUSION. WHEN THAT HAPPENS, LITTLE THINGS CAN TURN INTO LARGE DISASTERS.
BUT A MAN WHO AIMS TO RULE THE WORLD MUST RISE ABOVE THE CHAOS, SEE FAR INTO THE FUTURE, AND REALIZE THAT THE ANGER YOU FEEL RIGHT NOW IS FLEETING BECAUSE THE INSULT IS NOT A SERIOUS MATTER.
≥ SIGH ≤ ALL RIGHT. YOUR ADVICE IS REASONABLE.
I WILL TAKE YOUR WORD FOR IT AND CURB MY ANGER FOR NOW.

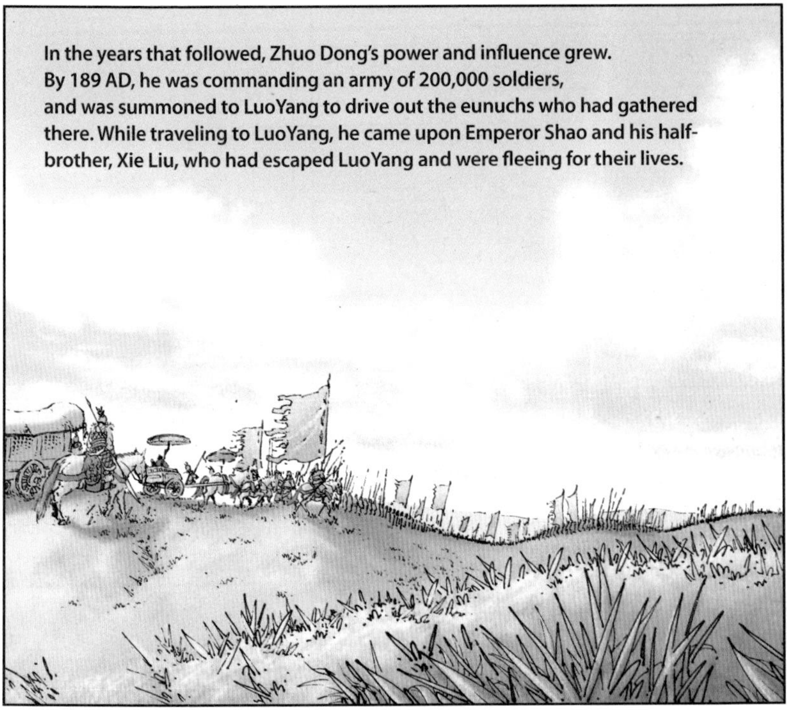
In the years that followed, Zhuo Dong's power and influence grew. By 189 AD, he was commanding an army of 200,000 soldiers, and was summoned to LuoYang to drive out the eunuchs who had gathered there. While traveling to LuoYang, he came upon Emperor Shao and his half-brother, Xie Liu, who had escaped LuoYang and were fleeing for their lives.

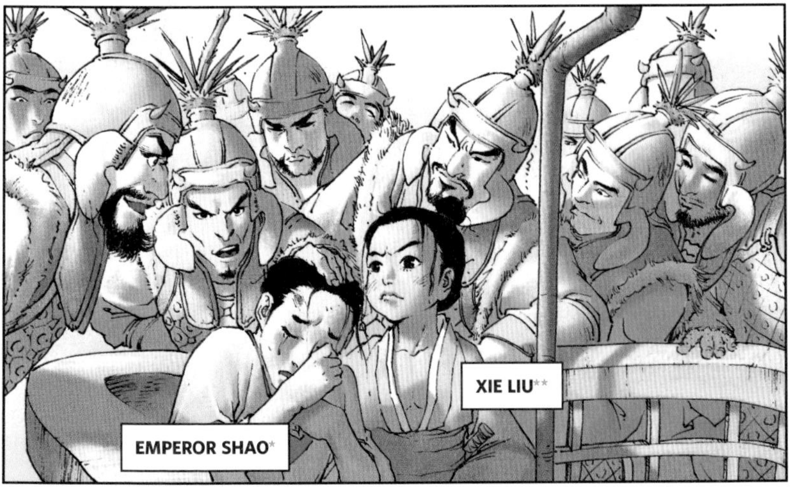
XIE LIU**
EMPEROR SHAO*

* The 13th Emperor of the Post-Han Dynasty

** To be crowned by Zhuo Dong as the 14th Emperor of the Post-Han Dynasty

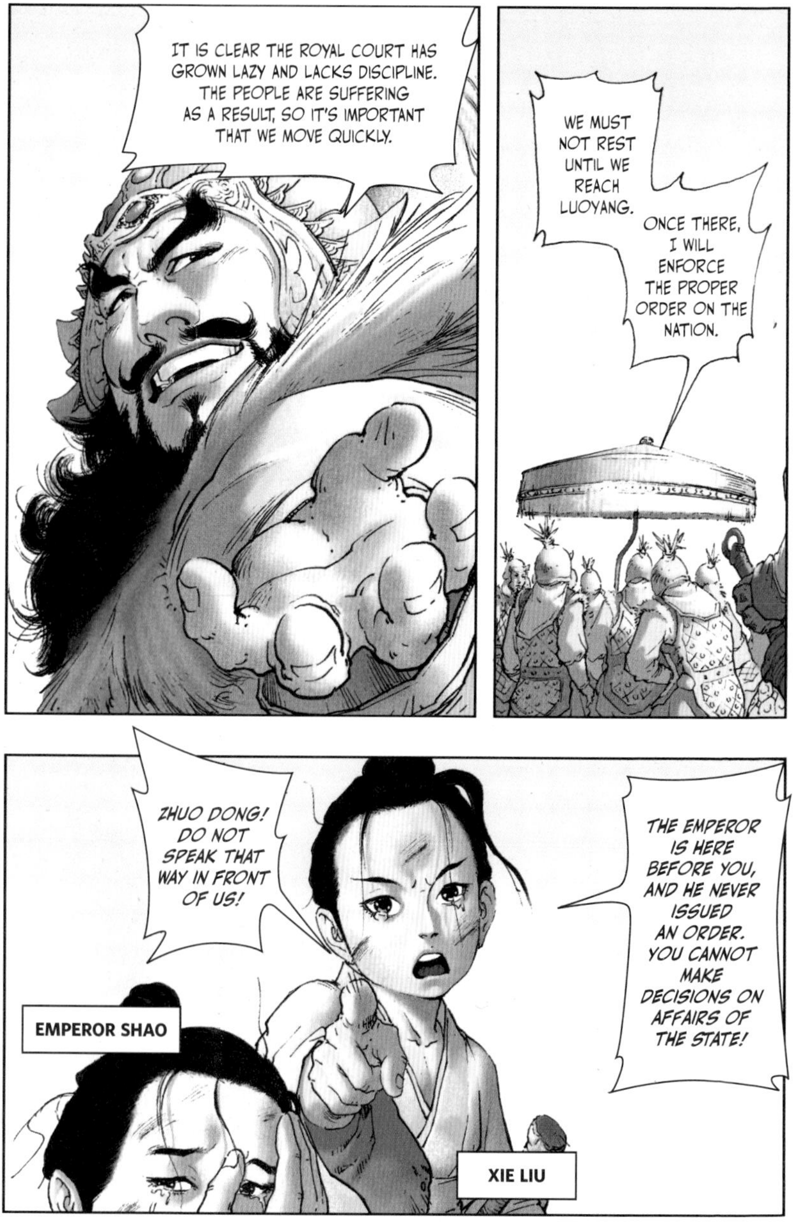
IT IS CLEAR THE ROYAL COURT HAS GROWN LAZY AND LACKS DISCIPLINE. THE PEOPLE ARE SUFFERING AS A RESULT, SO IT'S IMPORTANT THAT WE MOVE QUICKLY.
WE MUST NOT REST UNTIL WE REACH LUOYANG.
ONCE THERE, I WILL ENFORCE THE PROPER ORDER ON THE NATION.
ZHUO DONG! DO NOT SPEAK THAT WAY IN FRONT OF US!
THE EMPEROR IS HERE BEFORE YOU, AND HE NEVER ISSUED AN ORDER. YOU CANNOT MAKE DECISIONS ON AFFAIRS OF THE STATE!
EMPEROR SHAO
XIE LIU

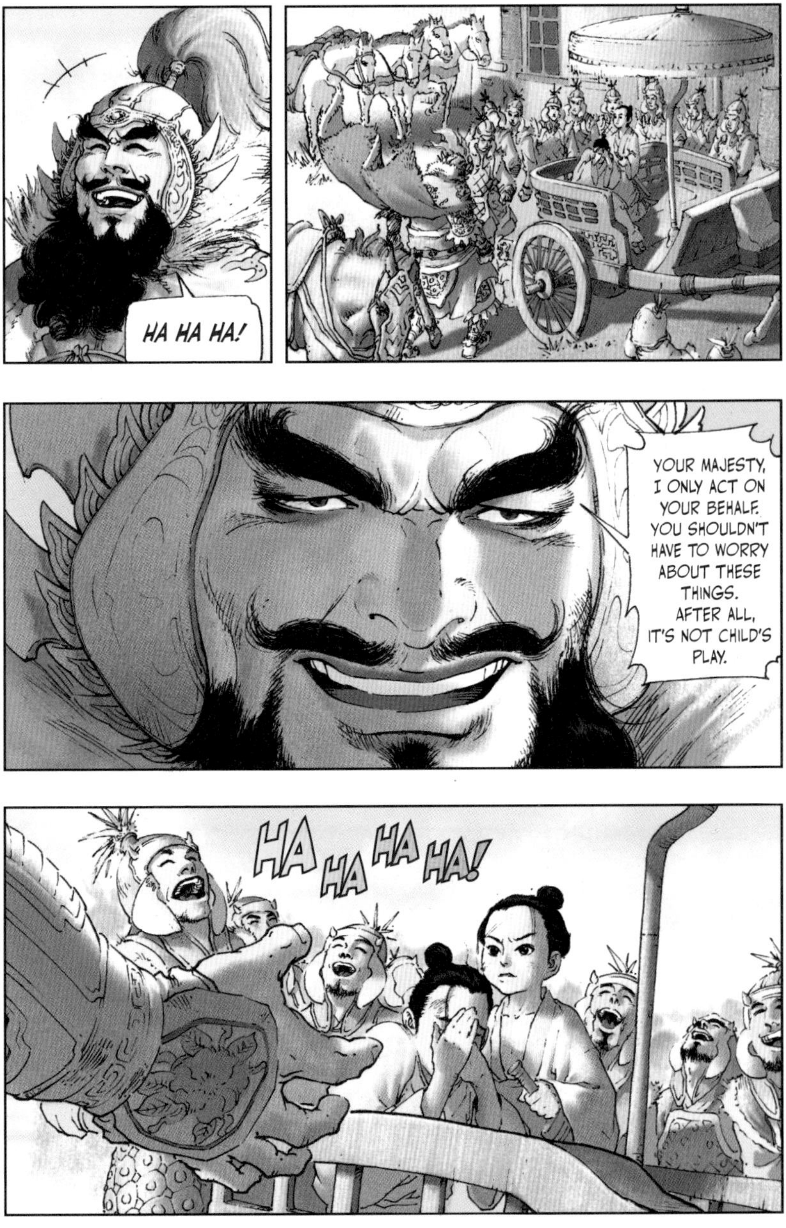
HA HA HA!
YOUR MAJESTY, I ONLY ACT ON YOUR BEHALF. YOU SHOULDN'T HAVE TO WORRY ABOUT THESE THINGS. AFTER ALL, IT'S NOT CHILD'S PLAY.
HA HA HA HA!

Once, LuoYang was a capital city that embodied the peace and prosperity of a nation. But once the nation began to crumble, ominous signs of danger appeared.

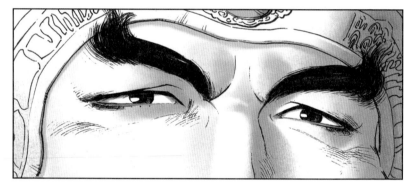

HA HA HA!

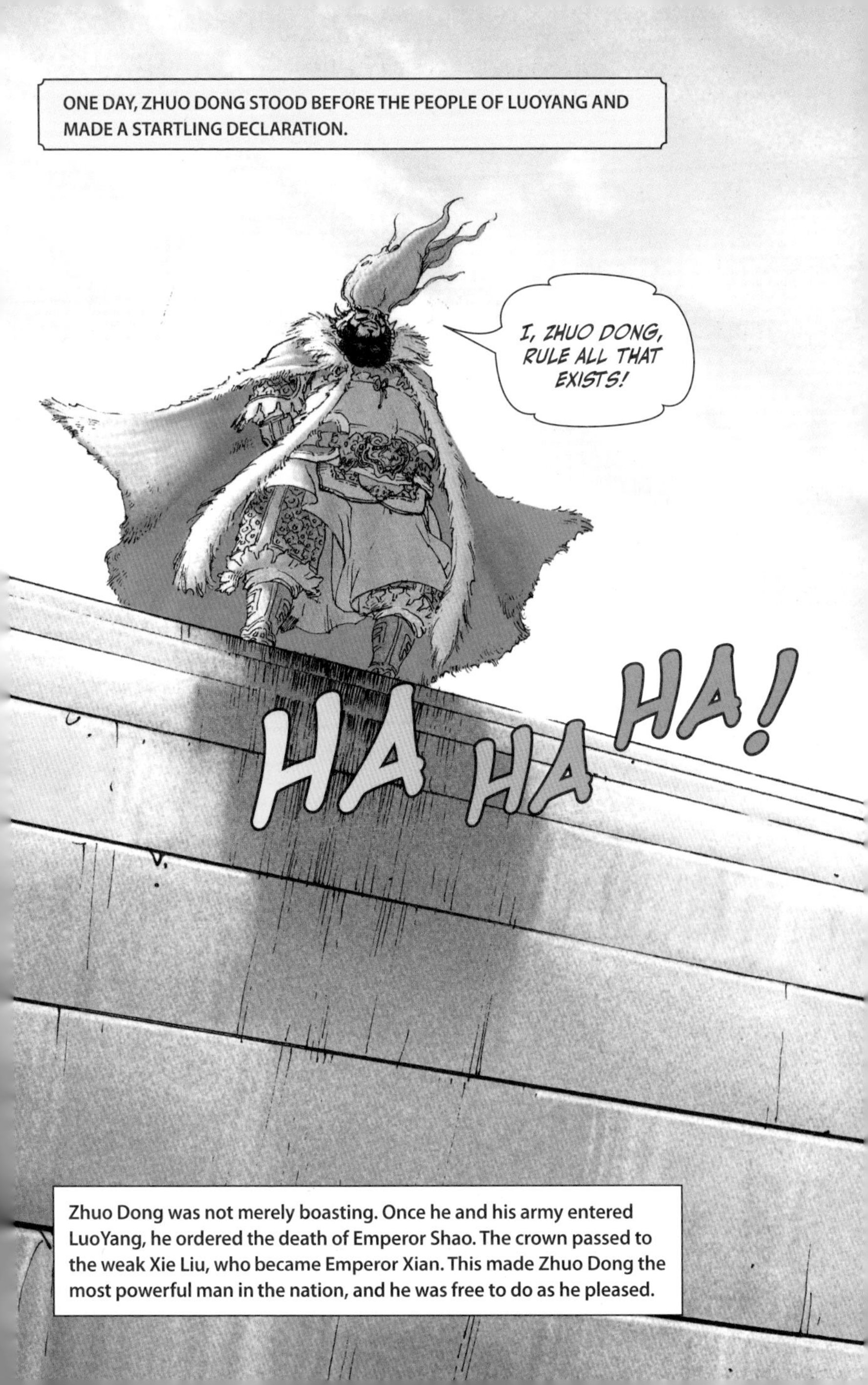
ONE DAY, ZHUO DONG STOOD BEFORE THE PEOPLE OF LUOYANG AND MADE A STARTLING DECLARATION.
I, ZHUO DONG, RULE ALL THAT EXISTS!
HA HA HA!
Zhuo Dong was not merely boasting. Once he and his army entered LuoYang, he ordered the death of Emperor Shao. The crown passed to the weak Xie Liu, who became Emperor Xian. This made Zhuo Dong the most powerful man in the nation, and he was free to do as he pleased.

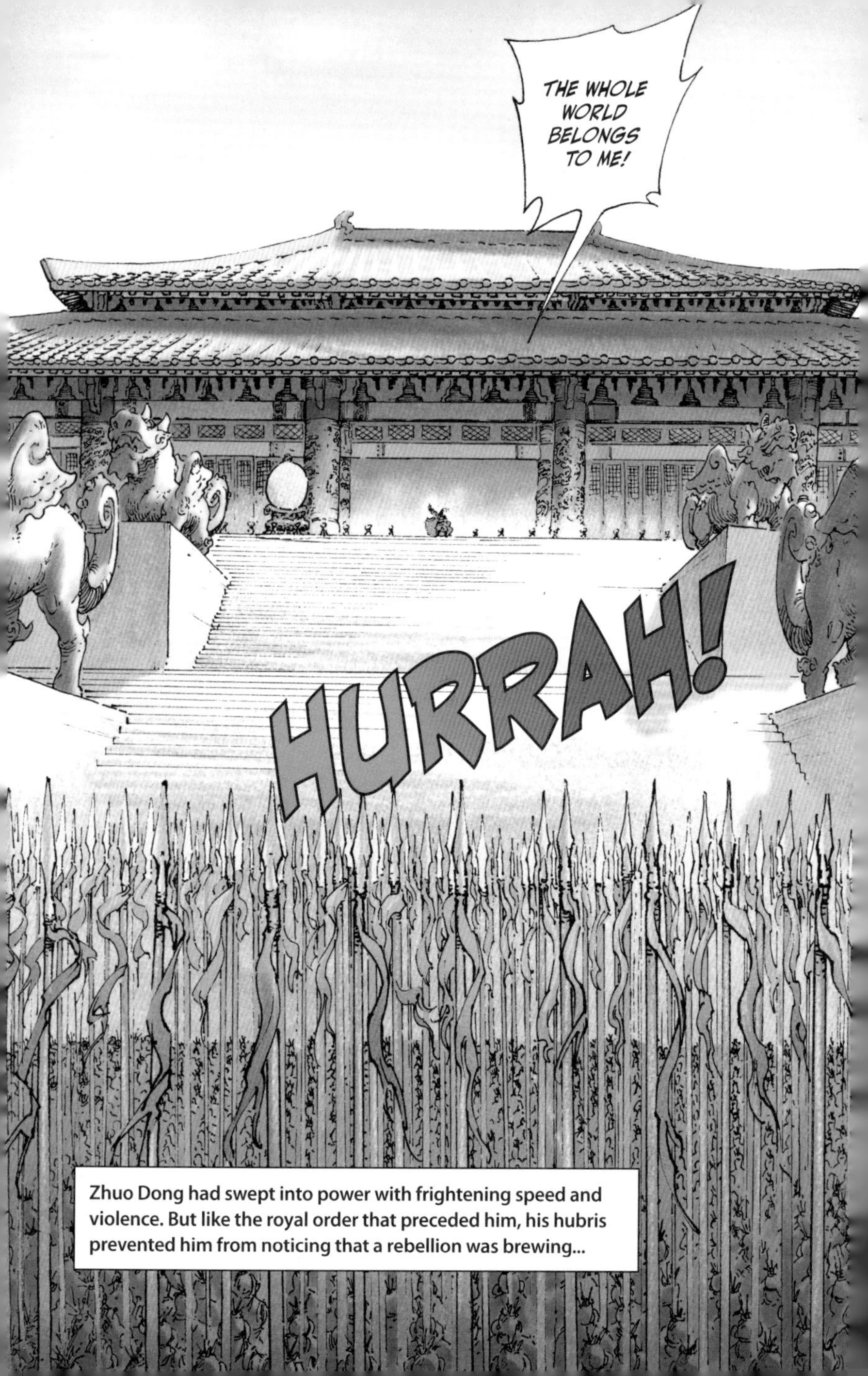
THE WHOLE WORLD BELONGS TO ME!
HURRAH!
Zhuo Dong had swept into power with frightening speed and violence. But like the royal order that preceded him, his hubris prevented him from noticing that a rebellion was brewing...

The 13 provinces of China at the end of the second century

YOU
BING
JI
QING
YAN
LIANG
SI LI
XU
YU
JING
YANG
YI
JIAO

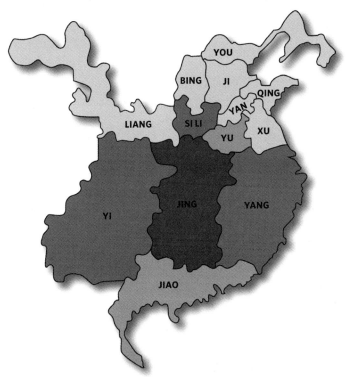

Before Zhuo Dong entered the city of LuoYang, Cao Cao and Shao Yuan, two royal military officers, had been summoned to the city to defeat the eunuchs. The two were run out of the city upon Zhuo Dong's arrival, and Cao Cao swore to take revenge. He raised a militia in his province and merged it with the militias of seventeen other feudal lords, creating a coalition army to defeat Zhuo Dong.

The coalition army selected Shao Yuan as their leader in the war against Zhuo Dong's forces. Meanwhile, a feudal lord named Zan GongSun counted among his fighters three men who recently had taken a blood oath to defend one another and restore the nation: Bei Liu, Yu Guan, and Fei Zhang.

Chapter 2

The Coalition Army Forms to do Battle with Zhuo Dong, and Bei Liu Makes a Name for Himself AD 190

Summary

Having entered the capital city of LuoYang, Zhuo Dong orders the execution of the emperor and the crowning of his weaker younger brother, who become the fourteenth emperor, Xian. In doing so, Zhuo Dong assumes almost unlimited power. Cao Cao, in an effort to wrestle control away from Zhuo Dong, forms a coalition army to do battle with the tyrant's forces.

In response to the coalition's attack, Zhuo Dong dispatches his best general, Xiong Hua, to do battle with coalition forces led by Jian Sun. The battle turns against the coalition when a shipment of desperately needed supplies does not reach the army. But just when it seems that all hope is lost, Bei Liu and his brothers make themselves known to the coalition when Yu Guan claims the head of Xiong Hua. Zhuo Dong desperately retreats, and orders Bu Lu, a legendary and much-feared warrior, to crush the coalition.

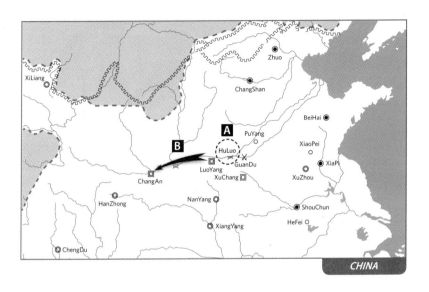

XiLiang
Zhuo
ChangShan
BeiHai
A
PuYang
XiaoPei
B
HuLuo
LuoYang
GuanDu
XiaPi
ChangAn
XuChang
XuZhou
HanZhong
NanYang
ShouChun
HeFei
XiangYang
ChengDu
CHINA

A The Battle of HuLuo

This is the battle where Xiong Hua is killed; Zhuo Dong is driven back to LuoYang; and Bei Liu, Yu Guan, and Fei Zhang make a name for themselves in the coalition army.

B Zhuo Dong Abandons LuoYang and Moves the Capital to ChangAn

After the battle of HuLuo, Zhuo Dong abandons LuoYang and sets the city ablaze. With the emperor in tow, he establishes a new capital in ChangAn.

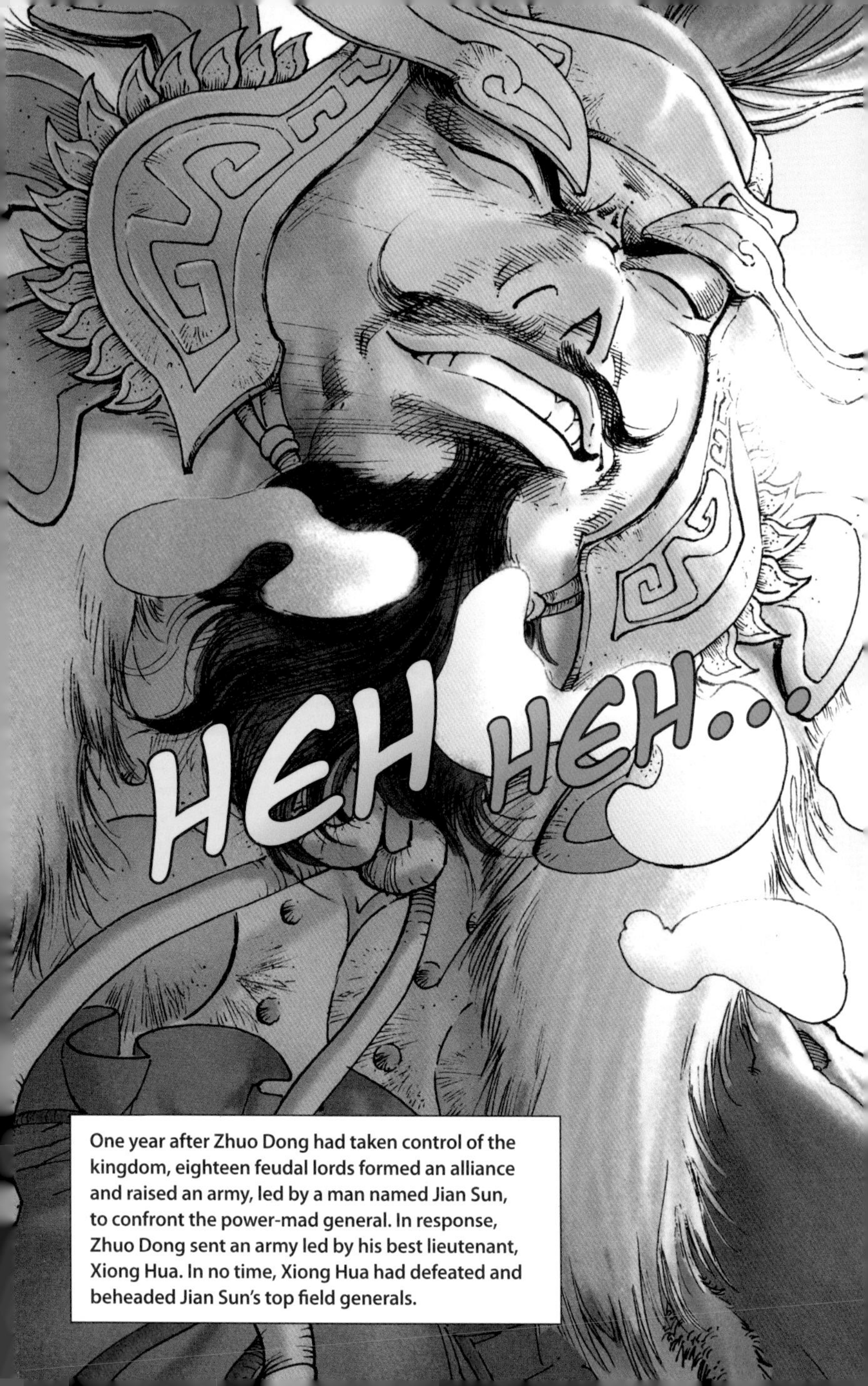
HEH HEH...
One year after Zhuo Dong had taken control of the kingdom, eighteen feudal lords formed an alliance and raised an army, led by a man named Jian Sun, to confront the power-mad general. In response, Zhuo Dong sent an army led by his best lieutenant, Xiong Hua. In no time, Xiong Hua had defeated and beheaded Jian Sun's top field generals.

XIONG HUA AND THE FIGHT AGAINST THE COALITION ARMY

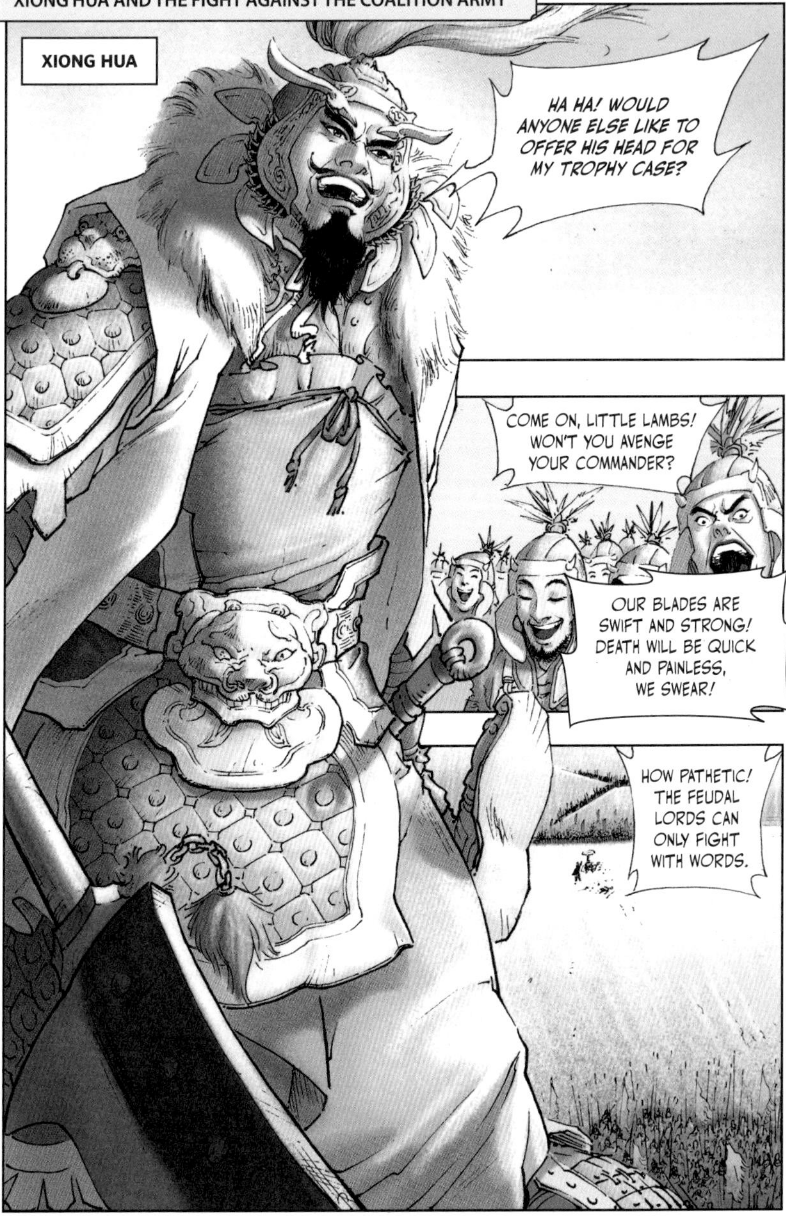
XIONG HUA
HA HA! WOULD ANYONE ELSE LIKE TO OFFER HIS HEAD FOR MY TROPHY CASE?
COME ON, LITTLE LAMBS! WON'T YOU AVENGE YOUR COMMANDER?
OUR BLADES ARE SWIFT AND STRONG! DEATH WILL BE QUICK AND PAINLESS, WE SWEAR!
HOW PATHETIC! THE FEUDAL LORDS CAN ONLY FIGHT WITH WORDS.

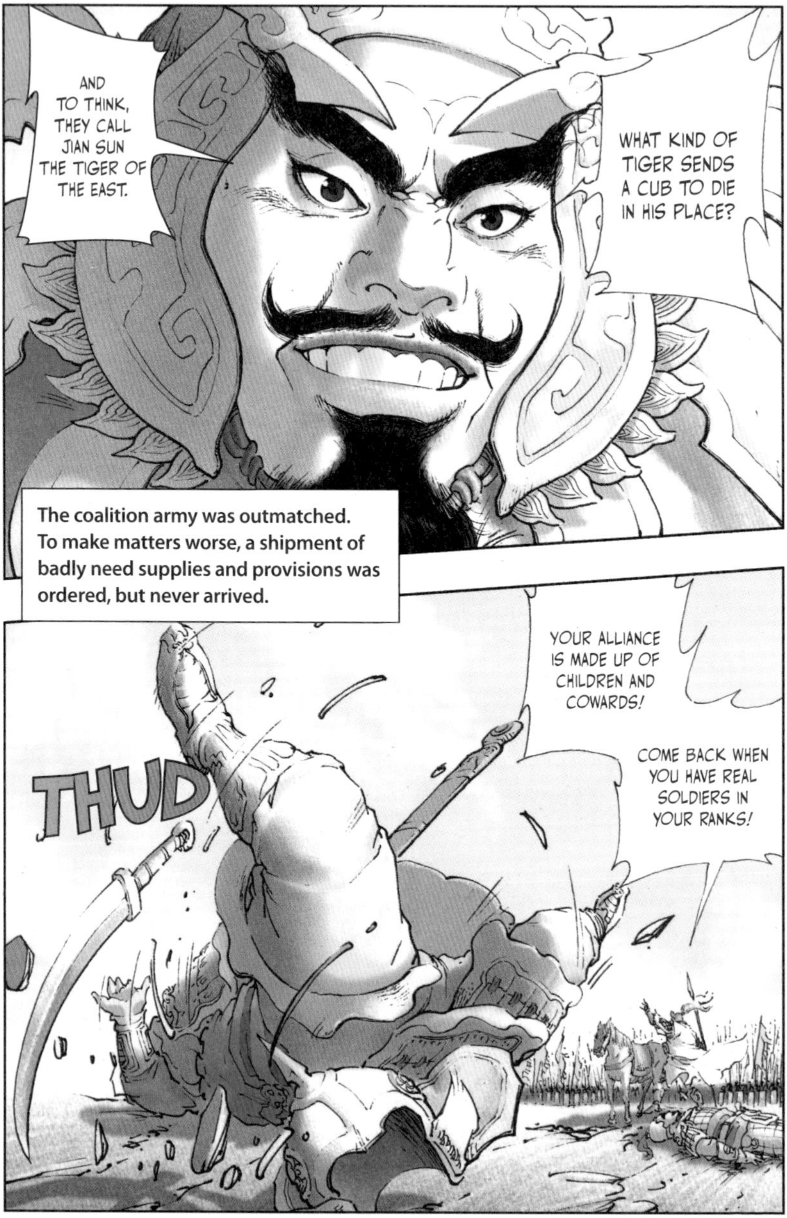
AND TO THINK, THEY CALL JIAN SUN THE TIGER OF THE EAST.
WHAT KIND OF TIGER SENDS A CUB TO DIE IN HIS PLACE?
The coalition army was outmatched. To make matters worse, a shipment of badly need supplies and provisions was ordered, but never arrived.
YOUR ALLIANCE IS MADE UP OF CHILDREN AND COWARDS!
COME BACK WHEN YOU HAVE REAL SOLDIERS IN YOUR RANKS!
THUD

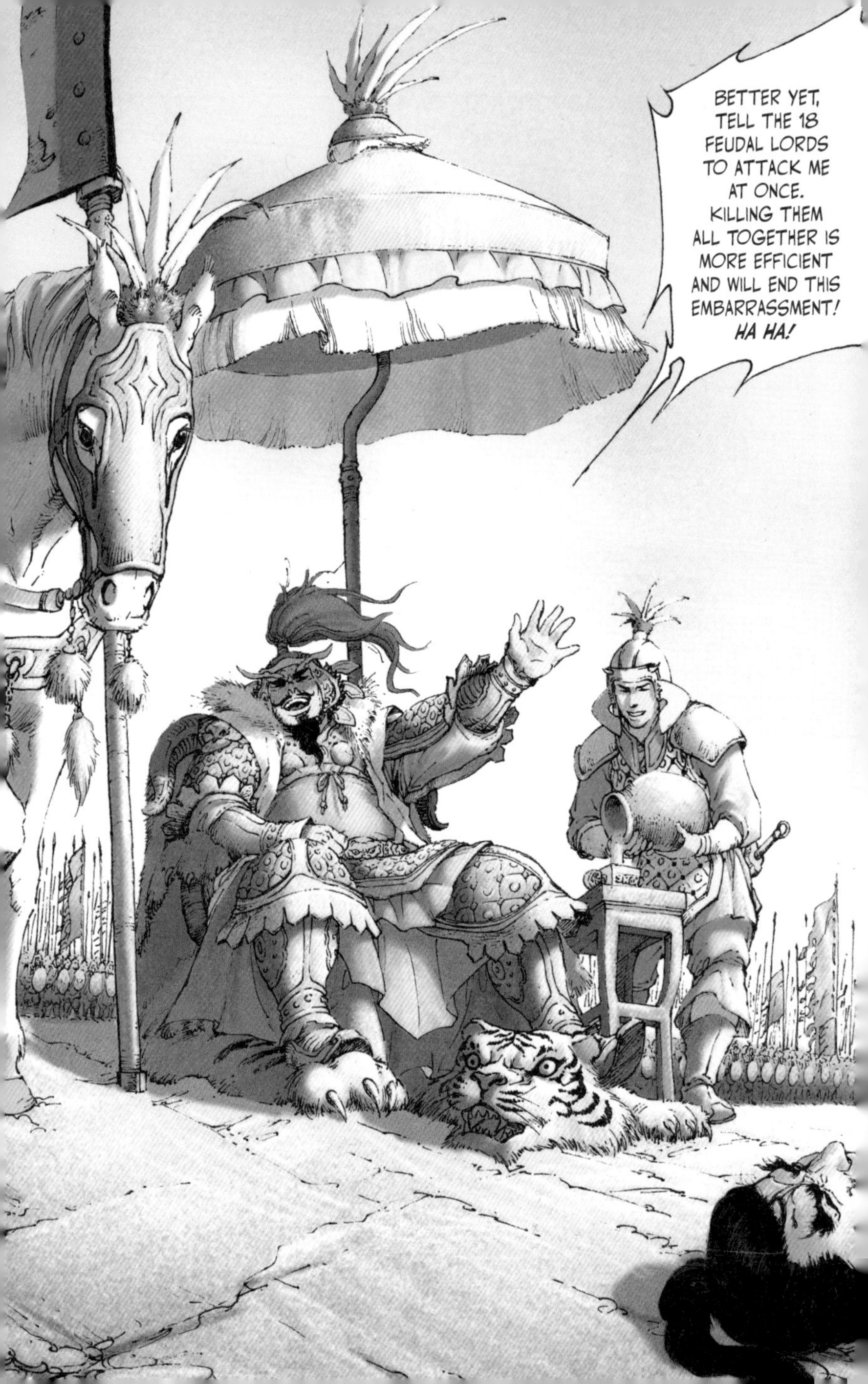
BETTER YET, TELL THE 18 FEUDAL LORDS TO ATTACK ME AT ONCE. KILLING THEM ALL TOGETHER IS MORE EFFICIENT AND WILL END THIS EMBARRASSMENT! *HA HA!*

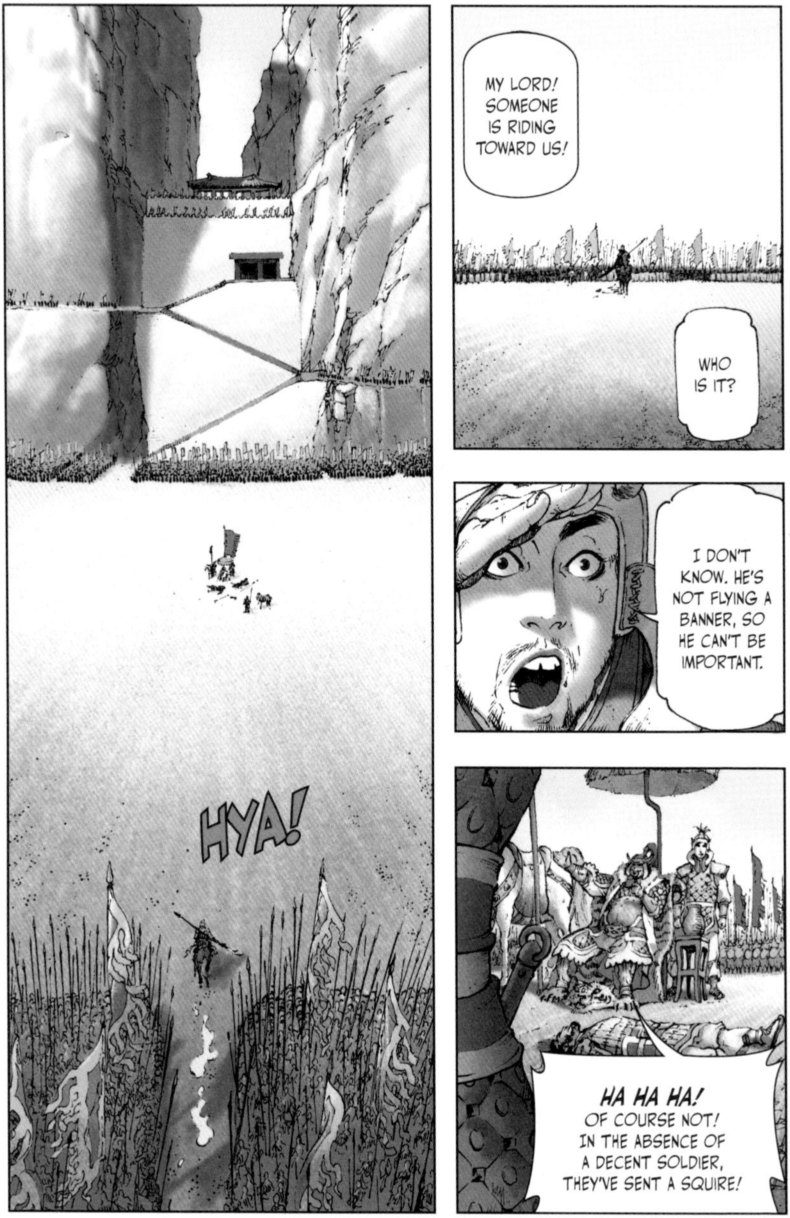
HYA!
MY LORD! SOMEONE IS RIDING TOWARD US!
WHO IS IT?
I DON'T KNOW. HE'S NOT FLYING A BANNER, SO HE CAN'T BE IMPORTANT.
HA HA HA! OF COURSE NOT! IN THE ABSENCE OF A DECENT SOLDIER, THEY'VE SENT A SQUIRE!

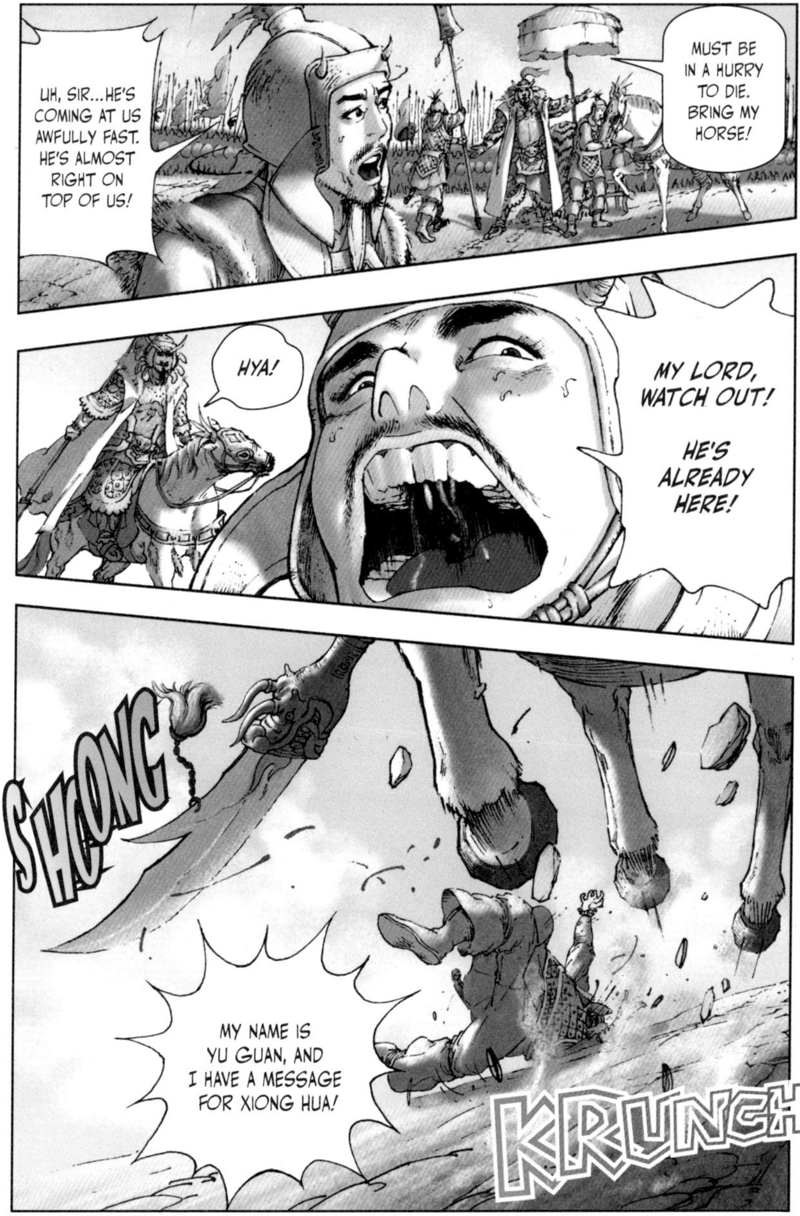
UH, SIR...HE'S COMING AT US AWFULLY FAST. HE'S ALMOST RIGHT ON TOP OF US!
MUST BE IN A HURRY TO DIE. BRING MY HORSE!
HYA!
MY LORD, WATCH OUT!
HE'S ALREADY HERE!
SHCONG
MY NAME IS YU GUAN, AND I HAVE A MESSAGE FOR XIONG HUA!
KRUNCH

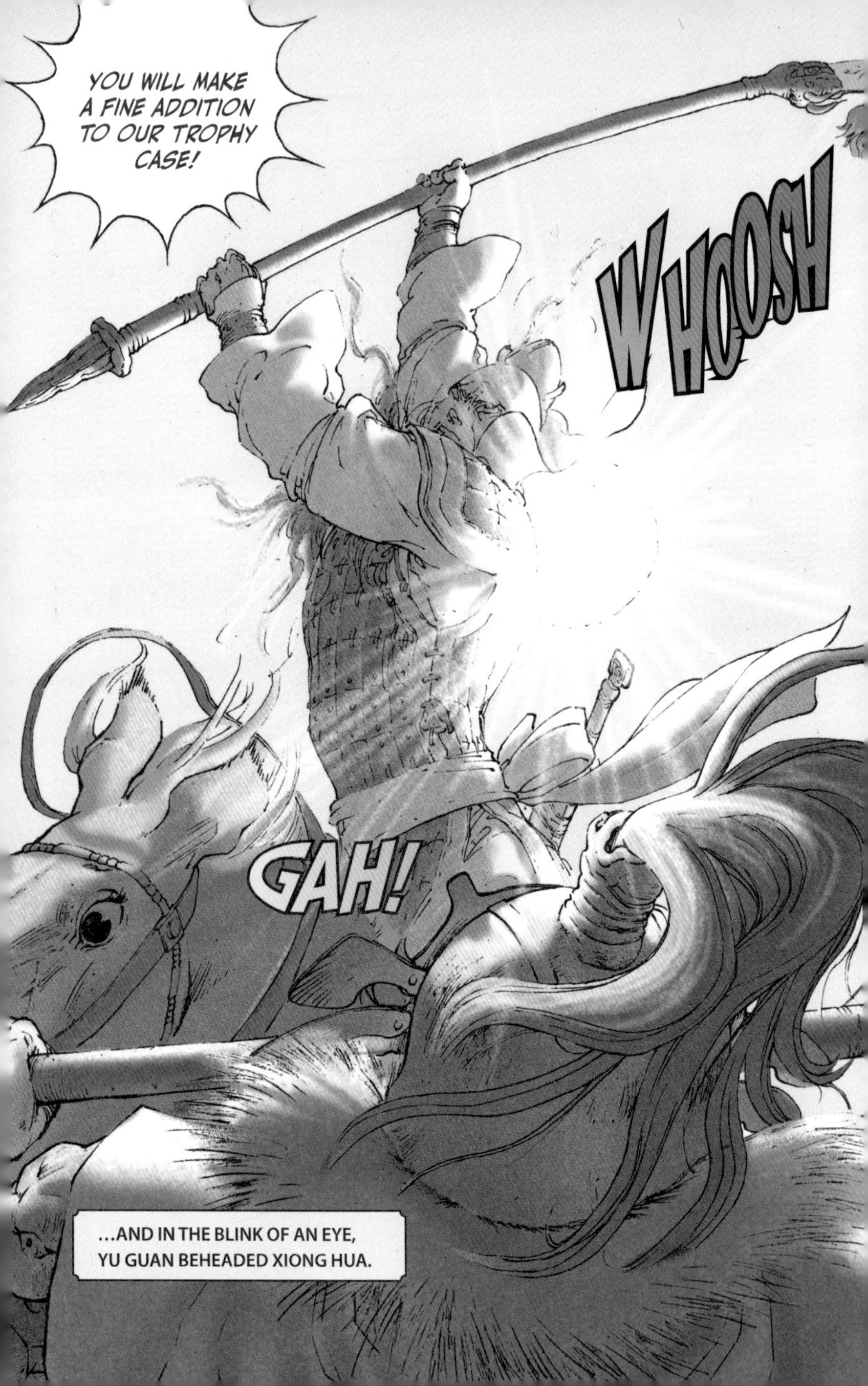
YOU WILL MAKE A FINE ADDITION TO OUR TROPHY CASE!
WHOOSH
GAH!
...AND IN THE BLINK OF AN EYE, YU GUAN BEHEADED XIONG HUA.

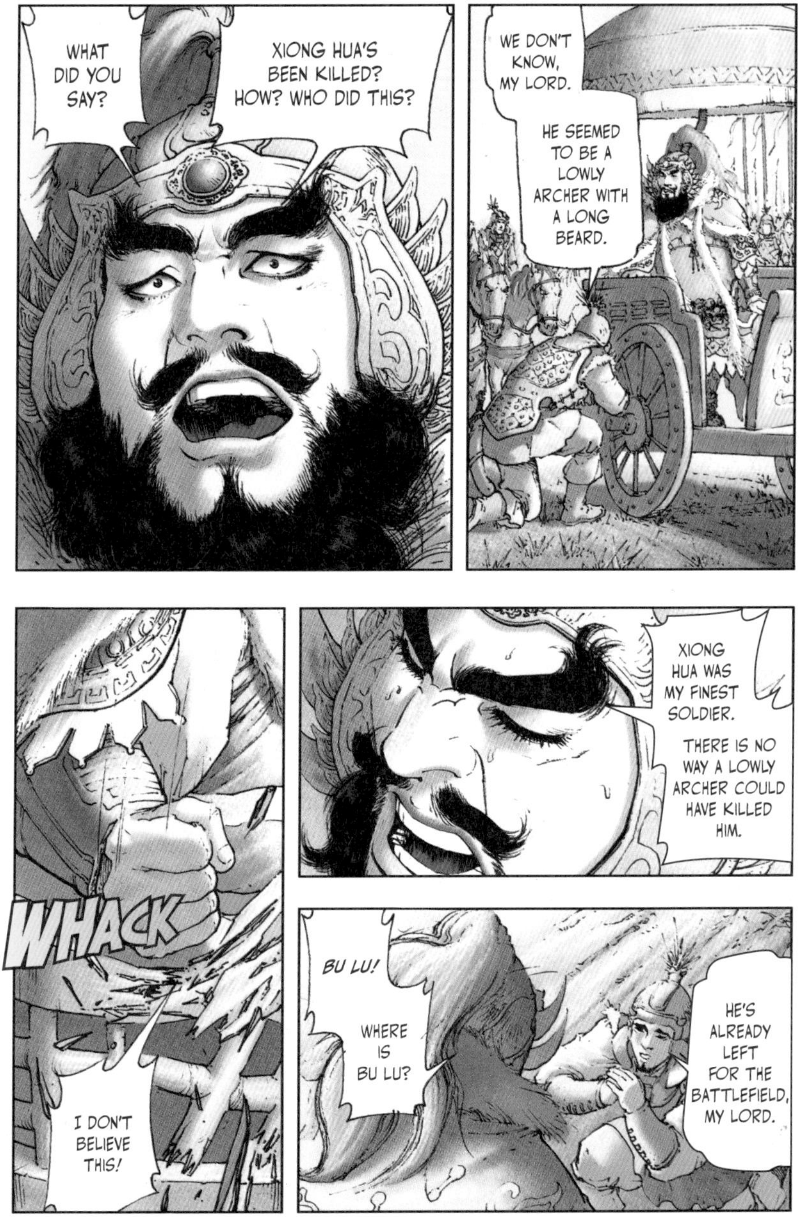
WHAT DID YOU SAY?
XIONG HUA'S BEEN KILLED? HOW? WHO DID THIS?
WE DON'T KNOW, MY LORD.
HE SEEMED TO BE A LOWLY ARCHER WITH A LONG BEARD.
WHACK
I DON'T BELIEVE THIS!
XIONG HUA WAS MY FINEST SOLDIER.
THERE IS NO WAY A LOWLY ARCHER COULD HAVE KILLED HIM.
BU LU!
WHERE IS BU LU?
HE'S ALREADY LEFT FOR THE BATTLEFIELD, MY LORD.

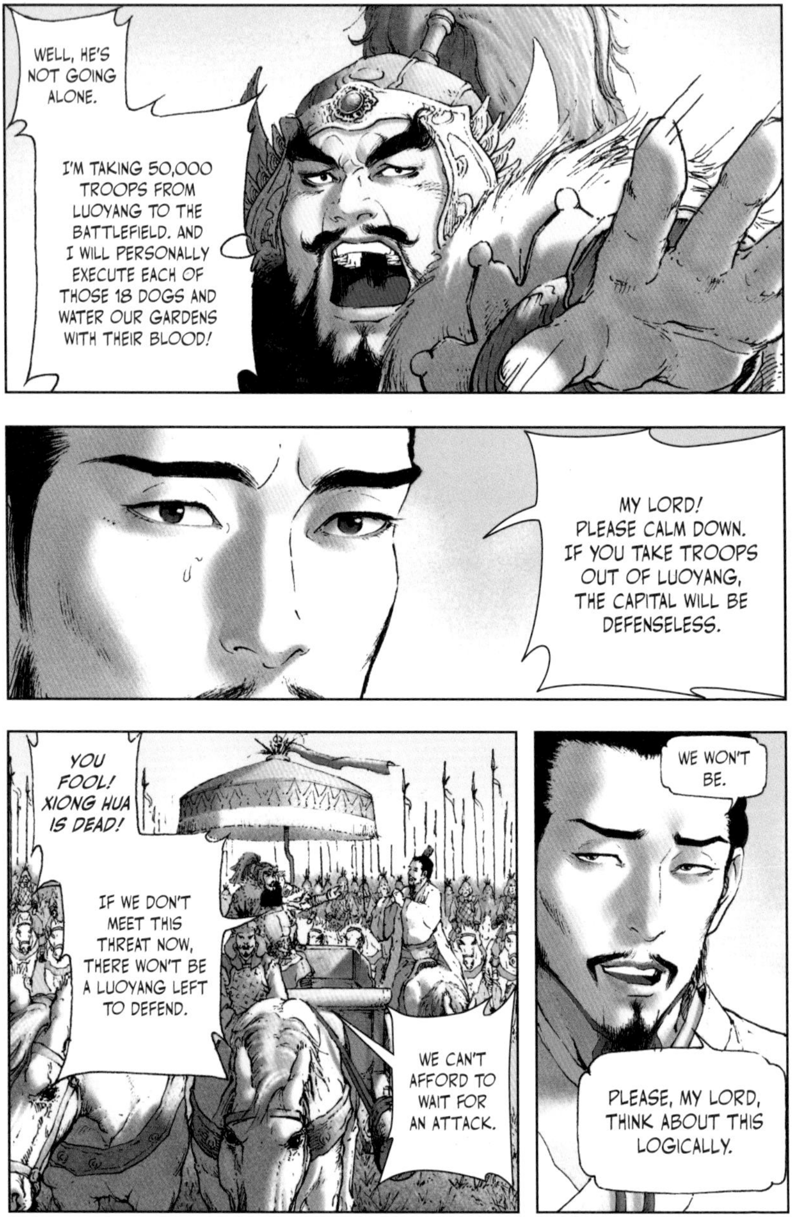
WELL, HE'S NOT GOING ALONE.
I'M TAKING 50,000 TROOPS FROM LUOYANG TO THE BATTLEFIELD. AND I WILL PERSONALLY EXECUTE EACH OF THOSE 18 DOGS AND WATER OUR GARDENS WITH THEIR BLOOD!
MY LORD! PLEASE CALM DOWN. IF YOU TAKE TROOPS OUT OF LUOYANG, THE CAPITAL WILL BE DEFENSELESS.
YOU FOOL! XIONG HUA IS DEAD!
IF WE DON'T MEET THIS THREAT NOW, THERE WON'T BE A LUOYANG LEFT TO DEFEND.
WE CAN'T AFFORD TO WAIT FOR AN ATTACK.
WE WON'T BE.
PLEASE, MY LORD, THINK ABOUT THIS LOGICALLY.

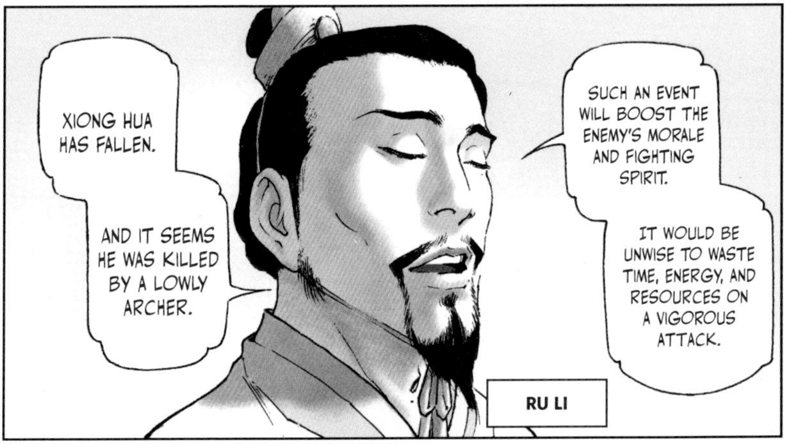
XIONG HUA HAS FALLEN.
AND IT SEEMS HE WAS KILLED BY A LOWLY ARCHER.
SUCH AN EVENT WILL BOOST THE ENEMY'S MORALE AND FIGHTING SPIRIT.
IT WOULD BE UNWISE TO WASTE TIME, ENERGY, AND RESOURCES ON A VIGOROUS ATTACK.
RU LI

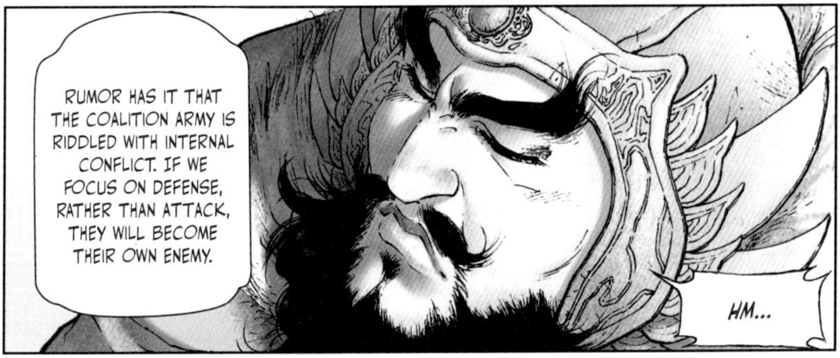
RUMOR HAS IT THAT THE COALITION ARMY IS RIDDLED WITH INTERNAL CONFLICT. IF WE FOCUS ON DEFENSE, RATHER THAN ATTACK, THEY WILL BECOME THEIR OWN ENEMY.
HM...

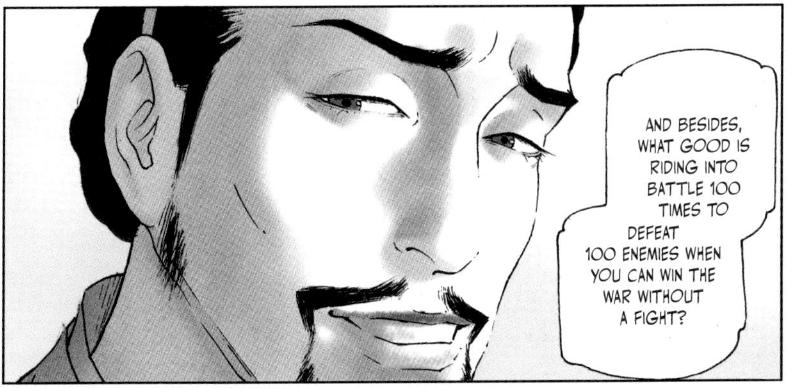
AND BESIDES, WHAT GOOD IS RIDING INTO BATTLE 100 TIMES TO DEFEAT 100 ENEMIES WHEN YOU CAN WIN THE WAR WITHOUT A FIGHT?

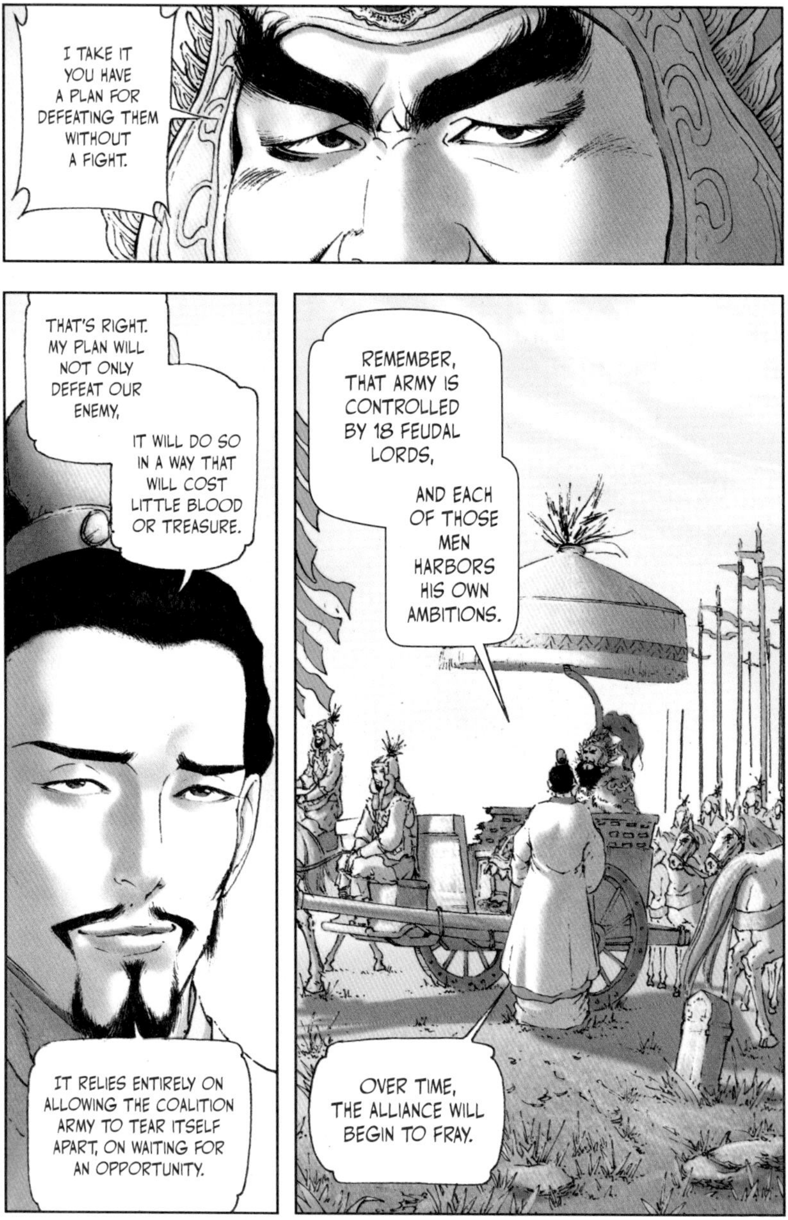
I TAKE IT YOU HAVE A PLAN FOR DEFEATING THEM WITHOUT A FIGHT.
THAT'S RIGHT. MY PLAN WILL NOT ONLY DEFEAT OUR ENEMY,
IT WILL DO SO IN A WAY THAT WILL COST LITTLE BLOOD OR TREASURE.
IT RELIES ENTIRELY ON ALLOWING THE COALITION ARMY TO TEAR ITSELF APART, ON WAITING FOR AN OPPORTUNITY.
REMEMBER, THAT ARMY IS CONTROLLED BY 18 FEUDAL LORDS,
AND EACH OF THOSE MEN HARBORS HIS OWN AMBITIONS.
OVER TIME, THE ALLIANCE WILL BEGIN TO FRAY.

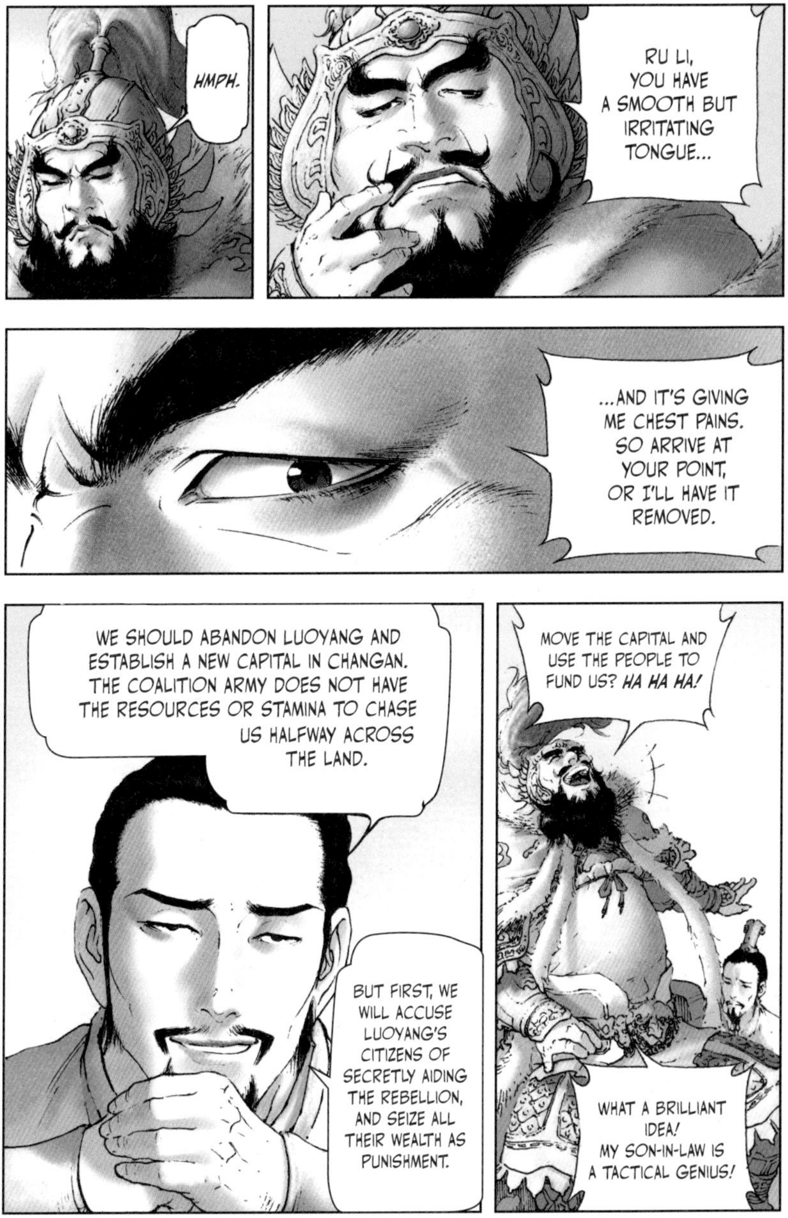
HMPH.
RU LI, YOU HAVE A SMOOTH BUT IRRITATING TONGUE...
...AND IT'S GIVING ME CHEST PAINS. SO ARRIVE AT YOUR POINT, OR I'LL HAVE IT REMOVED.
WE SHOULD ABANDON LUOYANG AND ESTABLISH A NEW CAPITAL IN CHANGAN. THE COALITION ARMY DOES NOT HAVE THE RESOURCES OR STAMINA TO CHASE US HALFWAY ACROSS THE LAND.
BUT FIRST, WE WILL ACCUSE LUOYANG'S CITIZENS OF SECRETLY AIDING THE REBELLION, AND SEIZE ALL THEIR WEALTH AS PUNISHMENT.
MOVE THE CAPITAL AND USE THE PEOPLE TO FUND US? HA HA HA!
WHAT A BRILLIANT IDEA! MY SON-IN-LAW IS A TACTICAL GENIUS!

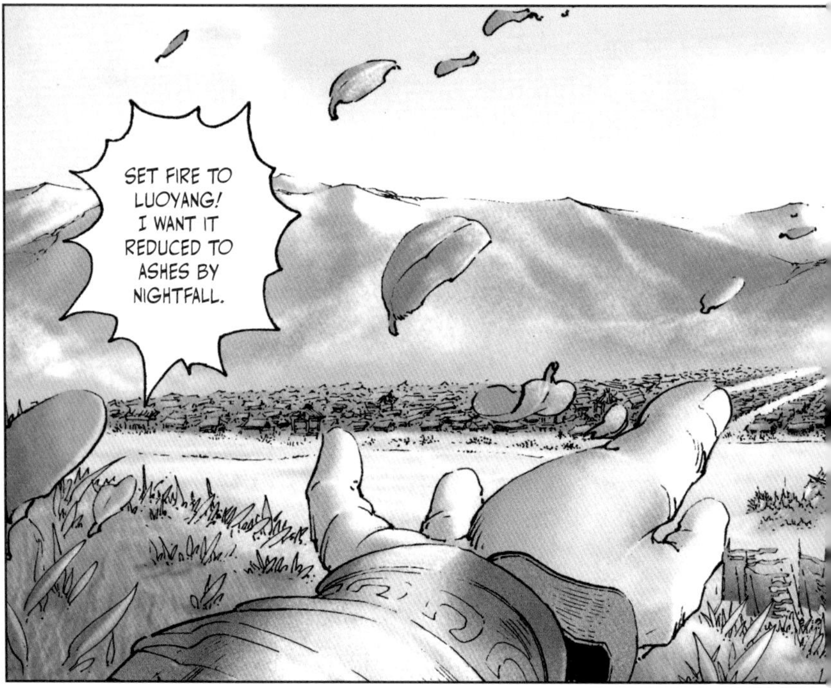
SET FIRE TO LUOYANG! I WANT IT REDUCED TO ASHES BY NIGHTFALL.

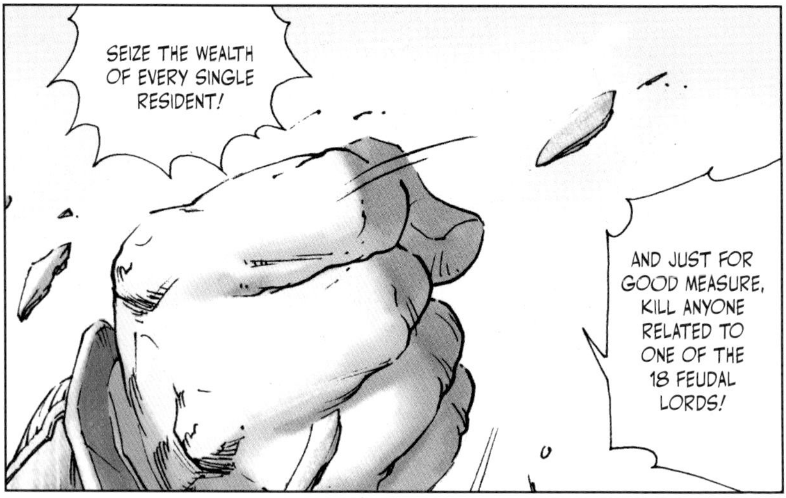
SEIZE THE WEALTH OF EVERY SINGLE RESIDENT!
AND JUST FOR GOOD MEASURE, KILL ANYONE RELATED TO ONE OF THE 18 FEUDAL LORDS!

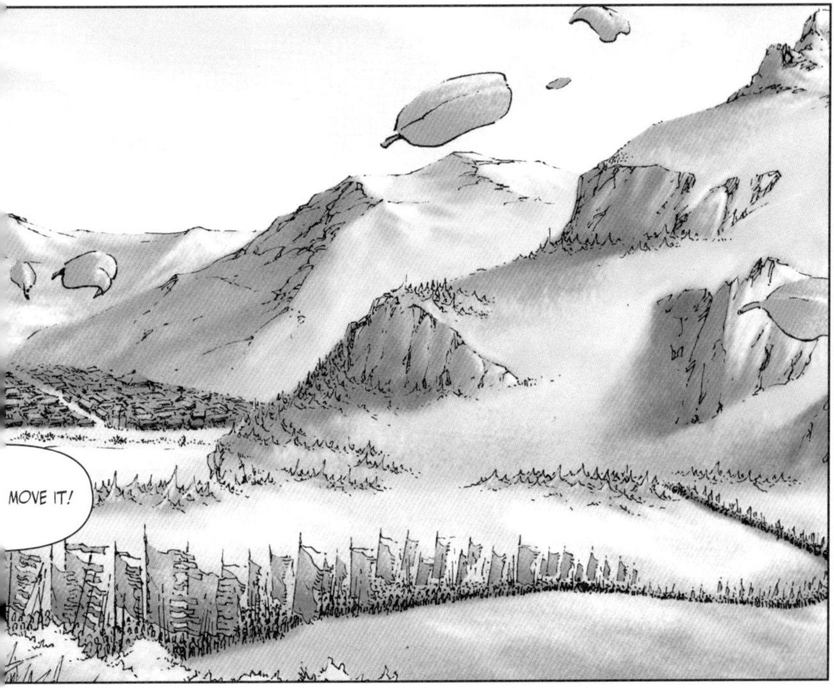
MOVE IT!

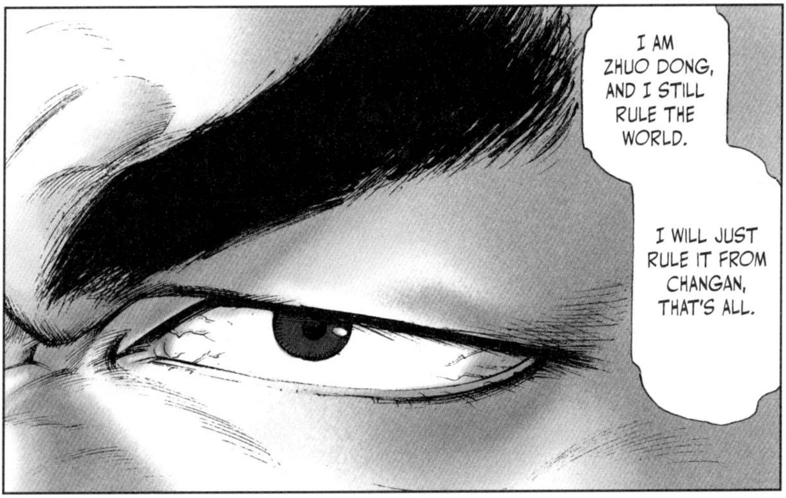
I AM ZHUO DONG, AND I STILL RULE THE WORLD.
I WILL JUST RULE IT FROM CHANGAN, THAT'S ALL.

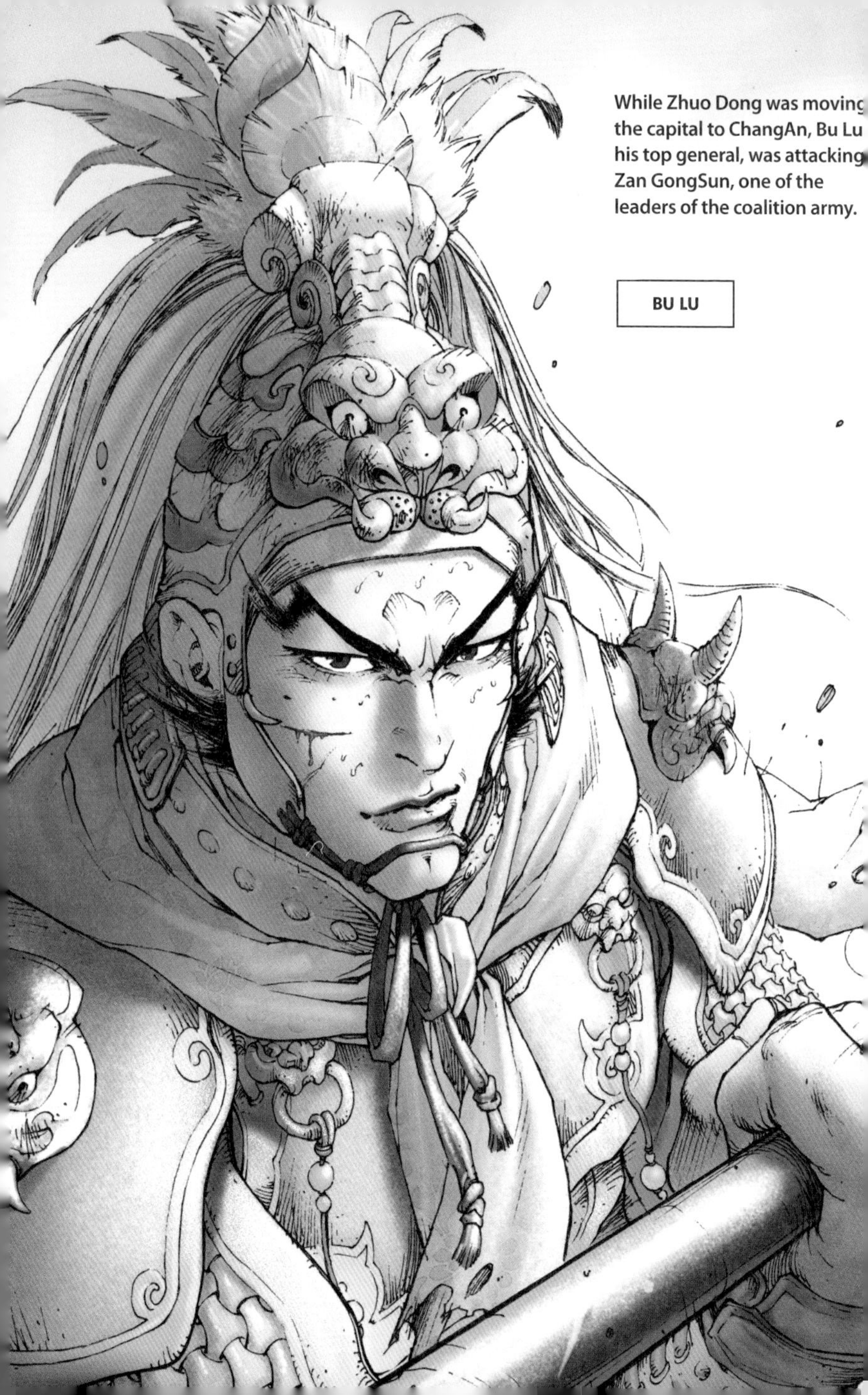
While Zhuo Dong was moving the capital to ChangAn, Bu Lu his top general, was attacking Zan GongSun, one of the leaders of the coalition army.
BU LU

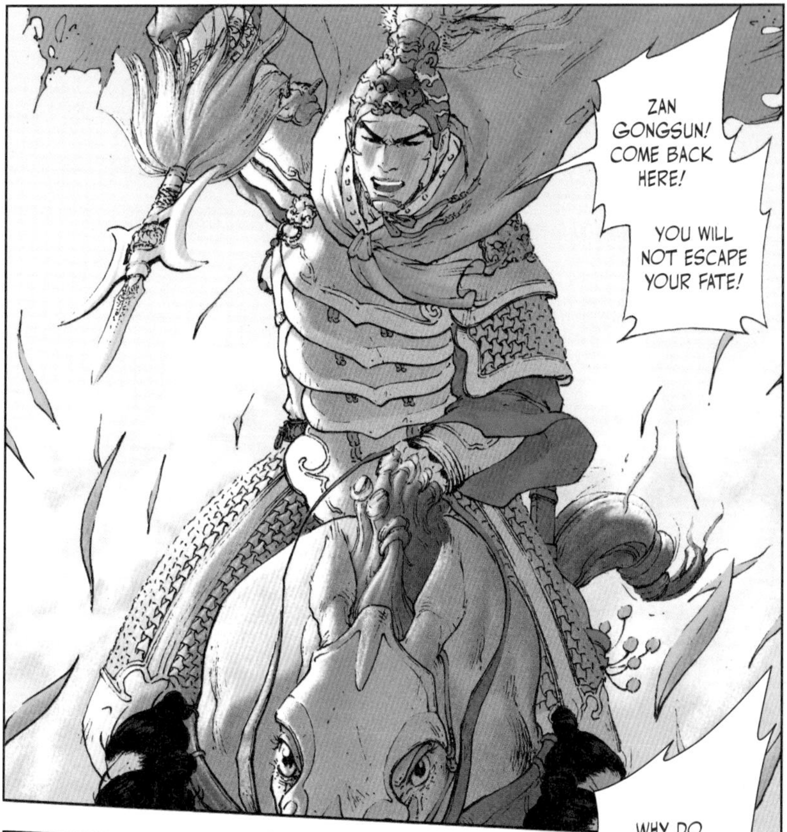
ZAN GONGSUN! COME BACK HERE!
YOU WILL NOT ESCAPE YOUR FATE!

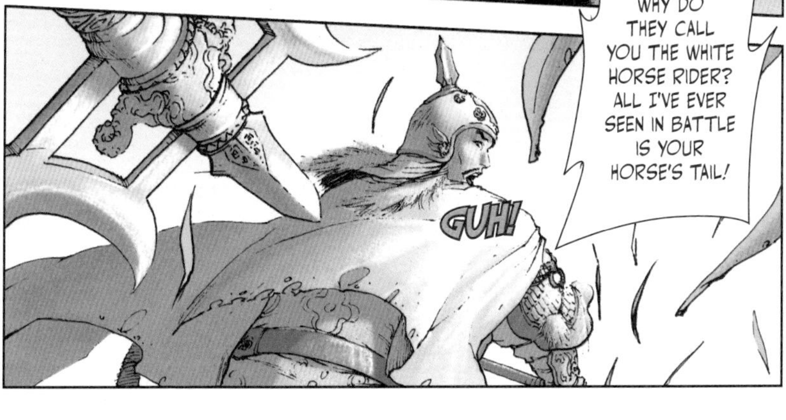
WHY DO THEY CALL YOU THE WHITE HORSE RIDER? ALL I'VE EVER SEEN IN BATTLE IS YOUR HORSE'S TAIL!
GUH!

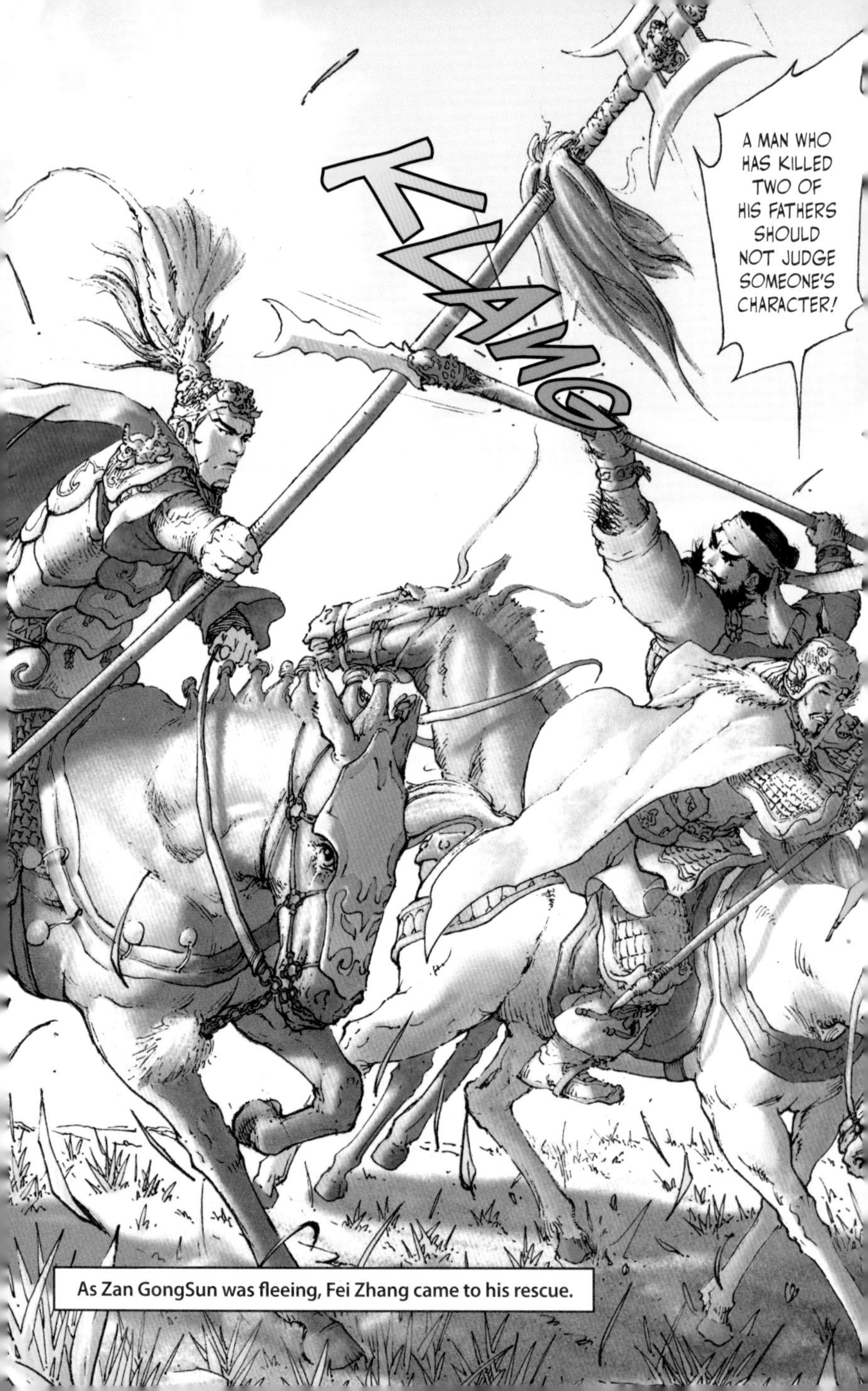
KLANG
A MAN WHO HAS KILLED TWO OF HIS FATHERS SHOULD NOT JUDGE SOMEONE'S CHARACTER!
As Zan GongSun was fleeing, Fei Zhang came to his rescue.

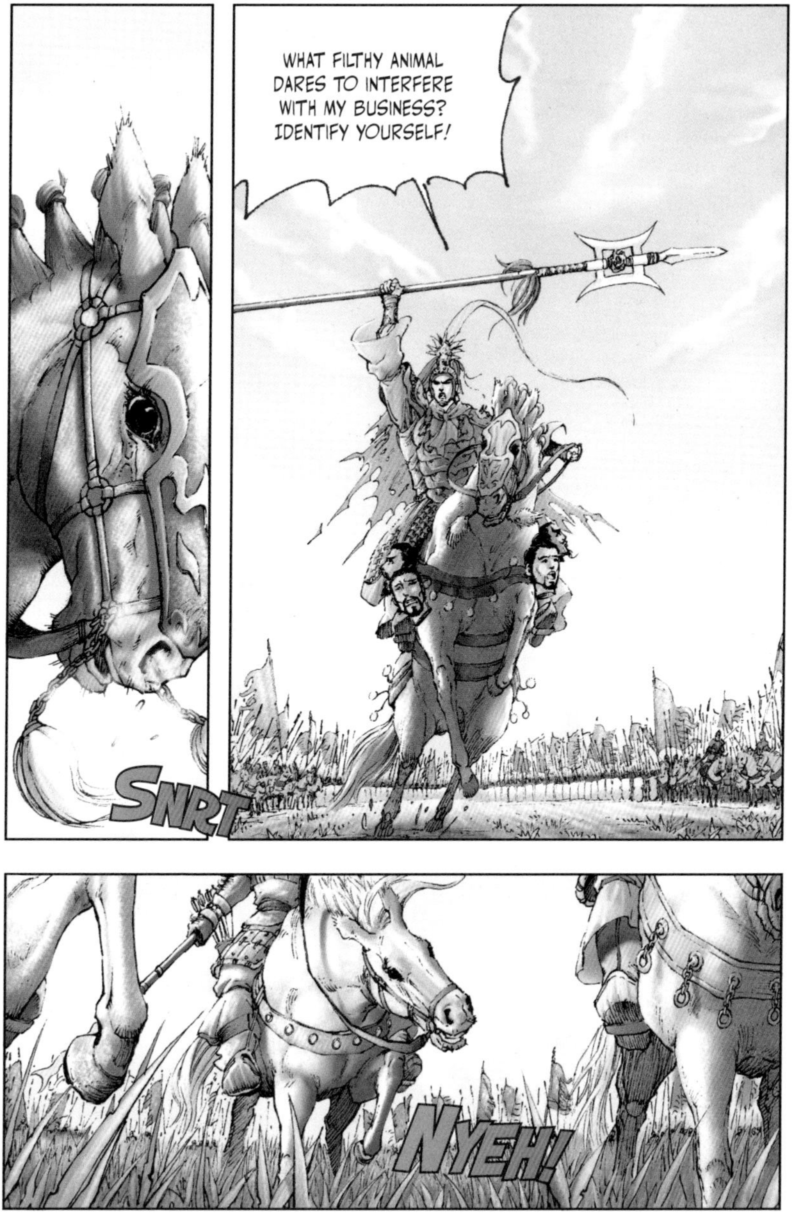
WHAT FILTHY ANIMAL DARES TO INTERFERE WITH MY BUSINESS? IDENTIFY YOURSELF!
SNRT
NYEH!

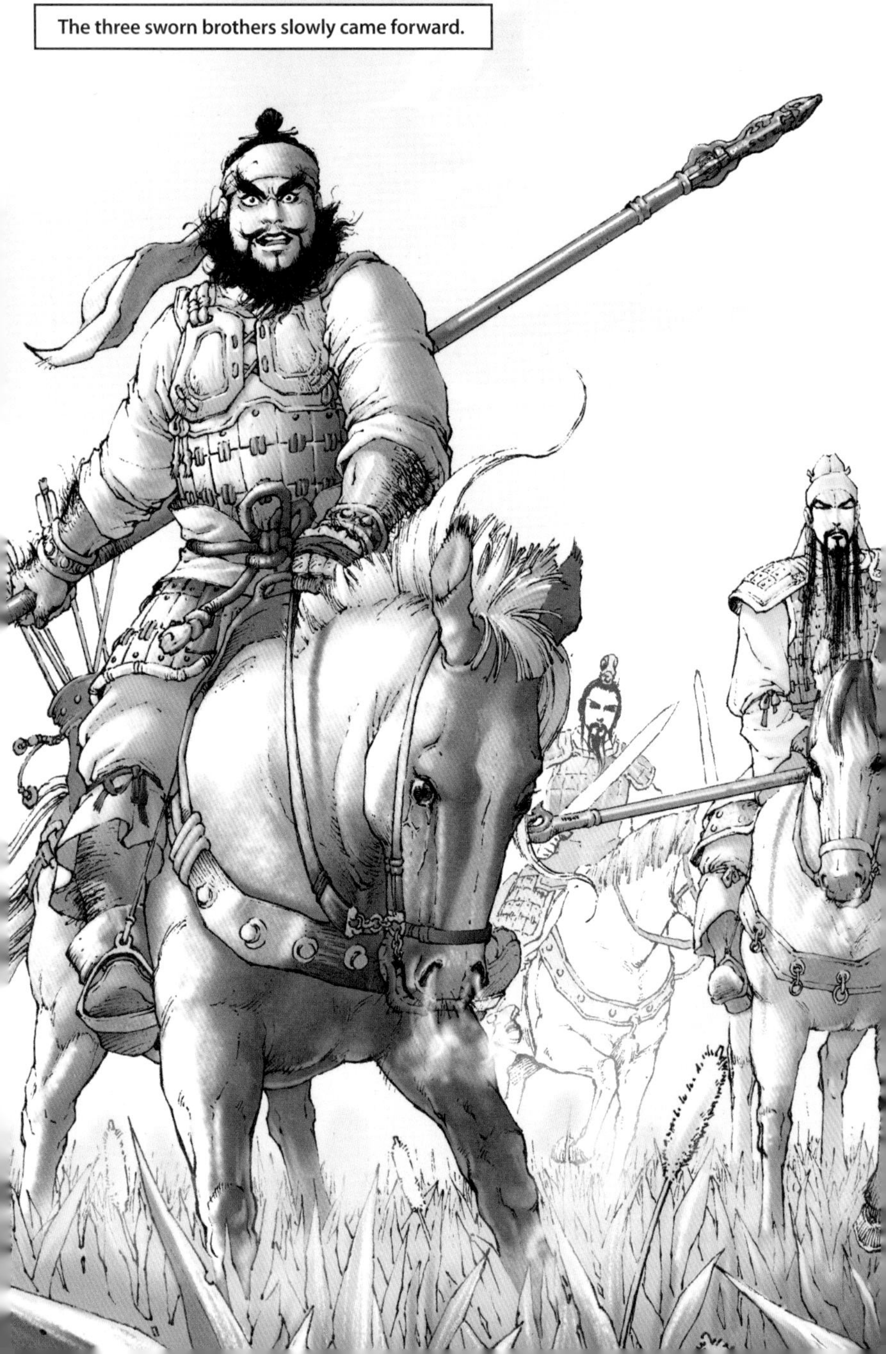
The three sworn brothers slowly came forward.

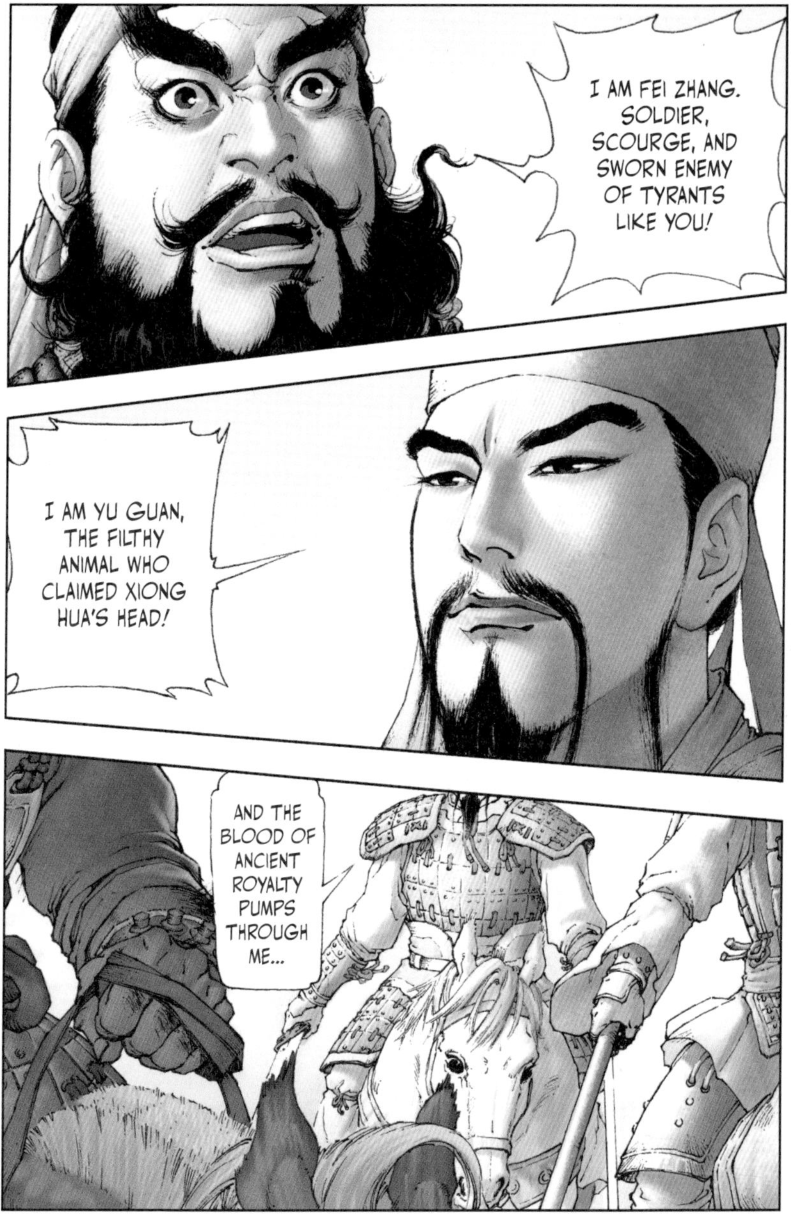
I AM FEI ZHANG. SOLDIER, SCOURGE, AND SWORN ENEMY OF TYRANTS LIKE YOU!
I AM YU GUAN, THE FILTHY ANIMAL WHO CLAIMED XIONG HUA'S HEAD!
AND THE BLOOD OF ANCIENT ROYALTY PUMPS THROUGH ME...

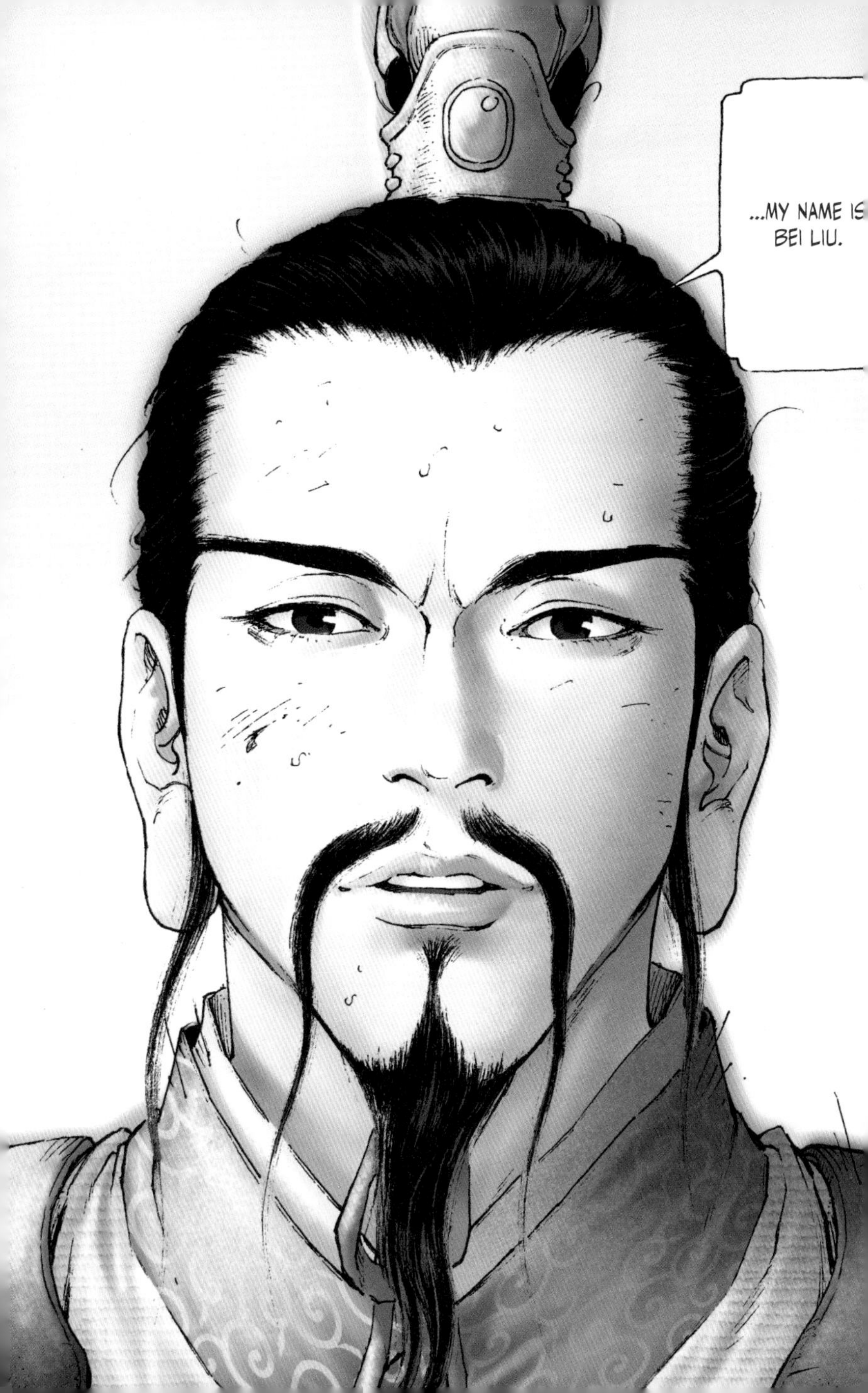
...MY NAME IS BEI LIU.

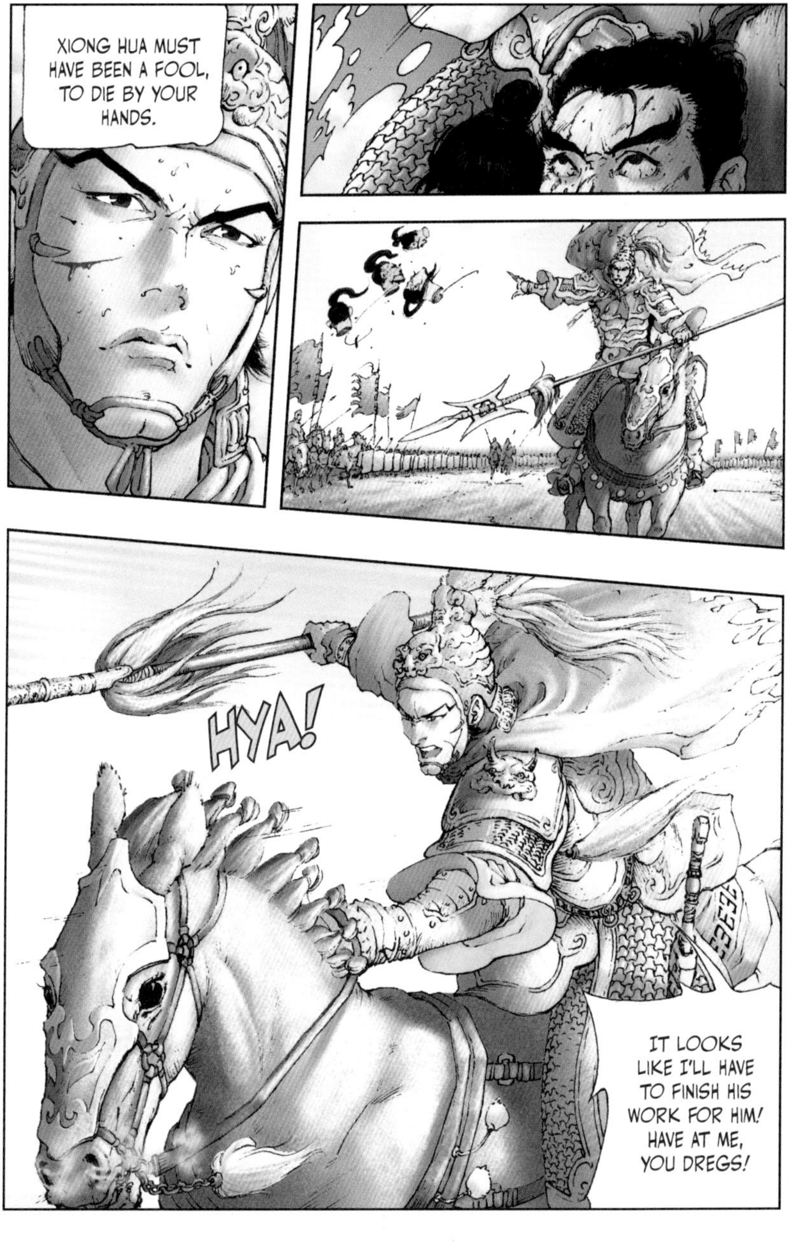
XIONG HUA MUST HAVE BEEN A FOOL, TO DIE BY YOUR HANDS.
HYA!
IT LOOKS LIKE I'LL HAVE TO FINISH HIS WORK FOR HIM! HAVE AT ME, YOU DREGS!

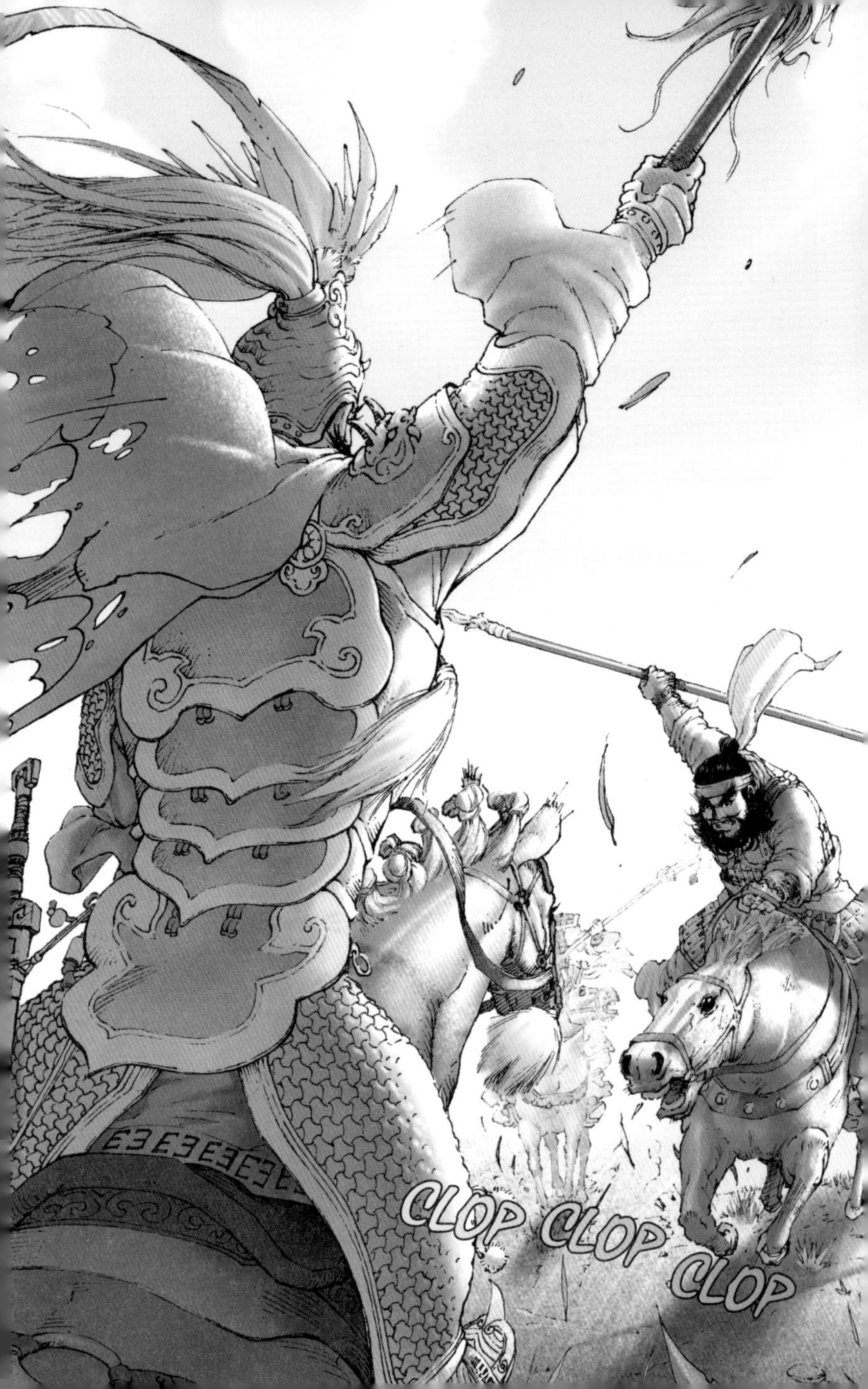
CLOP CLOP CLOP

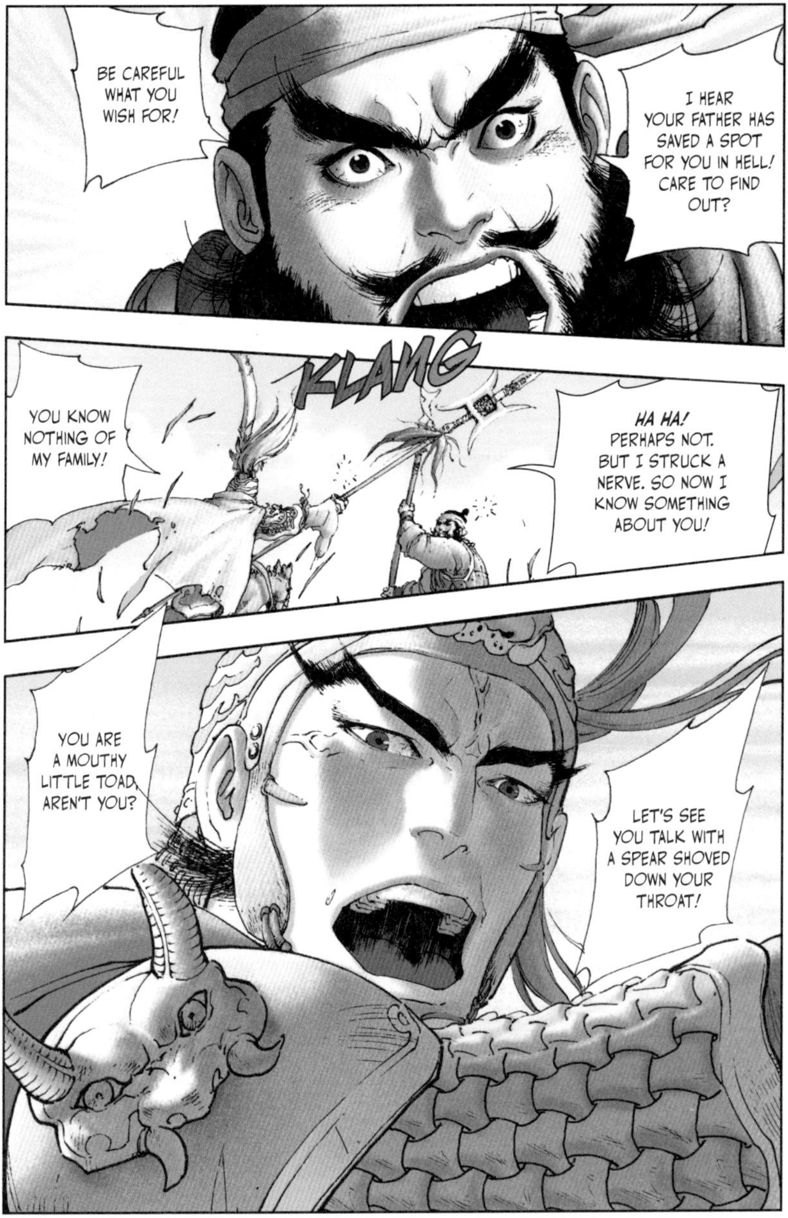
BE CAREFUL WHAT YOU WISH FOR!
I HEAR YOUR FATHER HAS SAVED A SPOT FOR YOU IN HELL! CARE TO FIND OUT?
KLANG
YOU KNOW NOTHING OF MY FAMILY!
HA HA! PERHAPS NOT. BUT I STRUCK A NERVE. SO NOW I KNOW SOMETHING ABOUT YOU!
YOU ARE A MOUTHY LITTLE TOAD, AREN'T YOU?
LET'S SEE YOU TALK WITH A SPEAR SHOVED DOWN YOUR THROAT!

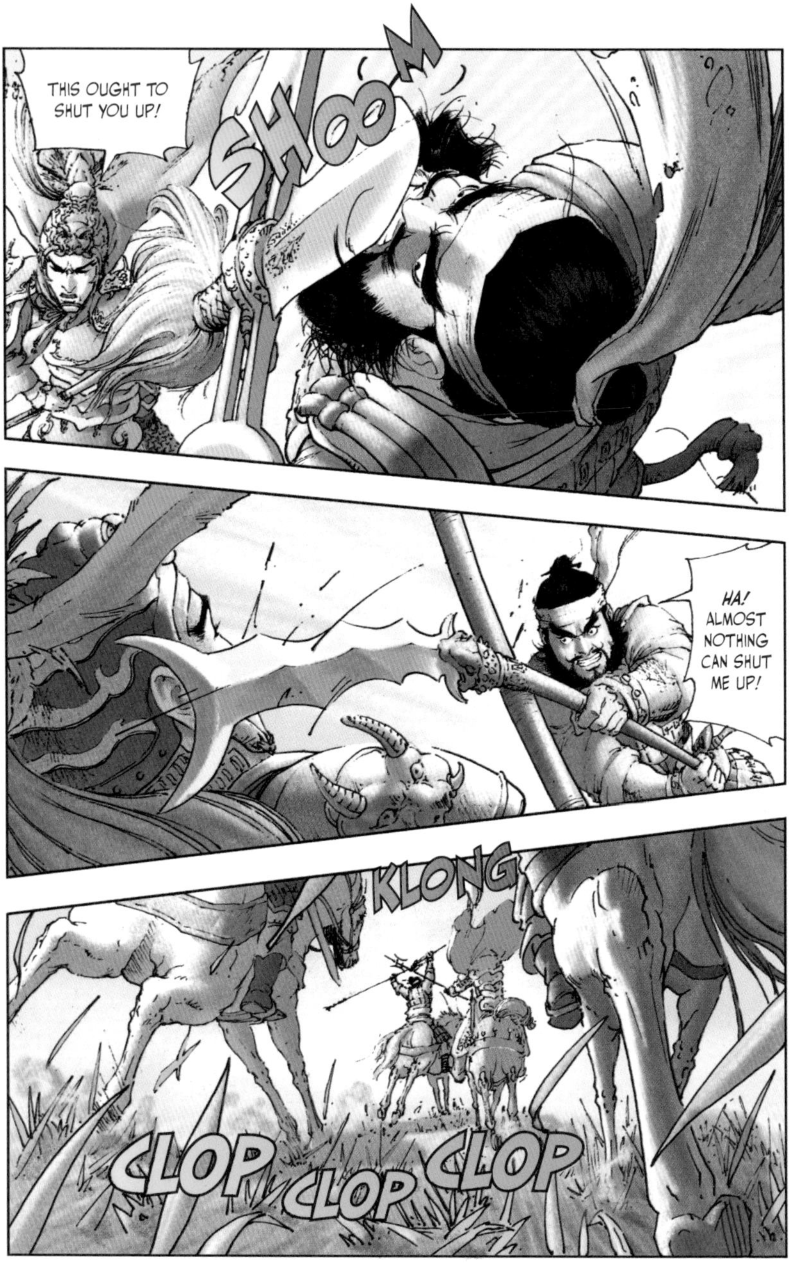
THIS OUGHT TO SHUT YOU UP!
SHOOOM
HA! ALMOST NOTHING CAN SHUT ME UP!
KLONG
CLOP CLOP CLOP

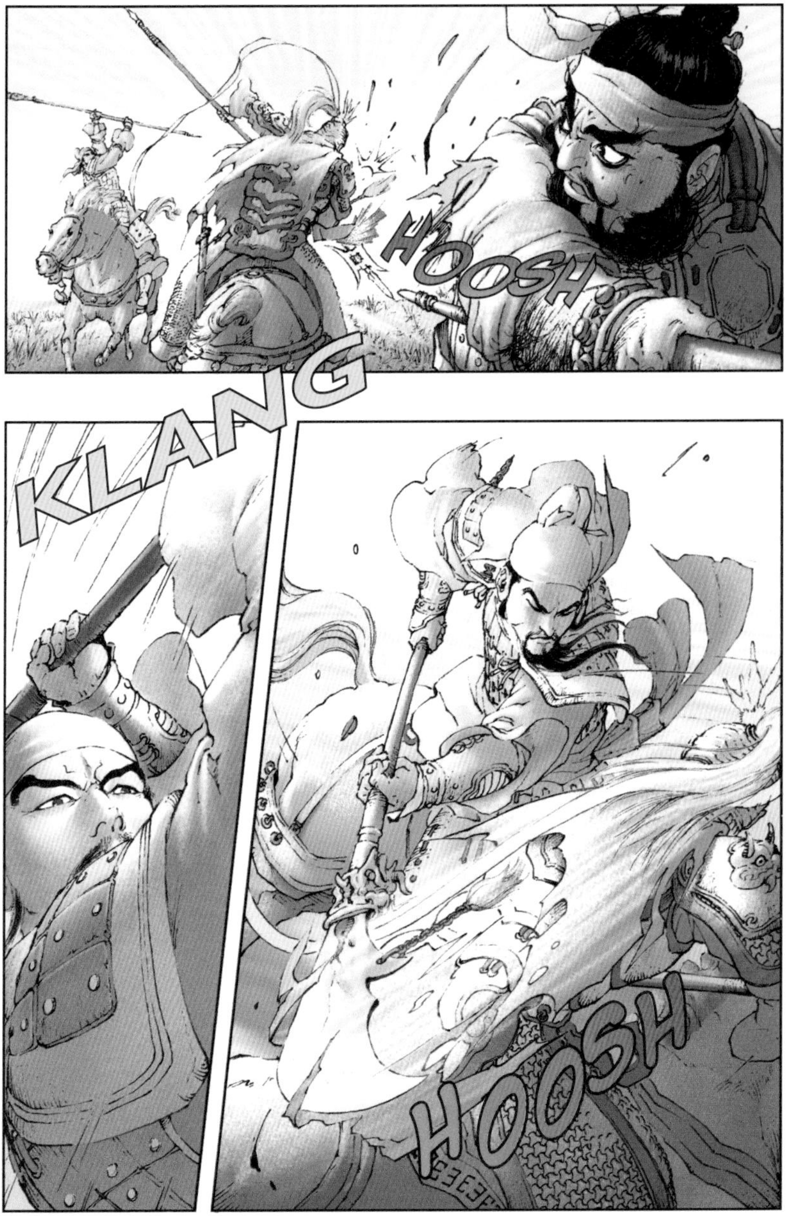
HOOSH
KLANG
HOOSH

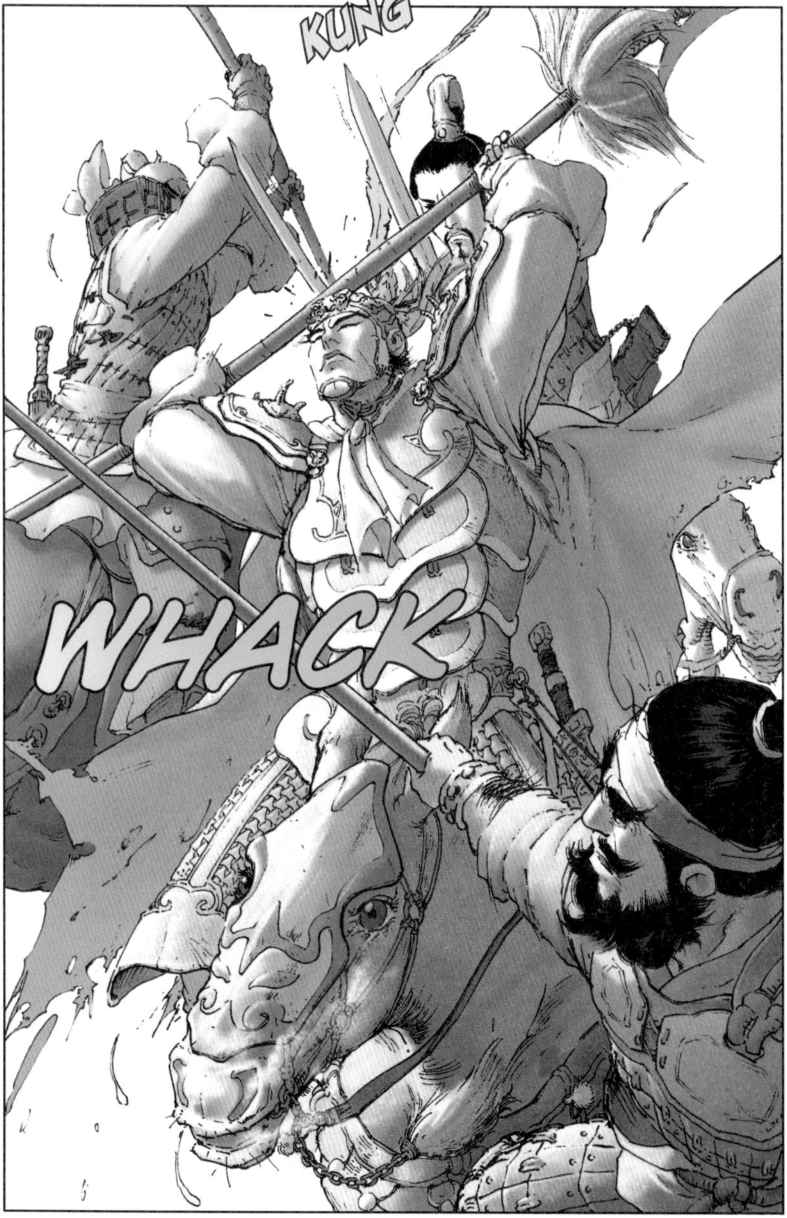
KUNG
WHACK

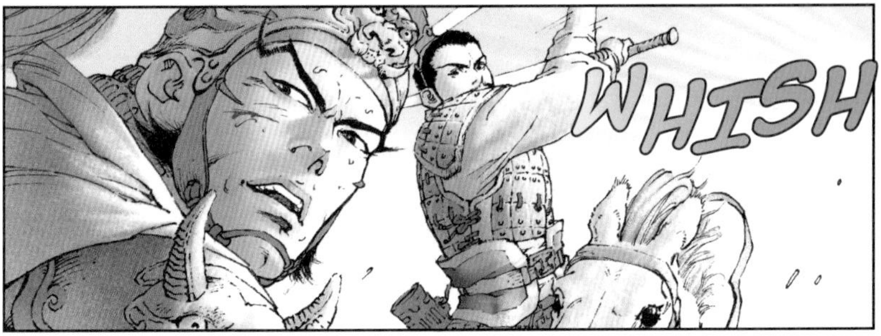
WHISH

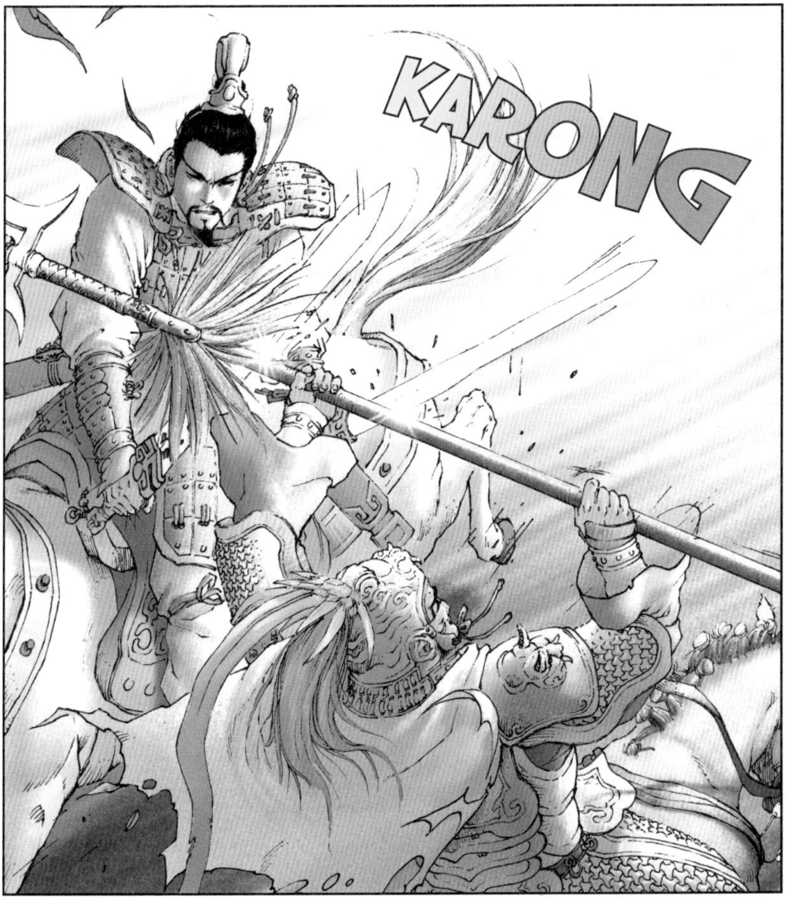
KARONG

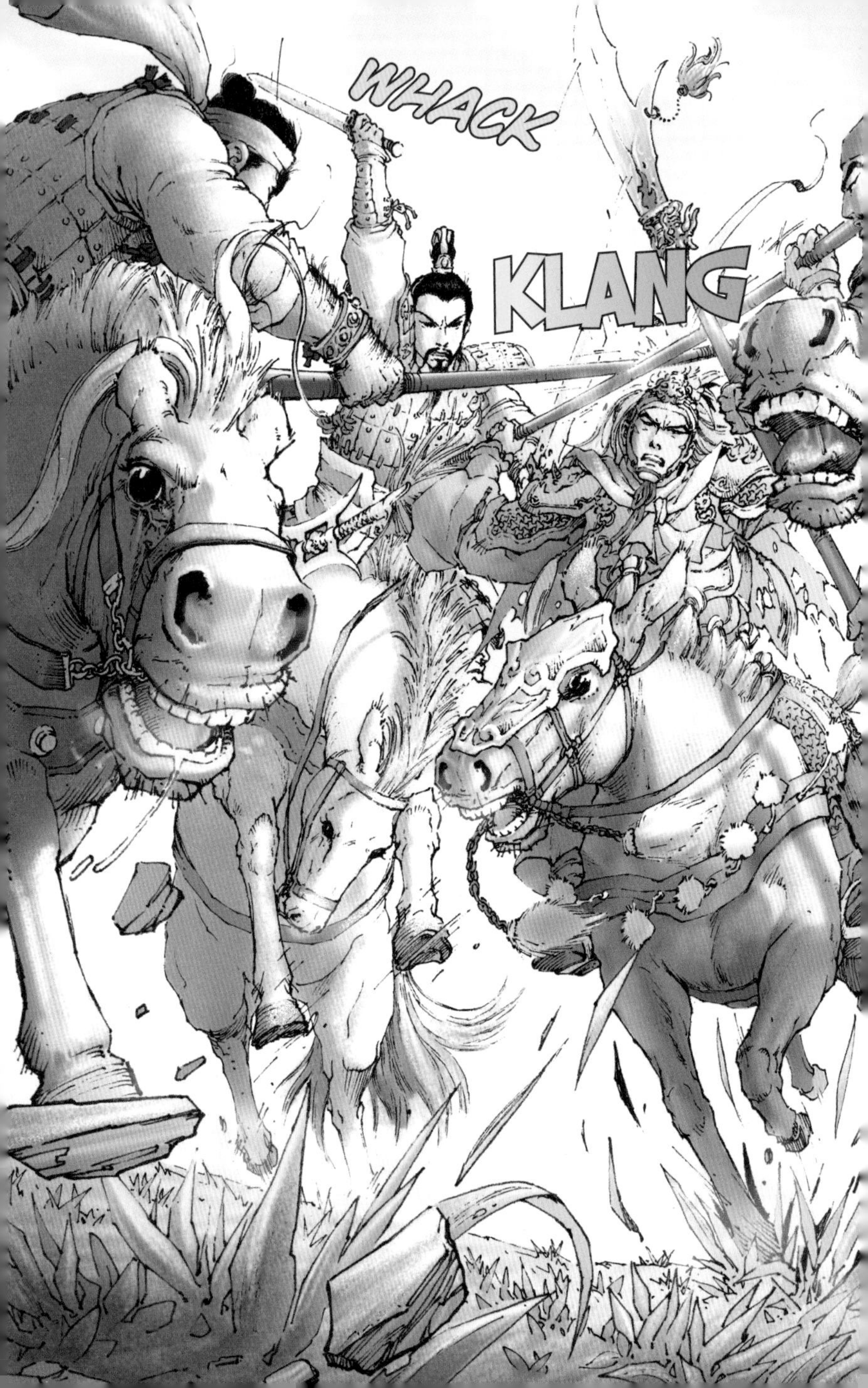
WHACK
KLANG

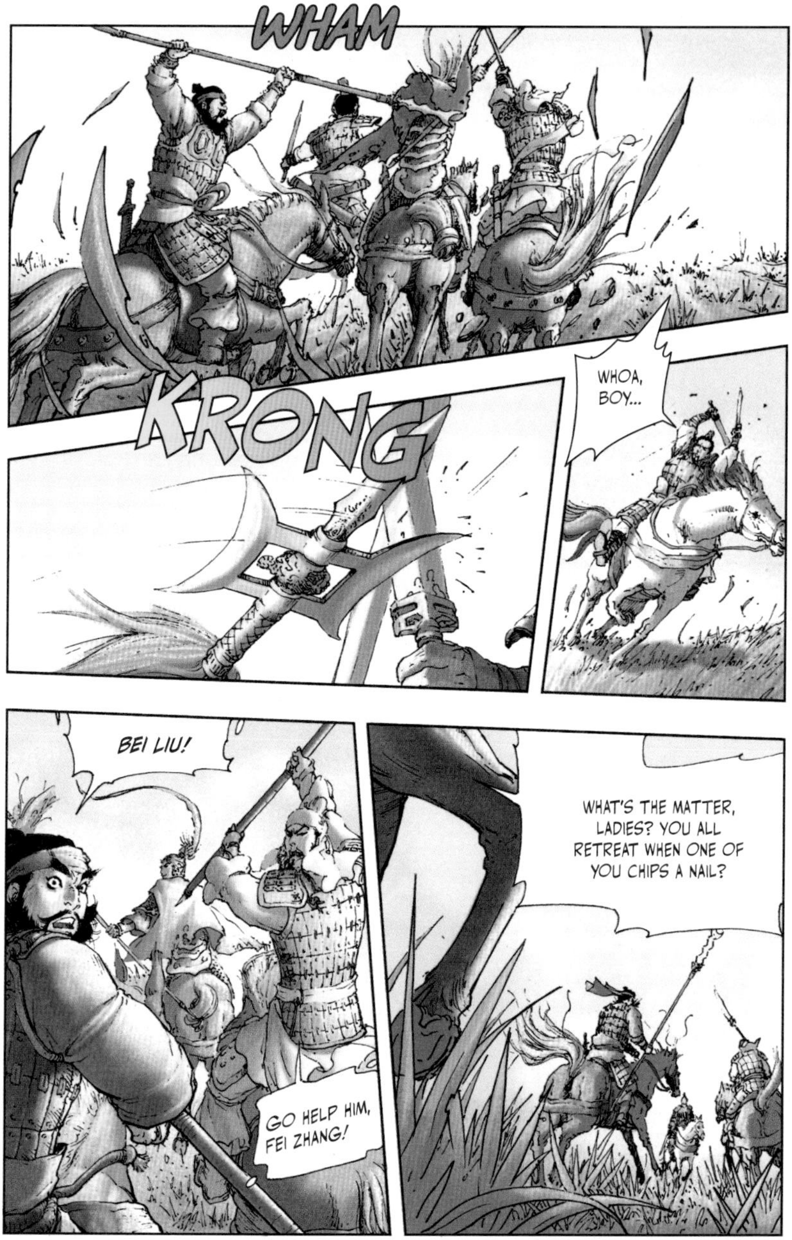
WHAM
KRONG
WHOA, BOY...
BEI LIU!
GO HELP HIM, FEI ZHANG!
WHAT'S THE MATTER, LADIES? YOU ALL RETREAT WHEN ONE OF YOU CHIPS A NAIL?

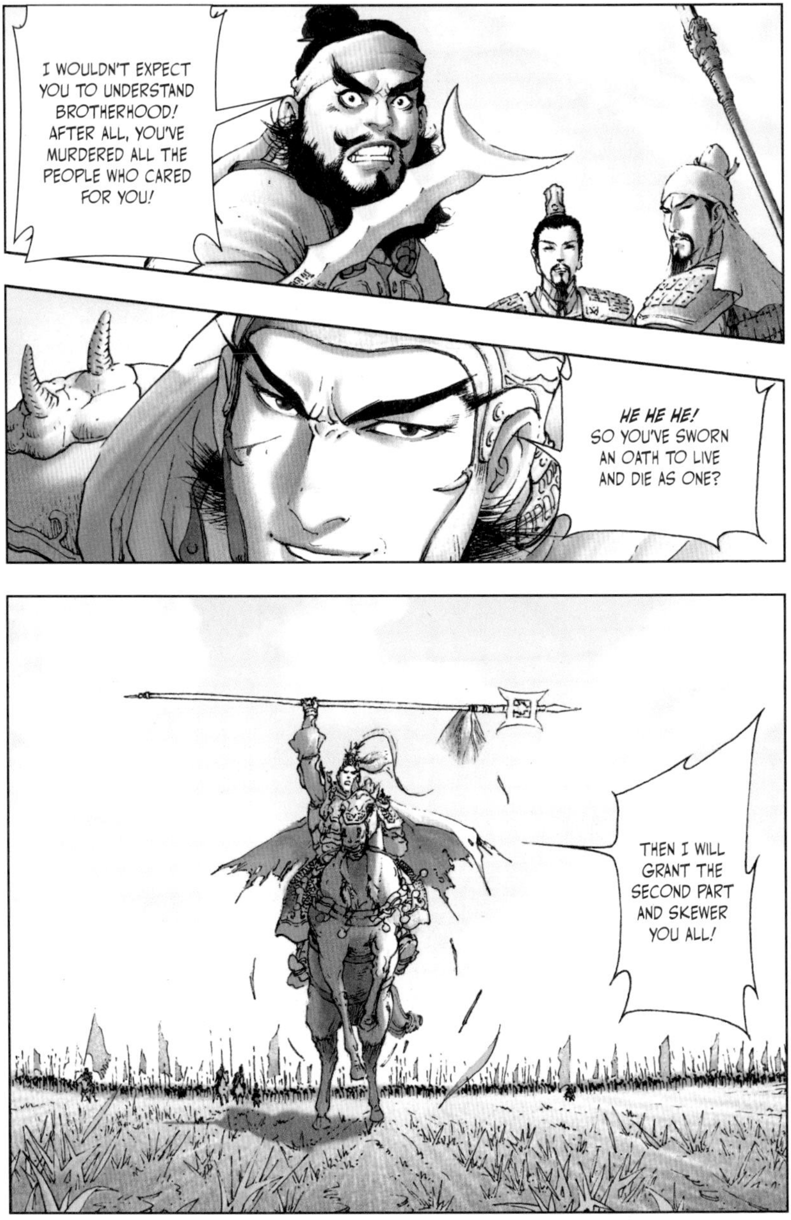
I WOULDN'T EXPECT YOU TO UNDERSTAND BROTHERHOOD! AFTER ALL, YOU'VE MURDERED ALL THE PEOPLE WHO CARED FOR YOU!
HE HE HE! SO YOU'VE SWORN AN OATH TO LIVE AND DIE AS ONE?
THEN I WILL GRANT THE SECOND PART AND SKEWER YOU ALL!

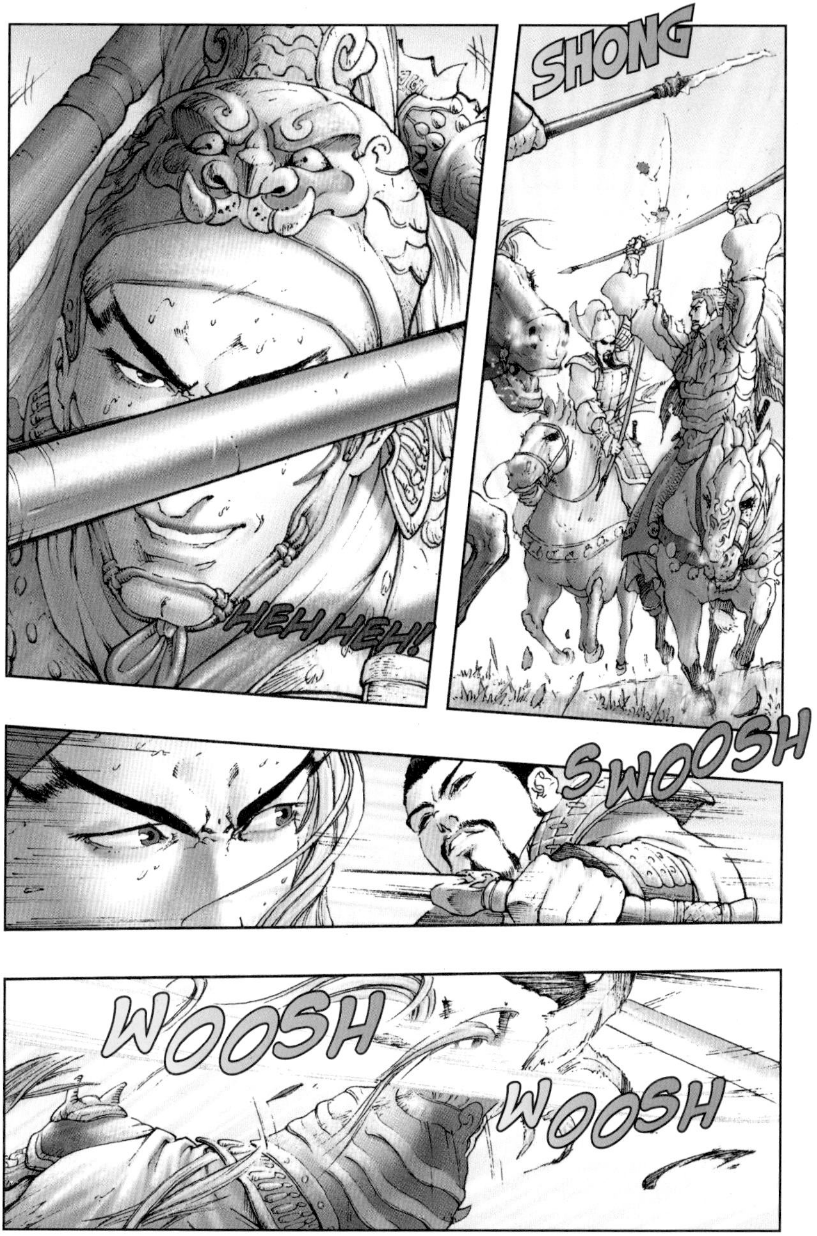
HEH HEH!
SHONG
SWOOSH
WOOSH
WOOSH

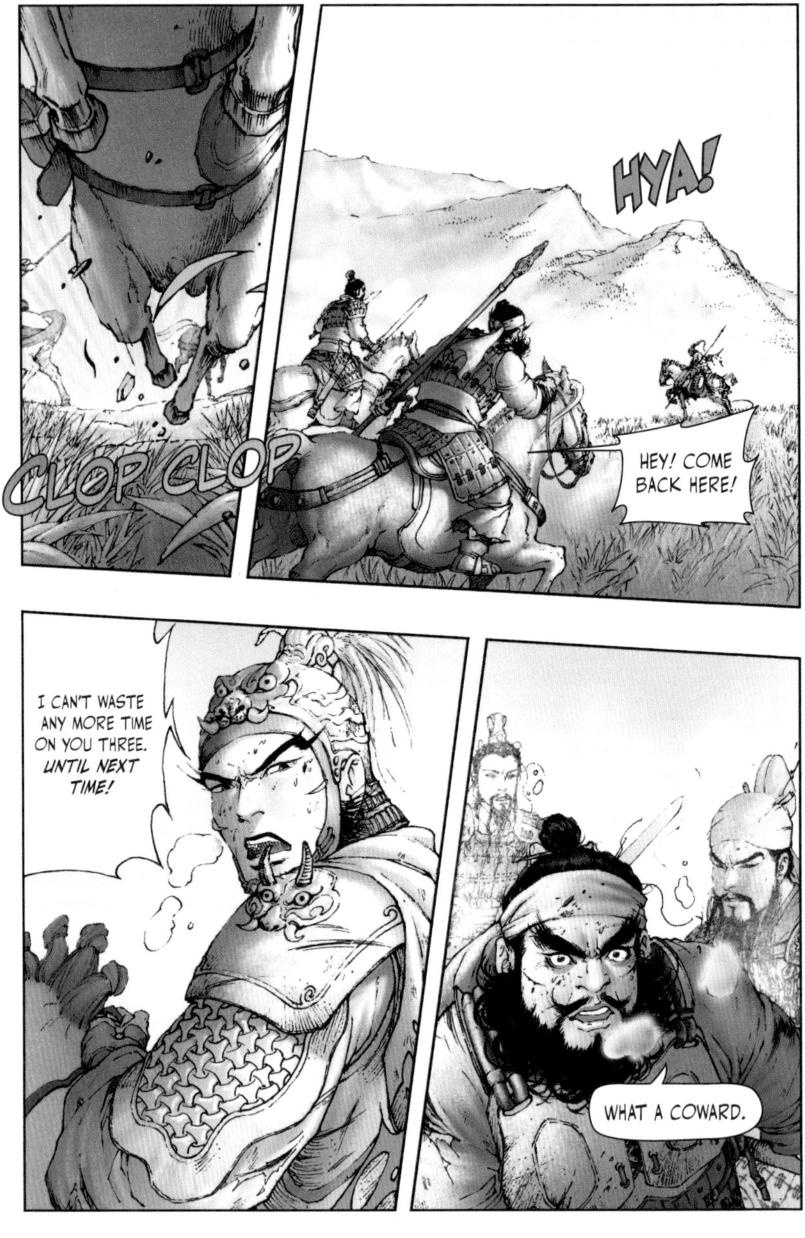
CLOP CLOP
HYA!
HEY! COME BACK HERE!
I CAN'T WASTE ANY MORE TIME ON YOU THREE. UNTIL NEXT TIME!
WHAT A COWARD.

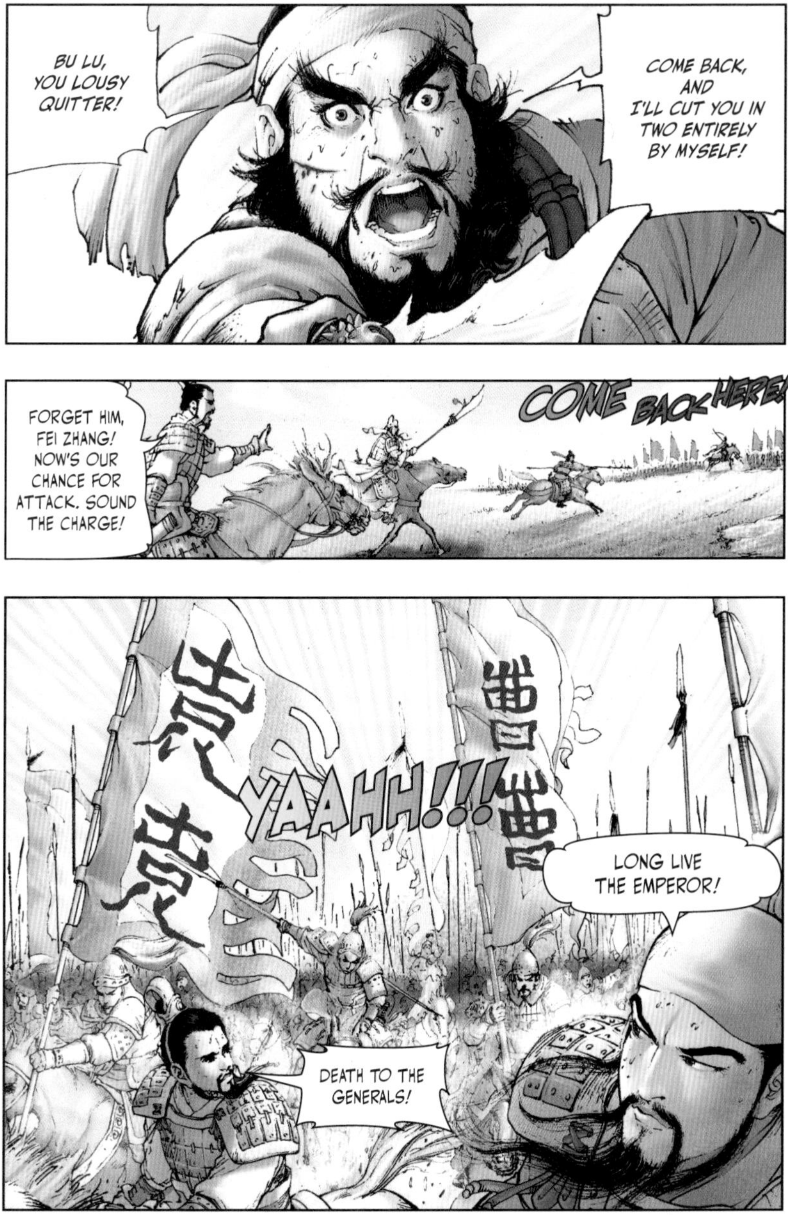
BU LU, YOU LOUSY QUITTER!
COME BACK, AND I'LL CUT YOU IN TWO ENTIRELY BY MYSELF!
FORGET HIM, FEI ZHANG! NOW'S OUR CHANCE FOR ATTACK. SOUND THE CHARGE!
COME BACK HERE!
YAAHH!!!
LONG LIVE THE EMPEROR!
DEATH TO THE GENERALS!

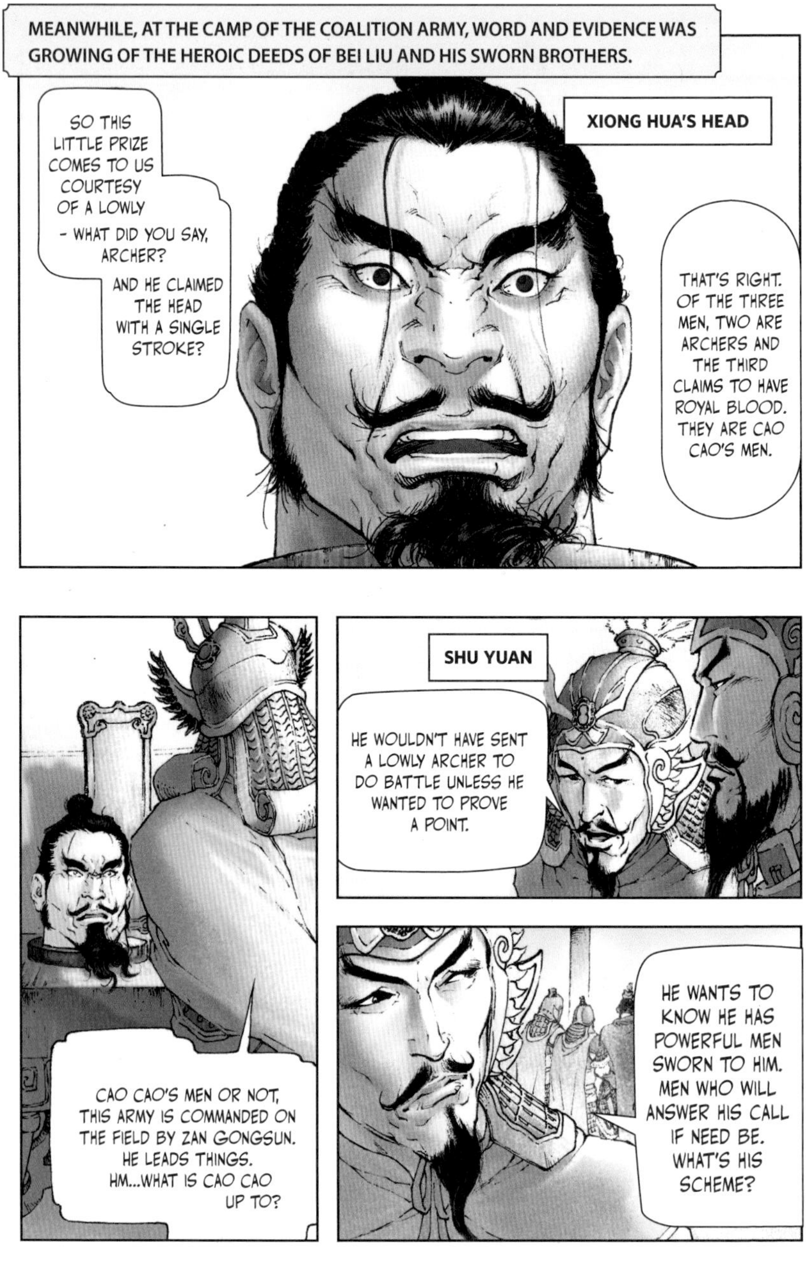
MEANWHILE, AT THE CAMP OF THE COALITION ARMY, WORD AND EVIDENCE WAS GROWING OF THE HEROIC DEEDS OF BEI LIU AND HIS SWORN BROTHERS.
SO THIS LITTLE PRIZE COMES TO US COURTESY OF A LOWLY - WHAT DID YOU SAY, ARCHER?
AND HE CLAIMED THE HEAD WITH A SINGLE STROKE?
XIONG HUA'S HEAD
THAT'S RIGHT. OF THE THREE MEN, TWO ARE ARCHERS AND THE THIRD CLAIMS TO HAVE ROYAL BLOOD. THEY ARE CAO CAO'S MEN.
CAO CAO'S MEN OR NOT, THIS ARMY IS COMMANDED ON THE FIELD BY ZAN GONGSUN. HE LEADS THINGS. HM...WHAT IS CAO CAO UP TO?
SHU YUAN
HE WOULDN'T HAVE SENT A LOWLY ARCHER TO DO BATTLE UNLESS HE WANTED TO PROVE A POINT.
HE WANTS TO KNOW HE HAS POWERFUL MEN SWORN TO HIM. MEN WHO WILL ANSWER HIS CALL IF NEED BE. WHAT'S HIS SCHEME?

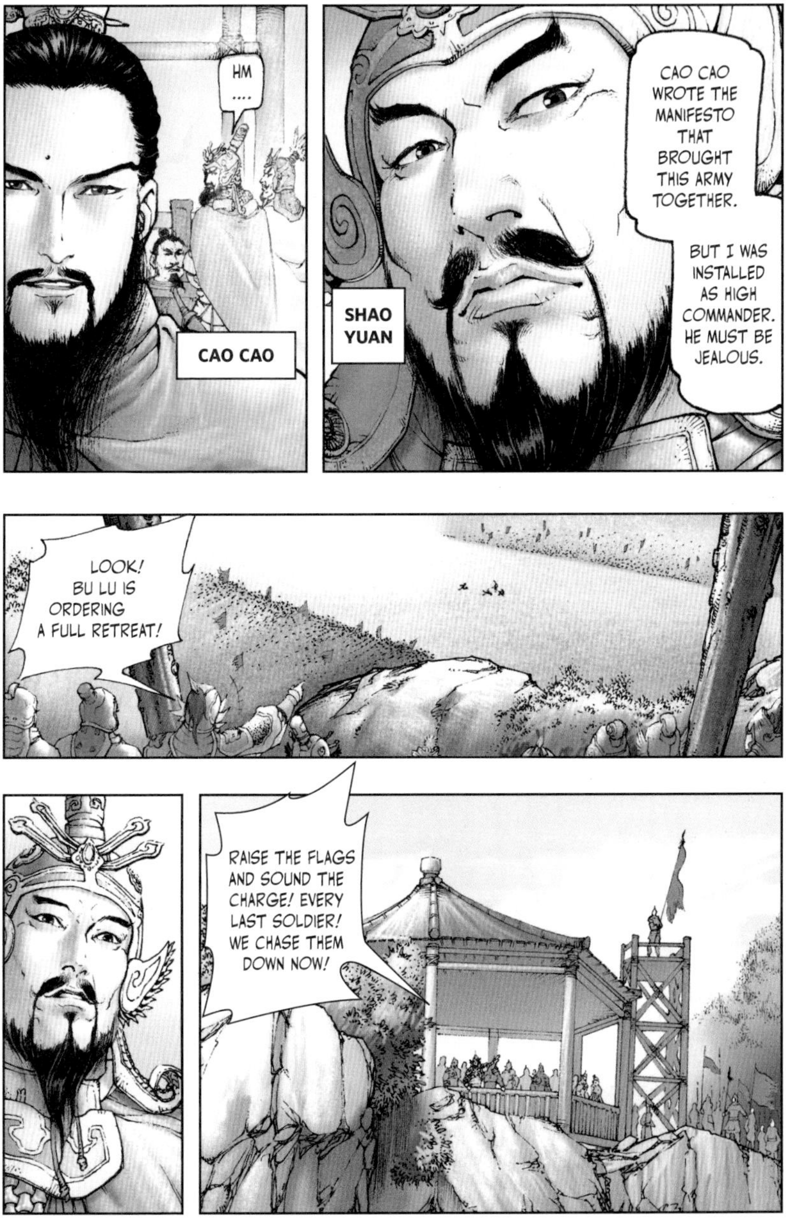
HM ....
CAO CAO
SHAO YUAN
CAO CAO WROTE THE MANIFESTO THAT BROUGHT THIS ARMY TOGETHER.
BUT I WAS INSTALLED AS HIGH COMMANDER. HE MUST BE JEALOUS.
LOOK! BU LU IS ORDERING A FULL RETREAT!
RAISE THE FLAGS AND SOUND THE CHARGE! EVERY LAST SOLDIER! WE CHASE THEM DOWN NOW!

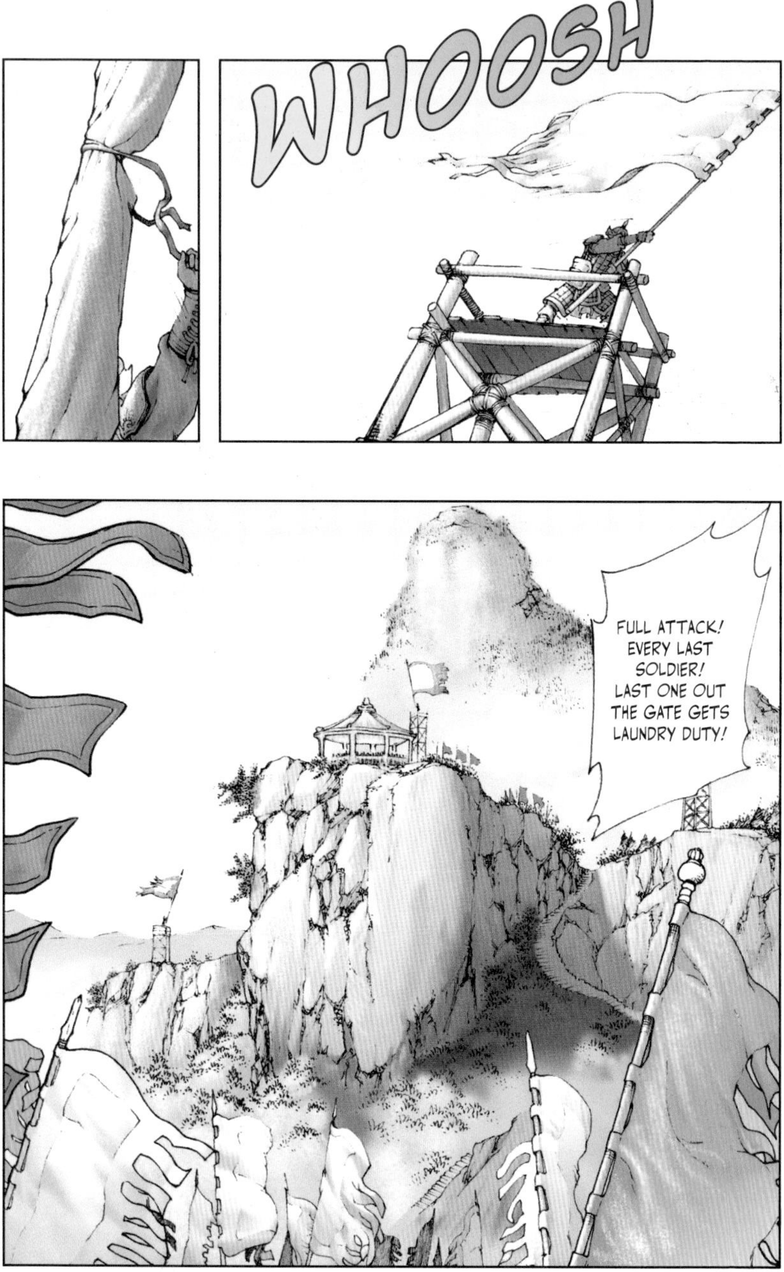
WHOOSH
FULL ATTACK! EVERY LAST SOLDIER! LAST ONE OUT THE GATE GETS LAUNDRY DUTY!

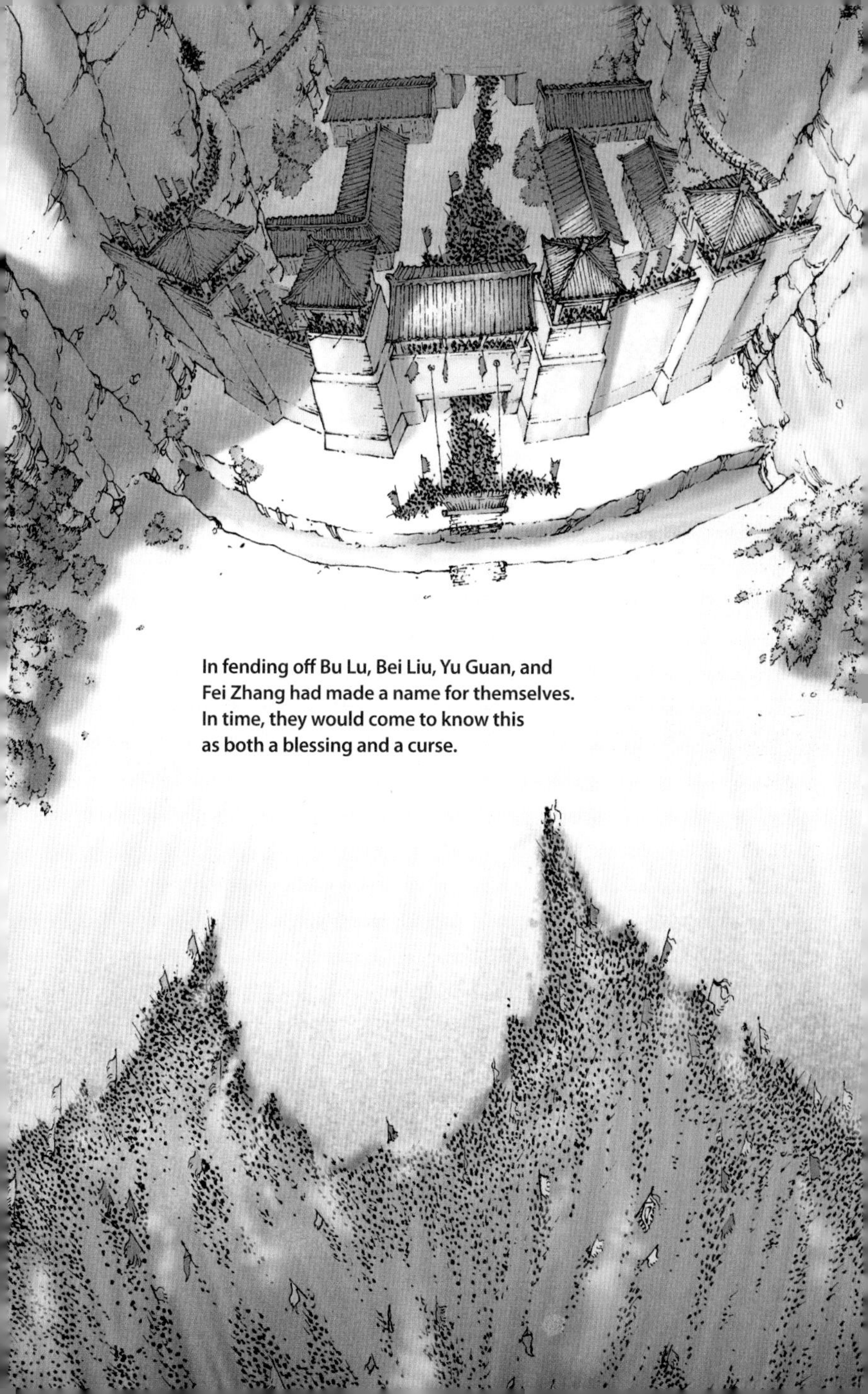
In fending off Bu Lu, Bei Liu, Yu Guan, and Fei Zhang had made a name for themselves. In time, they would come to know this as both a blessing and a curse.

Chapter 3

The Coalition Splinters AD 190 – 191

Summary

Bei Liu, Yu Guan, and Fei Zhang are highly praised for their roles in the battle against Zhuo Dong's forces, and are called to a feast of the council of feudal lords. During the feast, Jian Sun, who commanded the coalition forces during the battle, storms in and demands to know why Shu Yuan, who is responsible for sending supplies to the soldiers in the field, withheld an important and much-needed shipment during the battle. This leads to a series of squabbles among the lords, and it soon becomes clear that each of them have personal ambitions they put before the battle against Zhuo Dong. Bei Liu and his brothers are disillusioned by the pettiness on display, and when it becomes clear that the coalition has no plan for victory, they return to their homeland.

Meanwhile, Cao Cao takes it upon himself to chase down Zhuo Dong, who has fled LuoYang and is en route to ChangAn. Although he catches Zhuo Dong's army, Cao Cao's forces are vastly outnumbered, and the enemy forces are led by the dreaded Bu Lu. Cao Cao knows that a confrontation with Bu Lu could cost him his life, but still he charges into battle.

BEI LIU

Generals

YU GUAN

FEI ZHANG

Advisors

LIANG ZHUGE

TONG PANG

CAO CAO

Generals

DUN XIAHOU

HONG CAO

Advisors

XU JIA

JIA GUO

During the Han Dynasty, public officials fell into one of two categories: military officers and civil servants. Military officers handled matters of defense, and civil servants were in charge of public administration.

Some of the 18 feudal lords were military officers and some were civil servants. But at the point where the Han Dynasty fell apart, and each of them assumed leadership of a province and raised an army, they sought the assistance of another set of military and civil advisors. These men would provide the necessary military experience and expertise, as well as shrewd counsel on political strategy and maneuvers that didn't occur on the battlefield. As the Age of the Three Kingdoms comes to fruition, and adver-sarial relationships among the leaders intensify, these counselors will take on an ever-more-influential role in the course of events.

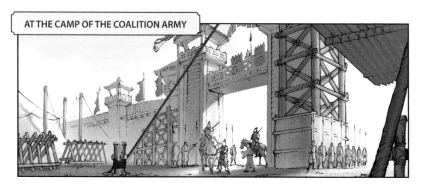

AT THE CAMP OF THE COALITION ARMY

SIRS! COMMANDER CAO CAO WOULD LIKE TO INVITE YOU TO A BANQUET, TO HONOR YOUR REMARKABLE ACHIEVEMENTS IN BATTLE.

A BANQUET? EXCELLENT! I'M SO HUNGRY I COULD EAT A DEAD MULE'S GUTS!

VERY WELL.

FEI ZHANG!

WHAT? WHAT DID I SAY?

PLEASE GIVE OUR SINCERE THANKS TO THE COMMANDER, AND TELL HIM WE WOULD BE HONORED TO ATTEND AFTER OUR BRIEFING.

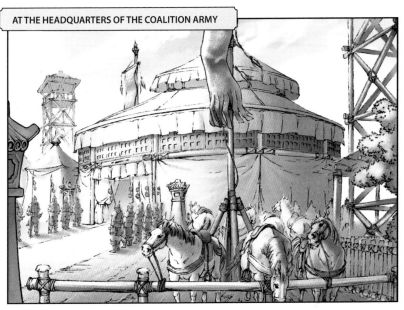

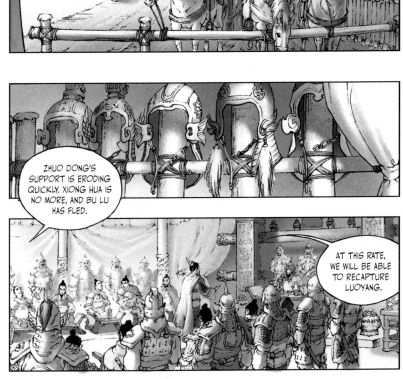

AT THE HEADQUARTERS OF THE COALITION ARMY
ZHUO DONG'S SUPPORT IS ERODING QUICKLY. XIONG HUA IS NO MORE, AND BU LU HAS FLED.
AT THIS RATE, WE WILL BE ABLE TO RECAPTURE LUOYANG.

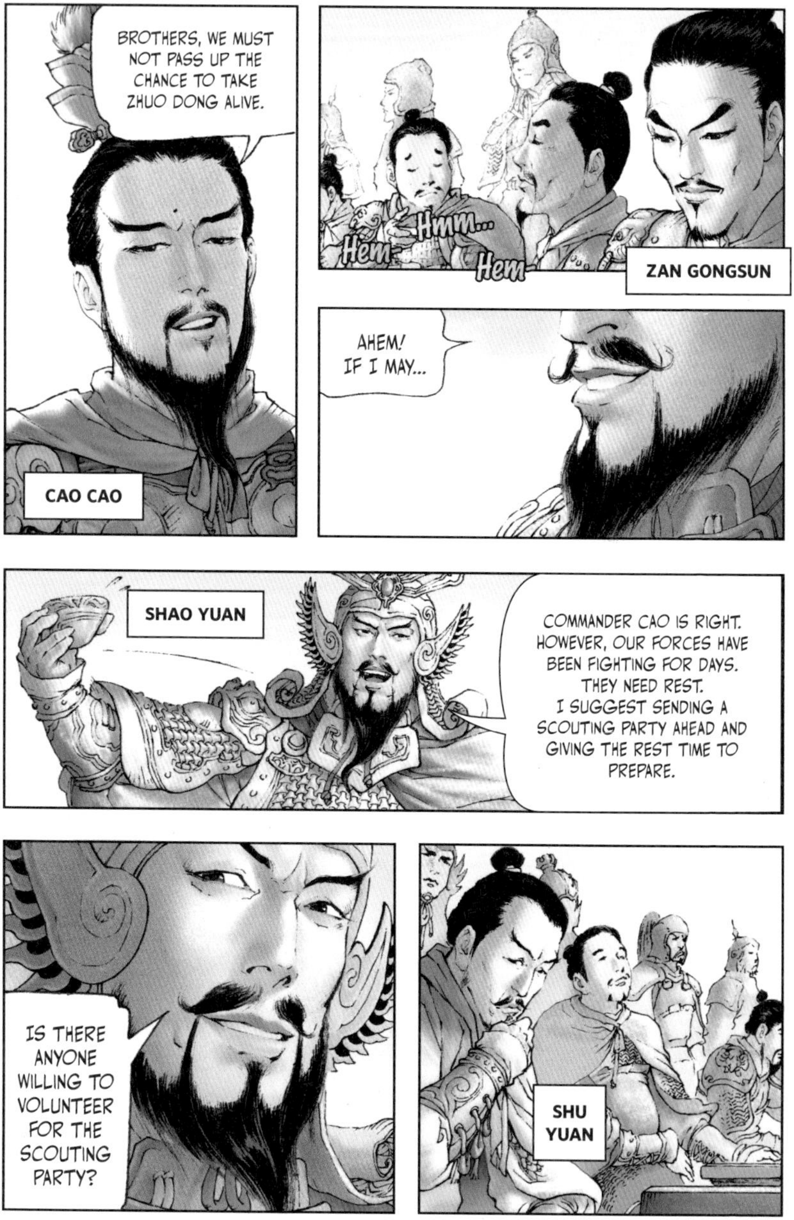
BROTHERS, WE MUST NOT PASS UP THE CHANCE TO TAKE ZHUO DONG ALIVE.
CAO CAO
Hem
Hmm...
Hem
ZAN GONGSUN
AHEM! IF I MAY...
SHAO YUAN
COMMANDER CAO IS RIGHT. HOWEVER, OUR FORCES HAVE BEEN FIGHTING FOR DAYS. THEY NEED REST. I SUGGEST SENDING A SCOUTING PARTY AHEAD AND GIVING THE REST TIME TO PREPARE.
IS THERE ANYONE WILLING TO VOLUNTEER FOR THE SCOUTING PARTY?
SHU YUAN

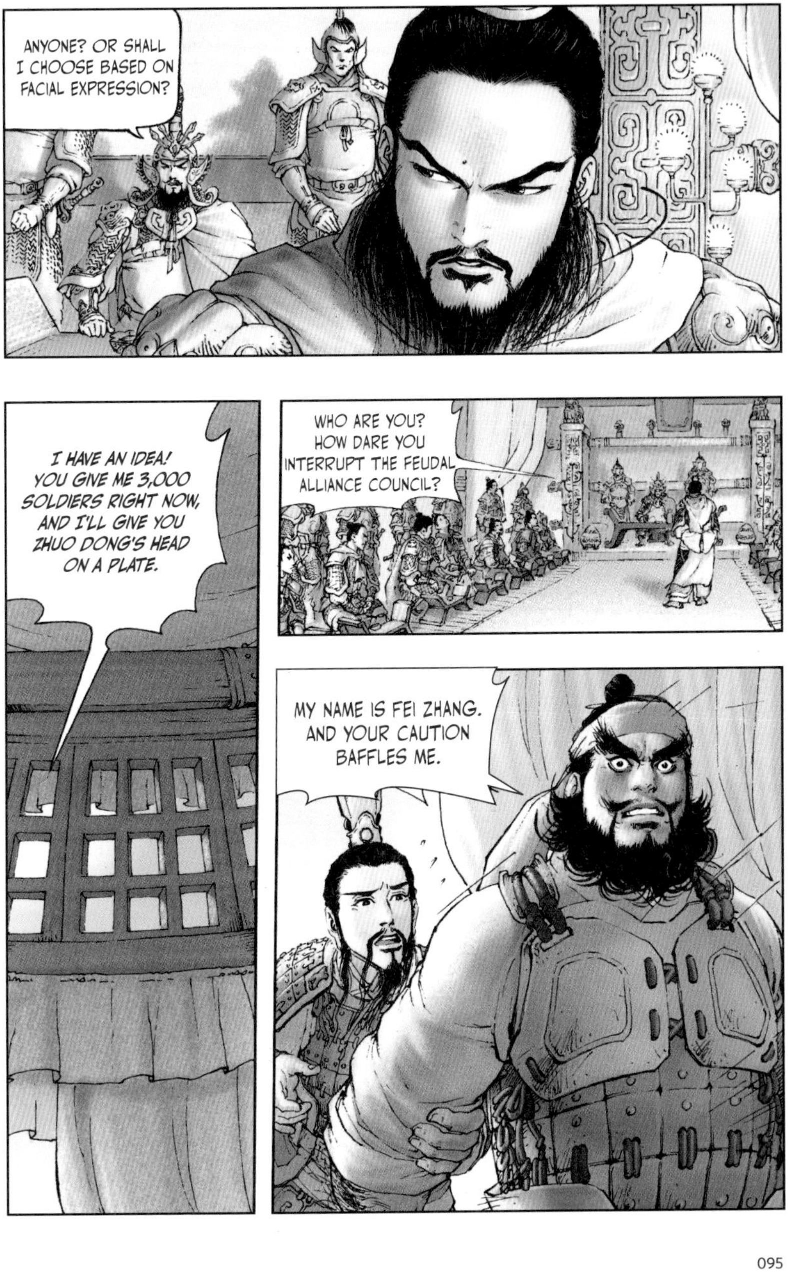
ANYONE? OR SHALL I CHOOSE BASED ON FACIAL EXPRESSION?
I HAVE AN IDEA! YOU GIVE ME 3,000 SOLDIERS RIGHT NOW, AND I'LL GIVE YOU ZHUO DONG'S HEAD ON A PLATE.
WHO ARE YOU? HOW DARE YOU INTERRUPT THE FEUDAL ALLIANCE COUNCIL?
MY NAME IS FEI ZHANG. AND YOUR CAUTION BAFFLES ME.

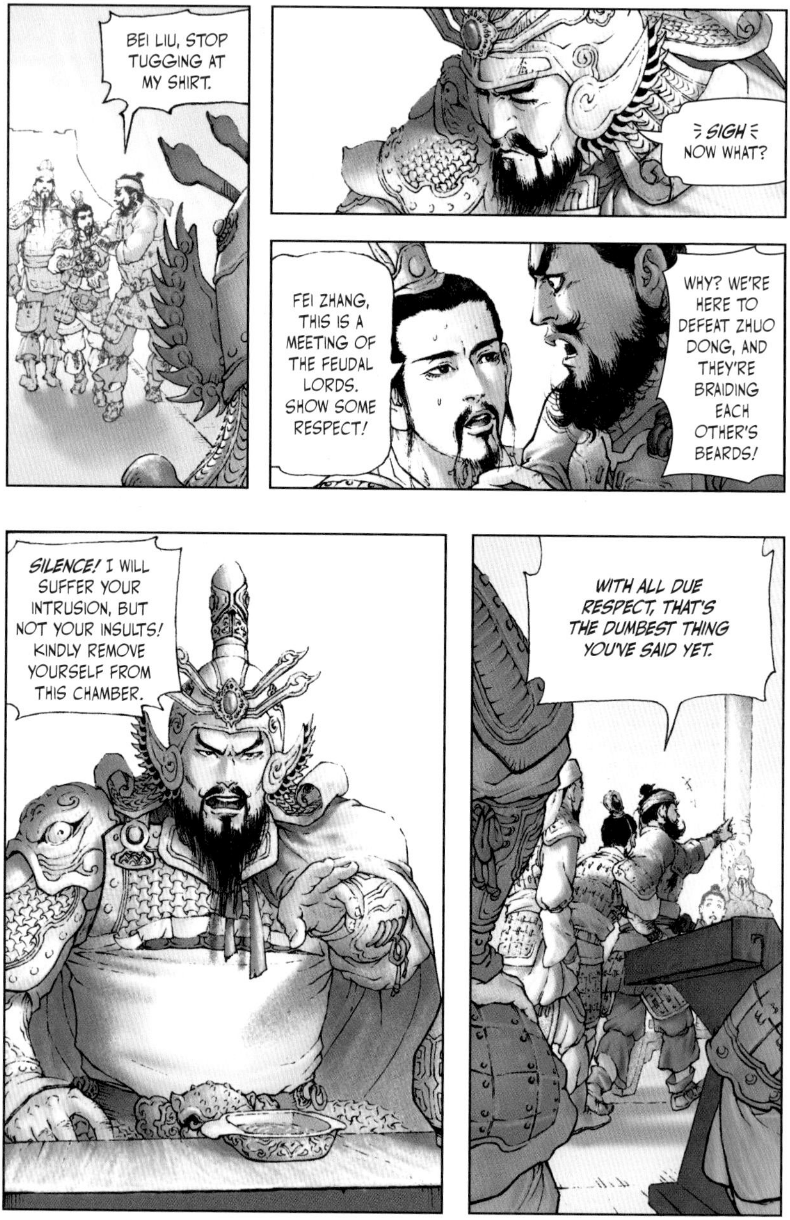
BEI LIU, STOP TUGGING AT MY SHIRT.
≈ SIGH ≈ NOW WHAT?
FEI ZHANG, THIS IS A MEETING OF THE FEUDAL LORDS. SHOW SOME RESPECT!
WHY? WE'RE HERE TO DEFEAT ZHUO DONG, AND THEY'RE BRAIDING EACH OTHER'S BEARDS!
SILENCE! I WILL SUFFER YOUR INTRUSION, BUT NOT YOUR INSULTS! KINDLY REMOVE YOURSELF FROM THIS CHAMBER.
WITH ALL DUE RESPECT, THAT'S THE DUMBEST THING YOU'VE SAID YET.

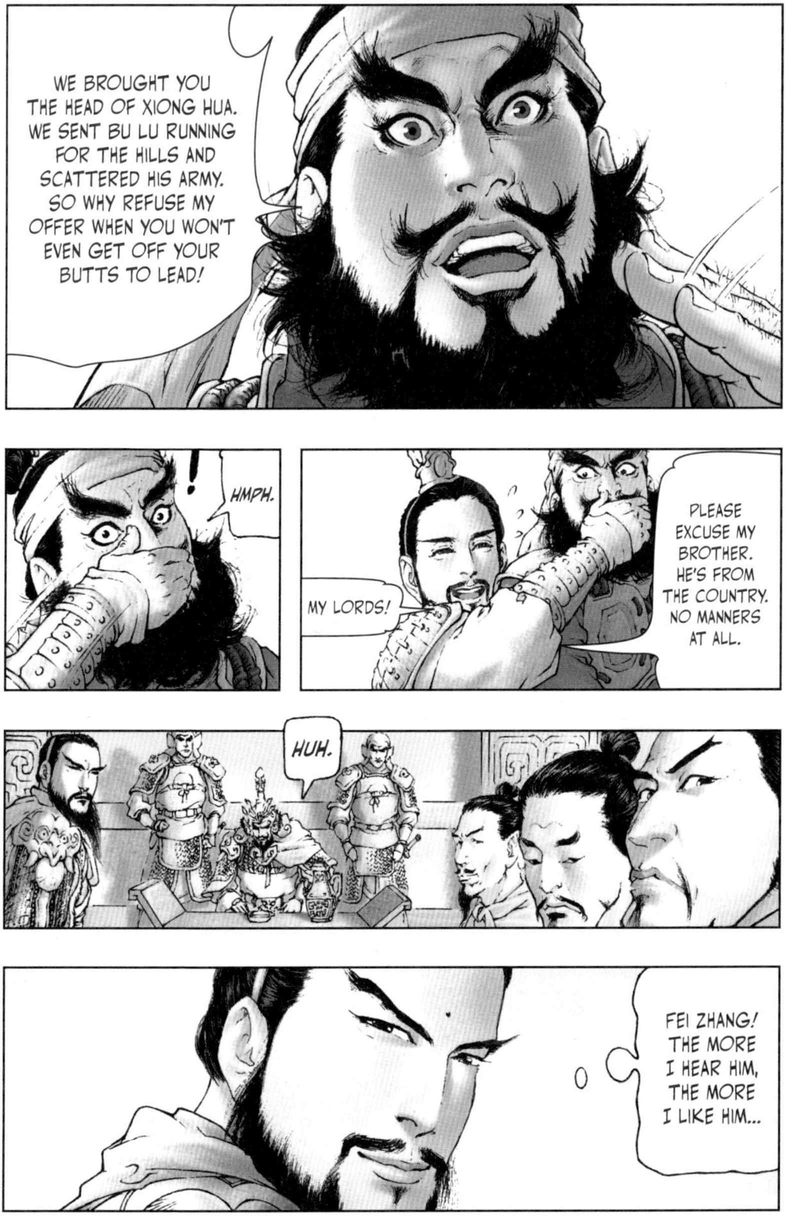

WE BROUGHT YOU THE HEAD OF XIONG HUA. WE SENT BU LU RUNNING FOR THE HILLS AND SCATTERED HIS ARMY. SO WHY REFUSE MY OFFER WHEN YOU WON'T EVEN GET OFF YOUR BUTTS TO LEAD!
!
HMPH.
MY LORDS!
PLEASE EXCUSE MY BROTHER. HE'S FROM THE COUNTRY. NO MANNERS AT ALL.
HUH.
FEI ZHANG! THE MORE I HEAR HIM, THE MORE I LIKE HIM...

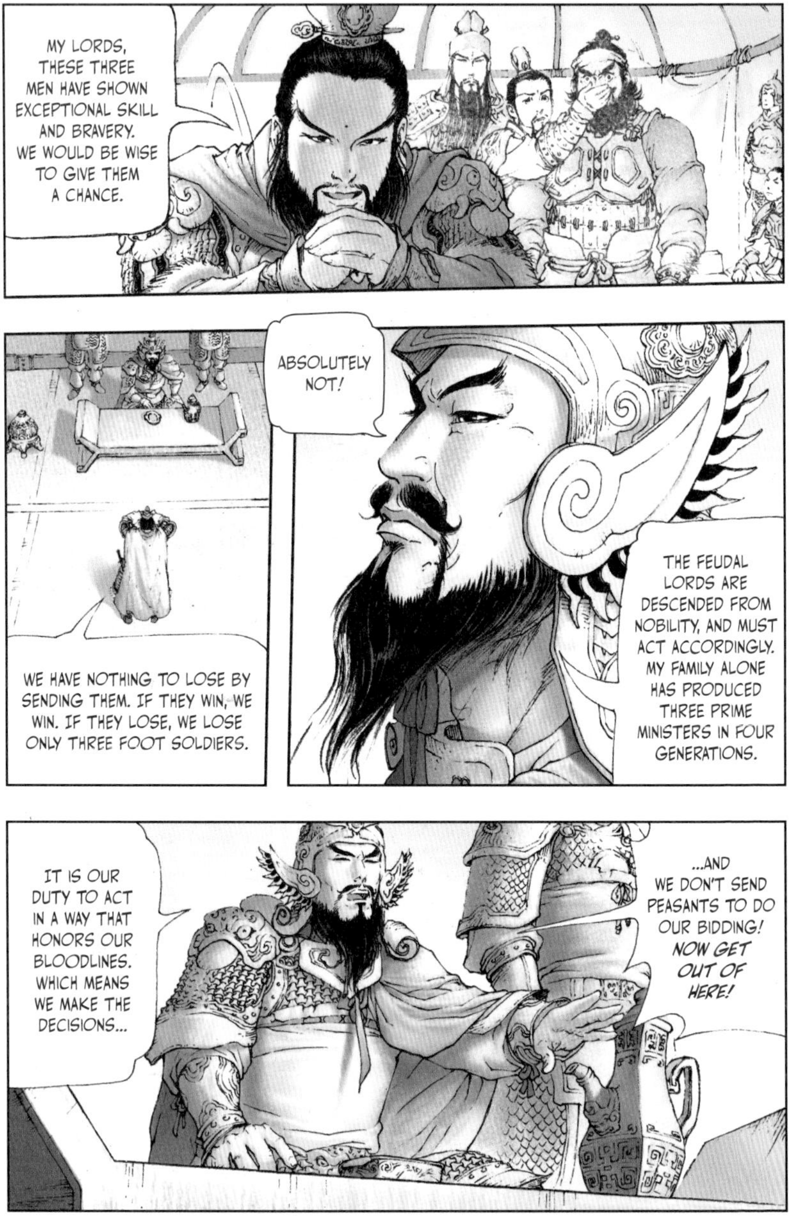
MY LORDS, THESE THREE MEN HAVE SHOWN EXCEPTIONAL SKILL AND BRAVERY. WE WOULD BE WISE TO GIVE THEM A CHANCE.
ABSOLUTELY NOT!
THE FEUDAL LORDS ARE DESCENDED FROM NOBILITY, AND MUST ACT ACCORDINGLY. MY FAMILY ALONE HAS PRODUCED THREE PRIME MINISTERS IN FOUR GENERATIONS.
WE HAVE NOTHING TO LOSE BY SENDING THEM. IF THEY WIN, WE WIN. IF THEY LOSE, WE LOSE ONLY THREE FOOT SOLDIERS.
IT IS OUR DUTY TO ACT IN A WAY THAT HONORS OUR BLOODLINES. WHICH MEANS WE MAKE THE DECISIONS...
...AND WE DON'T SEND PEASANTS TO DO OUR BIDDING! *NOW GET OUT OF HERE!*

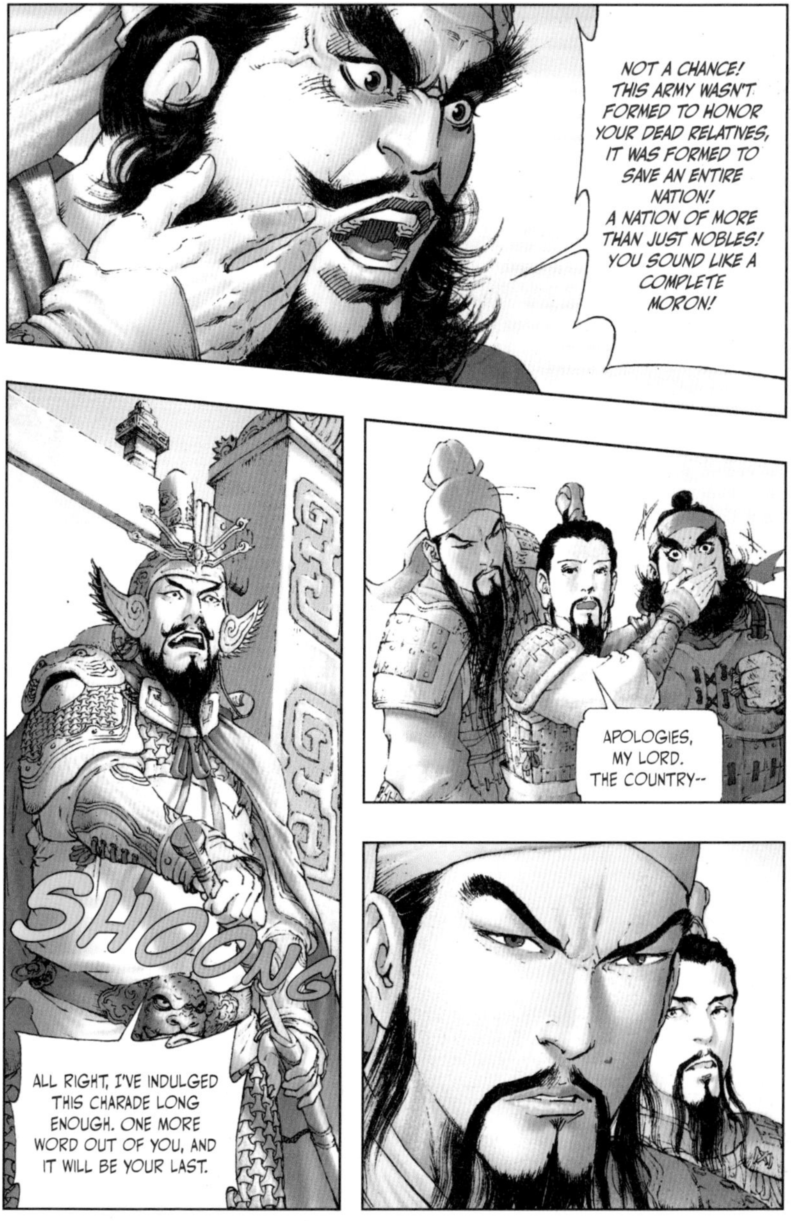
NOT A CHANCE! THIS ARMY WASN'T FORMED TO HONOR YOUR DEAD RELATIVES, IT WAS FORMED TO SAVE AN ENTIRE NATION! A NATION OF MORE THAN JUST NOBLES! YOU SOUND LIKE A COMPLETE MORON!
APOLOGIES, MY LORD. THE COUNTRY--
SHOONG
ALL RIGHT, I'VE INDULGED THIS CHARADE LONG ENOUGH. ONE MORE WORD OUT OF YOU, AND IT WILL BE YOUR LAST.

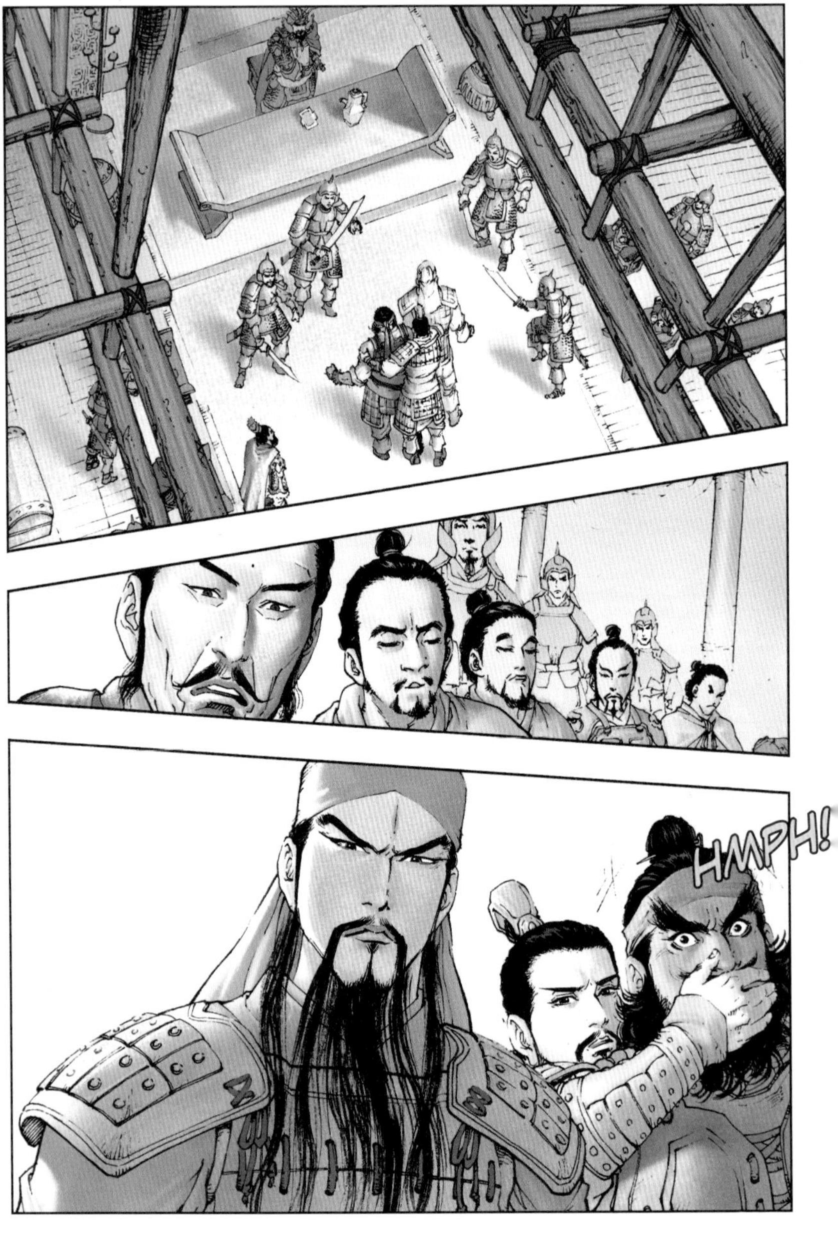
HMPH!

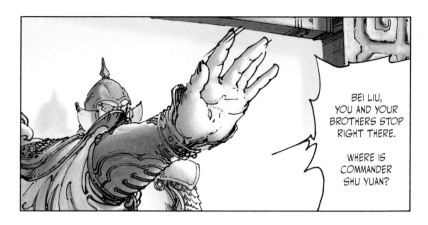

BEI LIU, YOU AND YOUR BROTHERS STOP RIGHT THERE.

WHERE IS COMMANDER SHU YUAN?

COMMANDER JIAN SUN! WHEN DID YOU GET BACK?

SHU YUAN

OH, NO...

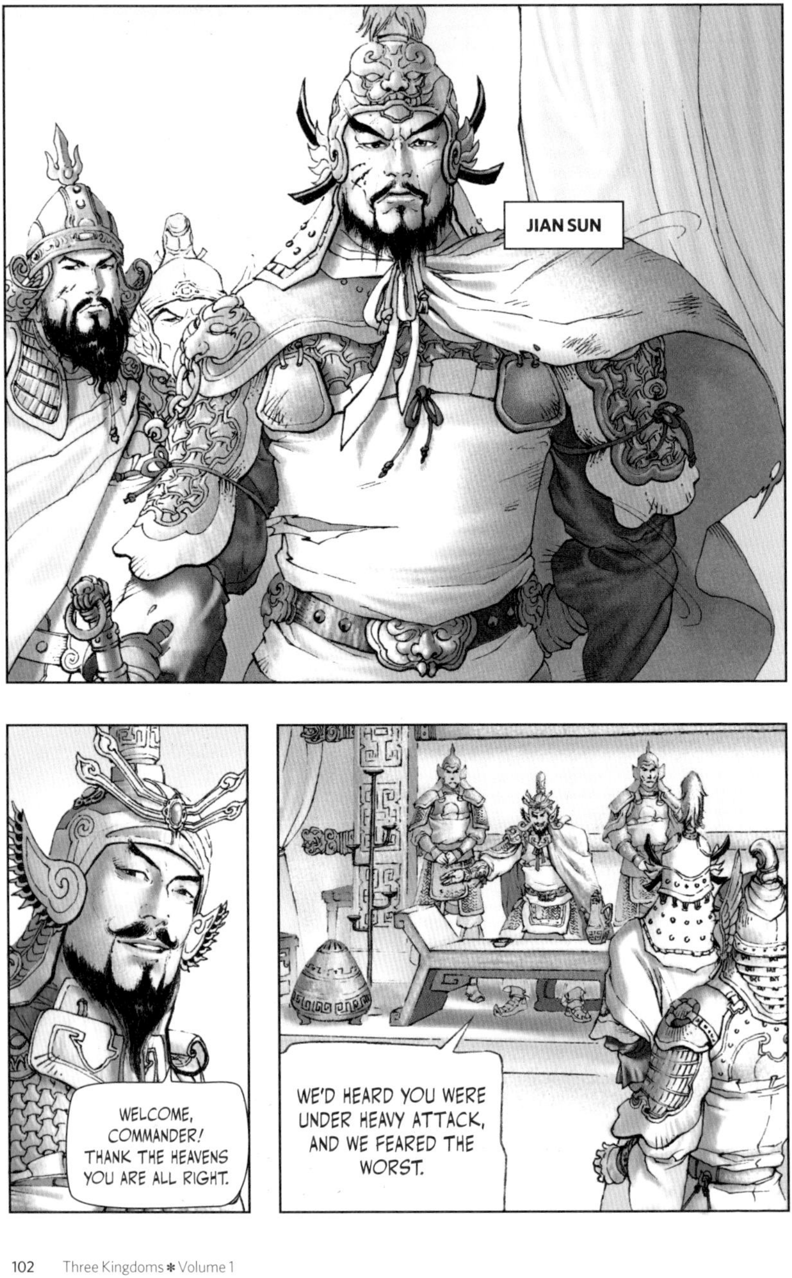
JIAN SUN
WELCOME, COMMANDER! THANK THE HEAVENS YOU ARE ALL RIGHT.
WE'D HEARD YOU WERE UNDER HEAVY ATTACK, AND WE FEARED THE WORST.

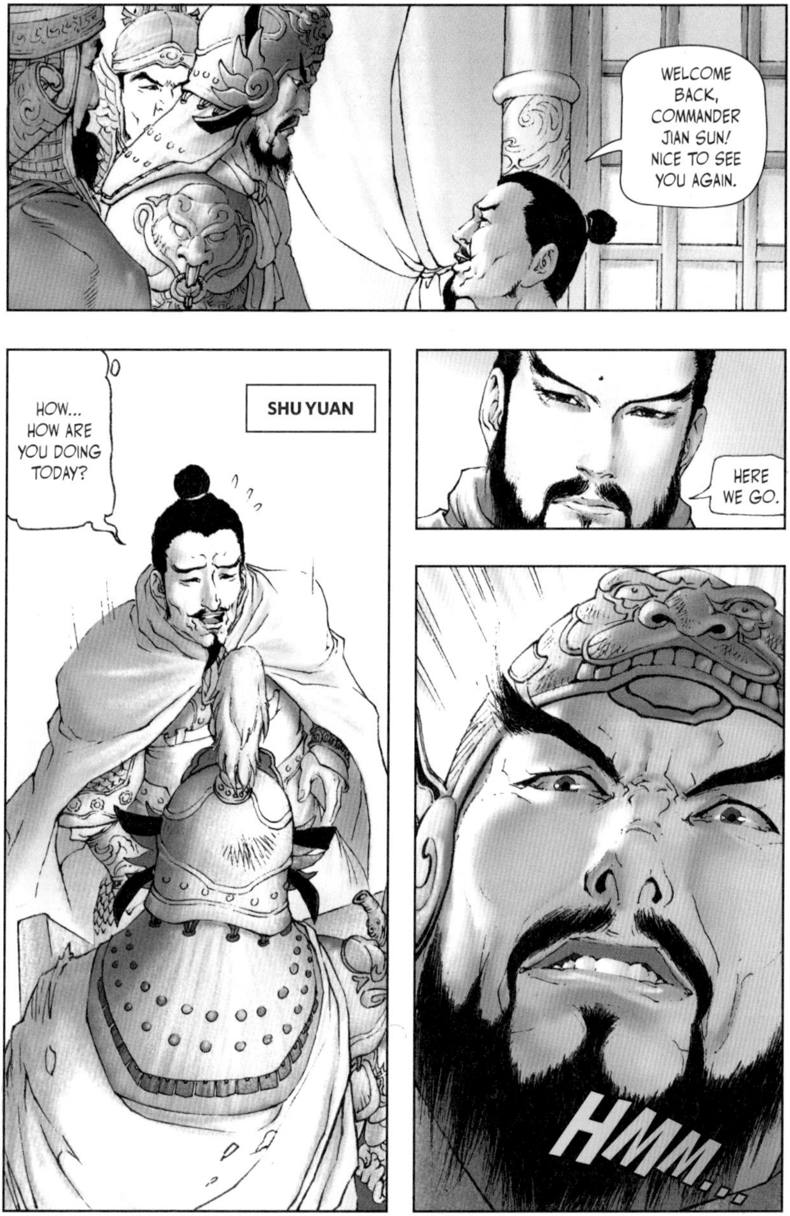
WELCOME BACK, COMMANDER JIAN SUN! NICE TO SEE YOU AGAIN.
SHU YUAN
HOW... HOW ARE YOU DOING TODAY?
HERE WE GO.
HMM...

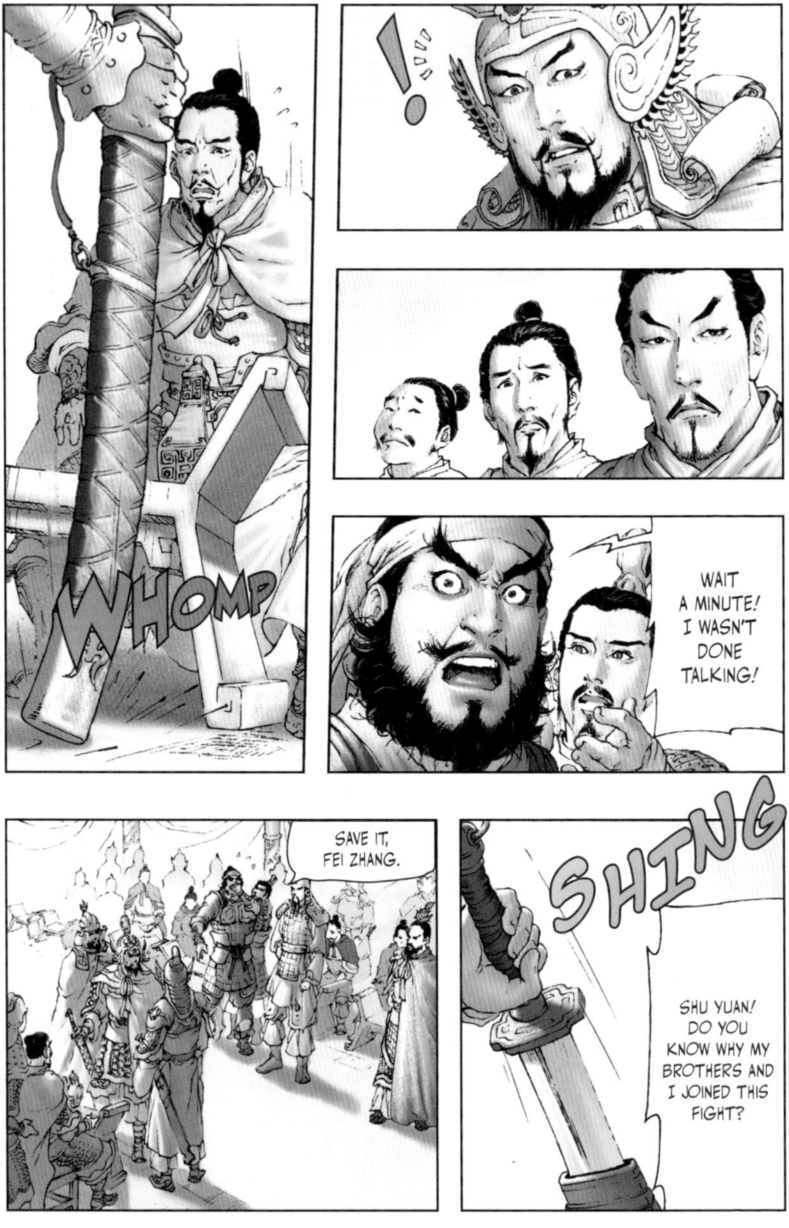

!
WHOMP
WAIT A MINUTE! I WASN'T DONE TALKING!
SAVE IT, FEI ZHANG.
SHING
SHU YUAN! DO YOU KNOW WHY MY BROTHERS AND I JOINED THIS FIGHT?

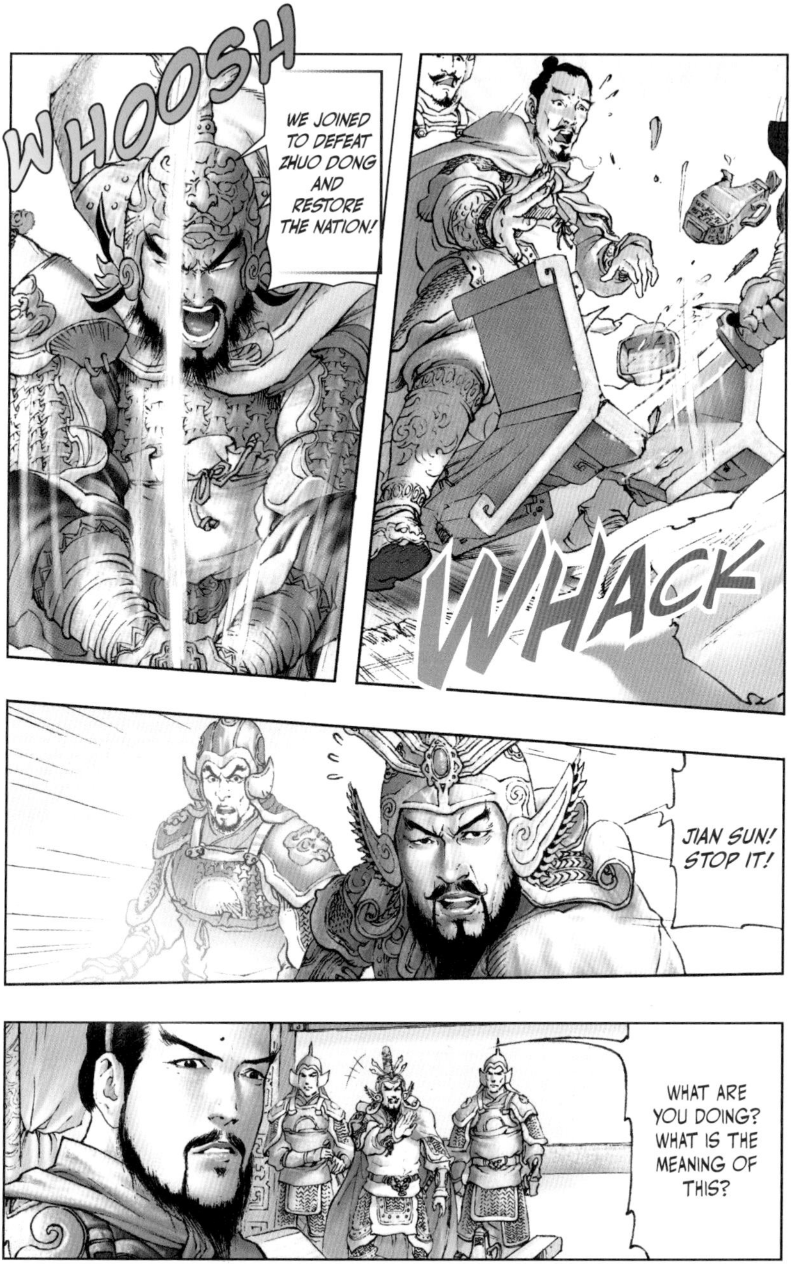
WHOOSH
WE JOINED TO DEFEAT ZHUO DONG AND RESTORE THE NATION!
WHACK
JIAN SUN! STOP IT!
WHAT ARE YOU DOING? WHAT IS THE MEANING OF THIS?

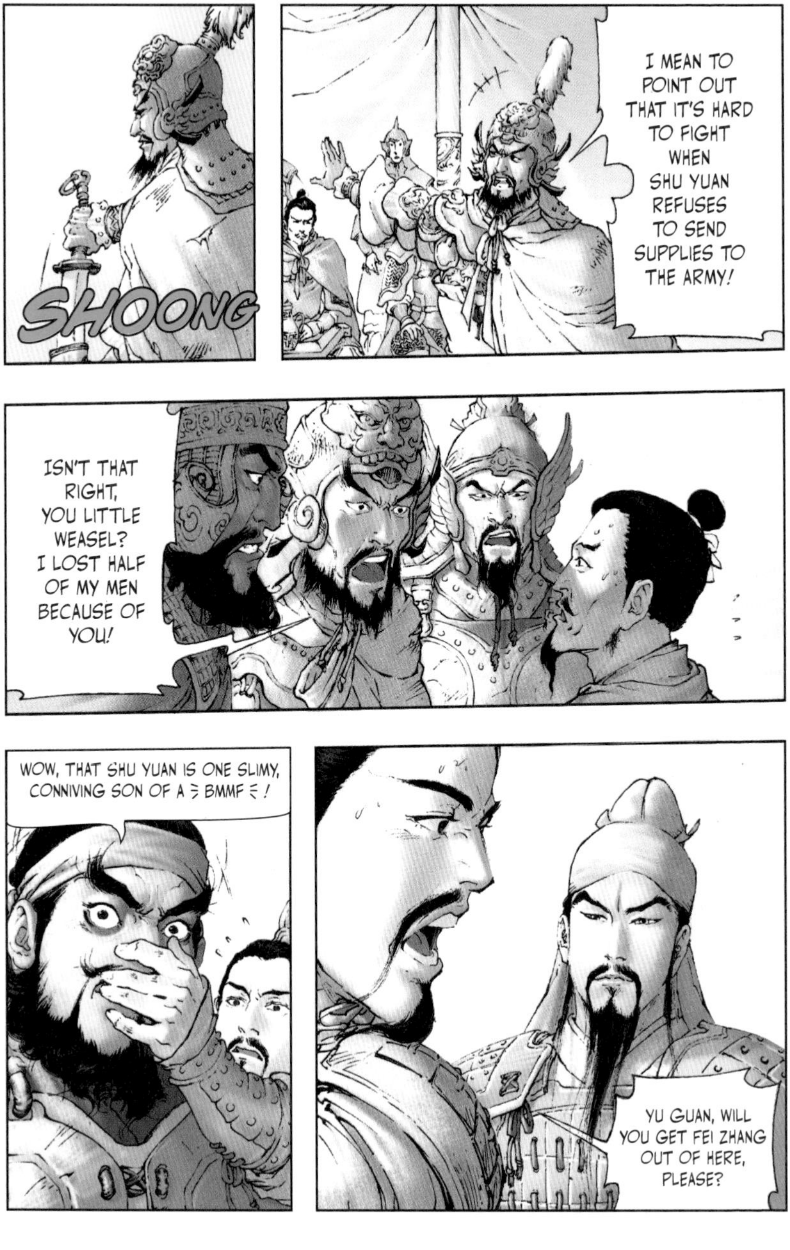
SHOONG
I MEAN TO POINT OUT THAT IT'S HARD TO FIGHT WHEN SHU YUAN REFUSES TO SEND SUPPLIES TO THE ARMY!
ISN'T THAT RIGHT, YOU LITTLE WEASEL? I LOST HALF OF MY MEN BECAUSE OF YOU!
WOW, THAT SHU YUAN IS ONE SLIMY, CONNIVING SON OF A ≡ BMMF ≡ !
YU GUAN, WILL YOU GET FEI ZHANG OUT OF HERE, PLEASE?

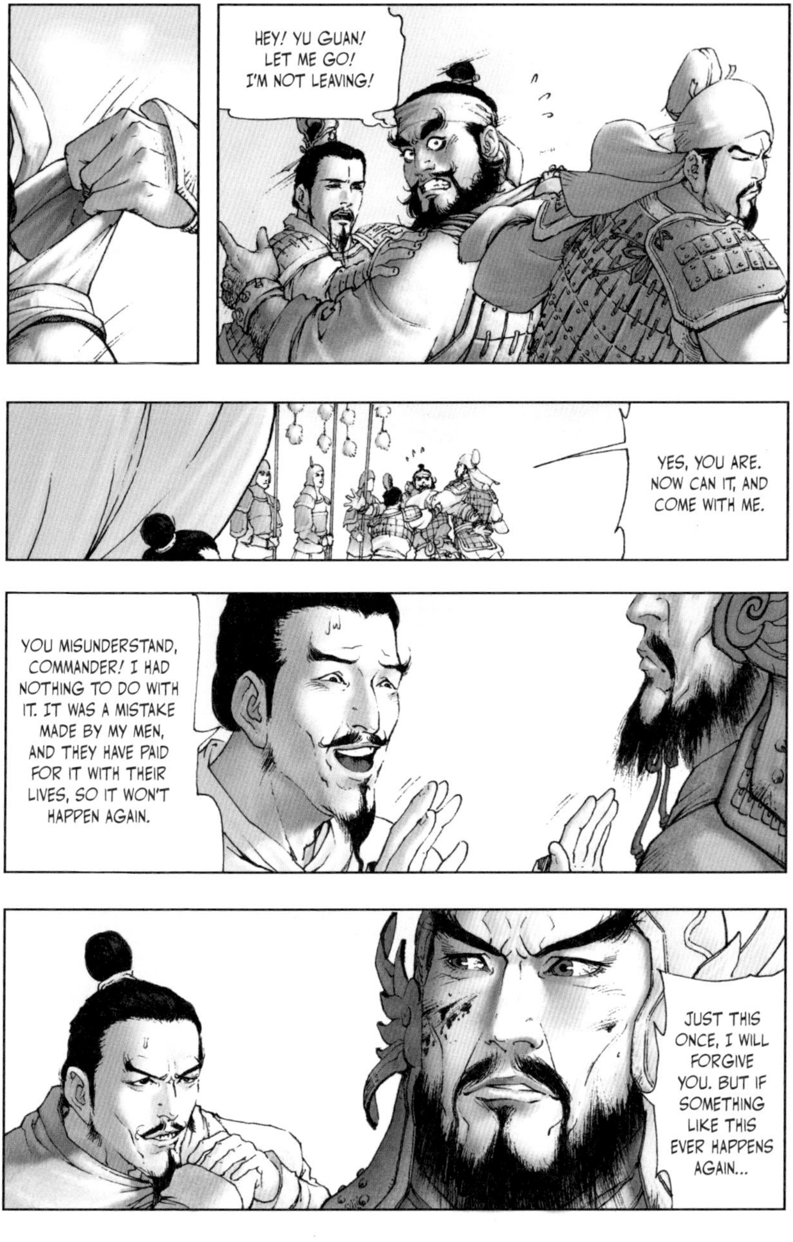
HEY! YU GUAN! LET ME GO! I'M NOT LEAVING!
YES, YOU ARE. NOW CAN IT, AND COME WITH ME.
YOU MISUNDERSTAND, COMMANDER! I HAD NOTHING TO DO WITH IT. IT WAS A MISTAKE MADE BY MY MEN, AND THEY HAVE PAID FOR IT WITH THEIR LIVES, SO IT WON'T HAPPEN AGAIN.
JUST THIS ONCE, I WILL FORGIVE YOU. BUT IF SOMETHING LIKE THIS EVER HAPPENS AGAIN...

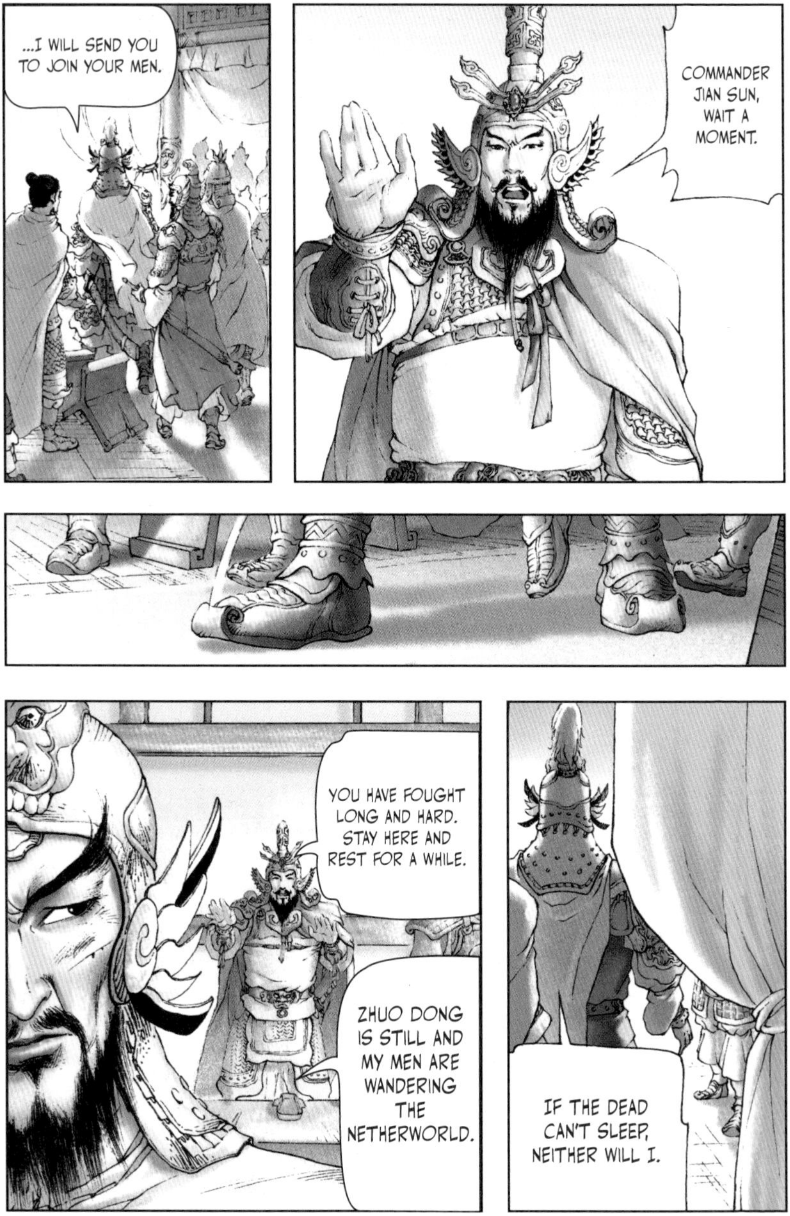
...I WILL SEND YOU TO JOIN YOUR MEN.
COMMANDER JIAN SUN, WAIT A MOMENT.
YOU HAVE FOUGHT LONG AND HARD. STAY HERE AND REST FOR A WHILE.
ZHUO DONG IS STILL AND MY MEN ARE WANDERING THE NETHERWORLD.
IF THE DEAD CAN'T SLEEP, NEITHER WILL I.

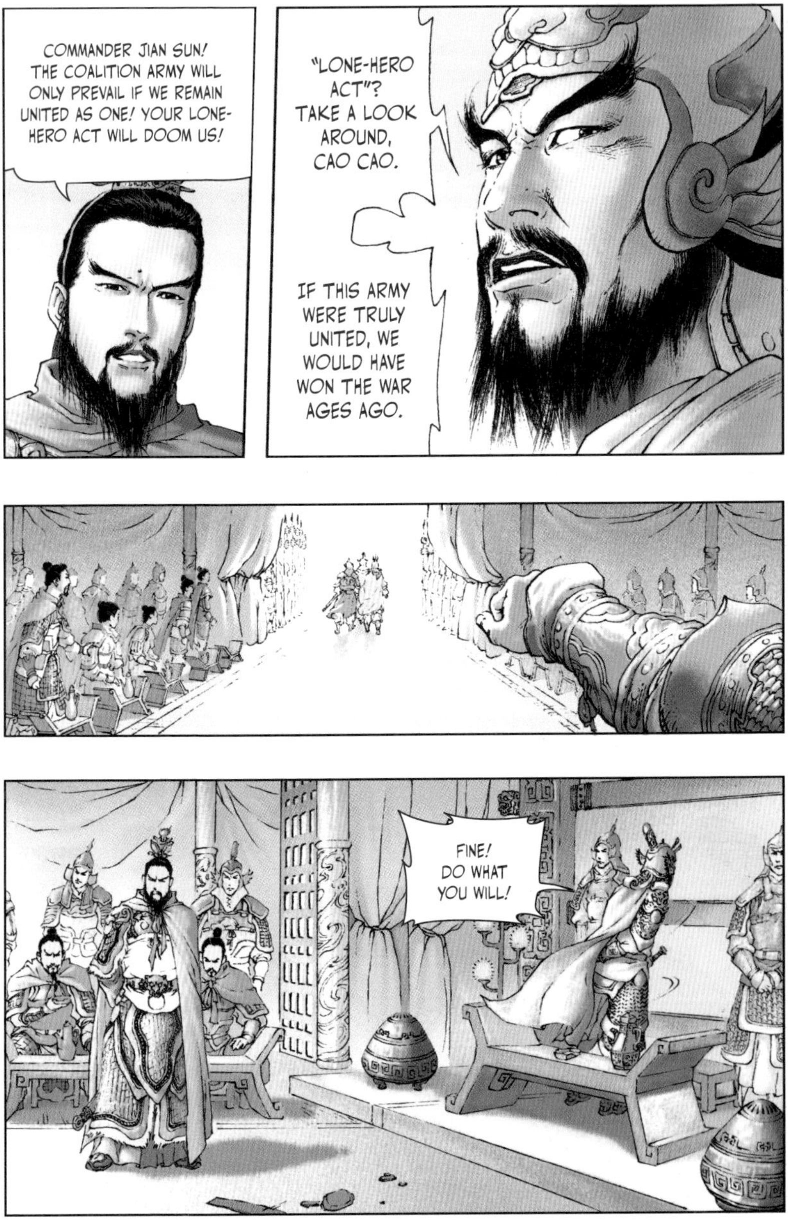
COMMANDER JIAN SUN! THE COALITION ARMY WILL ONLY PREVAIL IF WE REMAIN UNITED AS ONE! YOUR LONE-HERO ACT WILL DOOM US!
"LONE-HERO ACT"? TAKE A LOOK AROUND, CAO CAO.
IF THIS ARMY WERE TRULY UNITED, WE WOULD HAVE WON THE WAR AGES AGO.
FINE! DO WHAT YOU WILL!

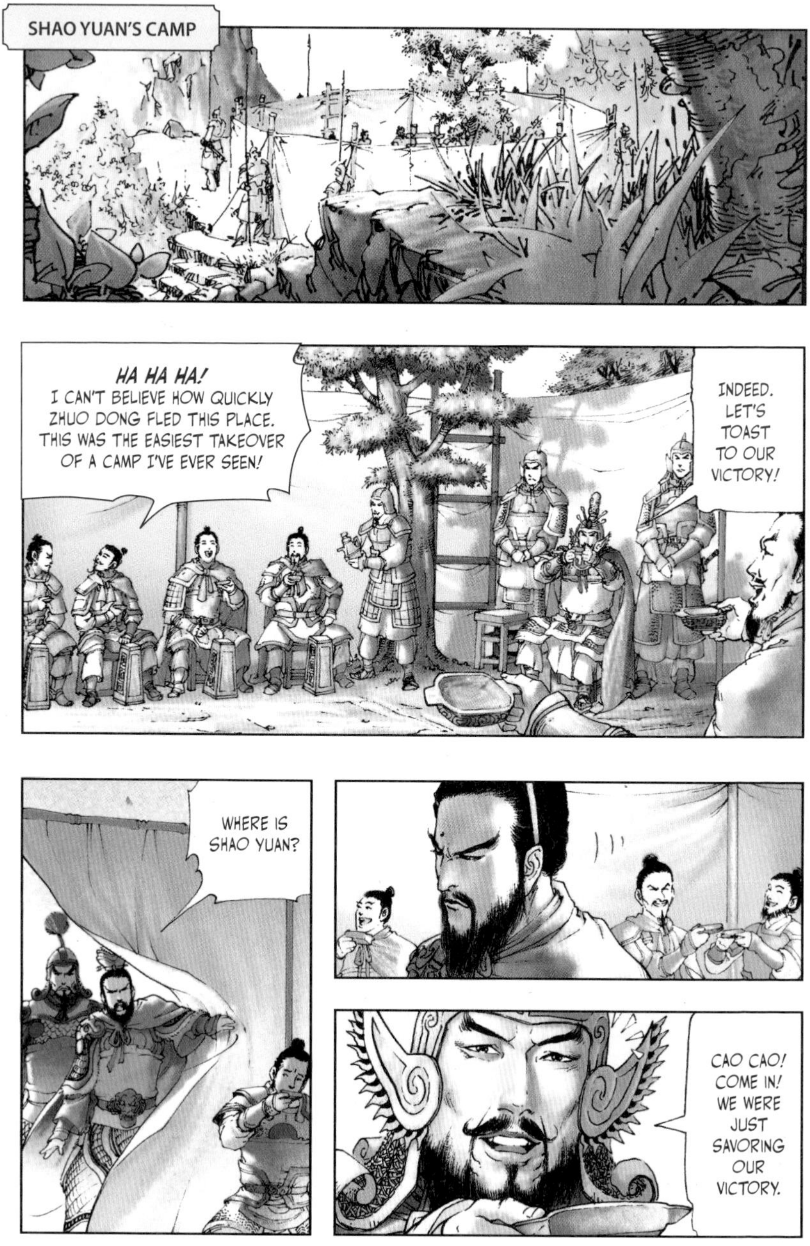
SHAO YUAN'S CAMP
HA HA HA! I CAN'T BELIEVE HOW QUICKLY ZHUO DONG FLED THIS PLACE. THIS WAS THE EASIEST TAKEOVER OF A CAMP I'VE EVER SEEN!
INDEED. LET'S TOAST TO OUR VICTORY!
WHERE IS SHAO YUAN?
CAO CAO! COME IN! WE WERE JUST SAVORING OUR VICTORY.

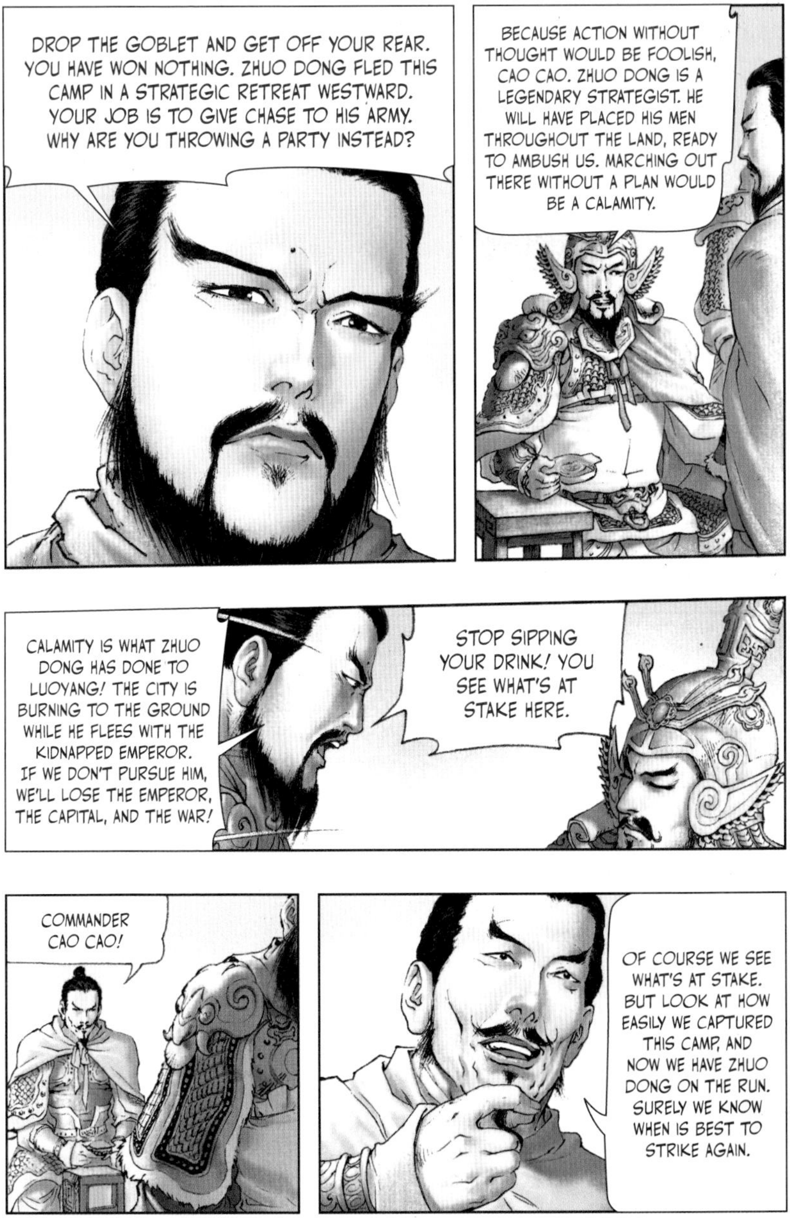
DROP THE GOBLET AND GET OFF YOUR REAR. YOU HAVE WON NOTHING. ZHUO DONG FLED THIS CAMP IN A STRATEGIC RETREAT WESTWARD. YOUR JOB IS TO GIVE CHASE TO HIS ARMY. WHY ARE YOU THROWING A PARTY INSTEAD?
BECAUSE ACTION WITHOUT THOUGHT WOULD BE FOOLISH, CAO CAO. ZHUO DONG IS A LEGENDARY STRATEGIST. HE WILL HAVE PLACED HIS MEN THROUGHOUT THE LAND, READY TO AMBUSH US. MARCHING OUT THERE WITHOUT A PLAN WOULD BE A CALAMITY.
CALAMITY IS WHAT ZHUO DONG HAS DONE TO LUOYANG! THE CITY IS BURNING TO THE GROUND WHILE HE FLEES WITH THE KIDNAPPED EMPEROR. IF WE DON'T PURSUE HIM, WE'LL LOSE THE EMPEROR, THE CAPITAL, AND THE WAR!
STOP SIPPING YOUR DRINK! YOU SEE WHAT'S AT STAKE HERE.
COMMANDER CAO CAO!
OF COURSE WE SEE WHAT'S AT STAKE. BUT LOOK AT HOW EASILY WE CAPTURED THIS CAMP, AND NOW WE HAVE ZHUO DONG ON THE RUN. SURELY WE KNOW WHEN IS BEST TO STRIKE AGAIN.

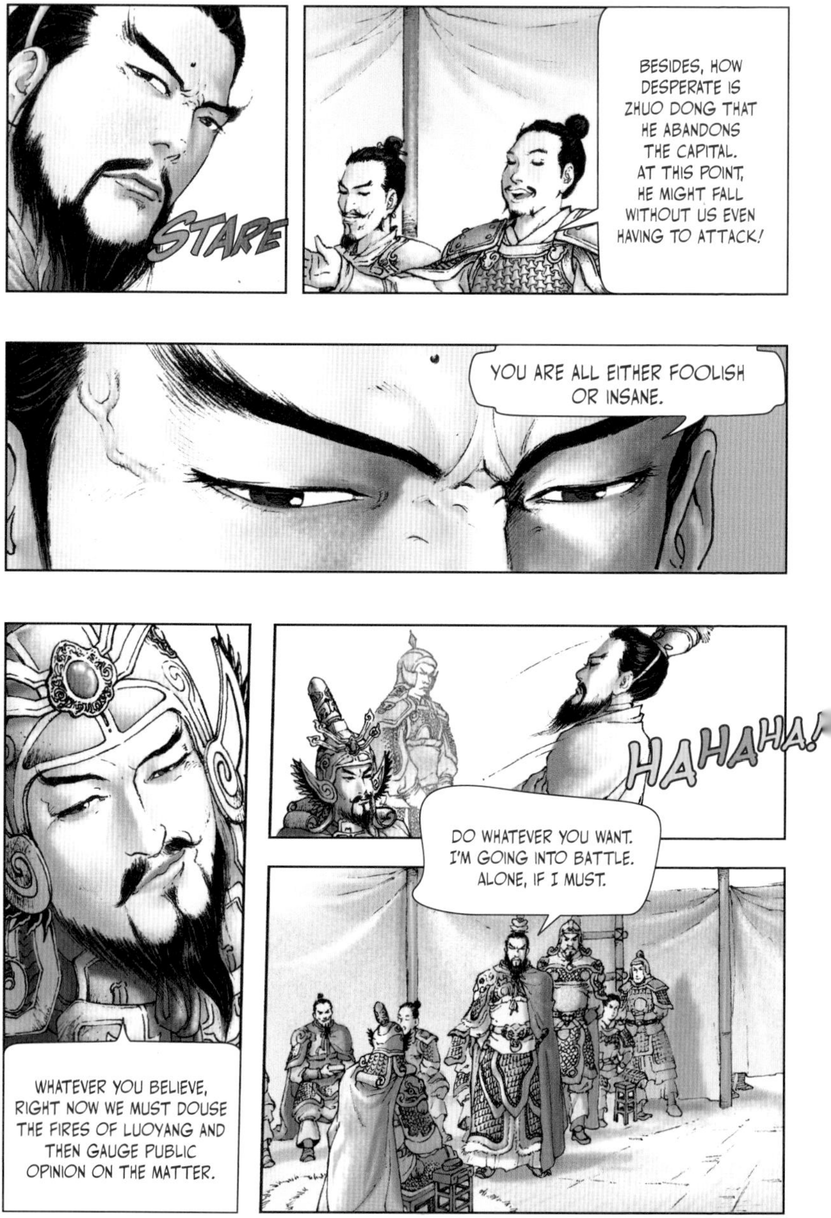
STARE
BESIDES, HOW DESPERATE IS ZHUO DONG THAT HE ABANDONS THE CAPITAL. AT THIS POINT, HE MIGHT FALL WITHOUT US EVEN HAVING TO ATTACK!
YOU ARE ALL EITHER FOOLISH OR INSANE.
HAHAHAHA!
DO WHATEVER YOU WANT. I'M GOING INTO BATTLE. ALONE, IF I MUST.
WHATEVER YOU BELIEVE, RIGHT NOW WE MUST DOUSE THE FIRES OF LUOYANG AND THEN GAUGE PUBLIC OPINION ON THE MATTER.

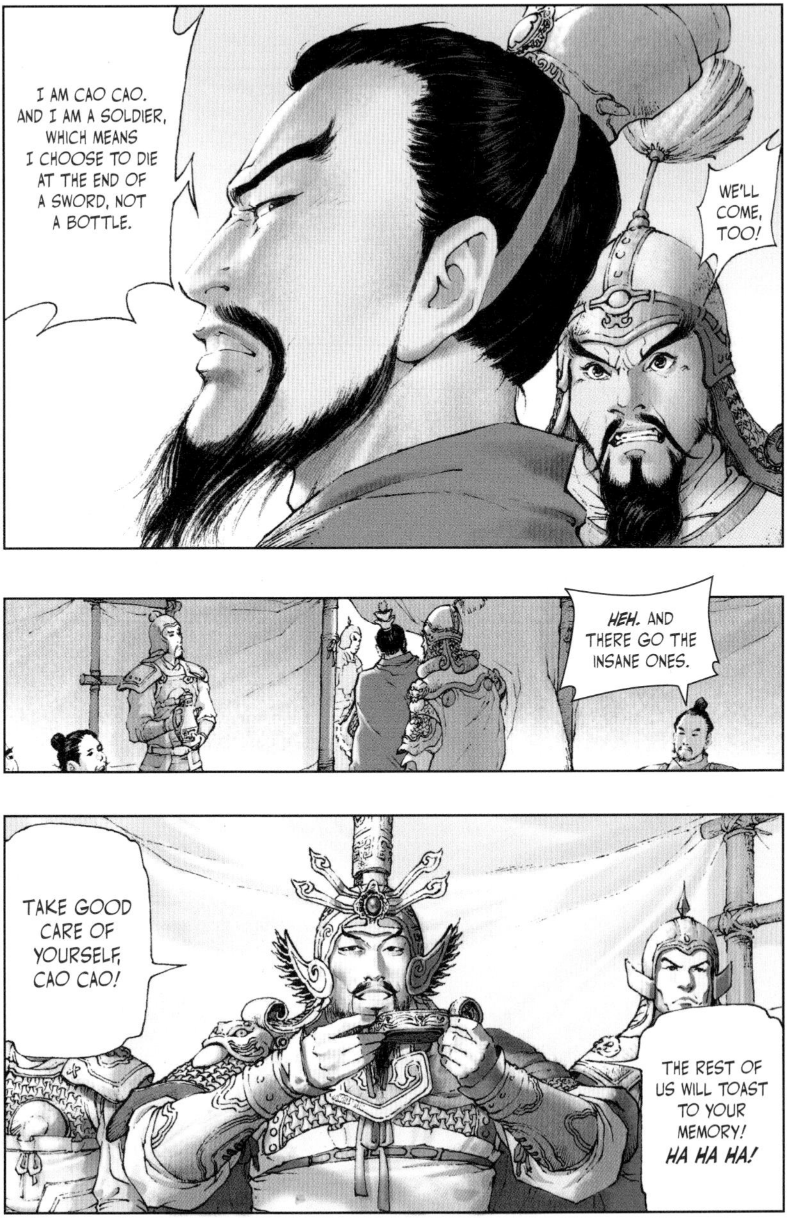
I AM CAO CAO. AND I AM A SOLDIER, WHICH MEANS I CHOOSE TO DIE AT THE END OF A SWORD, NOT A BOTTLE.
WE'LL COME, TOO!
HEH. AND THERE GO THE INSANE ONES.
TAKE GOOD CARE OF YOURSELF, CAO CAO!
THE REST OF US WILL TOAST TO YOUR MEMORY! HA HA HA!

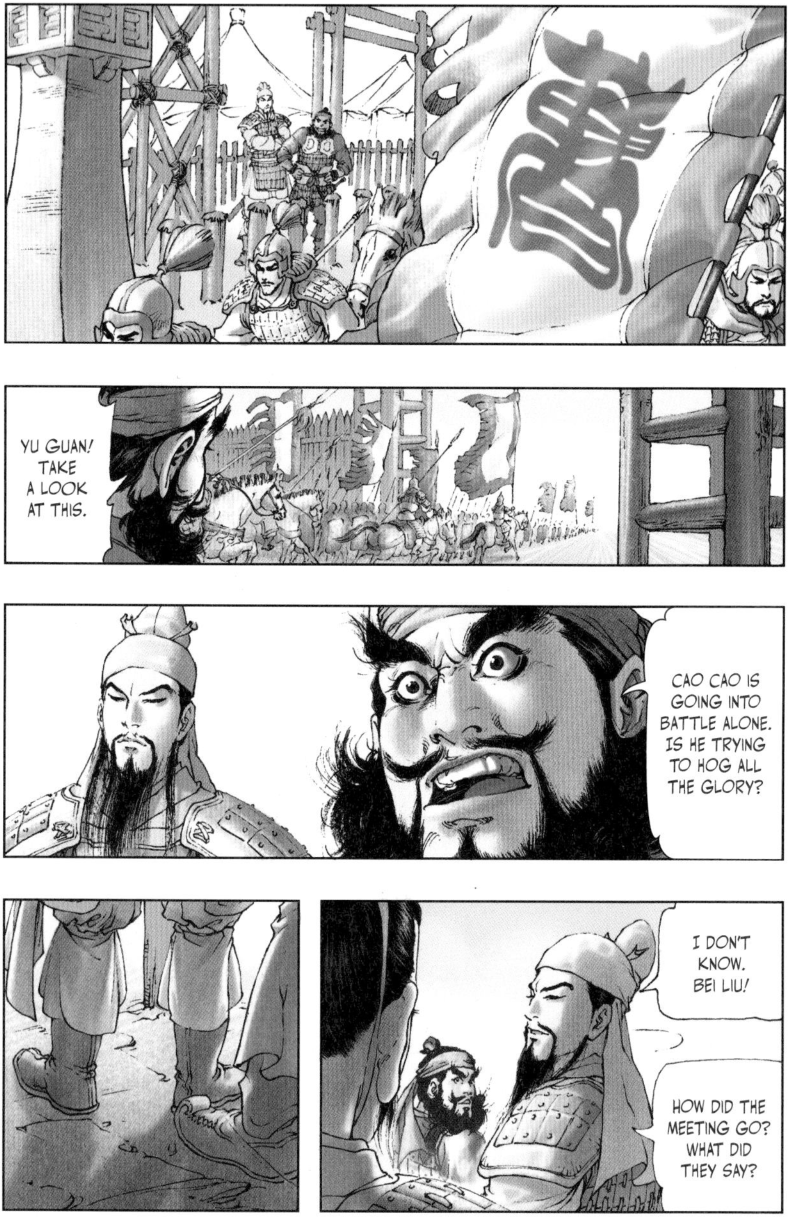
YU GUAN! TAKE A LOOK AT THIS.
CAO CAO IS GOING INTO BATTLE ALONE. IS HE TRYING TO HOG ALL THE GLORY?
I DON'T KNOW. BEI LIU!
HOW DID THE MEETING GO? WHAT DID THEY SAY?

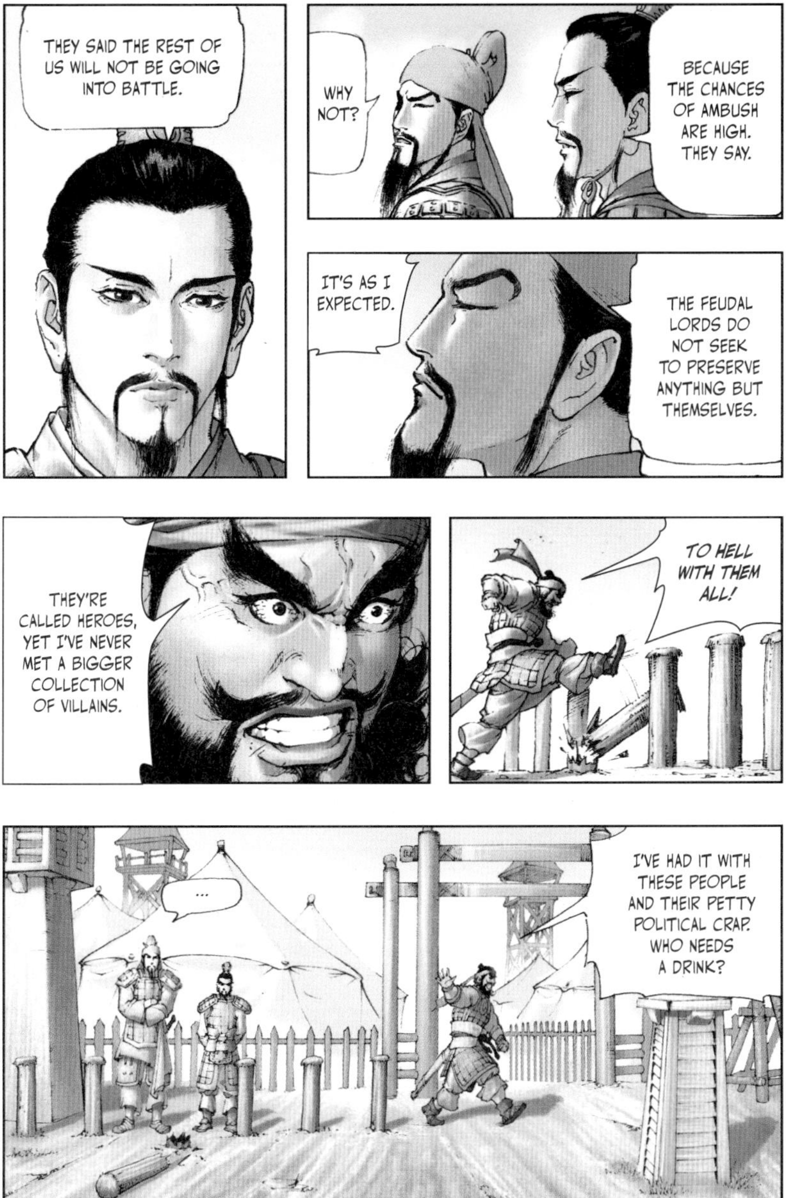
THEY SAID THE REST OF US WILL NOT BE GOING INTO BATTLE.
WHY NOT?
BECAUSE THE CHANCES OF AMBUSH ARE HIGH. THEY SAY.
IT'S AS I EXPECTED.
THE FEUDAL LORDS DO NOT SEEK TO PRESERVE ANYTHING BUT THEMSELVES.
THEY'RE CALLED HEROES, YET I'VE NEVER MET A BIGGER COLLECTION OF VILLAINS.
TO HELL WITH THEM ALL!
...
I'VE HAD IT WITH THESE PEOPLE AND THEIR PETTY POLITICAL CRAP. WHO NEEDS A DRINK?

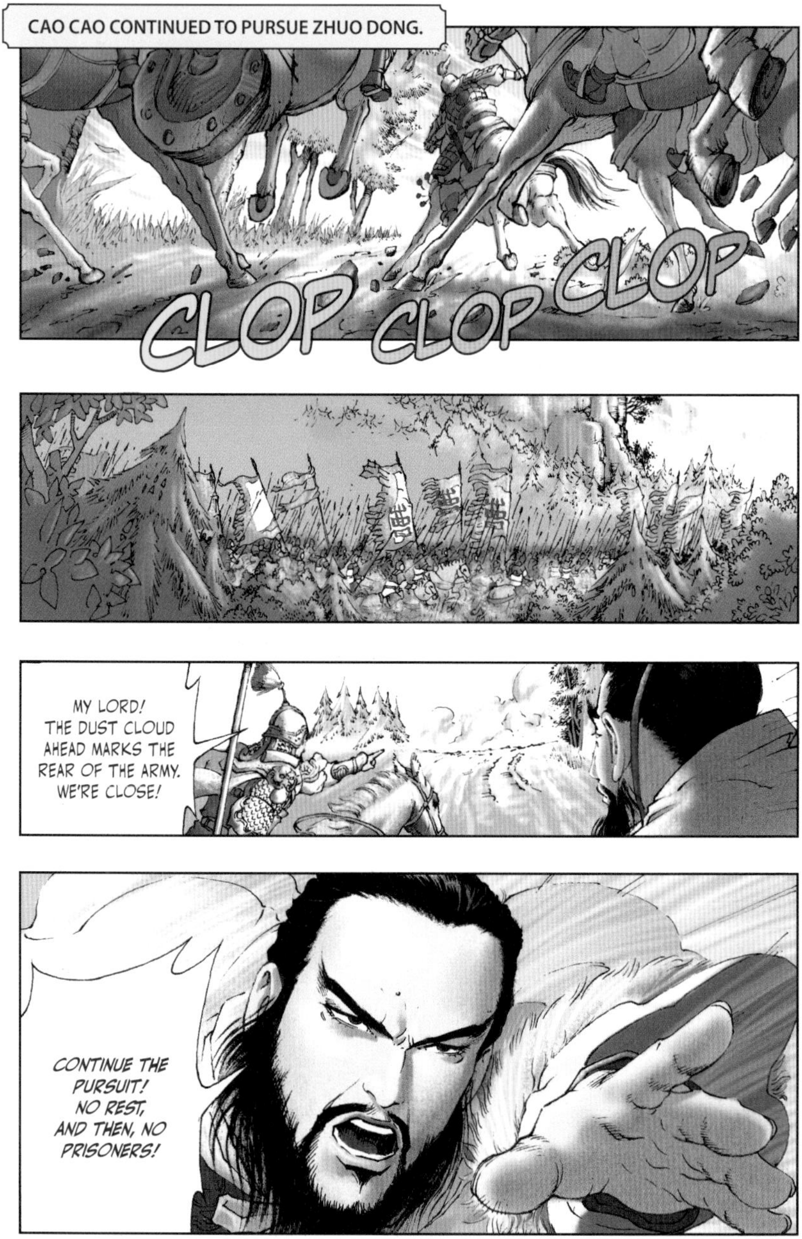
CAO CAO CONTINUED TO PURSUE ZHUO DONG.
CLOP CLOP CLOP
MY LORD! THE DUST CLOUD AHEAD MARKS THE REAR OF THE ARMY. WE'RE CLOSE!
CONTINUE THE PURSUIT! NO REST, AND THEN, NO PRISONERS!

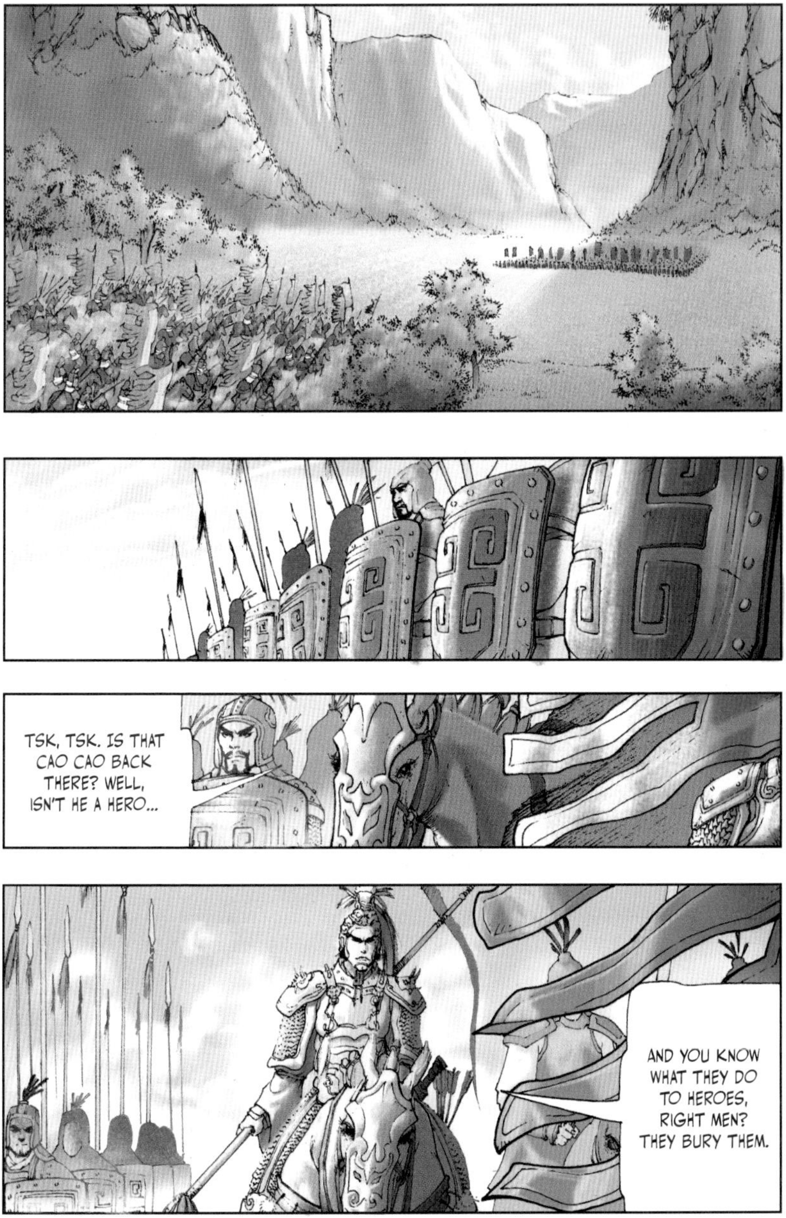
TSK, TSK. IS THAT CAO CAO BACK THERE? WELL, ISN'T HE A HERO...
AND YOU KNOW WHAT THEY DO TO HEROES, RIGHT MEN? THEY BURY THEM.

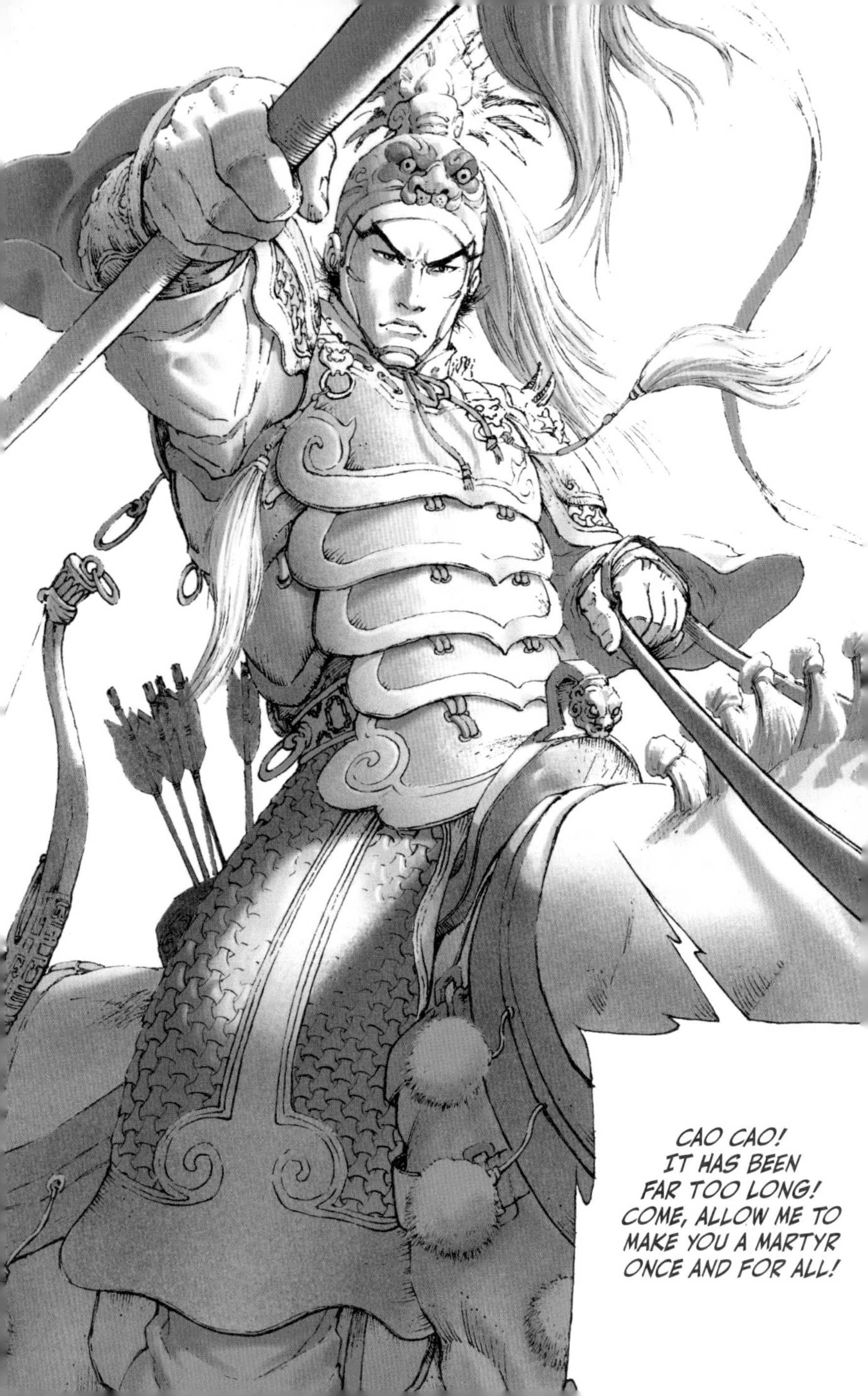
CAO CAO!
IT HAS BEEN
FAR TOO LONG!
COME, ALLOW ME TO
MAKE YOU A MARTYR
ONCE AND FOR ALL!

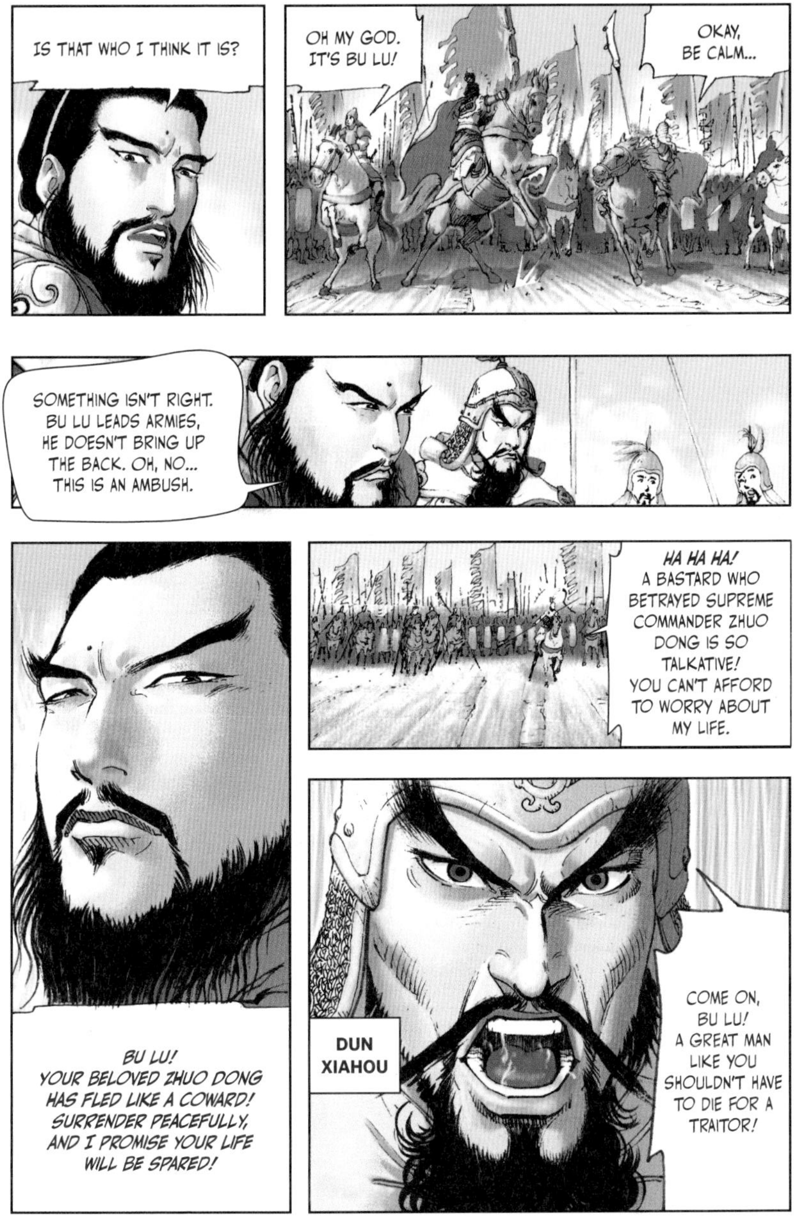
IS THAT WHO I THINK IT IS?
OH MY GOD. IT'S BU LU!
OKAY, BE CALM...
SOMETHING ISN'T RIGHT. BU LU LEADS ARMIES, HE DOESN'T BRING UP THE BACK. OH, NO... THIS IS AN AMBUSH.
BU LU! YOUR BELOVED ZHUO DONG HAS FLED LIKE A COWARD! SURRENDER PEACEFULLY, AND I PROMISE YOUR LIFE WILL BE SPARED!
HA HA HA! A BASTARD WHO BETRAYED SUPREME COMMANDER ZHUO DONG IS SO TALKATIVE! YOU CAN'T AFFORD TO WORRY ABOUT MY LIFE.
DUN XIAHOU
COME ON, BU LU! A GREAT MAN LIKE YOU SHOULDN'T HAVE TO DIE FOR A TRAITOR!

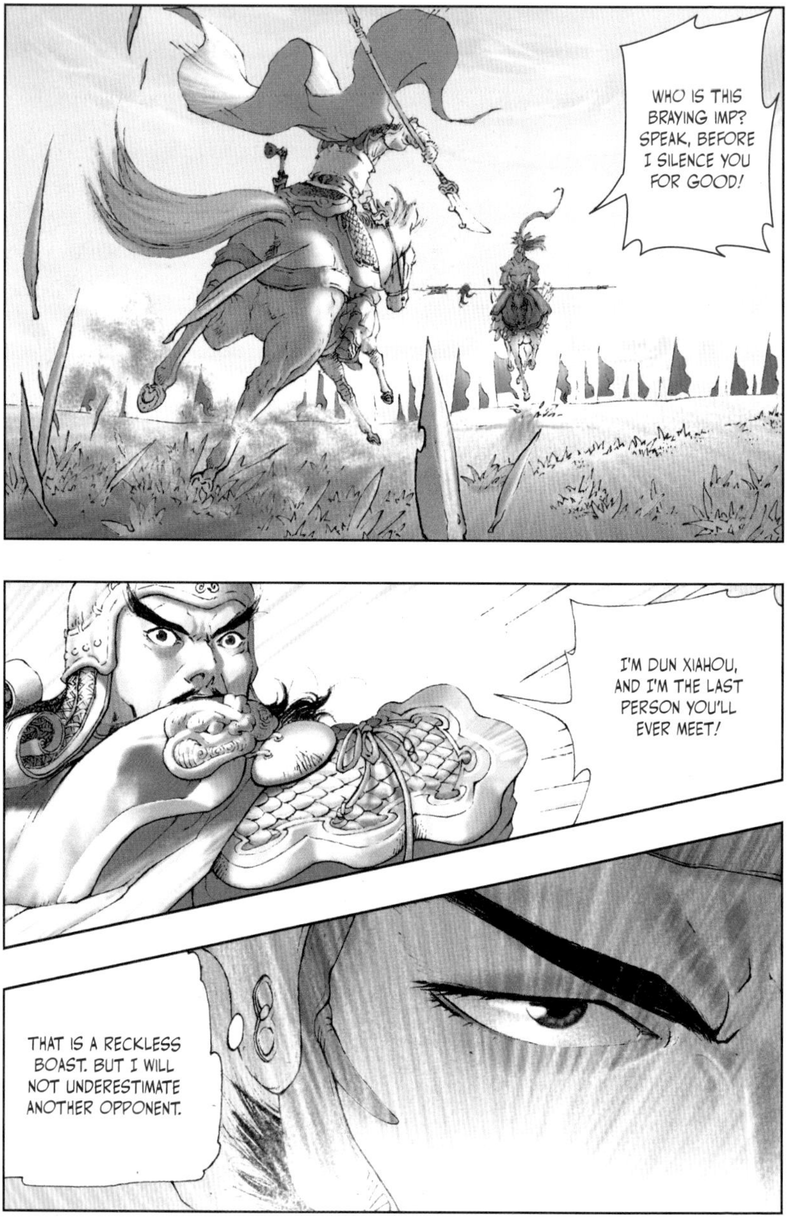
WHO IS THIS BRAYING IMP? SPEAK, BEFORE I SILENCE YOU FOR GOOD!
I'M DUN XIAHOU, AND I'M THE LAST PERSON YOU'LL EVER MEET!
THAT IS A RECKLESS BOAST. BUT I WILL NOT UNDERESTIMATE ANOTHER OPPONENT.

KLANG

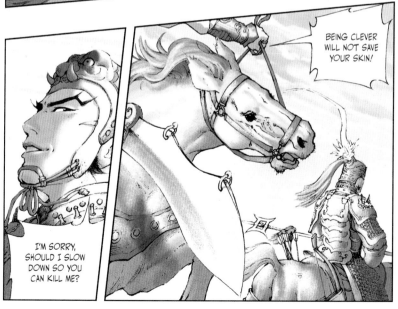

BEING CLEVER WILL NOT SAVE YOUR SKIN!

I'M SORRY, SHOULD I SLOW DOWN SO YOU CAN KILL ME?

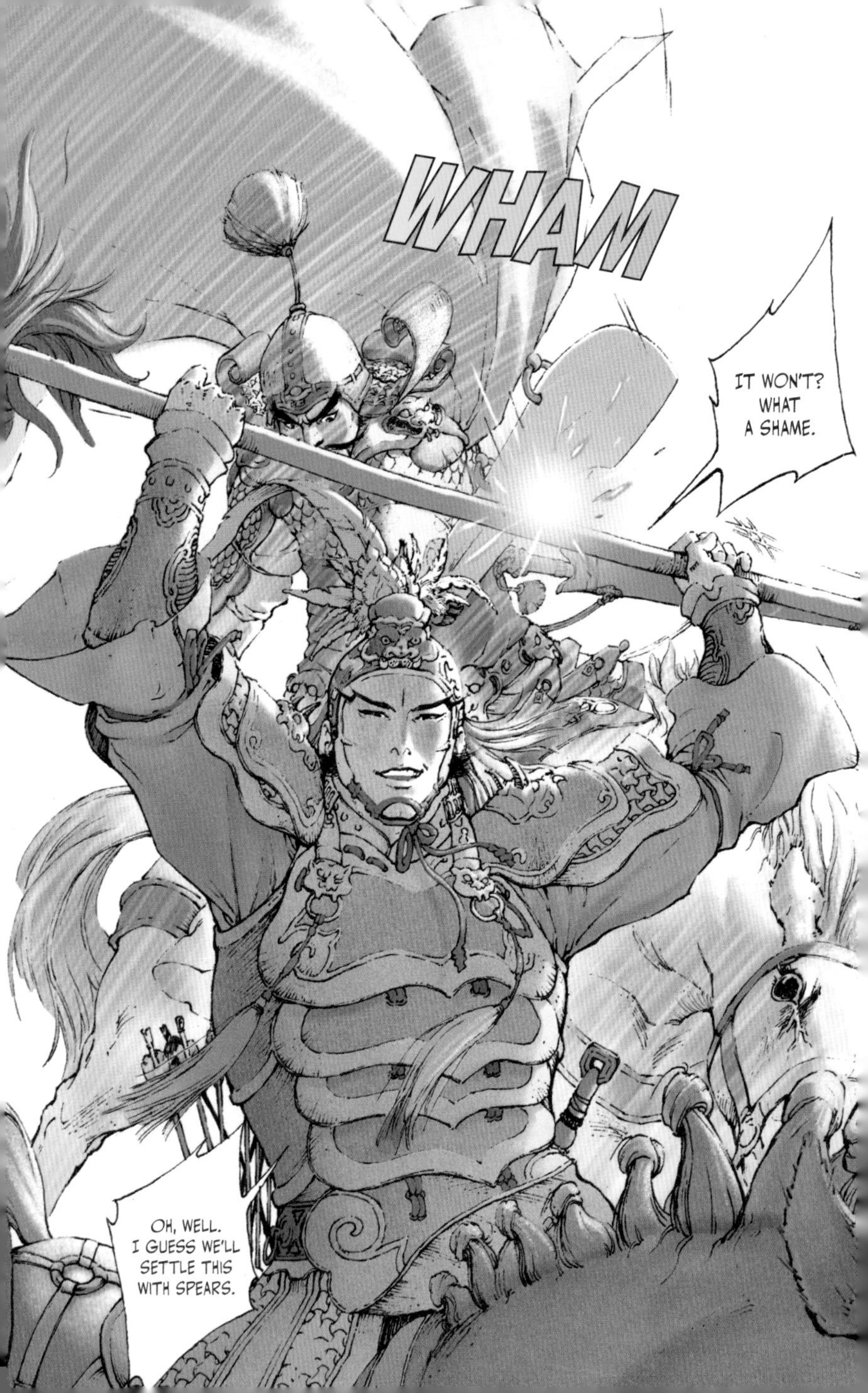
WHAM
IT WON'T? WHAT A SHAME.
OH, WELL. I GUESS WE'LL SETTLE THIS WITH SPEARS.

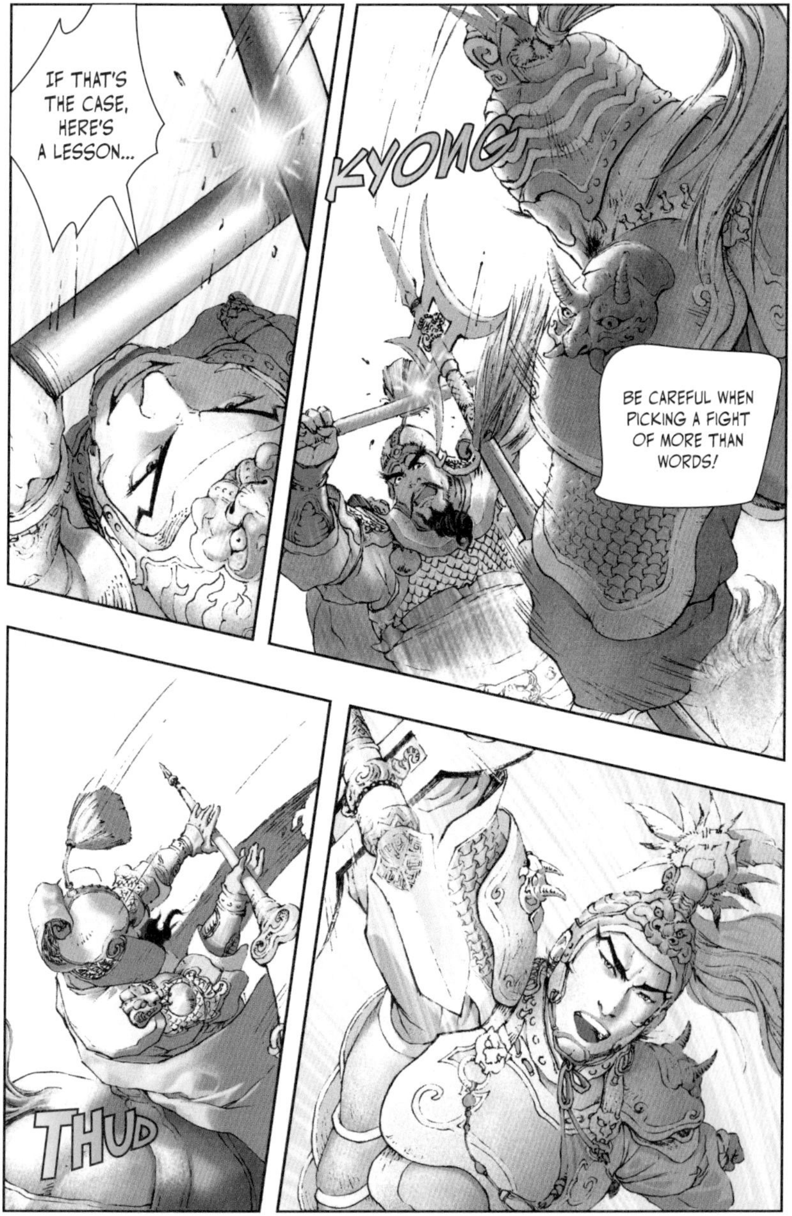
IF THAT'S THE CASE, HERE'S A LESSON...
KYONG
BE CAREFUL WHEN PICKING A FIGHT OF MORE THAN WORDS!
THUD

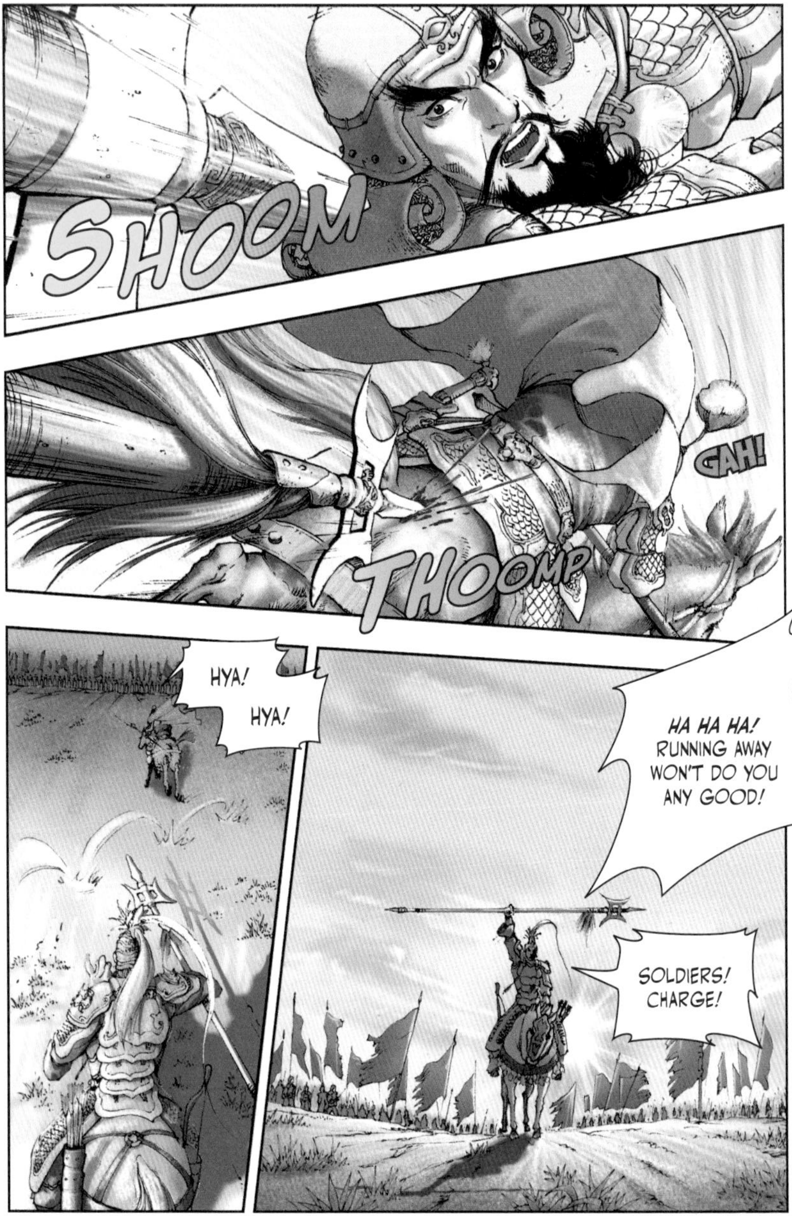
SHOOM
GAH!
THOOMP
HYA!
HYA!
HA HA HA! RUNNING AWAY WON'T DO YOU ANY GOOD!
SOLDIERS! CHARGE!

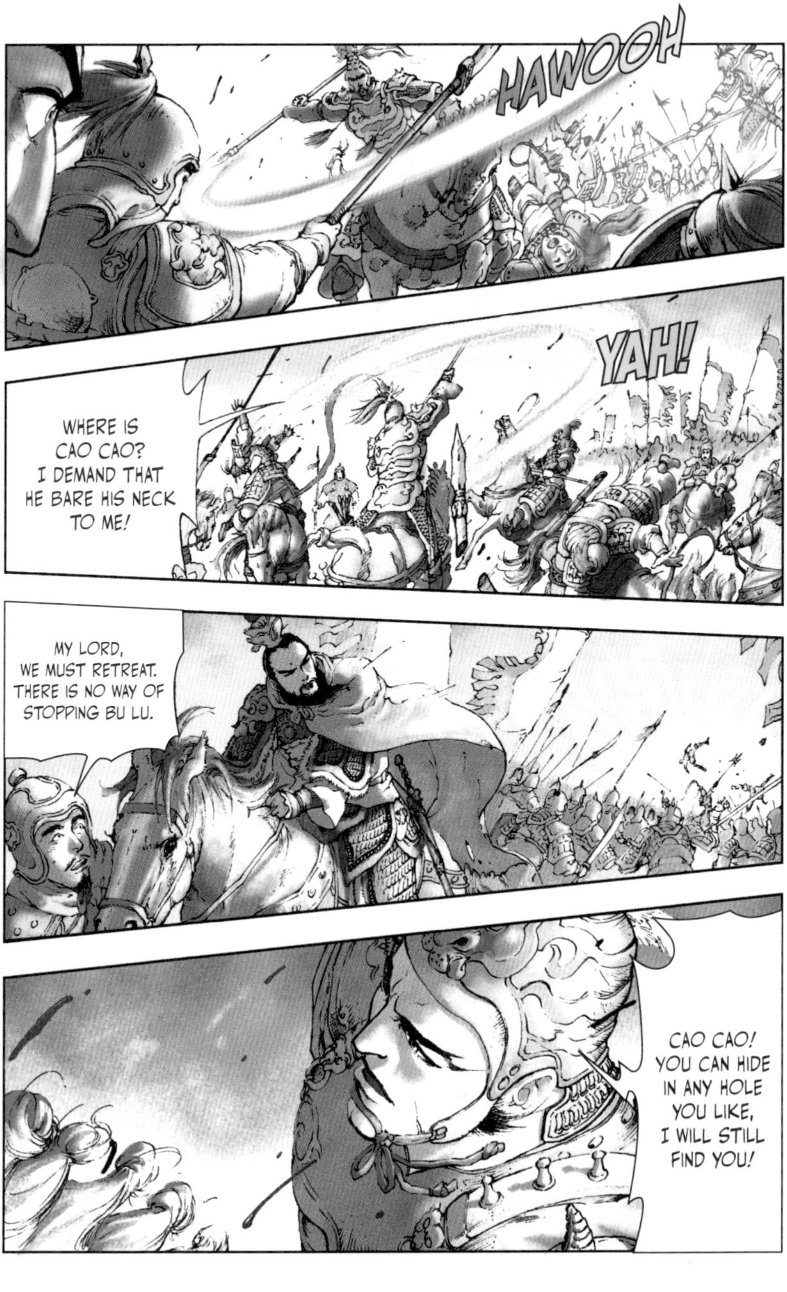
HAWOOH
YAH!
WHERE IS CAO CAO? I DEMAND THAT HE BARE HIS NECK TO ME!
MY LORD, WE MUST RETREAT. THERE IS NO WAY OF STOPPING BU LU.
CAO CAO! YOU CAN HIDE IN ANY HOLE YOU LIKE, I WILL STILL FIND YOU!

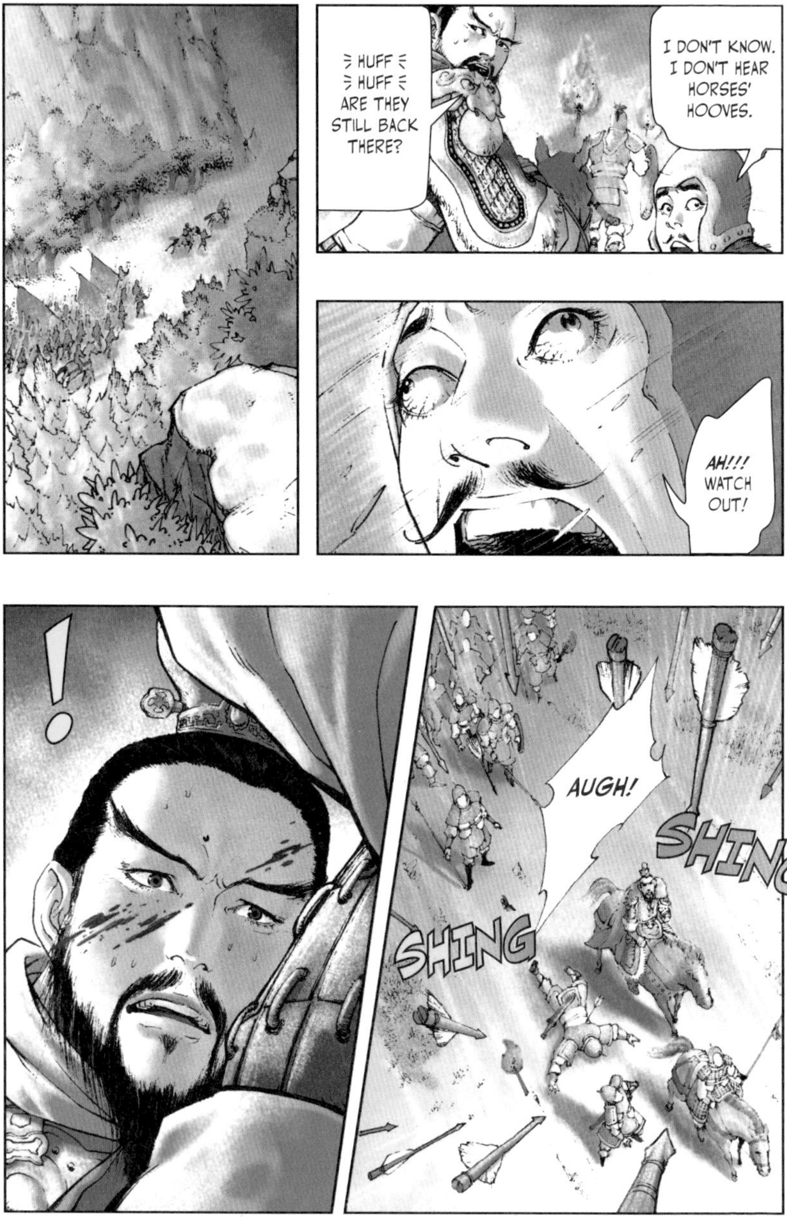
≡ HUFF ≡
≡ HUFF ≡
ARE THEY
STILL BACK
THERE?
I DON'T KNOW.
I DON'T HEAR
HORSES'
HOOVES.
AH!!!
WATCH
OUT!
!
AUGH!
SHING
SHING

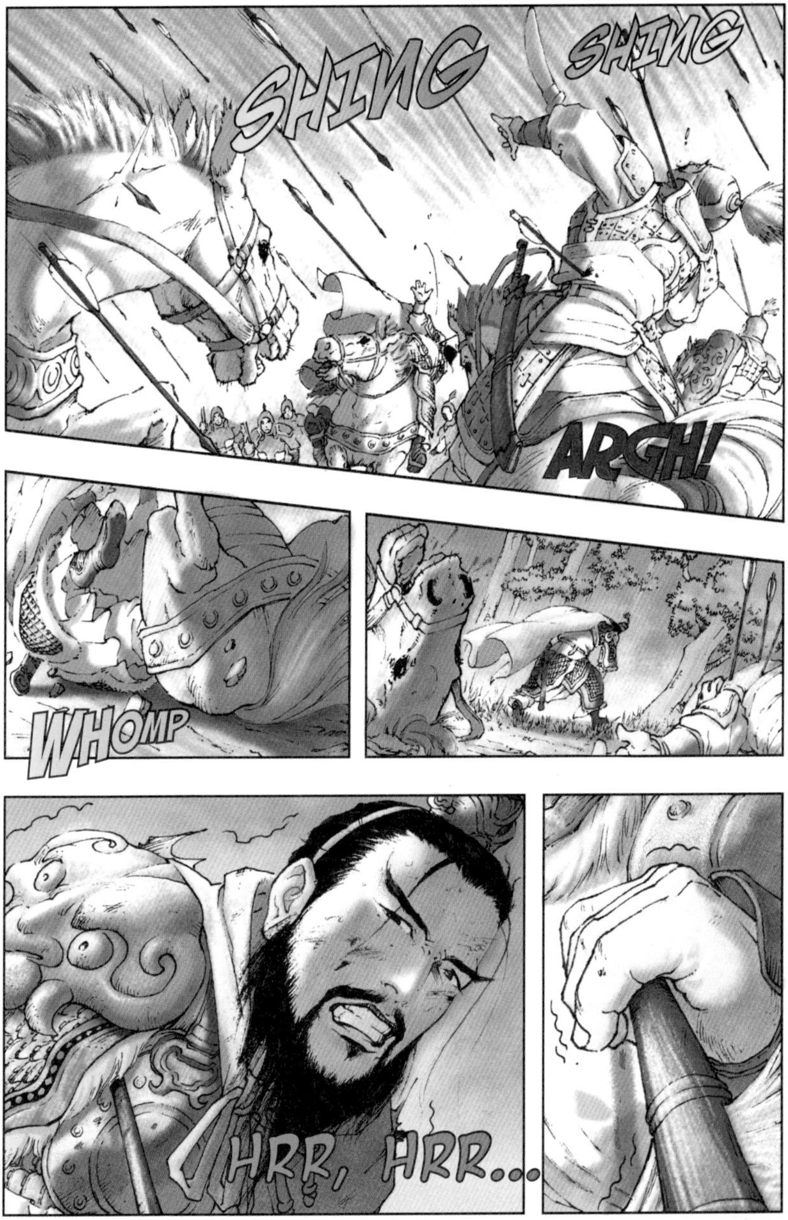
SHING
SHING
ARGH!
WHOMP
HRR, HRR...

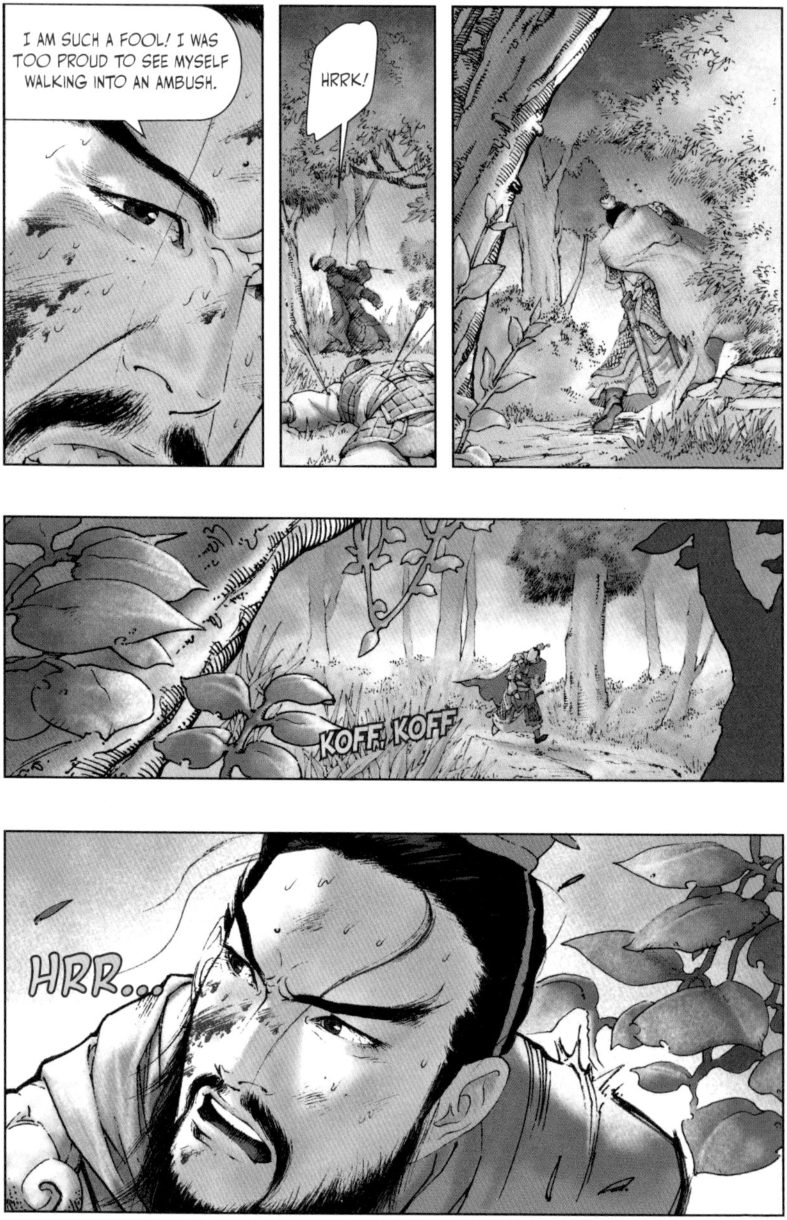
I AM SUCH A FOOL! I WAS TOO PROUD TO SEE MYSELF WALKING INTO AN AMBUSH.
HRRK!
KOFF, KOFF
HRR...

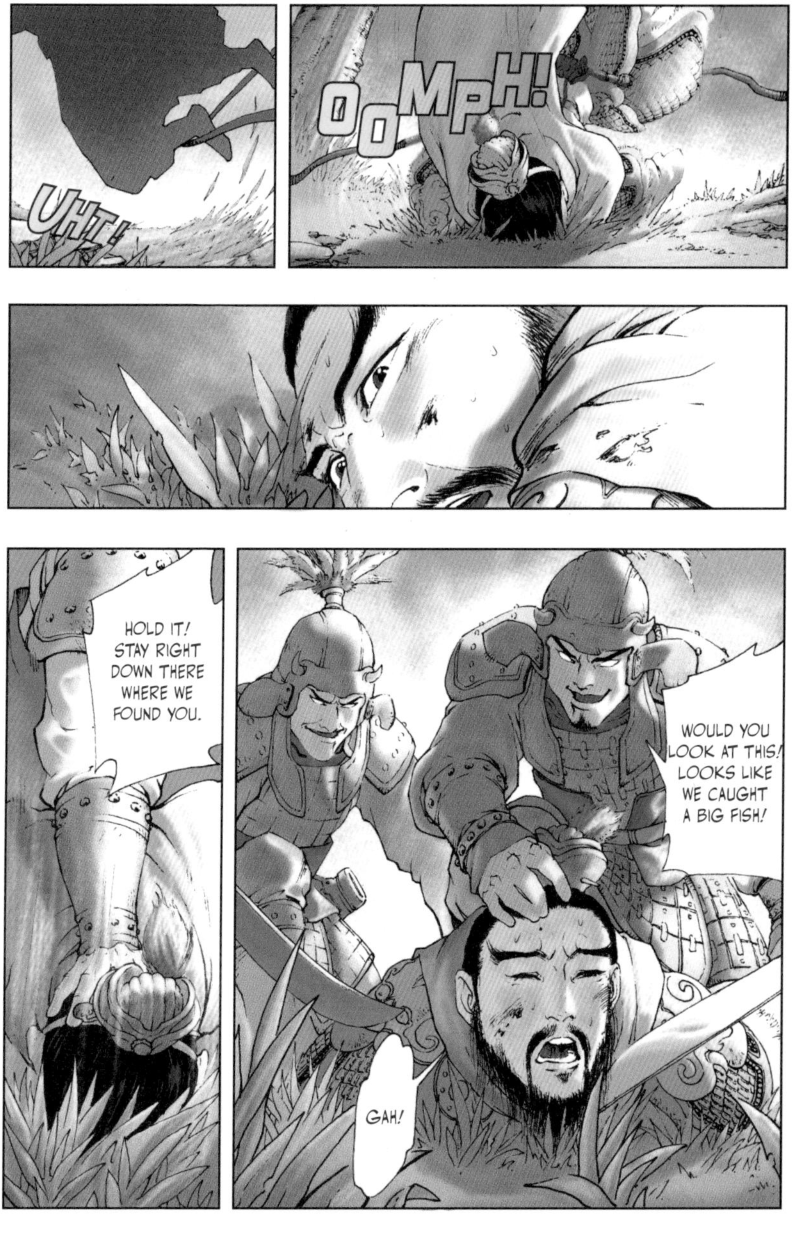
UHT!
OOMPH!
HOLD IT! STAY RIGHT DOWN THERE WHERE WE FOUND YOU.
WOULD YOU LOOK AT THIS! LOOKS LIKE WE CAUGHT A BIG FISH!
GAH!

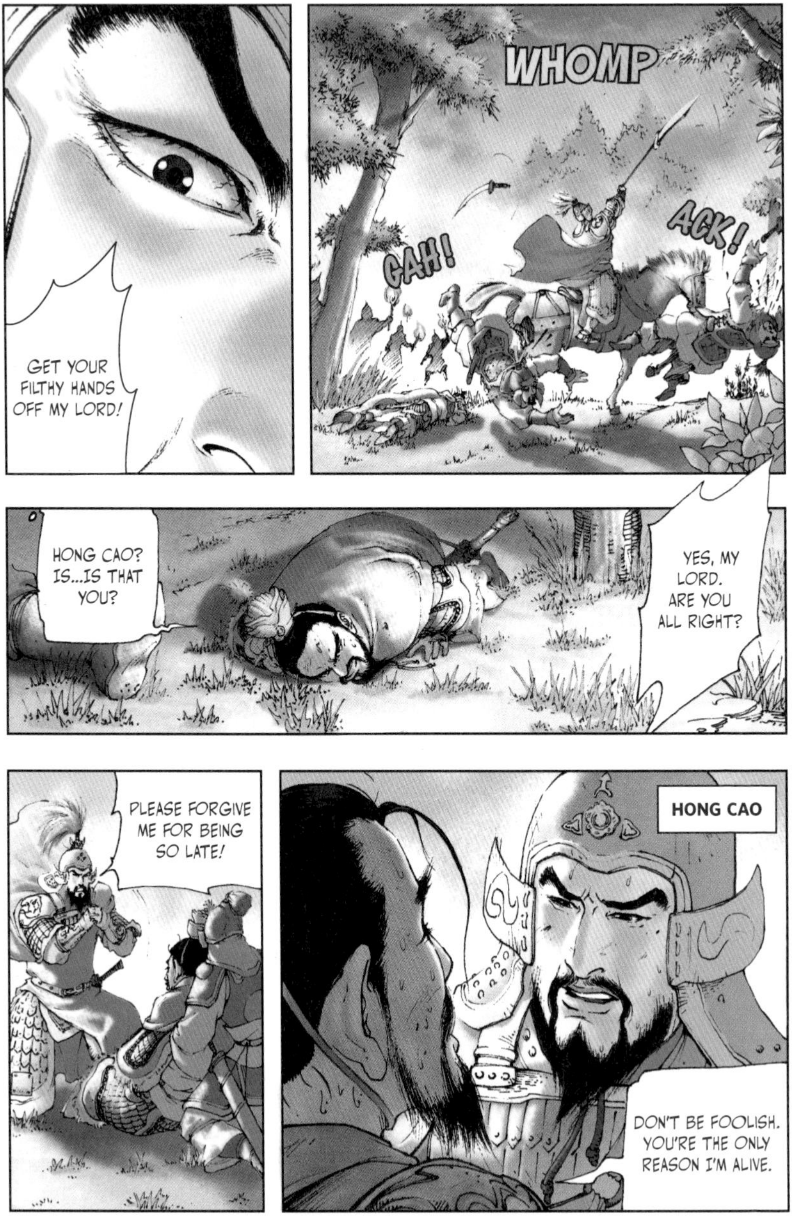
GET YOUR FILTHY HANDS OFF MY LORD!
WHOMP
GAH!
ACK!
HONG CAO? IS...IS THAT YOU?
YES, MY LORD. ARE YOU ALL RIGHT?
PLEASE FORGIVE ME FOR BEING SO LATE!
HONG CAO
DON'T BE FOOLISH. YOU'RE THE ONLY REASON I'M ALIVE.

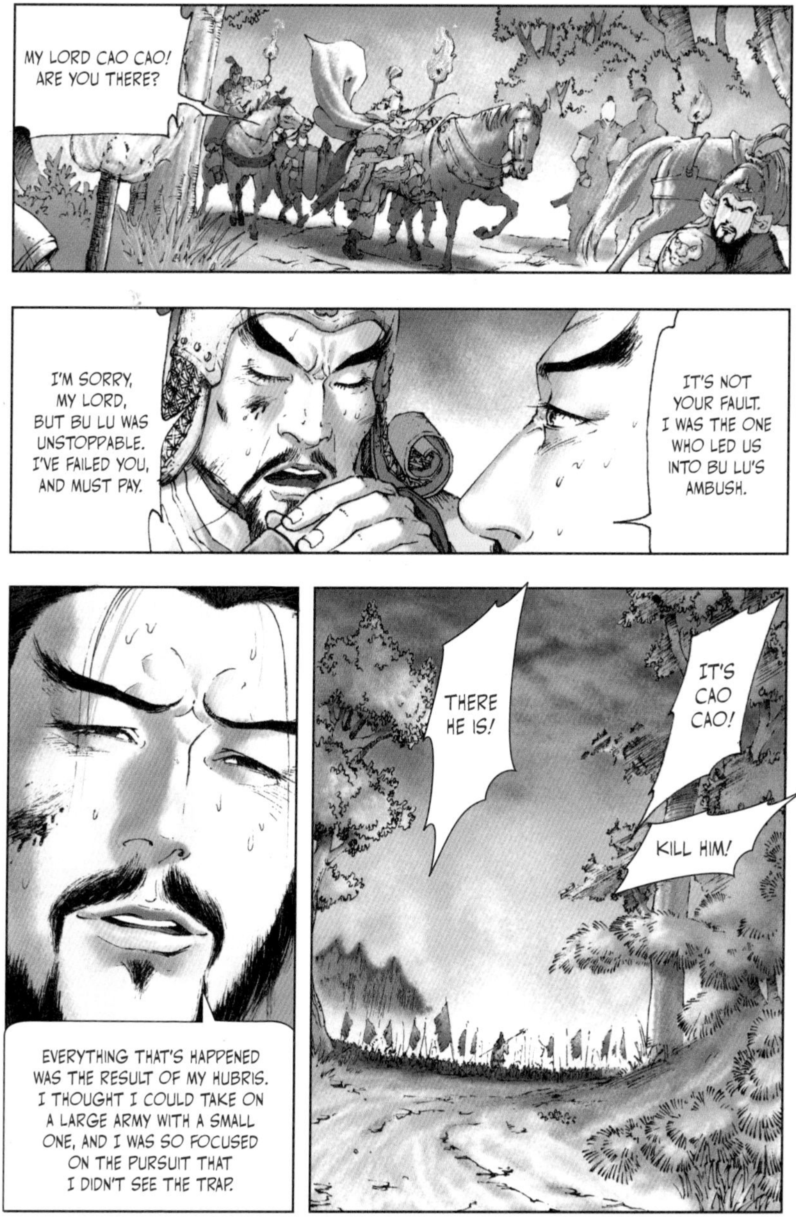
MY LORD CAO CAO! ARE YOU THERE?
I'M SORRY, MY LORD, BUT BU LU WAS UNSTOPPABLE. I'VE FAILED YOU, AND MUST PAY.
IT'S NOT YOUR FAULT. I WAS THE ONE WHO LED US INTO BU LU'S AMBUSH.
EVERYTHING THAT'S HAPPENED WAS THE RESULT OF MY HUBRIS. I THOUGHT I COULD TAKE ON A LARGE ARMY WITH A SMALL ONE, AND I WAS SO FOCUSED ON THE PURSUIT THAT I DIDN'T SEE THE TRAP.
THERE HE IS!
IT'S CAO CAO!
KILL HIM!

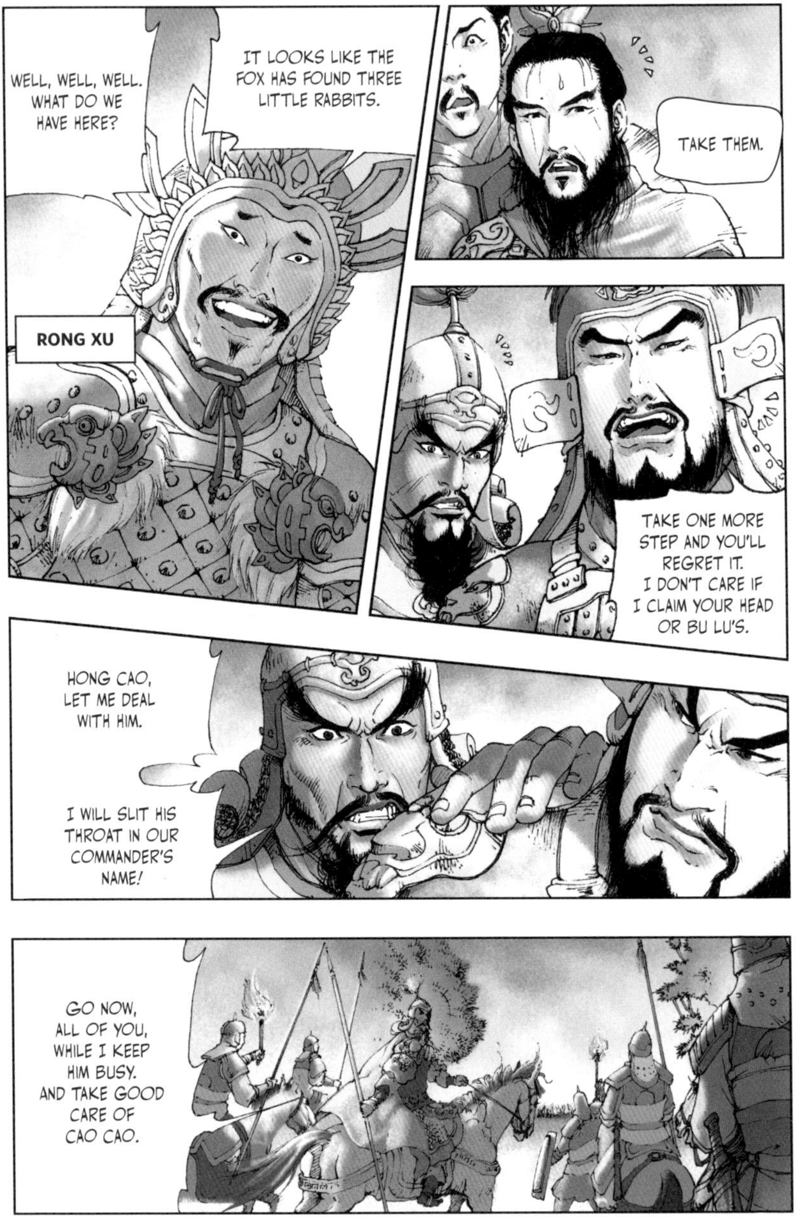
WELL, WELL, WELL. WHAT DO WE HAVE HERE?
IT LOOKS LIKE THE FOX HAS FOUND THREE LITTLE RABBITS.
RONG XU
TAKE THEM.
TAKE ONE MORE STEP AND YOU'LL REGRET IT. I DON'T CARE IF I CLAIM YOUR HEAD OR BU LU'S.
HONG CAO, LET ME DEAL WITH HIM.
I WILL SLIT HIS THROAT IN OUR COMMANDER'S NAME!
GO NOW, ALL OF YOU, WHILE I KEEP HIM BUSY. AND TAKE GOOD CARE OF CAO CAO.

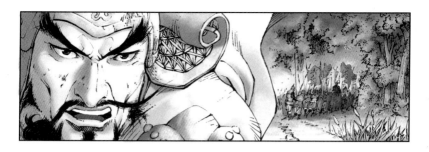

DUN XIAHOU

REST IN PEACE.

SHOONK

133

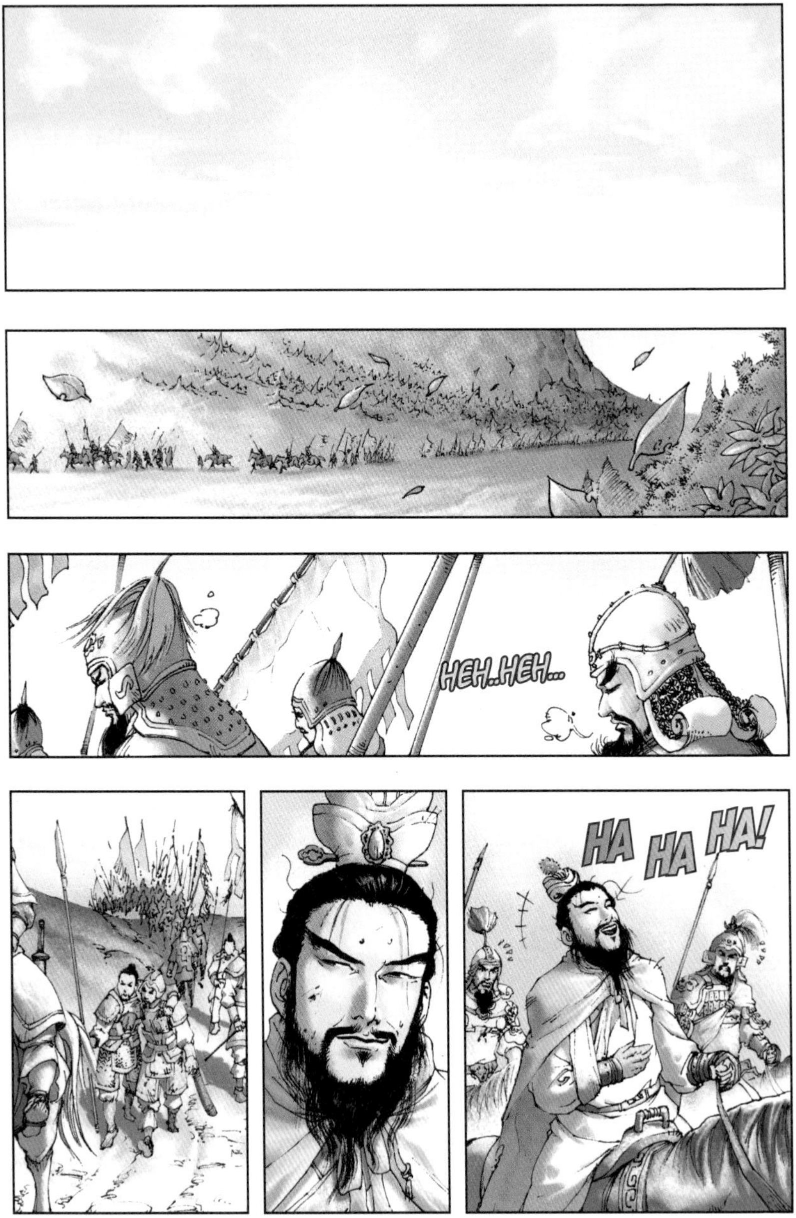
HEH..HEH...
HA HA HA!

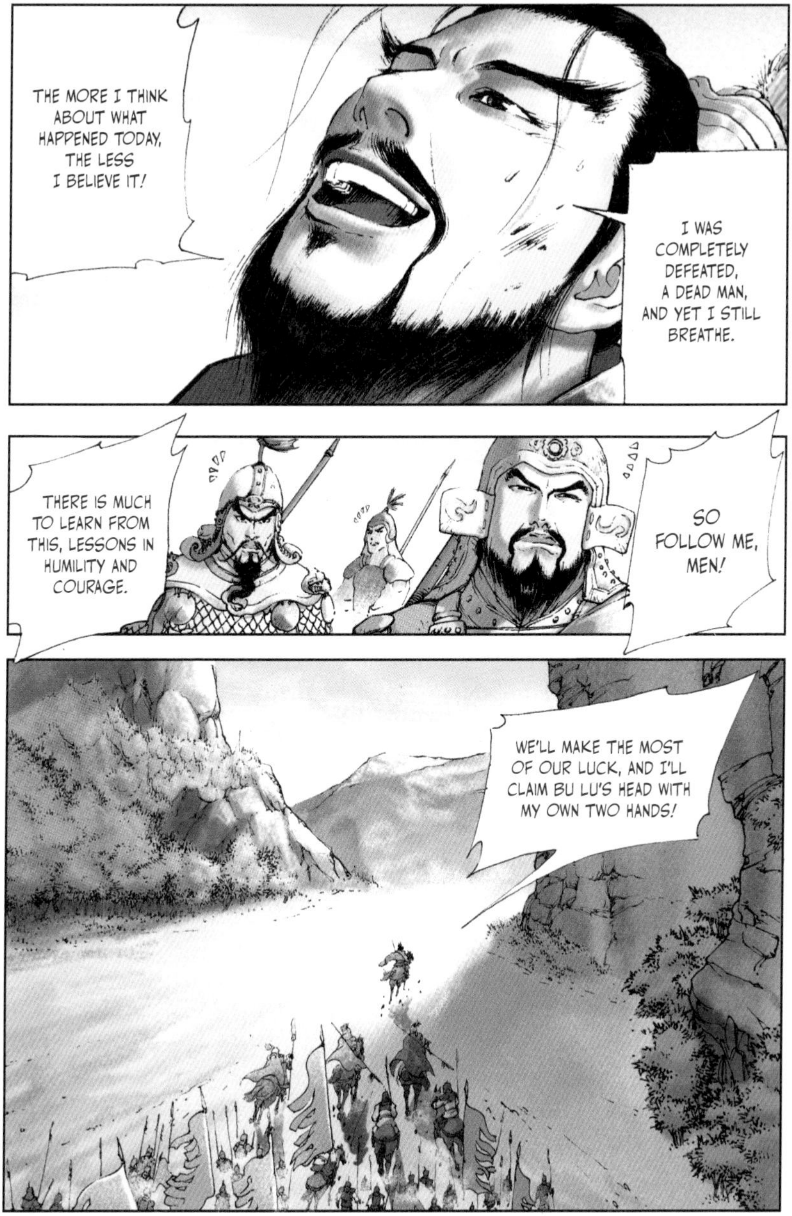
THE MORE I THINK ABOUT WHAT HAPPENED TODAY, THE LESS I BELIEVE IT!
I WAS COMPLETELY DEFEATED, A DEAD MAN, AND YET I STILL BREATHE.
THERE IS MUCH TO LEARN FROM THIS, LESSONS IN HUMILITY AND COURAGE.
SO FOLLOW ME, MEN!
WE'LL MAKE THE MOST OF OUR LUCK, AND I'LL CLAIM BU LU'S HEAD WITH MY OWN TWO HANDS!

Chapter 4

Jian Sun's Theft of the Royal Seal and the Rivalry of the Yuan Brothers AD 191–192

Summary

Zhuo Dong has fled the capital of LuoYang and set fire to the city on his way out. He is bound for ChangAn, which he will convert into a new capital. Jian Sun leads his men into the city, and for days they attempt to put out the fires. While fighting the inferno, Jian Sun discovers an item on the body of a dead woman: the Emperor's Hereditary Seal, an extremely powerful and precious royal token. Shao Yuan, the supreme commander of the coalition army, hears of Jian Sun's newest possession and accuses him of theft. The two men fight, and Jian Sun flees, wounded, to his homeland.

Later, Shao Yuan's younger brother, Shu, approaches his brother and asks him to provide supplies for his army. Shao tells him that such a thing is impossible, because doing so would require asking a favor of Fu Han, the head of Ji Province, a region Shao Yuan plans to conquer. With the help of Zan GongSun, Shao Yuan conquers Ji Province. But Shao Yuan rejects GongSun's request that they share the region, and the two sides do battle. Zan GongSun is having a difficult time against Shao Yuan's forces, and asks Bei Liu and his sworn brothers to come to his aid.

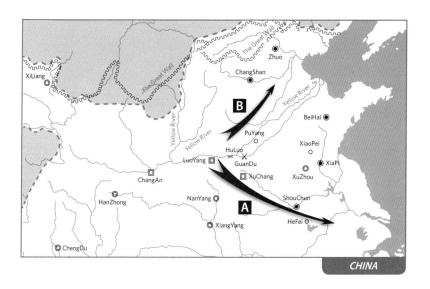

The Great Wall
The Great Wall
Zhuo
XiLiang
ChangShan
B
Yellow River
Yellow River
Yellow River
BeiHai
PuYang
XiaoPei
HuLuo
LuoYang
GuanDu
XiaPi
XuChang
XuZhou
ChangAn
HanZhong
NanYang
ShouChun
A
HeFei
XiangYang
ChengDu
CHINA

A Jian Sun returns to his homeland

Having taken possession of the Emperor's Hereditary Seal from the ruins of LuoYang, Jian Sun abandons the coalition army and heads to his homeland. But he is intercepted by two of Shao Yuan's commanders.

B Shao Yuan moves to conquer the Ji Province

After the coalition forces fall apart, Shao Yuan decides to conquer Ji Province. The head of the province hears of the plan and flees the region, and Shao Yuan is able to make the province his seat of power.

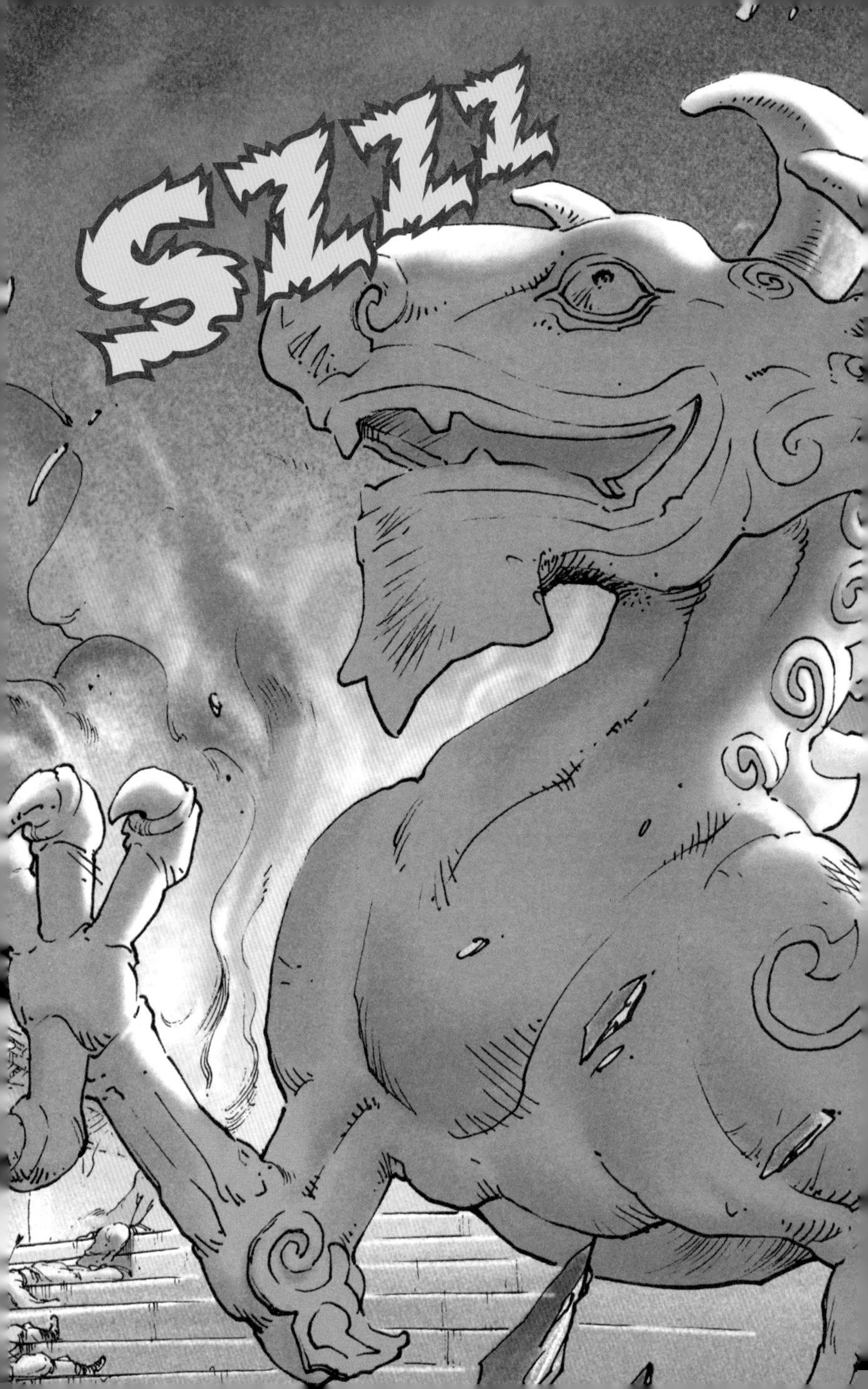
SZZZ

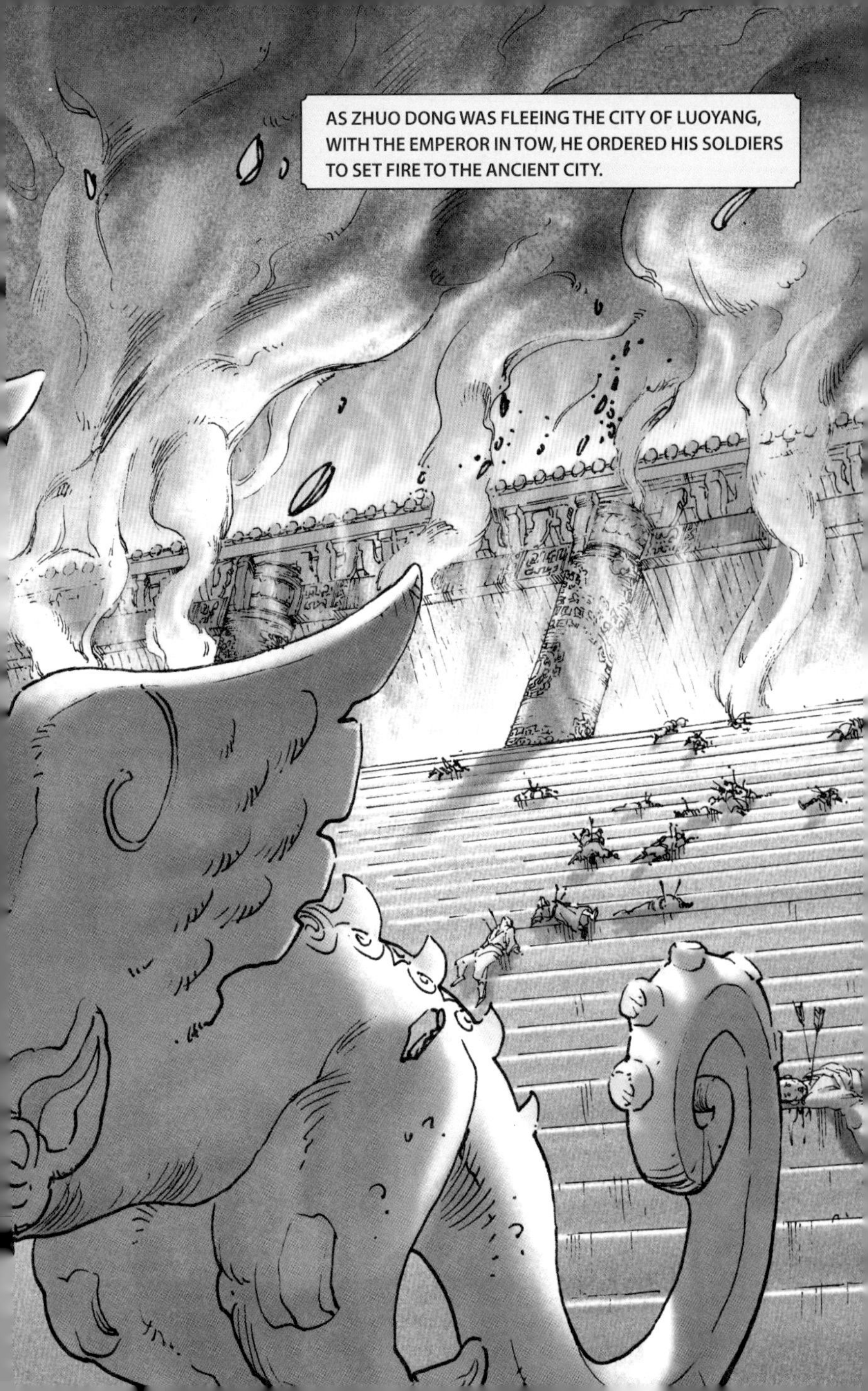
AS ZHUO DONG WAS FLEEING THE CITY OF LUOYANG, WITH THE EMPEROR IN TOW, HE ORDERED HIS SOLDIERS TO SET FIRE TO THE ANCIENT CITY.

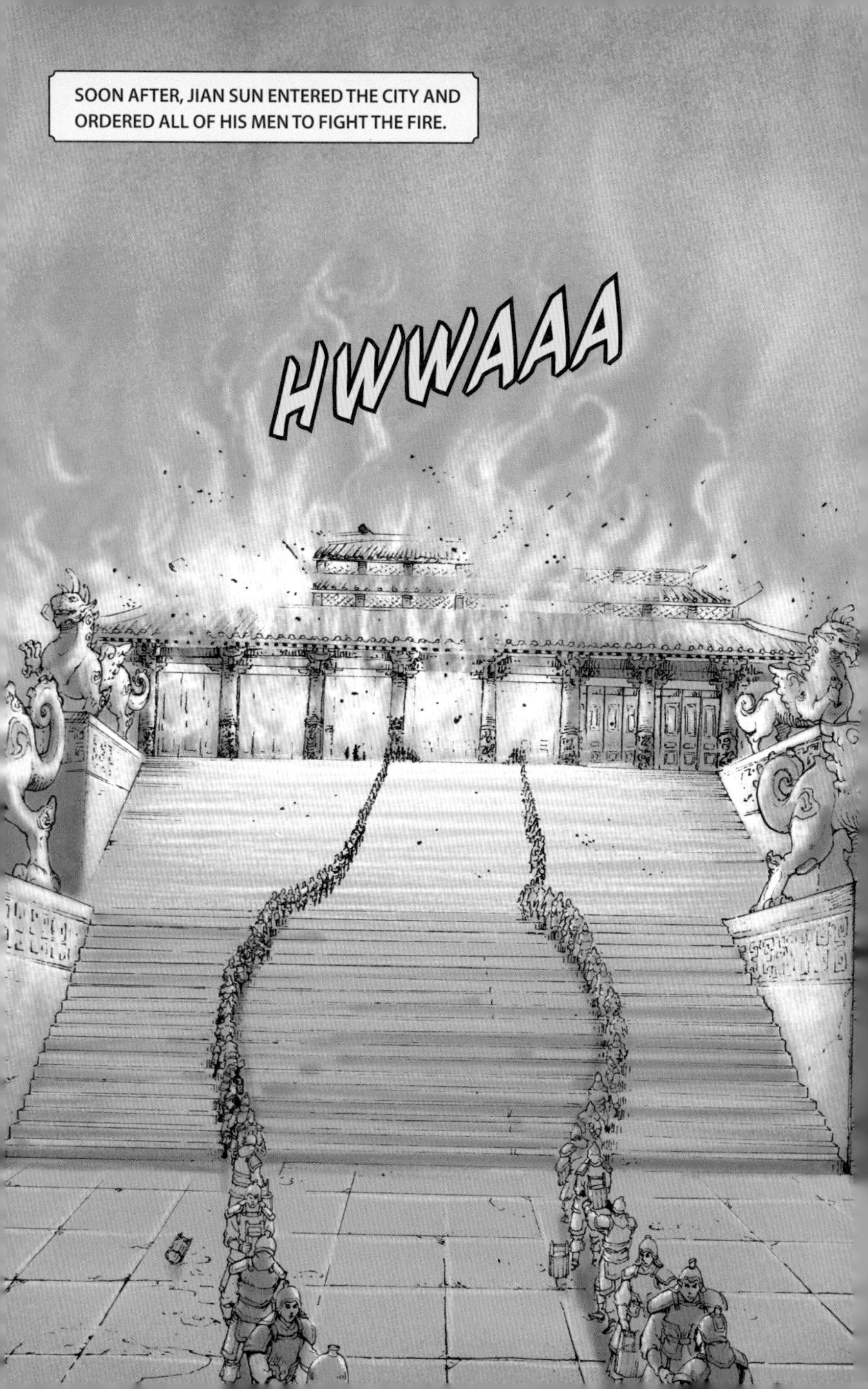
SOON AFTER, JIAN SUN ENTERED THE CITY AND ORDERED ALL OF HIS MEN TO FIGHT THE FIRE.
HWWAAA

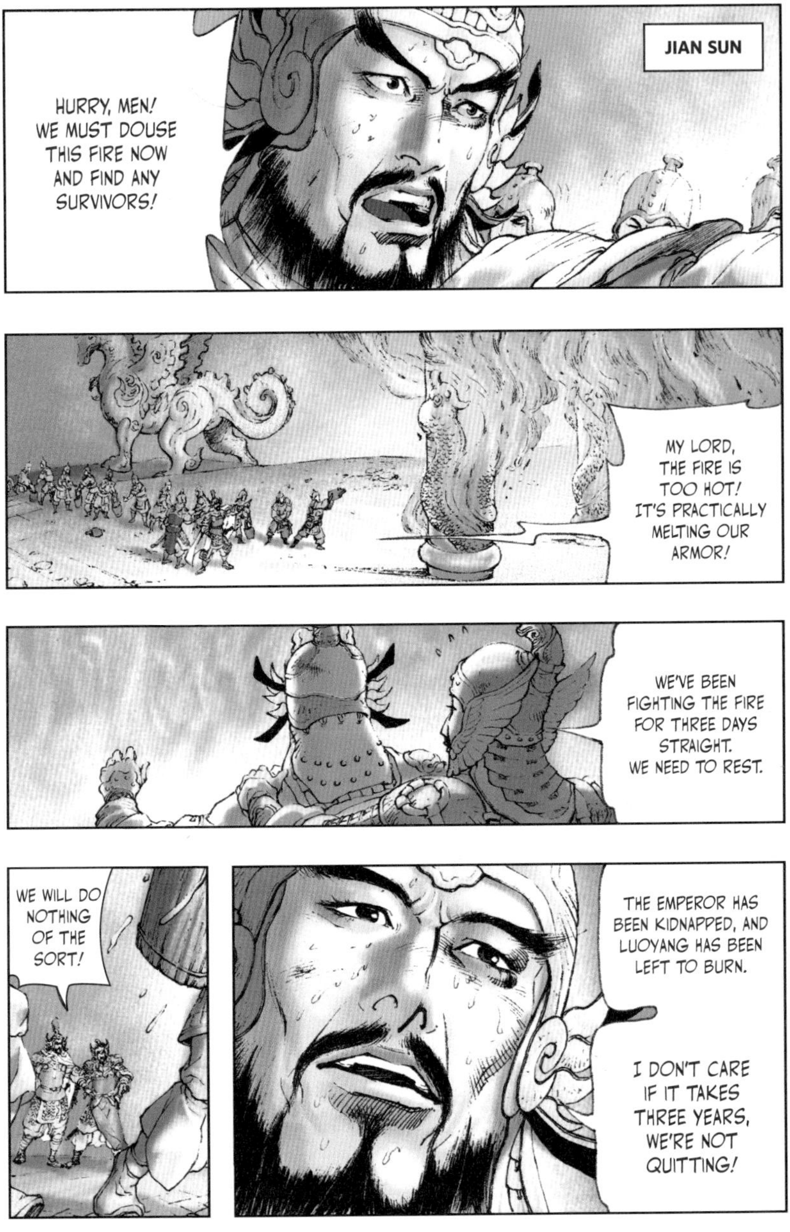
JIAN SUN
HURRY, MEN! WE MUST DOUSE THIS FIRE NOW AND FIND ANY SURVIVORS!
MY LORD, THE FIRE IS TOO HOT! IT'S PRACTICALLY MELTING OUR ARMOR!
WE'VE BEEN FIGHTING THE FIRE FOR THREE DAYS STRAIGHT. WE NEED TO REST.
WE WILL DO NOTHING OF THE SORT!
THE EMPEROR HAS BEEN KIDNAPPED, AND LUOYANG HAS BEEN LEFT TO BURN.
I DON'T CARE IF IT TAKES THREE YEARS, WE'RE NOT QUITTING!

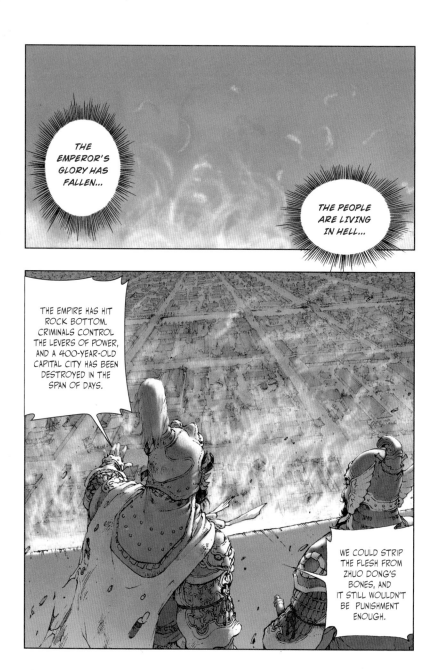

THE EMPEROR'S GLORY HAS FALLEN...

THE PEOPLE ARE LIVING IN HELL...

THE EMPIRE HAS HIT ROCK BOTTOM. CRIMINALS CONTROL THE LEVERS OF POWER, AND A 400-YEAR-OLD CAPITAL CITY HAS BEEN DESTROYED IN THE SPAN OF DAYS.

WE COULD STRIP THE FLESH FROM ZHUO DONG'S BONES, AND IT STILL WOULDN'T BE PUNISHMENT ENOUGH.

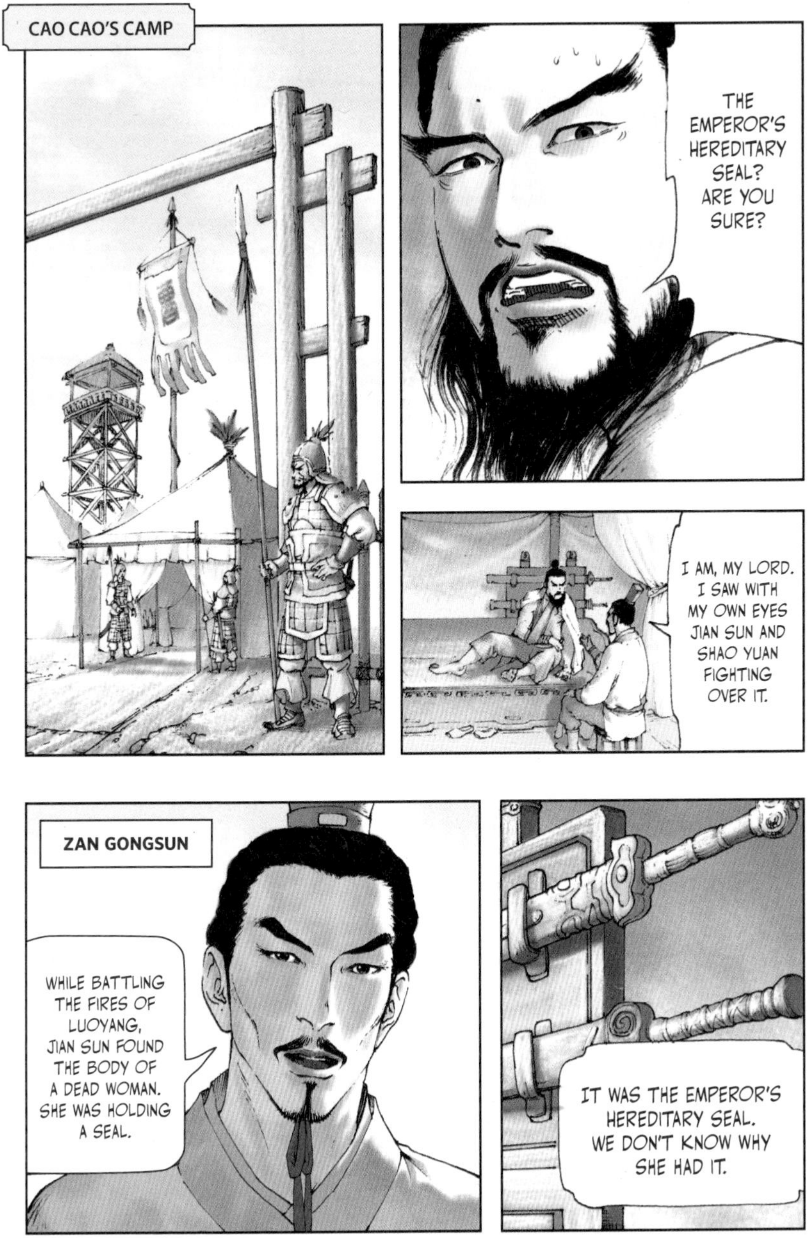
CAO CAO'S CAMP
THE EMPEROR'S HEREDITARY SEAL? ARE YOU SURE?
I AM, MY LORD. I SAW WITH MY OWN EYES JIAN SUN AND SHAO YUAN FIGHTING OVER IT.
ZAN GONGSUN
WHILE BATTLING THE FIRES OF LUOYANG, JIAN SUN FOUND THE BODY OF A DEAD WOMAN. SHE WAS HOLDING A SEAL.
IT WAS THE EMPEROR'S HEREDITARY SEAL. WE DON'T KNOW WHY SHE HAD IT.

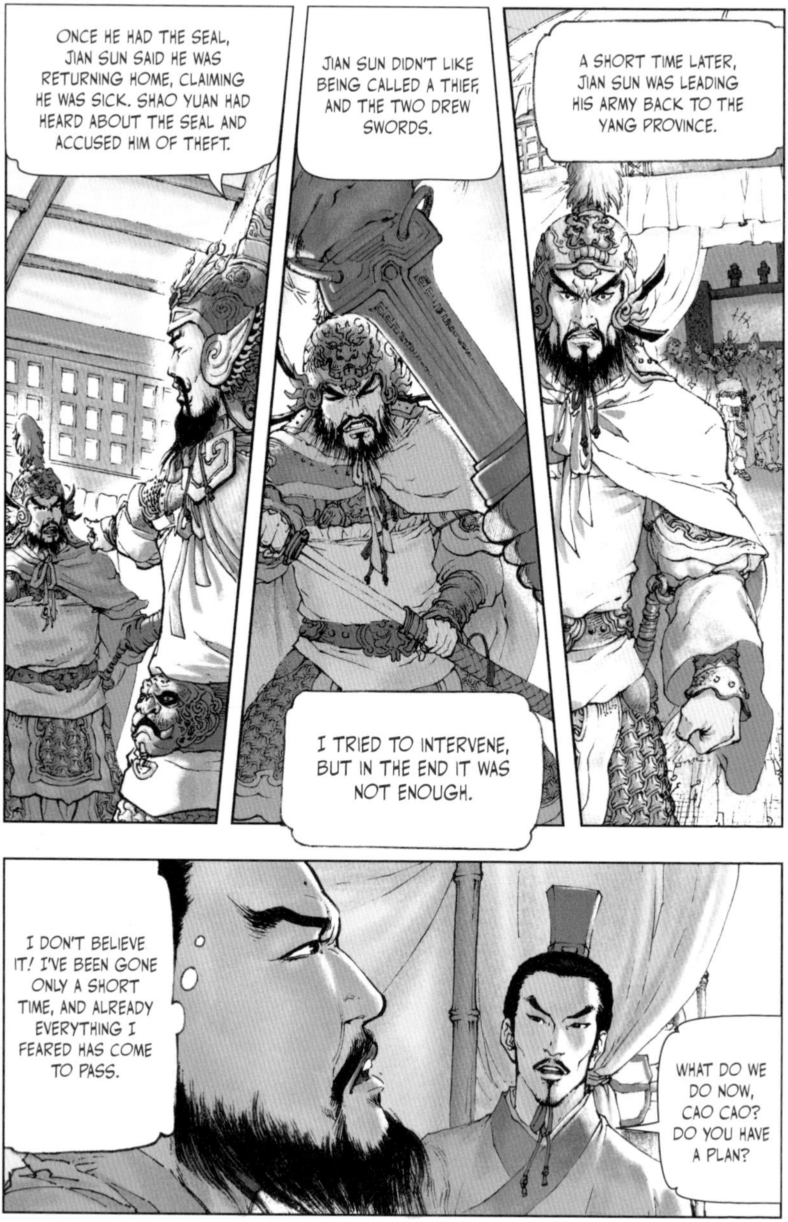
ONCE HE HAD THE SEAL, JIAN SUN SAID HE WAS RETURNING HOME, CLAIMING HE WAS SICK. SHAO YUAN HAD HEARD ABOUT THE SEAL AND ACCUSED HIM OF THEFT.
JIAN SUN DIDN'T LIKE BEING CALLED A THIEF, AND THE TWO DREW SWORDS.
I TRIED TO INTERVENE, BUT IN THE END IT WAS NOT ENOUGH.
A SHORT TIME LATER, JIAN SUN WAS LEADING HIS ARMY BACK TO THE YANG PROVINCE.
I DON'T BELIEVE IT! I'VE BEEN GONE ONLY A SHORT TIME, AND ALREADY EVERYTHING I FEARED HAS COME TO PASS.
WHAT DO WE DO NOW, CAO CAO? DO YOU HAVE A PLAN?

YES. TELL THE ENTIRE ARMY TO RETURN HOME. WE ARE DISBANDING.

YES, SIR!

WAIT, EVEN YOU ARE GIVING UP?

DON'T YOU SEE WHAT'S HAPPENING, GONGSUN? WE WERE TOLD THAT THE SOLE OBJECTIVE OF THIS ARMY WAS TO DEFEAT ZHUO DONG. BUT IT'S OBVIOUS THAT WAS A LIE. FIRST SHU YUAN CUTS OFF SUPPLIES TO THE BATTLEFIELD, THEN NO ONE COMES FORWARD TO HELP ME CHASE ZHUO DONG.

AND NOW JIAN SUN HAS TAKEN THE EMPEROR'S SEAL FOR HIMSELF. THIS ALLIANCE IS AND HAS ALWAYS BEEN A COMPLETE FARCE, AND THE LONGER WE SWEAR TO UPHOLD IT, THE MORE DANGER WE FACE. IF WE TRY TO HOLD THIS THING TOGETHER, WE'RE AS GOOD AS DEAD.

I AM RETURNING HOME WITH MY MEN IMMEDIATELY. I WILL MONITOR EVENTS FROM THERE.

Cao Cao left, and led his army back to the Yan Province.

HM...

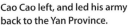

145

I KNEW THIS WOULD HAPPEN! FIRST JIAN SUN FLEES. NOW IT'S CAO CAO!

THE COALITION IS UNRAVELING BEFORE OUR EYES! WE'LL NEVER DEFEAT ZHUO DONG NOW.

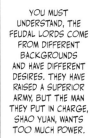

YOU MUST UNDERSTAND, THE FEUDAL LORDS COME FROM DIFFERENT BACKGROUNDS AND HAVE DIFFERENT DESIRES. THEY HAVE RAISED A SUPERIOR ARMY, BUT THE MAN THEY PUT IN CHARGE, SHAO YUAN, WANTS TOO MUCH POWER.

BUT THE OTHER LORDS ARE TOO TIMID AND INDECISIVE TO CONFRONT HIM. TO MAKE MATTERS WORSE, SHAO YUAN'S BROTHER, SHU, IS COMPLETELY INCOMPETENT AND UNTRUSTWORTHY.

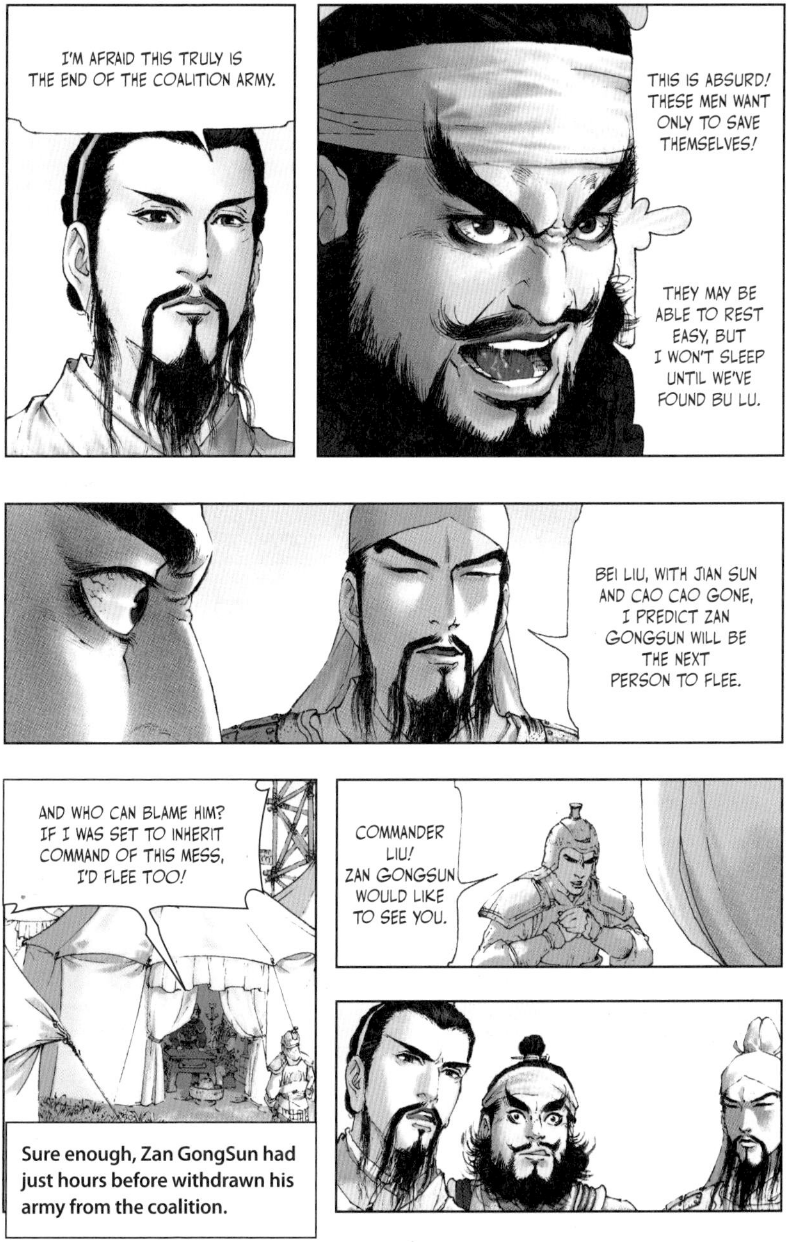
I'M AFRAID THIS TRULY IS THE END OF THE COALITION ARMY.
THIS IS ABSURD! THESE MEN WANT ONLY TO SAVE THEMSELVES!
THEY MAY BE ABLE TO REST EASY, BUT I WON'T SLEEP UNTIL WE'VE FOUND BU LU.
BEI LIU, WITH JIAN SUN AND CAO CAO GONE, I PREDICT ZAN GONGSUN WILL BE THE NEXT PERSON TO FLEE.
AND WHO CAN BLAME HIM? IF I WAS SET TO INHERIT COMMAND OF THIS MESS, I'D FLEE TOO!
Sure enough, Zan GongSun had just hours before withdrawn his army from the coalition.
COMMANDER LIU! ZAN GONGSUN WOULD LIKE TO SEE YOU.

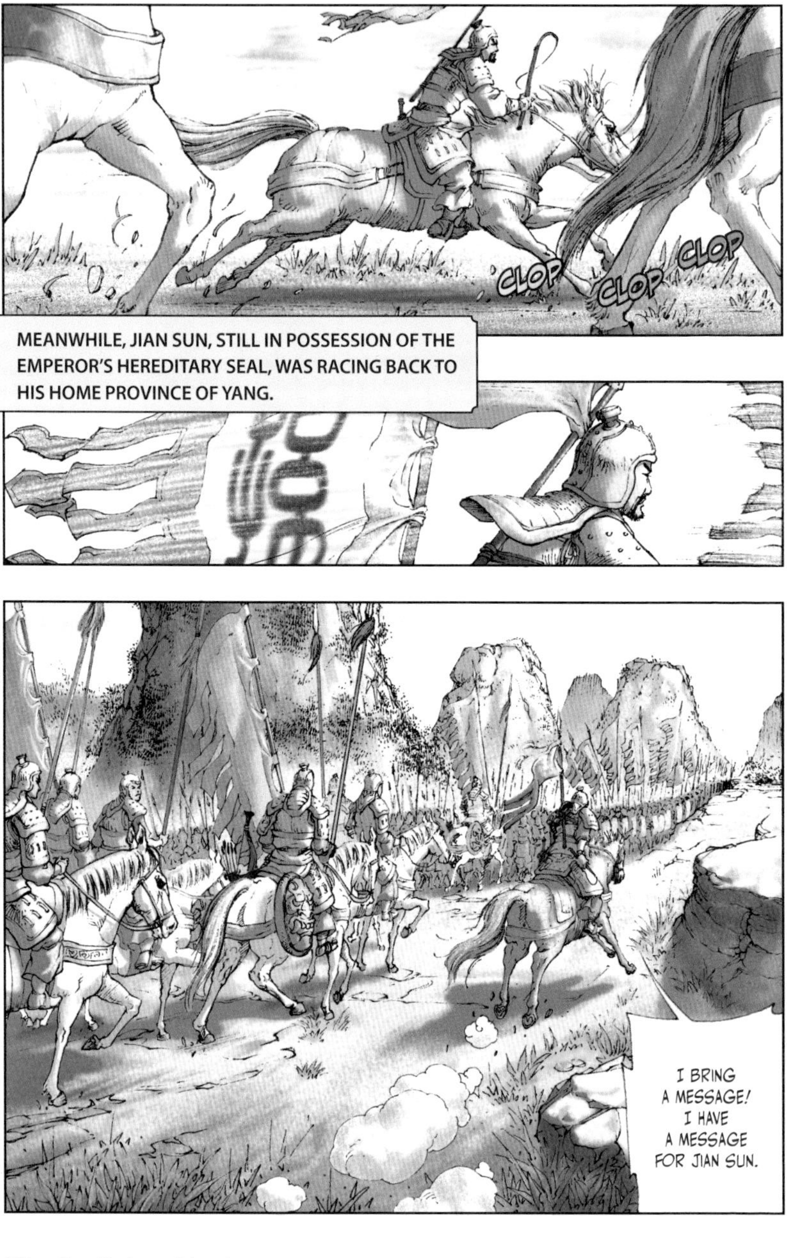
CLOP
CLOP
CLOP
MEANWHILE, JIAN SUN, STILL IN POSSESSION OF THE EMPEROR'S HEREDITARY SEAL, WAS RACING BACK TO HIS HOME PROVINCE OF YANG.
I BRING A MESSAGE! I HAVE A MESSAGE FOR JIAN SUN.

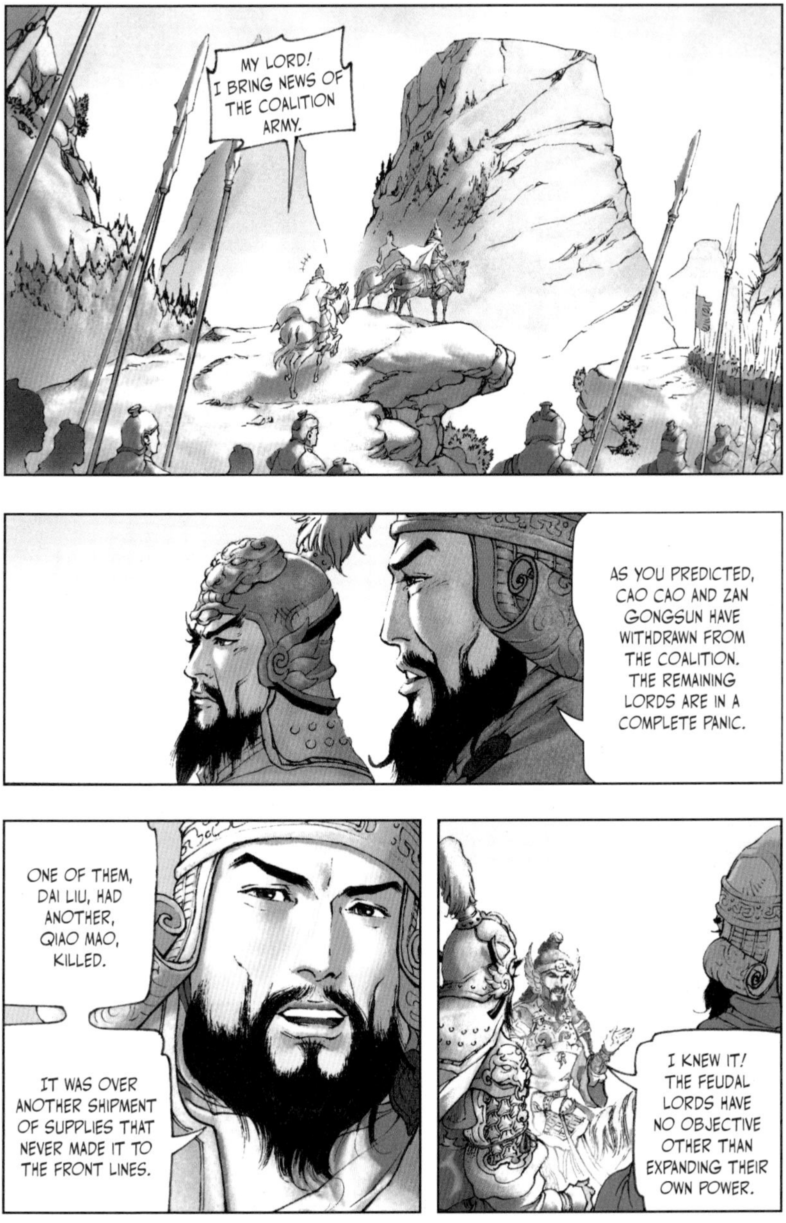
MY LORD! I BRING NEWS OF THE COALITION ARMY.
AS YOU PREDICTED, CAO CAO AND ZAN GONGSUN HAVE WITHDRAWN FROM THE COALITION. THE REMAINING LORDS ARE IN A COMPLETE PANIC.
ONE OF THEM, DAI LIU, HAD ANOTHER, QIAO MAO, KILLED.
IT WAS OVER ANOTHER SHIPMENT OF SUPPLIES THAT NEVER MADE IT TO THE FRONT LINES.
I KNEW IT! THE FEUDAL LORDS HAVE NO OBJECTIVE OTHER THAN EXPANDING THEIR OWN POWER.

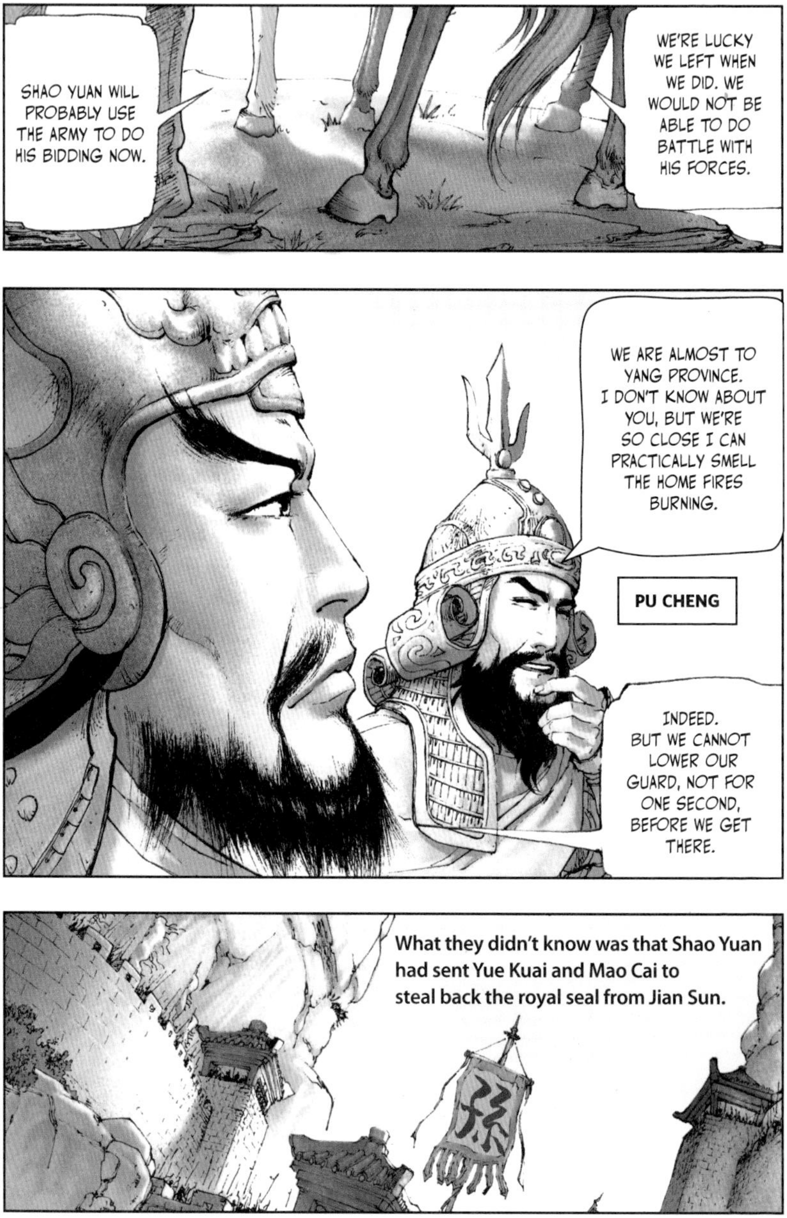
SHAO YUAN WILL PROBABLY USE THE ARMY TO DO HIS BIDDING NOW.
WE'RE LUCKY WE LEFT WHEN WE DID. WE WOULD NOT BE ABLE TO DO BATTLE WITH HIS FORCES.
WE ARE ALMOST TO YANG PROVINCE. I DON'T KNOW ABOUT YOU, BUT WE'RE SO CLOSE I CAN PRACTICALLY SMELL THE HOME FIRES BURNING.
PU CHENG
INDEED. BUT WE CANNOT LOWER OUR GUARD, NOT FOR ONE SECOND, BEFORE WE GET THERE.
What they didn't know was that Shao Yuan had sent Yue Kuai and Mao Cai to steal back the royal seal from Jian Sun.
孫

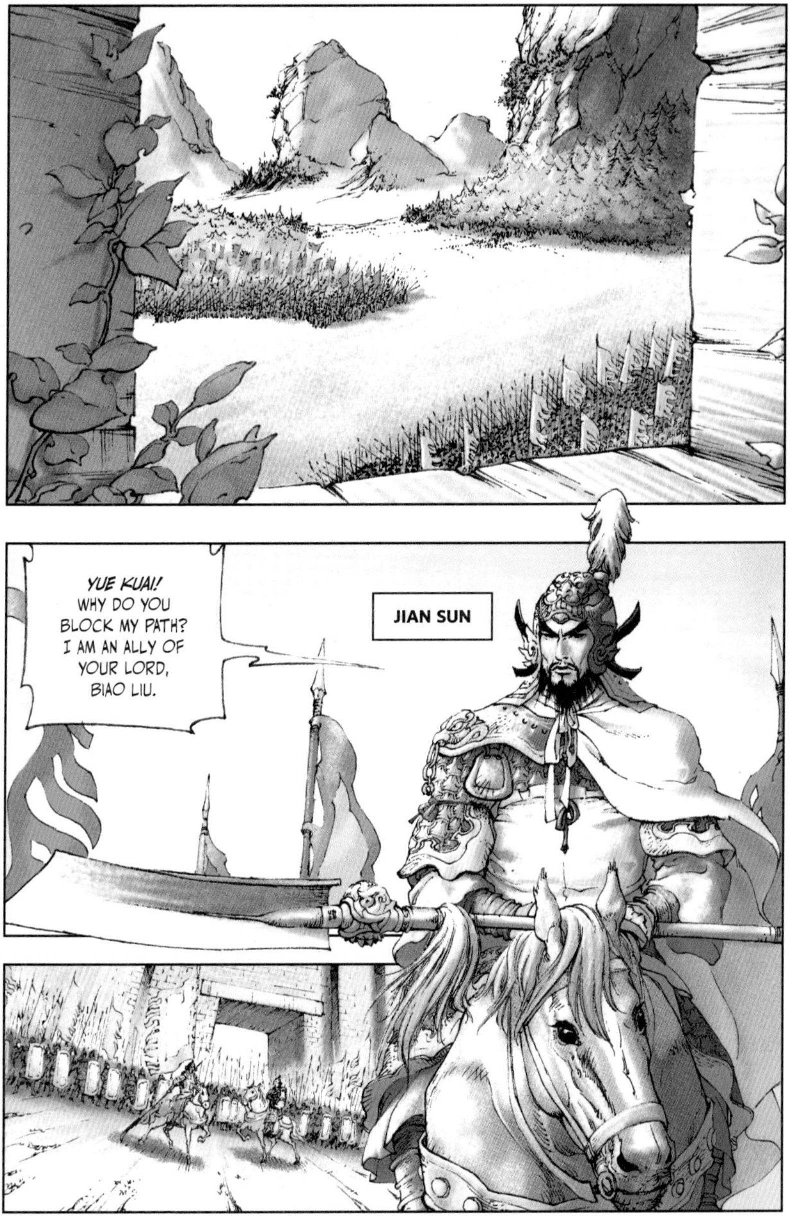
YUE KUAI! WHY DO YOU BLOCK MY PATH? I AM AN ALLY OF YOUR LORD, BIAO LIU.
JIAN SUN

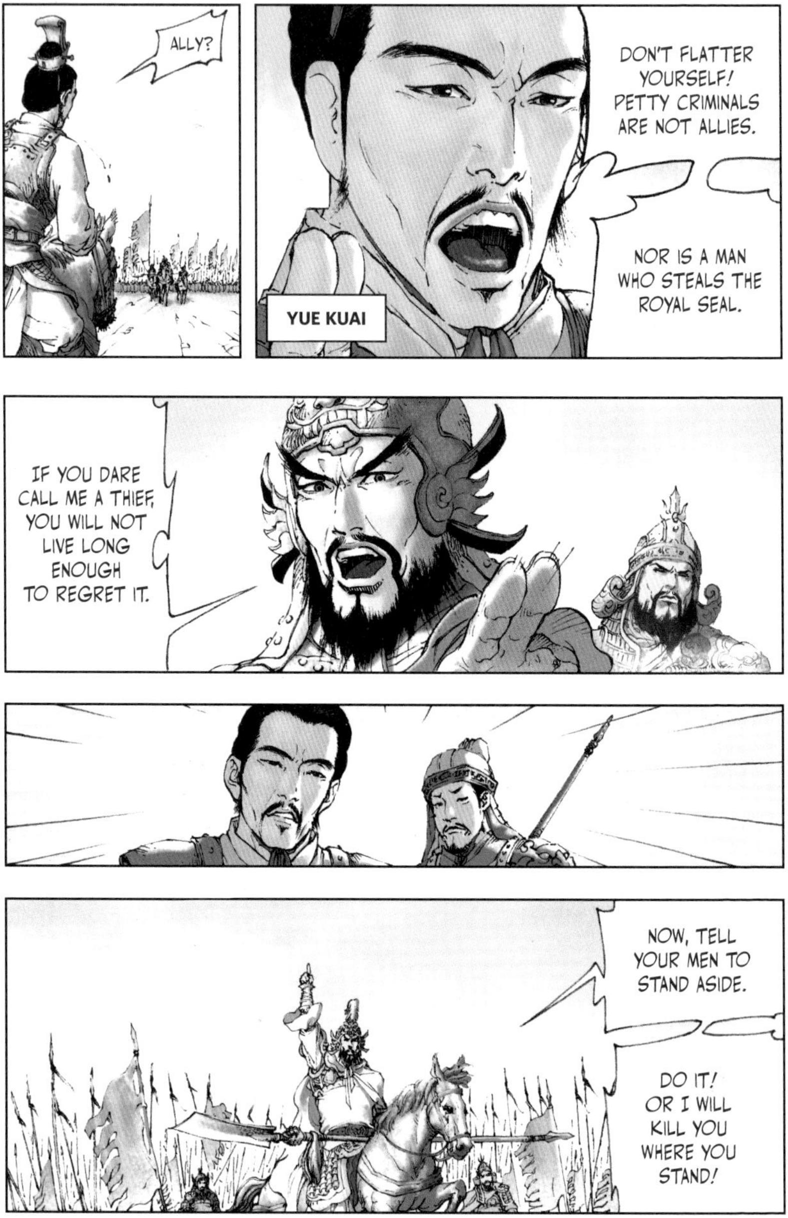
ALLY?
DON'T FLATTER YOURSELF! PETTY CRIMINALS ARE NOT ALLIES.
NOR IS A MAN WHO STEALS THE ROYAL SEAL.
YUE KUAI
IF YOU DARE CALL ME A THIEF, YOU WILL NOT LIVE LONG ENOUGH TO REGRET IT.
NOW, TELL YOUR MEN TO STAND ASIDE.
DO IT! OR I WILL KILL YOU WHERE YOU STAND!

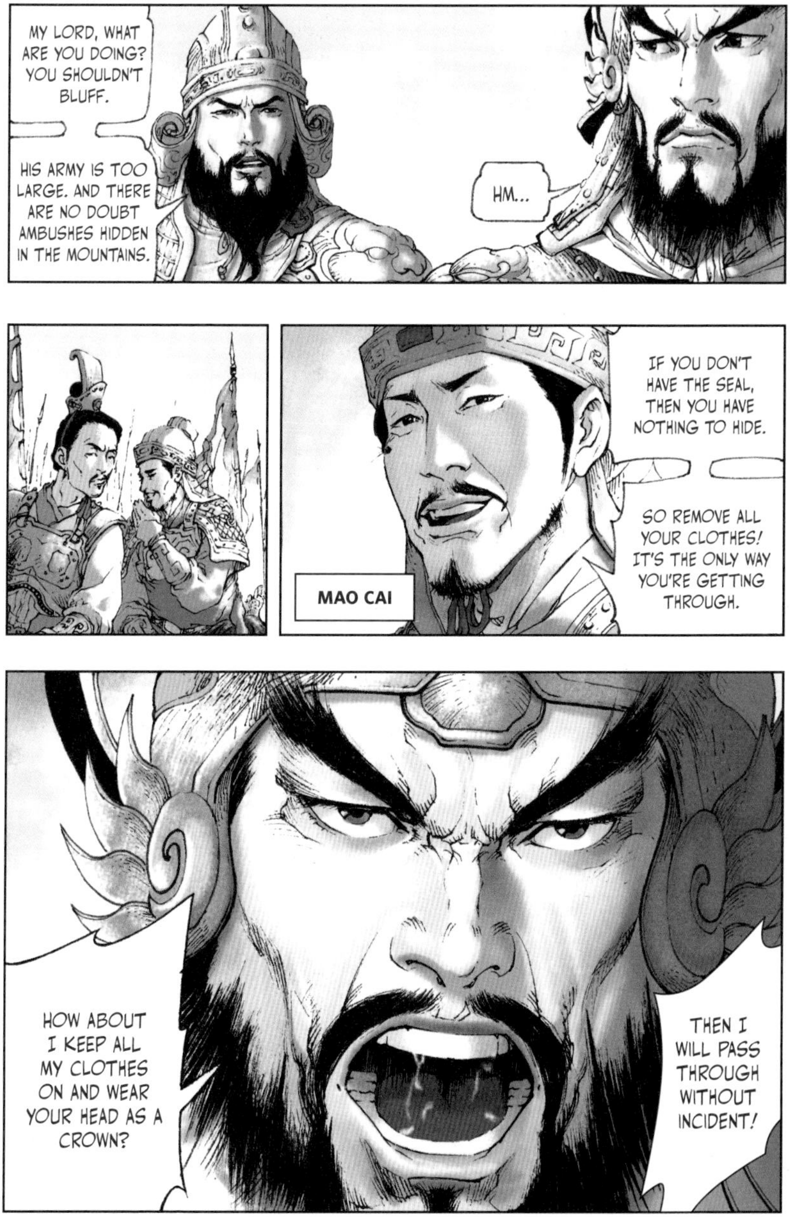
MY LORD, WHAT ARE YOU DOING? YOU SHOULDN'T BLUFF.
HIS ARMY IS TOO LARGE. AND THERE ARE NO DOUBT AMBUSHES HIDDEN IN THE MOUNTAINS.
HM...
MAO CAI
IF YOU DON'T HAVE THE SEAL, THEN YOU HAVE NOTHING TO HIDE.
SO REMOVE ALL YOUR CLOTHES! IT'S THE ONLY WAY YOU'RE GETTING THROUGH.
HOW ABOUT I KEEP ALL MY CLOTHES ON AND WEAR YOUR HEAD AS A CROWN?
THEN I WILL PASS THROUGH WITHOUT INCIDENT!

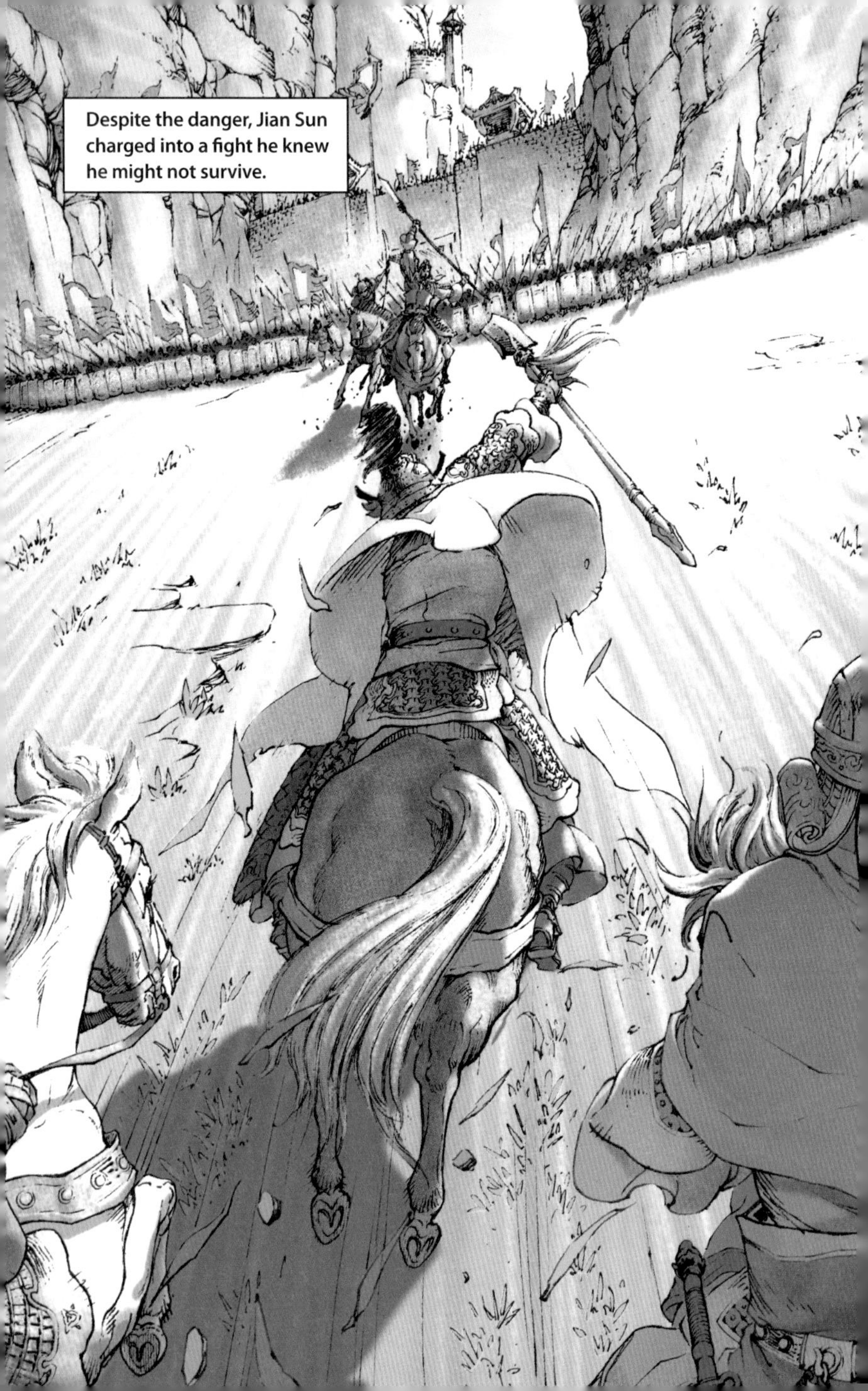
Despite the danger, Jian Sun charged into a fight he knew he might not survive.

VARIOUS HELMETS

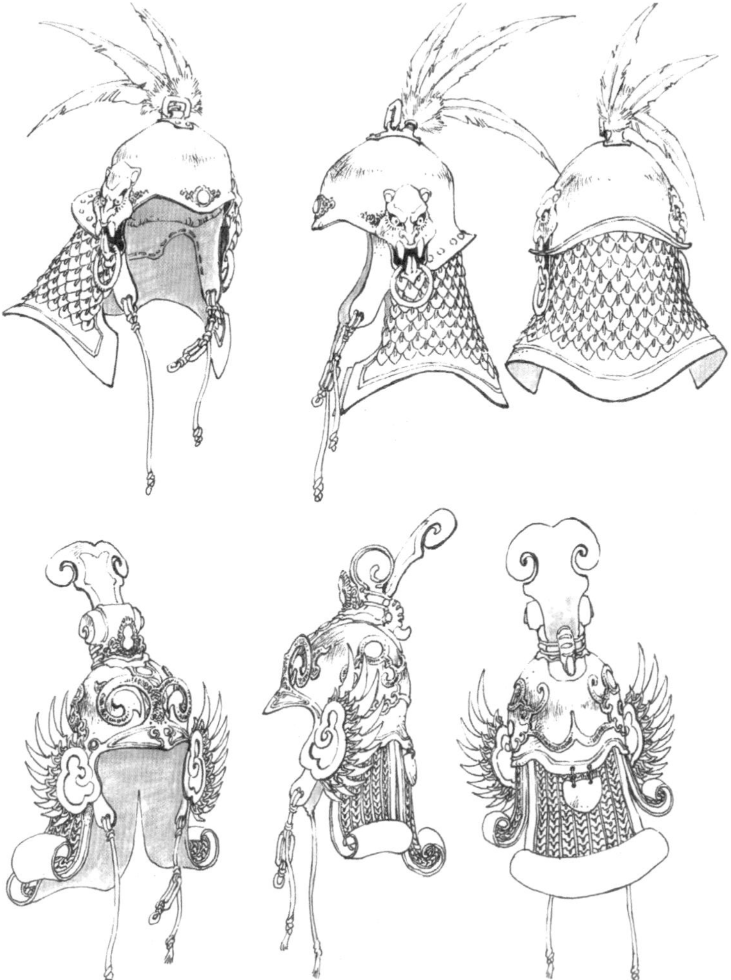

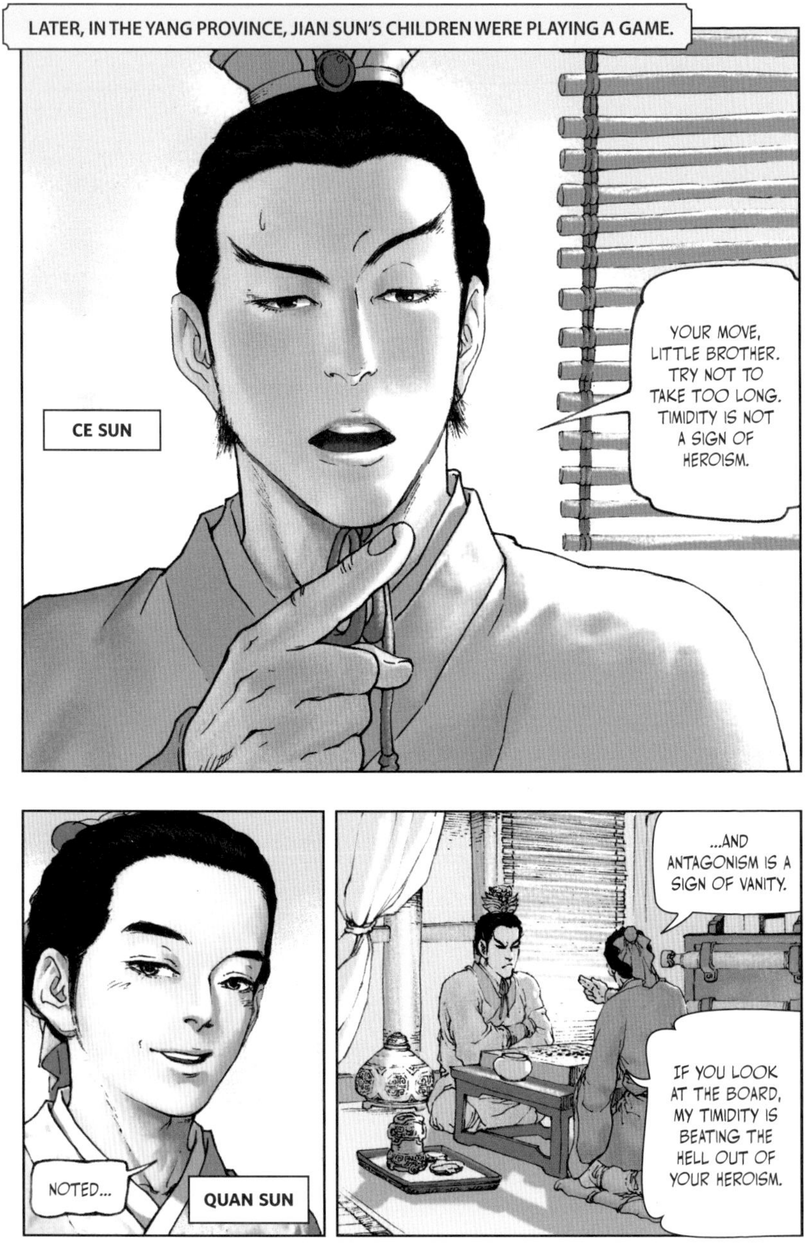
LATER, IN THE YANG PROVINCE, JIAN SUN'S CHILDREN WERE PLAYING A GAME.
CE SUN
YOUR MOVE, LITTLE BROTHER. TRY NOT TO TAKE TOO LONG. TIMIDITY IS NOT A SIGN OF HEROISM.
NOTED...
QUAN SUN
...AND ANTAGONISM IS A SIGN OF VANITY.
IF YOU LOOK AT THE BOARD, MY TIMIDITY IS BEATING THE HELL OUT OF YOUR HEROISM.

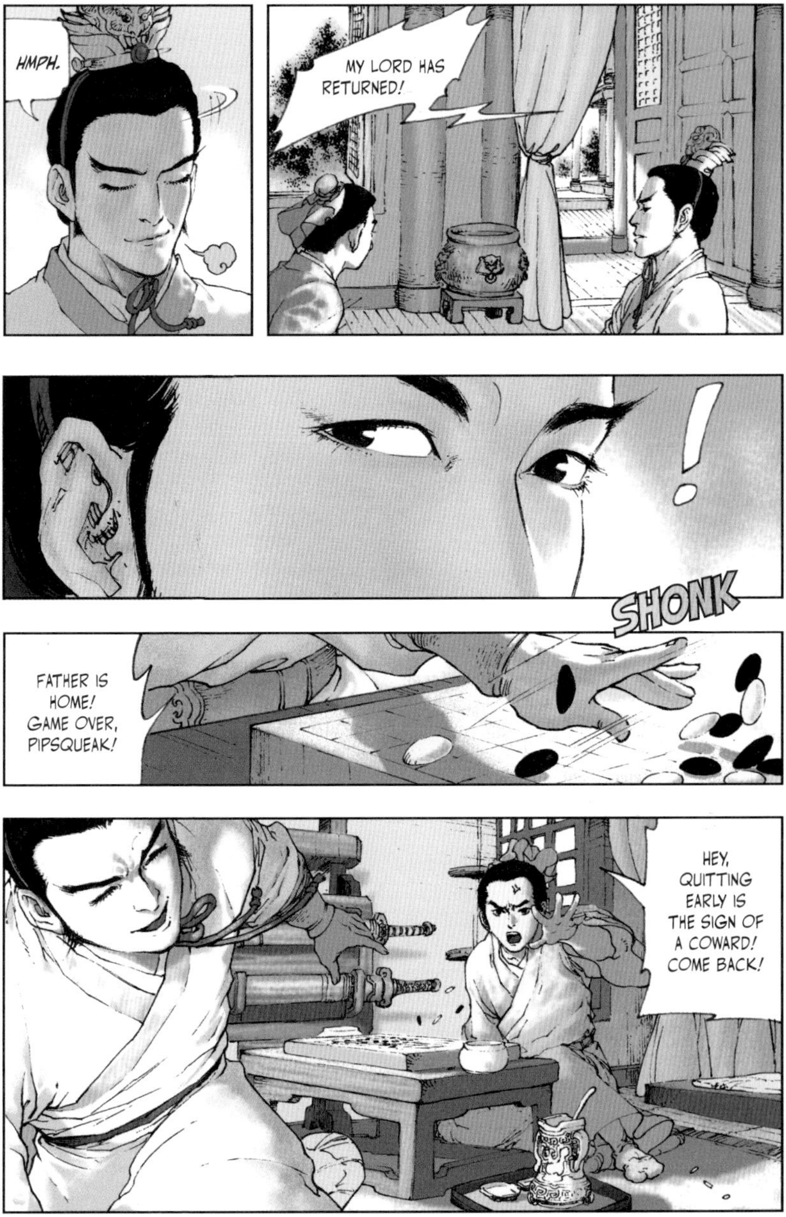
HMPH.
MY LORD HAS RETURNED!
!
SHONK
FATHER IS HOME! GAME OVER, PIPSQUEAK!
HEY, QUITTING EARLY IS THE SIGN OF A COWARD! COME BACK!

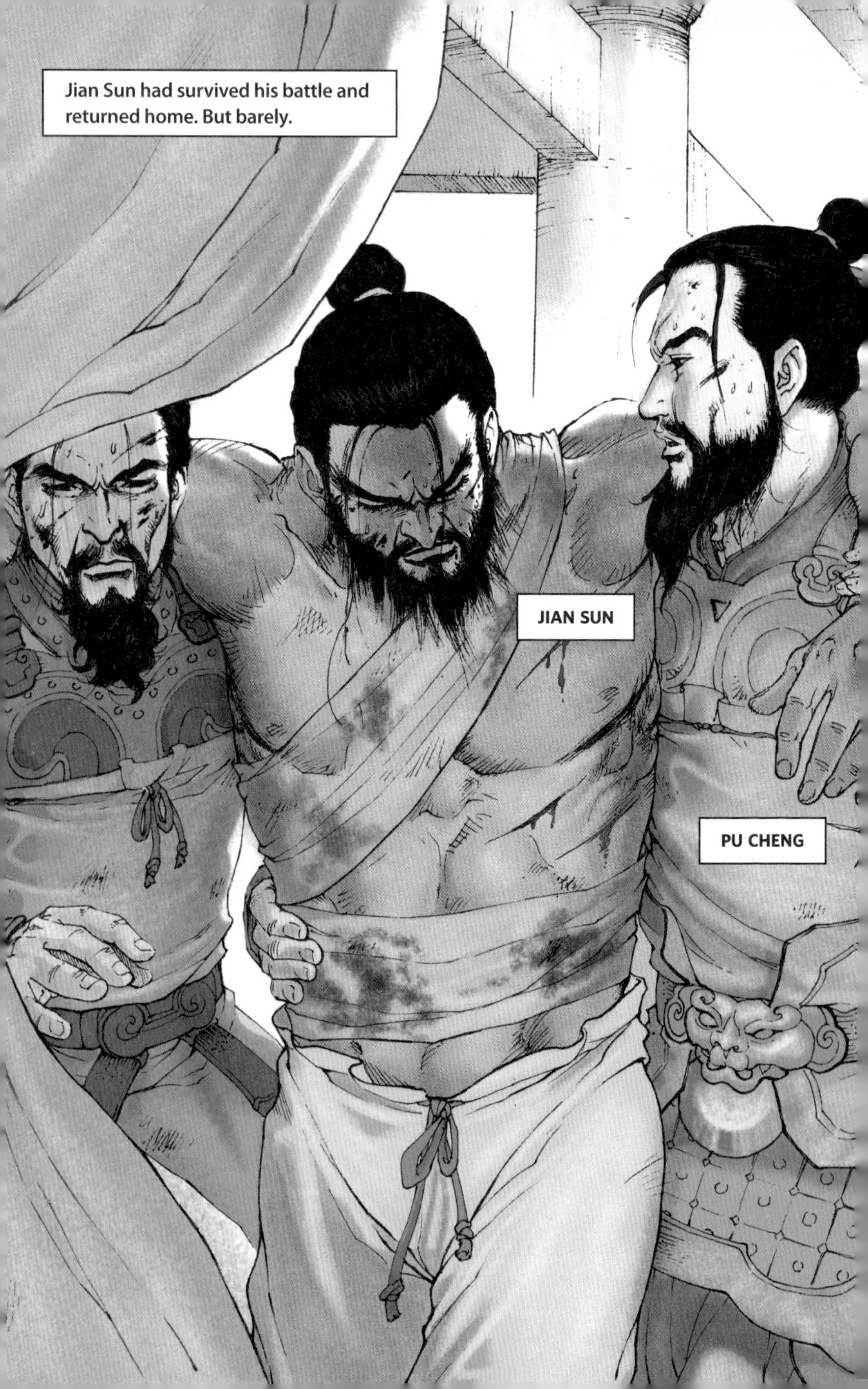
Jian Sun had survived his battle and returned home. But barely.
JIAN SUN
PU CHENG

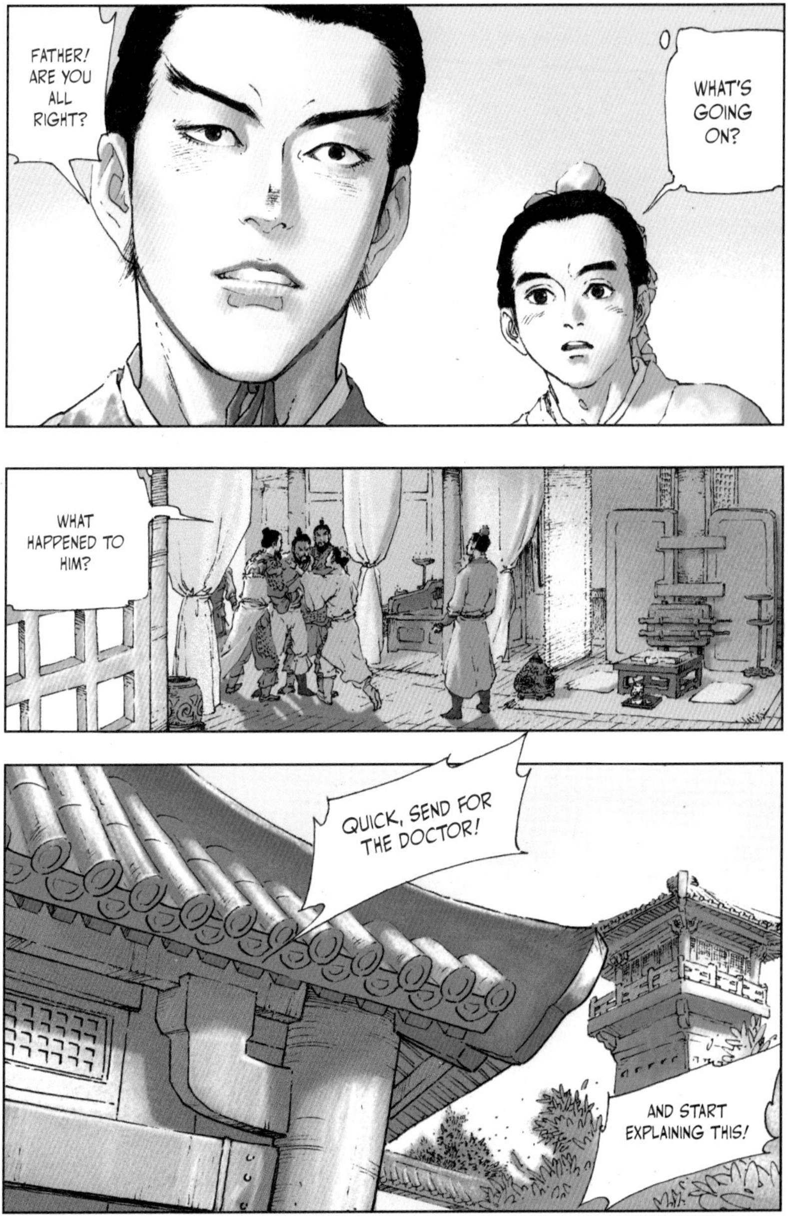
FATHER! ARE YOU ALL RIGHT?
WHAT'S GOING ON?
WHAT HAPPENED TO HIM?
QUICK, SEND FOR THE DOCTOR!
AND START EXPLAINING THIS!

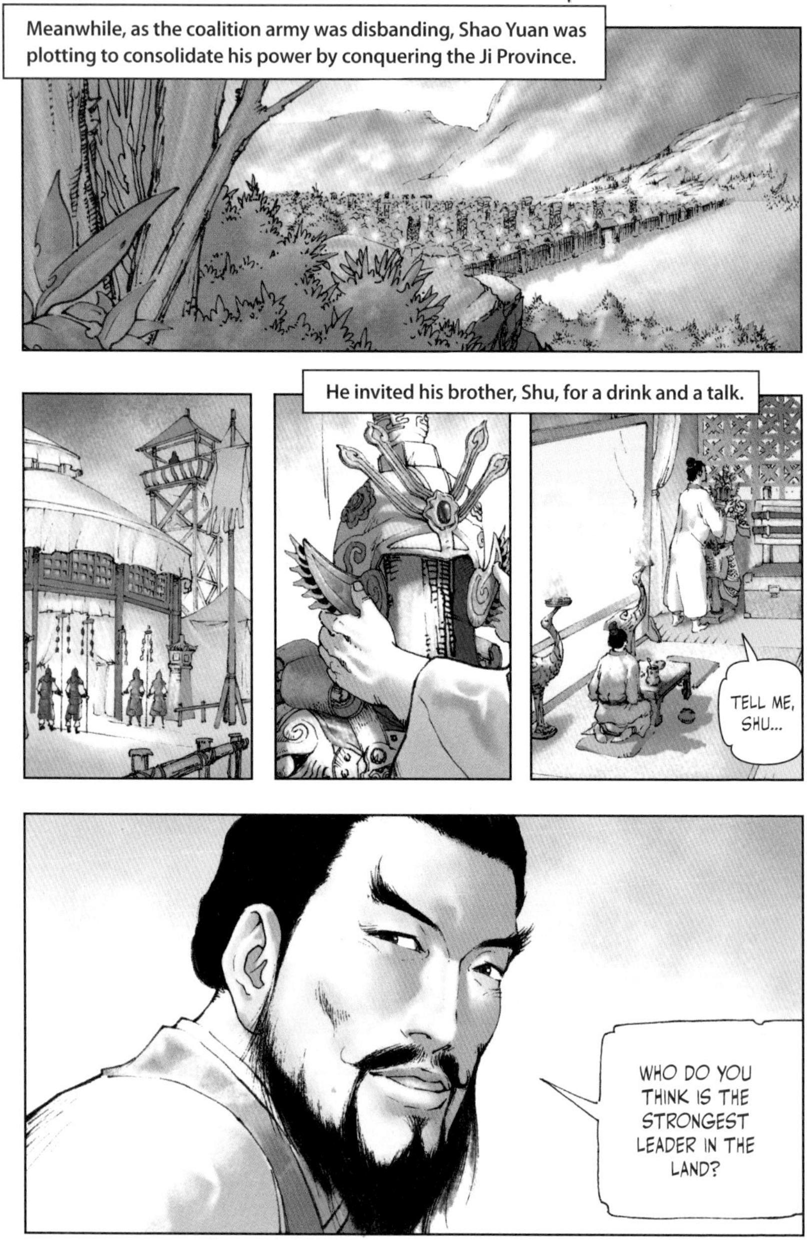
Meanwhile, as the coalition army was disbanding, Shao Yuan was plotting to consolidate his power by conquering the Ji Province.
He invited his brother, Shu, for a drink and a talk.
TELL ME, SHU...
WHO DO YOU THINK IS THE STRONGEST LEADER IN THE LAND?

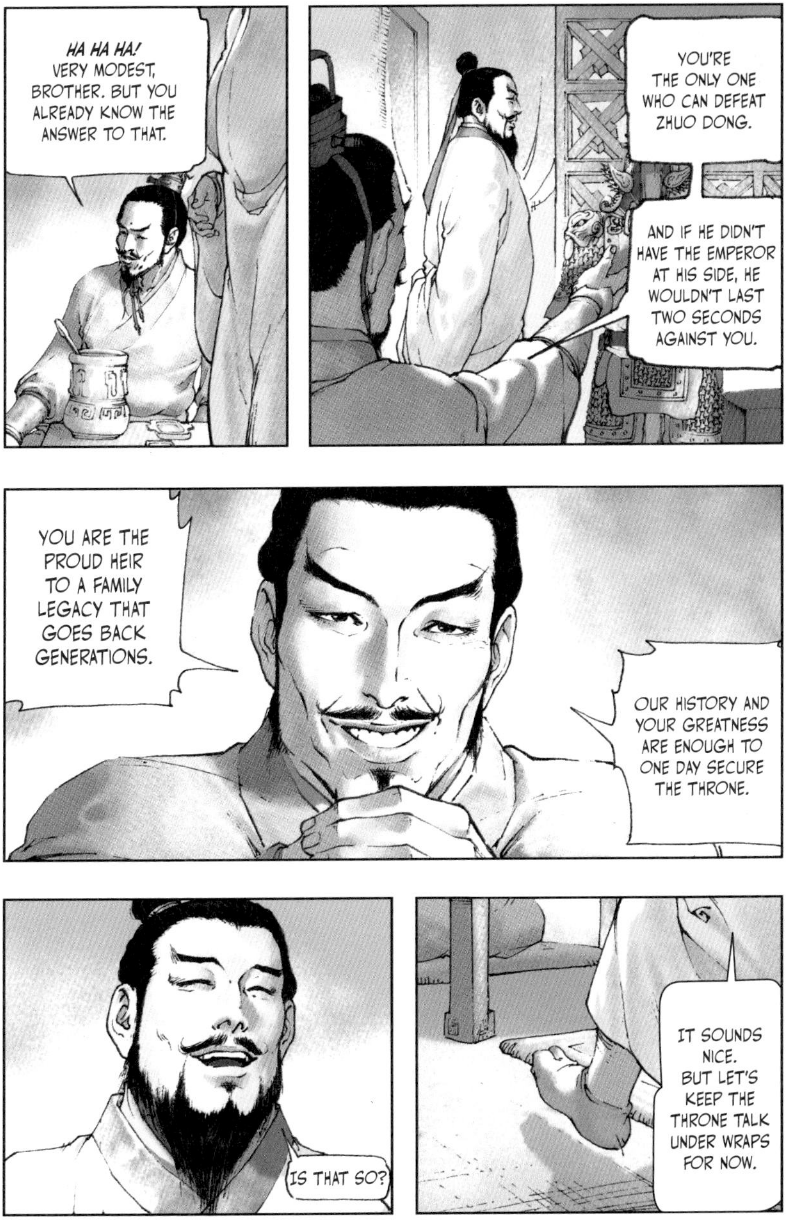
HA HA HA! VERY MODEST, BROTHER. BUT YOU ALREADY KNOW THE ANSWER TO THAT.
YOU'RE THE ONLY ONE WHO CAN DEFEAT ZHUO DONG.
AND IF HE DIDN'T HAVE THE EMPEROR AT HIS SIDE, HE WOULDN'T LAST TWO SECONDS AGAINST YOU.
YOU ARE THE PROUD HEIR TO A FAMILY LEGACY THAT GOES BACK GENERATIONS.
OUR HISTORY AND YOUR GREATNESS ARE ENOUGH TO ONE DAY SECURE THE THRONE.
IS THAT SO?
IT SOUNDS NICE. BUT LET'S KEEP THE THRONE TALK UNDER WRAPS FOR NOW.

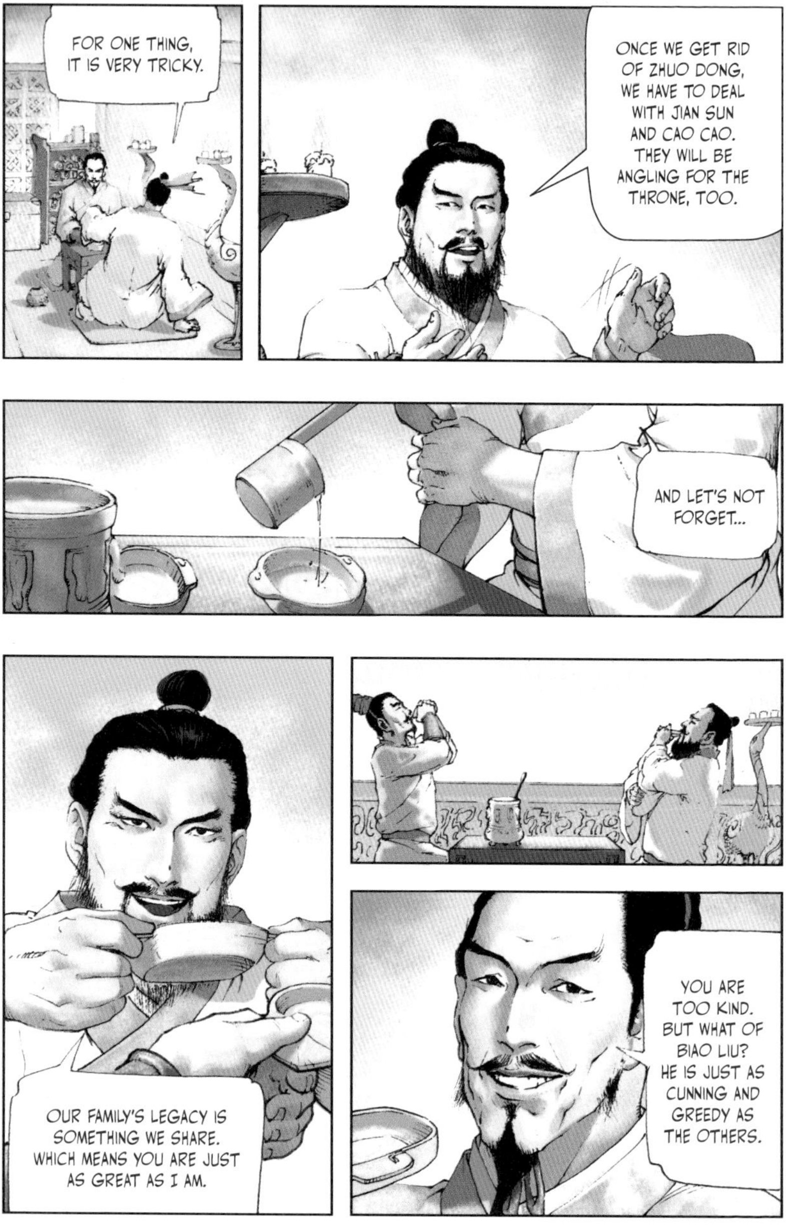
FOR ONE THING, IT IS VERY TRICKY.
ONCE WE GET RID OF ZHUO DONG, WE HAVE TO DEAL WITH JIAN SUN AND CAO CAO. THEY WILL BE ANGLING FOR THE THRONE, TOO.
AND LET'S NOT FORGET...
OUR FAMILY'S LEGACY IS SOMETHING WE SHARE. WHICH MEANS YOU ARE JUST AS GREAT AS I AM.
YOU ARE TOO KIND. BUT WHAT OF BIAO LIU? HE IS JUST AS CUNNING AND GREEDY AS THE OTHERS.

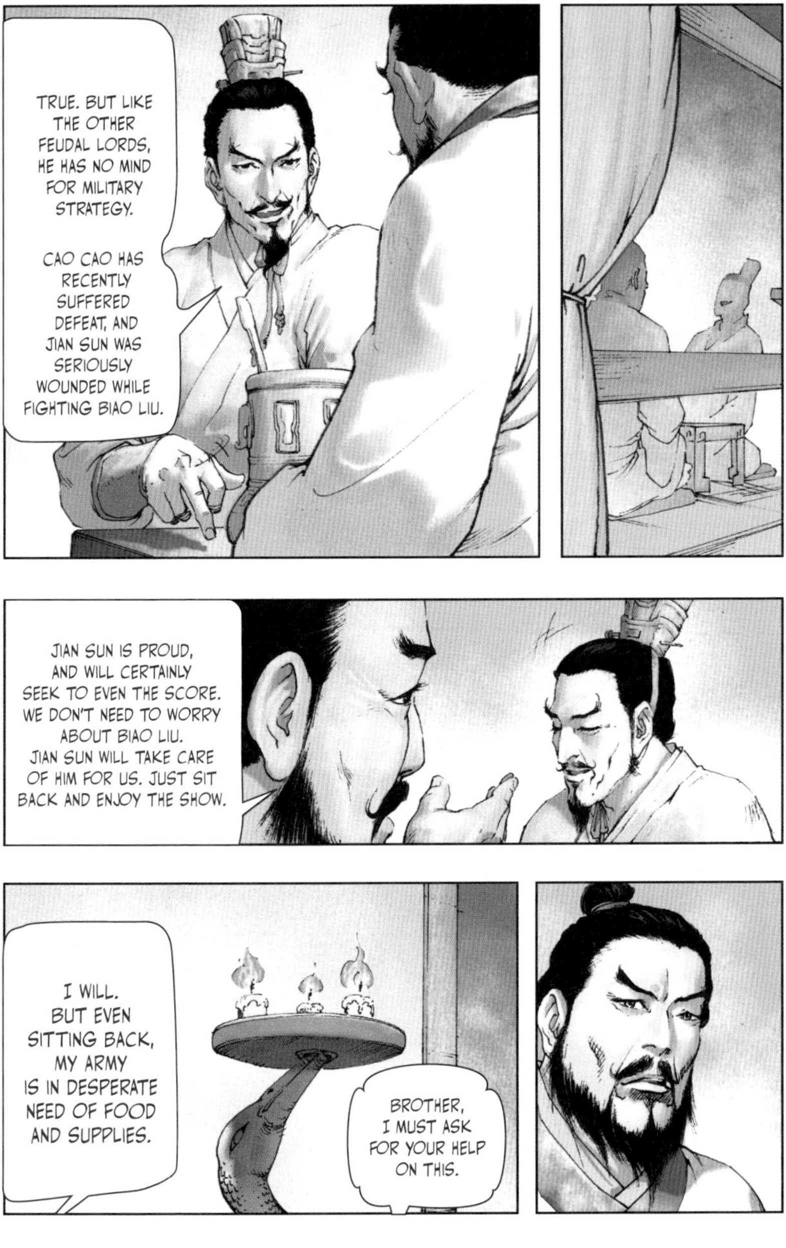
TRUE. BUT LIKE THE OTHER FEUDAL LORDS, HE HAS NO MIND FOR MILITARY STRATEGY.
CAO CAO HAS RECENTLY SUFFERED DEFEAT, AND JIAN SUN WAS SERIOUSLY WOUNDED WHILE FIGHTING BIAO LIU.
JIAN SUN IS PROUD, AND WILL CERTAINLY SEEK TO EVEN THE SCORE. WE DON'T NEED TO WORRY ABOUT BIAO LIU. JIAN SUN WILL TAKE CARE OF HIM FOR US. JUST SIT BACK AND ENJOY THE SHOW.
I WILL. BUT EVEN SITTING BACK, MY ARMY IS IN DESPERATE NEED OF FOOD AND SUPPLIES.
BROTHER, I MUST ASK FOR YOUR HELP ON THIS.

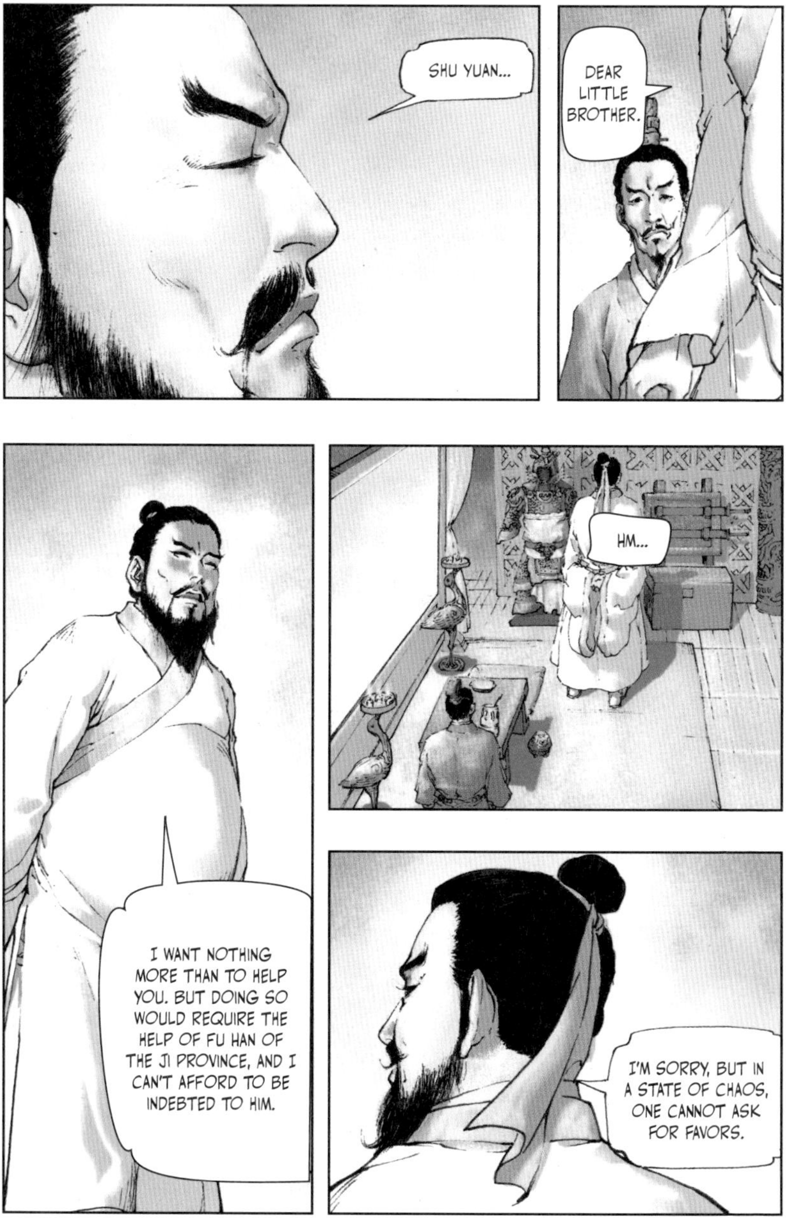
SHU YUAN...
DEAR LITTLE BROTHER.
HM...
I WANT NOTHING MORE THAN TO HELP YOU. BUT DOING SO WOULD REQUIRE THE HELP OF FU HAN OF THE JI PROVINCE, AND I CAN'T AFFORD TO BE INDEBTED TO HIM.
I'M SORRY, BUT IN A STATE OF CHAOS, ONE CANNOT ASK FOR FAVORS.

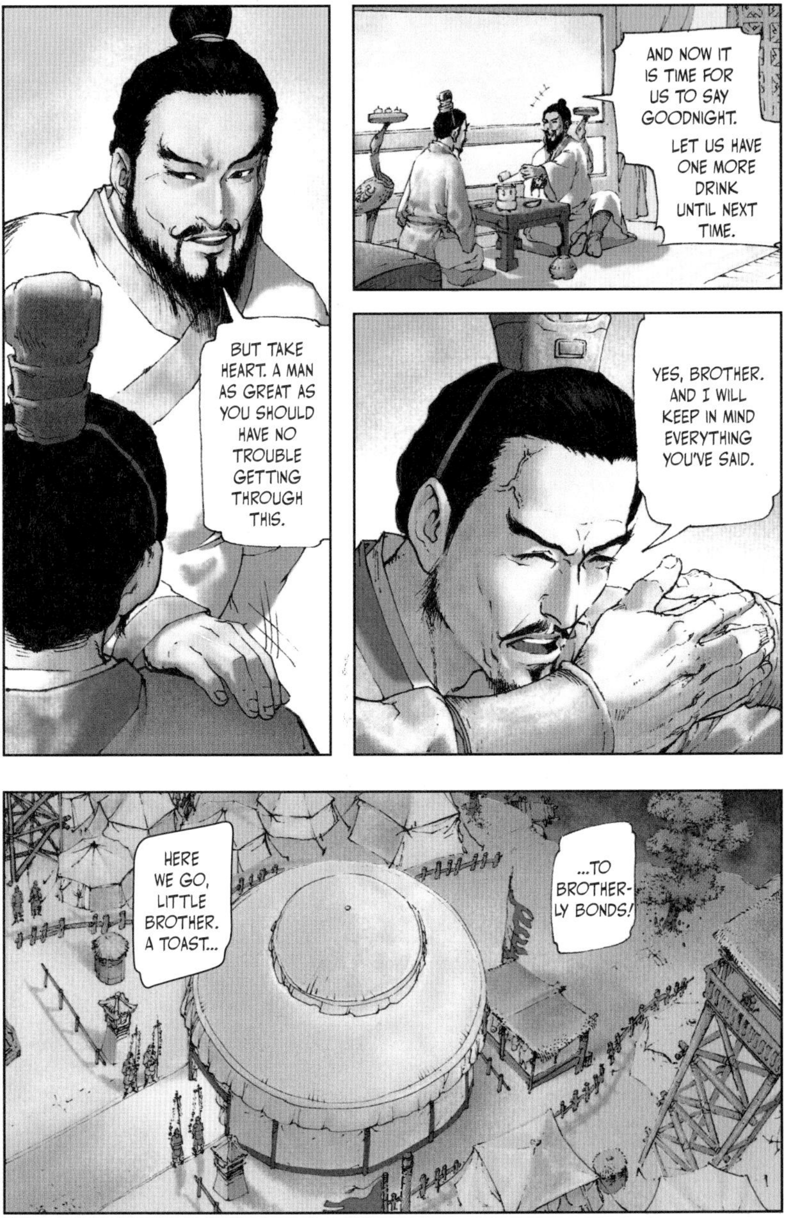
BUT TAKE HEART. A MAN AS GREAT AS YOU SHOULD HAVE NO TROUBLE GETTING THROUGH THIS.
AND NOW IT IS TIME FOR US TO SAY GOODNIGHT.
LET US HAVE ONE MORE DRINK UNTIL NEXT TIME.
YES, BROTHER. AND I WILL KEEP IN MIND EVERYTHING YOU'VE SAID.
HERE WE GO, LITTLE BROTHER. A TOAST...
...TO BROTHERLY BONDS!

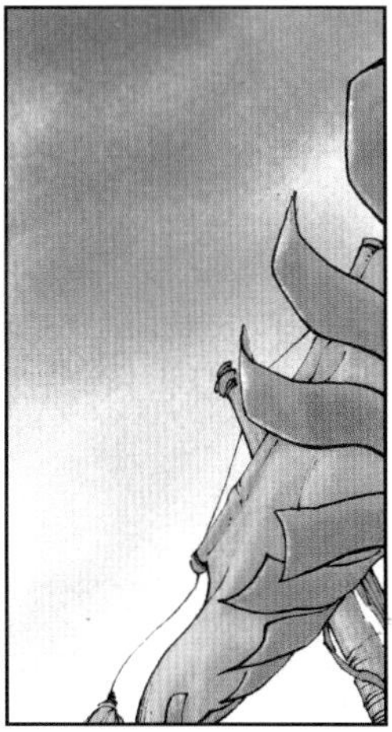

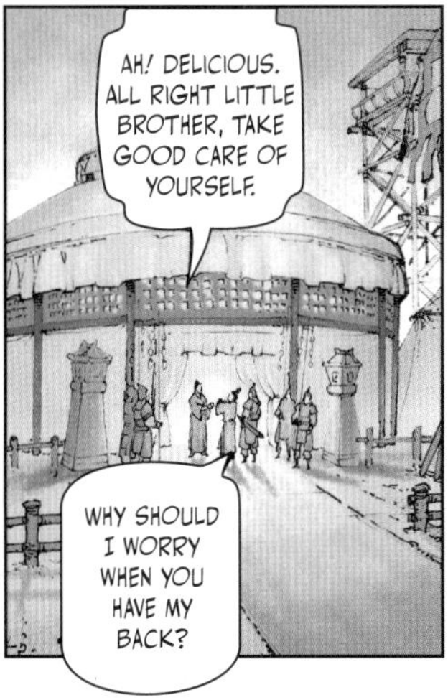
AH! DELICIOUS. ALL RIGHT LITTLE BROTHER, TAKE GOOD CARE OF YOURSELF.
WHY SHOULD I WORRY WHEN YOU HAVE MY BACK?

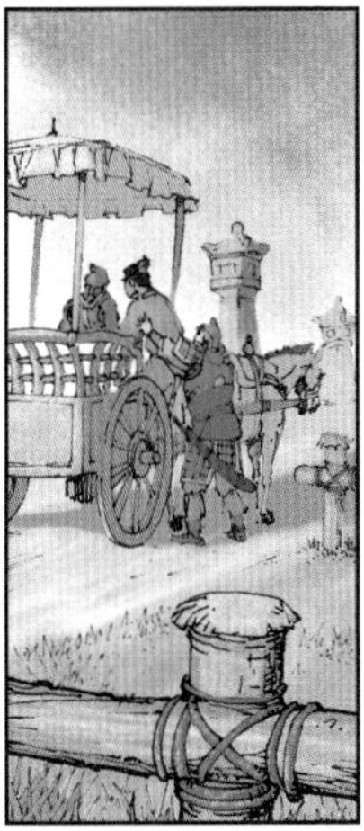

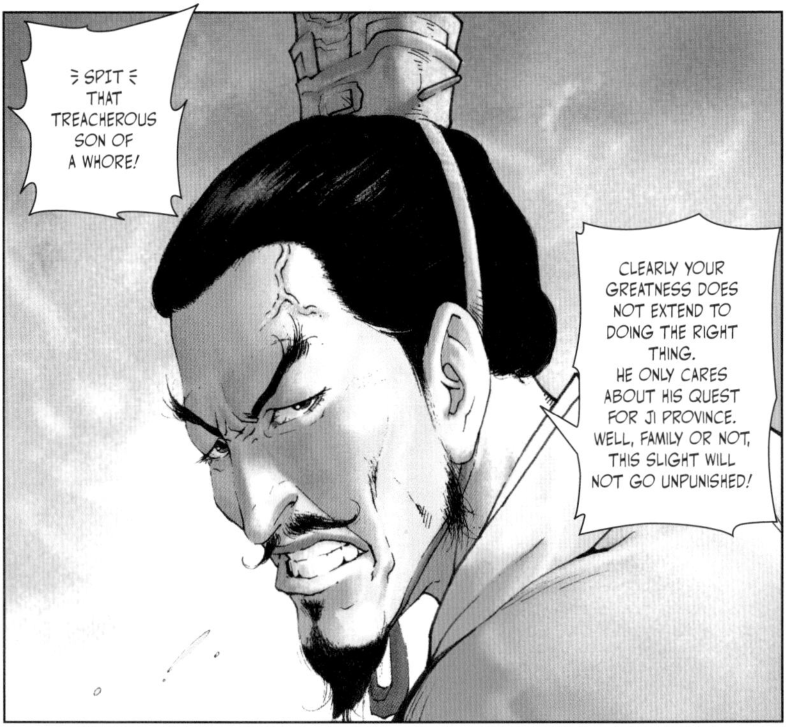
≋ SPIT ≋ THAT TREACHEROUS SON OF A WHORE!
CLEARLY YOUR GREATNESS DOES NOT EXTEND TO DOING THE RIGHT THING. HE ONLY CARES ABOUT HIS QUEST FOR JI PROVINCE. WELL, FAMILY OR NOT, THIS SLIGHT WILL NOT GO UNPUNISHED!

NATIONS IN CHINA

The Warring States Period	Spring and Autumn Period	770 BC – 476 BC
	Warring States Period	475 BC – 221 BC
Qin		221 BC – 206 BC
Han	Pre-Han	206 BC – 23 AD
	Post-Han	25 AD – 220
Three Kingdoms Period	Wei	220 – 265
	Shu	221 – 263
	Wu	222 – 280
Jin	Western Jin	265 – 317
	Eastern Jin	317 – 420
16 Kingdoms		304 – 439
Southern and Northern Dynasties	Southern Dynasty	420 – 589
	Northern Dynasty	386 – 581
Sui		581 – 618
Tang		618 – 907
5 Dynasties and 10 Kingdoms		907 – 960
Song	Northern Song	960 – 1127
	Southern Song	1127 – 1279
Liao		907 – 1125
Western Xia		1032 – 1227
Jin		1115 – 1234
Yuan		1206 – 1368
Ming		1368 – 1644
Qing		1616 – 1911
The Republic of China		1912 – 1949
The People's Republic of China		1949 – Present

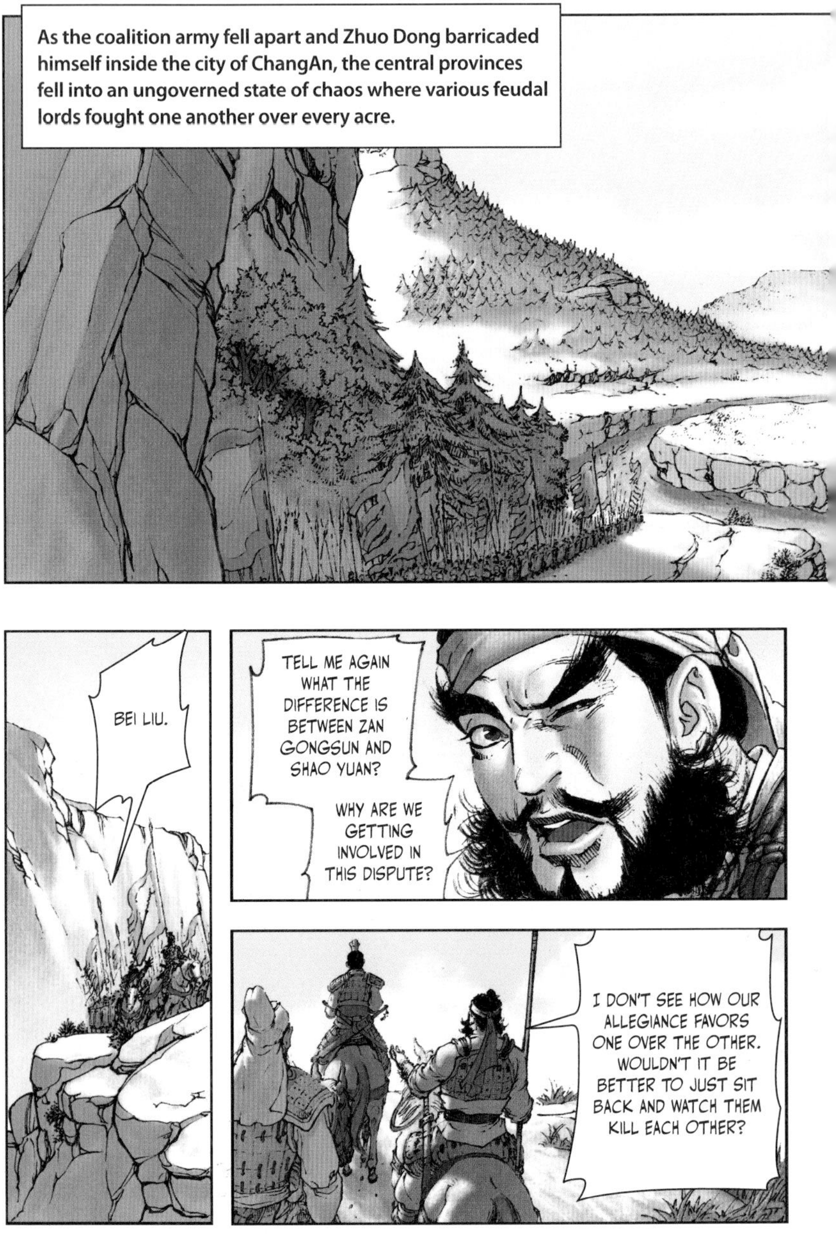
As the coalition army fell apart and Zhuo Dong barricaded himself inside the city of ChangAn, the central provinces fell into an ungoverned state of chaos where various feudal lords fought one another over every acre.
BEI LIU.
TELL ME AGAIN WHAT THE DIFFERENCE IS BETWEEN ZAN GONGSUN AND SHAO YUAN?
WHY ARE WE GETTING INVOLVED IN THIS DISPUTE?
I DON'T SEE HOW OUR ALLEGIANCE FAVORS ONE OVER THE OTHER. WOULDN'T IT BE BETTER TO JUST SIT BACK AND WATCH THEM KILL EACH OTHER?

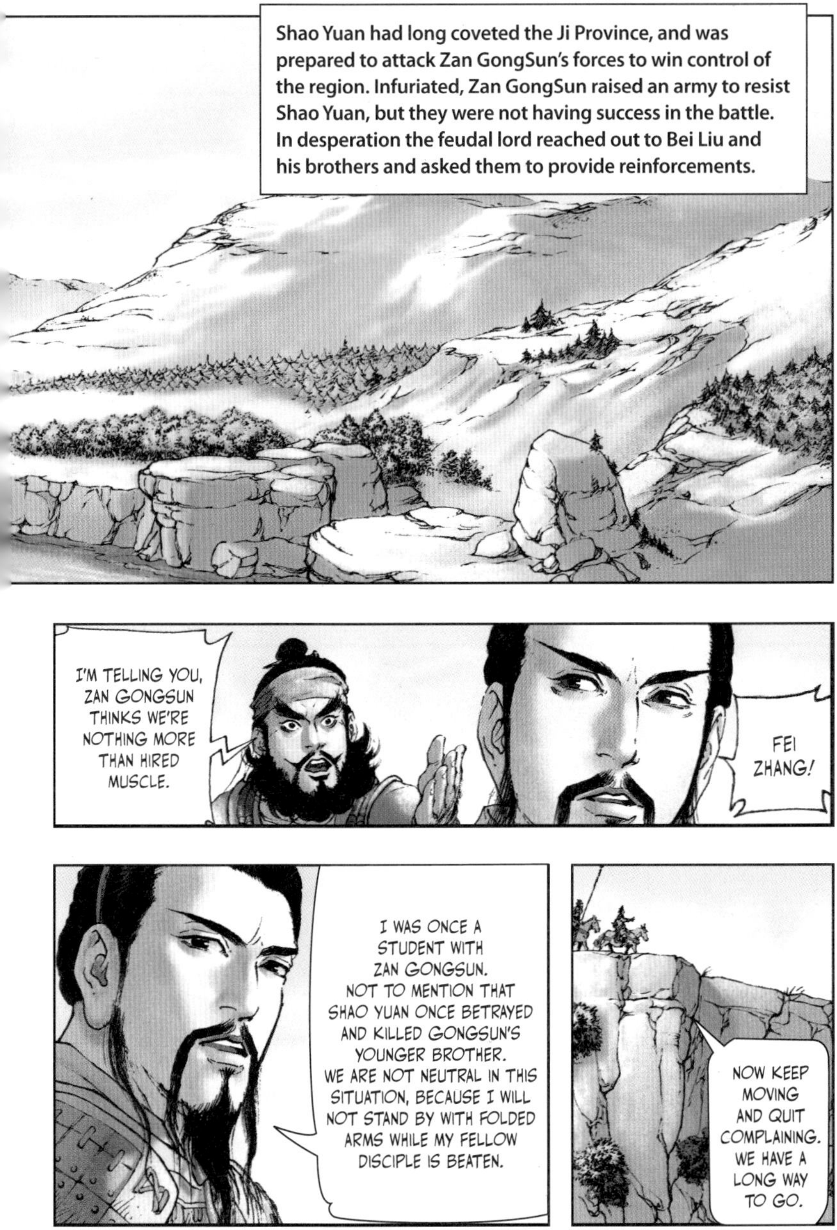
Shao Yuan had long coveted the Ji Province, and was prepared to attack Zan GongSun's forces to win control of the region. Infuriated, Zan GongSun raised an army to resist Shao Yuan, but they were not having success in the battle. In desperation the feudal lord reached out to Bei Liu and his brothers and asked them to provide reinforcements.
I'M TELLING YOU, ZAN GONGSUN THINKS WE'RE NOTHING MORE THAN HIRED MUSCLE.
FEI ZHANG!
I WAS ONCE A STUDENT WITH ZAN GONGSUN. NOT TO MENTION THAT SHAO YUAN ONCE BETRAYED AND KILLED GONGSUN'S YOUNGER BROTHER. WE ARE NOT NEUTRAL IN THIS SITUATION, BECAUSE I WILL NOT STAND BY WITH FOLDED ARMS WHILE MY FELLOW DISCIPLE IS BEATEN.
NOW KEEP MOVING AND QUIT COMPLAINING. WE HAVE A LONG WAY TO GO.

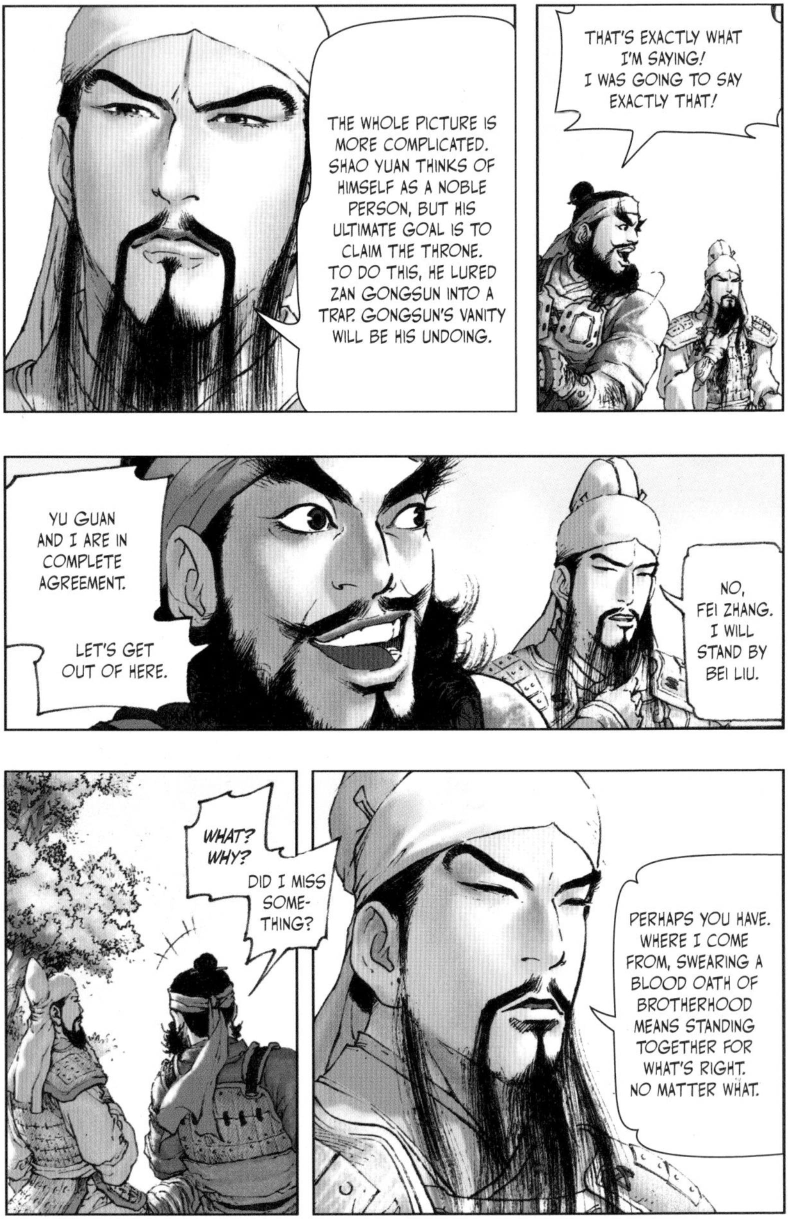
THE WHOLE PICTURE IS MORE COMPLICATED. SHAO YUAN THINKS OF HIMSELF AS A NOBLE PERSON, BUT HIS ULTIMATE GOAL IS TO CLAIM THE THRONE. TO DO THIS, HE LURED ZAN GONGSUN INTO A TRAP. GONGSUN'S VANITY WILL BE HIS UNDOING.
THAT'S EXACTLY WHAT I'M SAYING! I WAS GOING TO SAY EXACTLY THAT!
YU GUAN AND I ARE IN COMPLETE AGREEMENT.
LET'S GET OUT OF HERE.
NO, FEI ZHANG. I WILL STAND BY BEI LIU.
WHAT? WHY?
DID I MISS SOME-THING?
PERHAPS YOU HAVE. WHERE I COME FROM, SWEARING A BLOOD OATH OF BROTHERHOOD MEANS STANDING TOGETHER FOR WHAT'S RIGHT. NO MATTER WHAT.

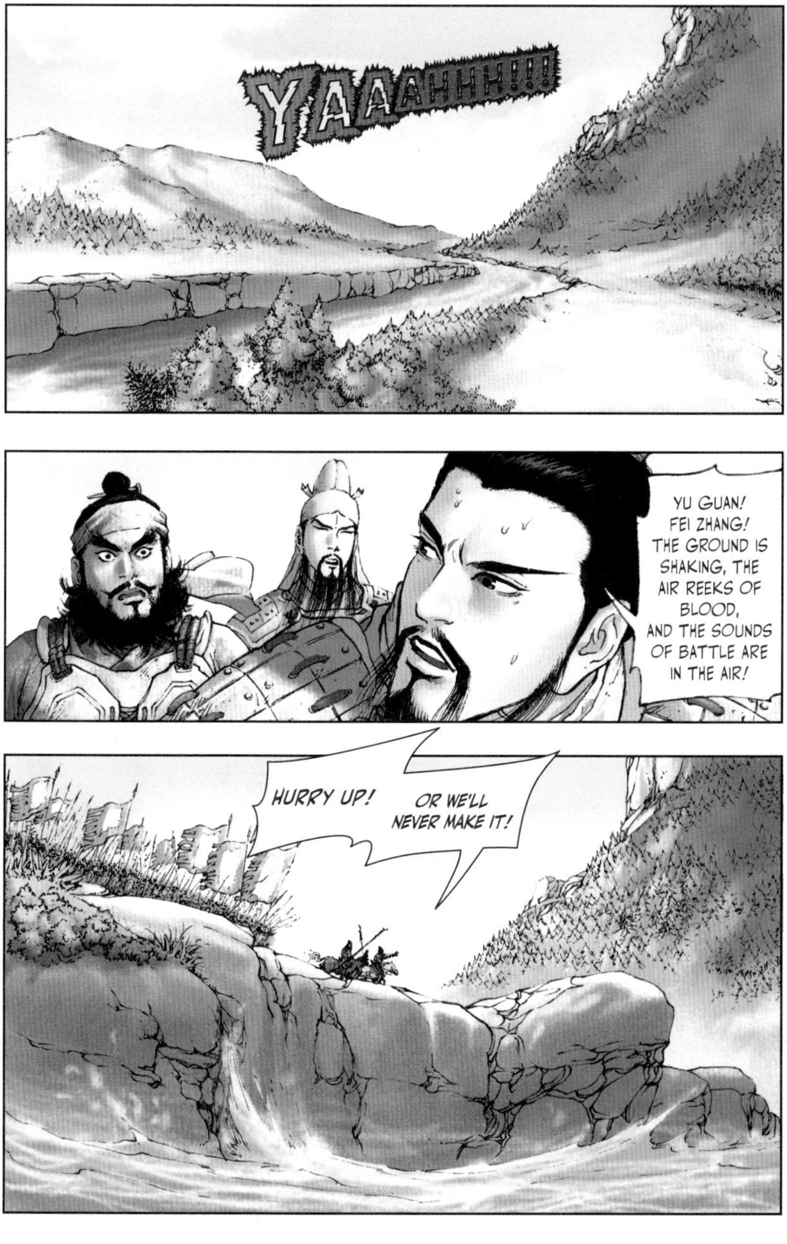
YAAAHHH!!!
YU GUAN! FEI ZHANG! THE GROUND IS SHAKING, THE AIR REEKS OF BLOOD, AND THE SOUNDS OF BATTLE ARE IN THE AIR!
HURRY UP! OR WE'LL NEVER MAKE IT!

THE TIMELESS WORLD OF THREE KINGDOMS

Three Kingdoms is the epic story of a very specific period of Chinese history: the end of the Han Dynasty and the Age of the Three Kingdoms. All told, the story covers several hundred years of Chinese history, up to the dawn of the fourth century AD. But Three Kingdoms is not an antiquated story that has no relevance to the modern world: even though the multi-generation struggle for power – complete with bloody conflict and political intrigue, selfish ambition and selfless heroism – took place more than 1,700 years ago, the world of the Three Kingdoms looks very much like the world we live in today.

While we no longer live in a world of feudal lords and emperors, it is not difficult to see that Three Kingdoms is, at its heart, a story of civil war. And civil war is not an event exclusive to ancient China: they run like a blood vessel throughout history, from the earliest oral histories of tribal Africa to the nightly news coverage of twenty-first-century Libya, from the decline and fall of the Roman Empire to

Abraham Lincoln's preservation of the American union. Like Three Kingdoms, these various events teach us valuable lessons about power and its influence: specifically, they remind us how easy it is to declare war against a powerful institution considered to be corrupt, but also how difficult it is to not be corrupted by personal ambition and the pursuit of power. Perhaps the most important lesson of Three Kingdoms is that people instinctively serve themselves, which makes serving others a constant source of struggle.

Three Kingdoms is the story of a time and place that no longer exists except in museums and in our imaginations, but the themes of the story are not exclusive to the age of feudal lords, blood brothers, and ruthless warriors. We may not wear armor or carry swords anymore, but our struggle to attain power and govern an unruly land remains very much unchanged.

Bei Liu

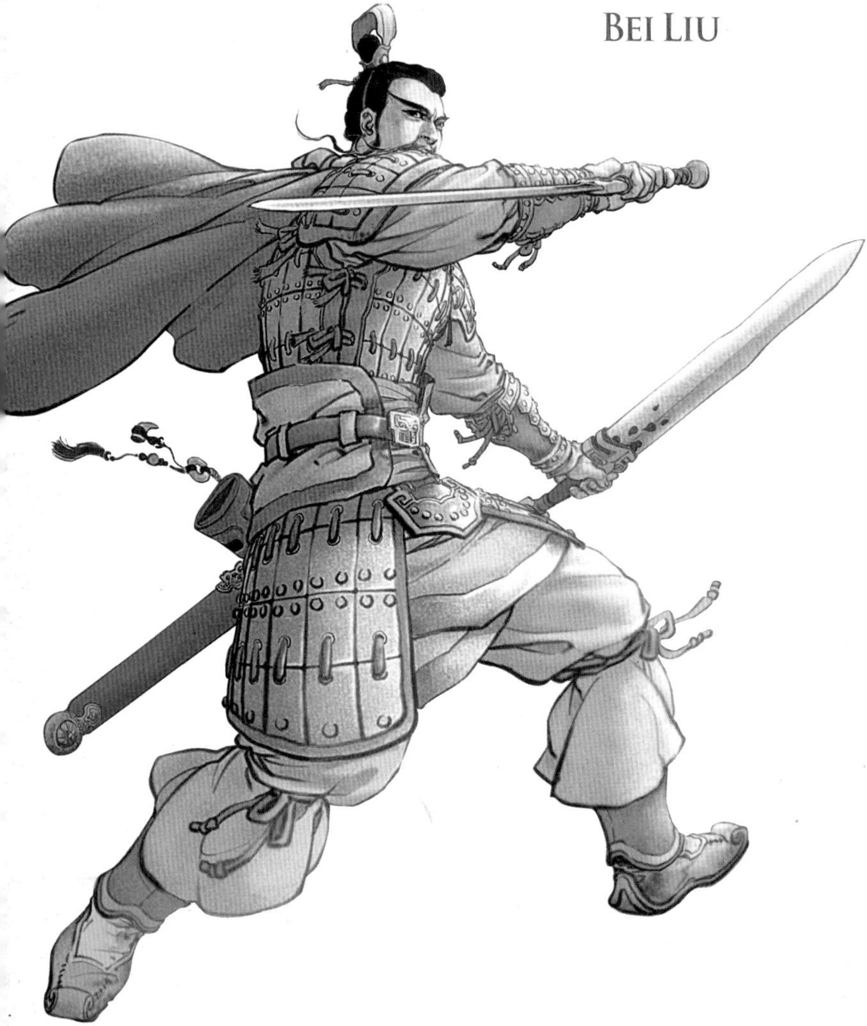

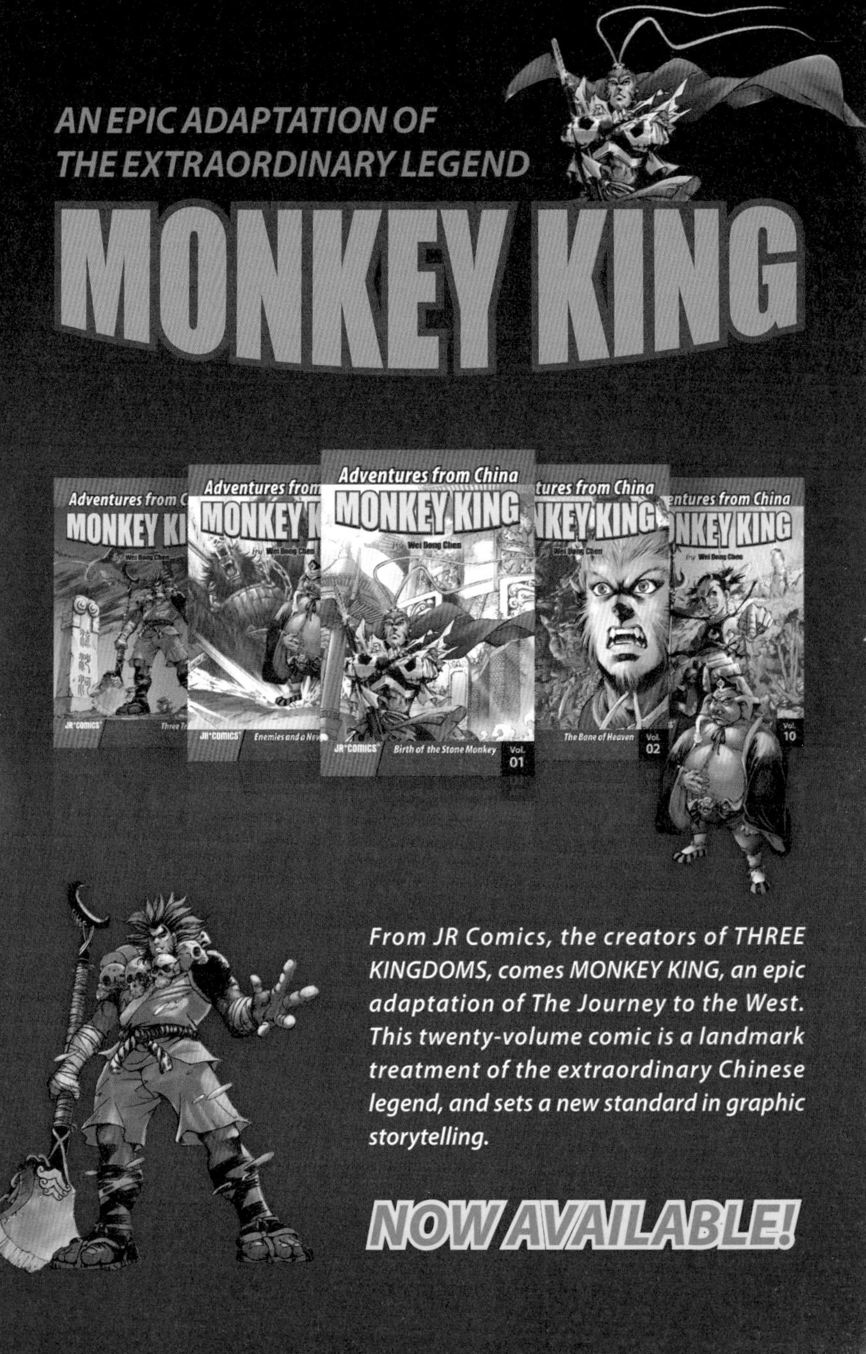

AN EPIC ADAPTATION OF
THE EXTRAORDINARY LEGEND
MONKEY KING
Adventures from China
MONKEY KING
by Wei Dong Chen
JR*COMICS
Birth of the Stone Monkey
Vol. 01
The Bone of Heaven
Vol. 02
Vol. 10
From JR Comics, the creators of THREE KINGDOMS, comes MONKEY KING, an epic adaptation of The Journey to the West. This twenty-volume comic is a landmark treatment of the extraordinary Chinese legend, and sets a new standard in graphic storytelling.
NOW AVAILABLE!

01 13

Legends from China THREE KINGDOMS

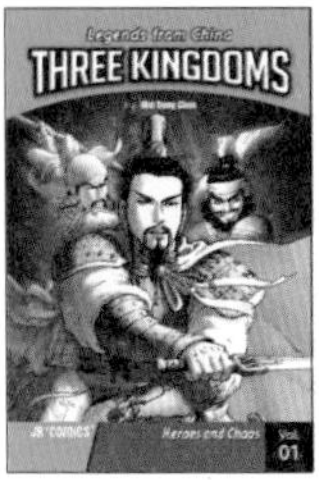
Legends from China
THREE KINGDOMS
JR COMICS
Heroes and Chaos
Vol. 01

Vol. 01

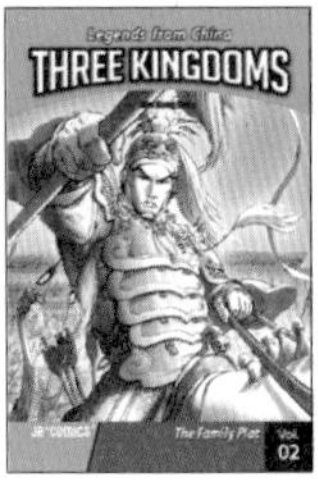
Legends from China
THREE KINGDOMS
JR COMICS
The Family Plot
Vol. 02

Vol. 02

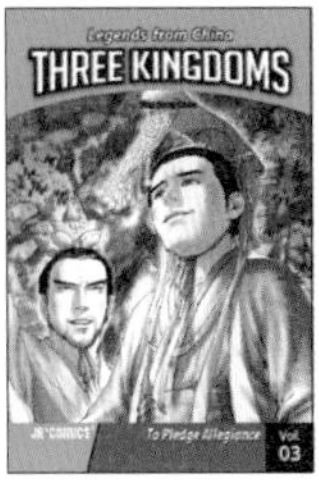
Legends from China
THREE KINGDOMS
JR COMICS
To Pledge Allegiance
Vol. 03

Vol. 03

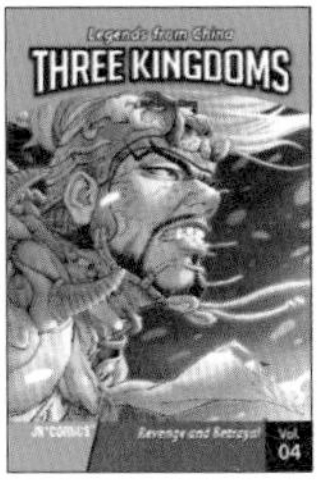
Legends from China
THREE KINGDOMS
JR COMICS
Revenge and Betrayal
Vol. 04

Vol. 04

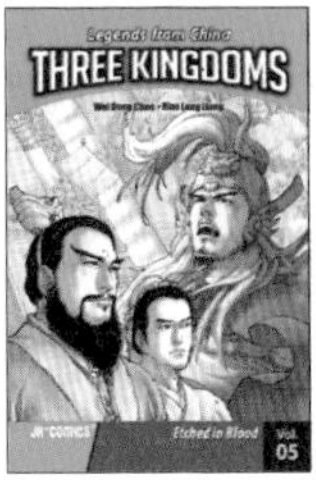
Legends from China
THREE KINGDOMS
JR COMICS
Etched in Blood
Vol. 05

Vol. 05

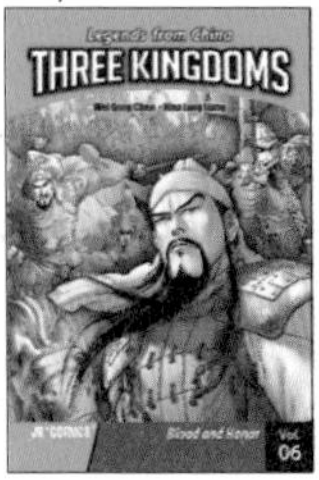
Legends from China
THREE KINGDOMS
JR COMICS
Blood and Honor
Vol. 06

Vol. 06

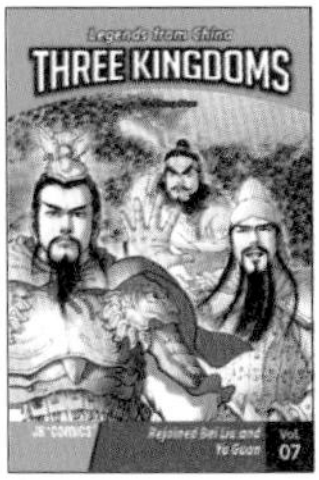
Legends from China
THREE KINGDOMS
JR COMICS
Rejoined Bei Liu and Yu Guan
Vol. 07

Vol. 07

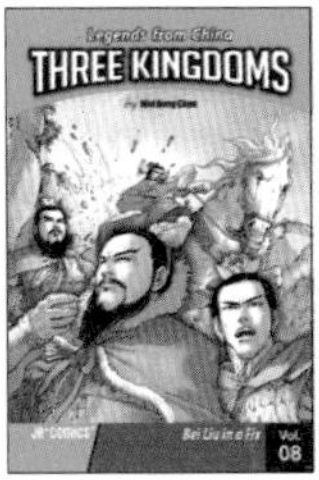
Legends from China
THREE KINGDOMS
JR COMICS
Bei Liu in a Fix
Vol. 08

Vol. 08

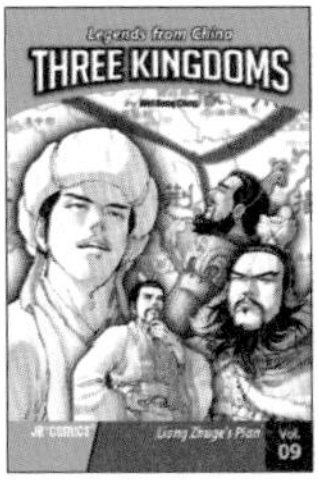
Legends from China
THREE KINGDOMS
JR COMICS
Liang Zhuge's Plan
Vol. 09

Vol. 09

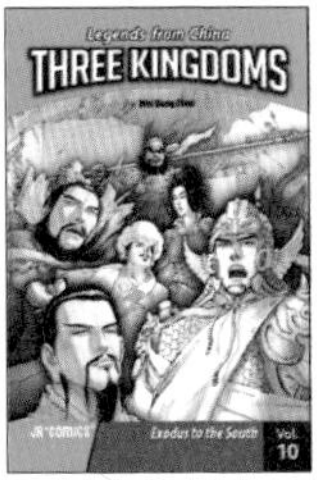
Legends from China
THREE KINGDOMS
JR COMICS
Exodus to the South
Vol. 10

Vol. 10

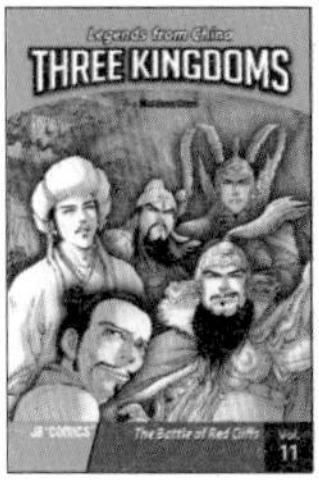
Legends from China
THREE KINGDOMS
JR COMICS
The Battle of Red Cliffs
Vol. 11

Vol. 11

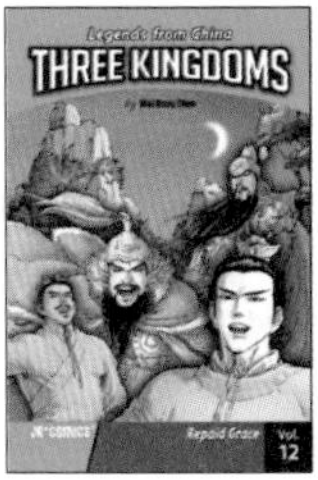
Legends from China
THREE KINGDOMS
JR COMICS
Repaid Grace
Vol. 12

Vol. 12

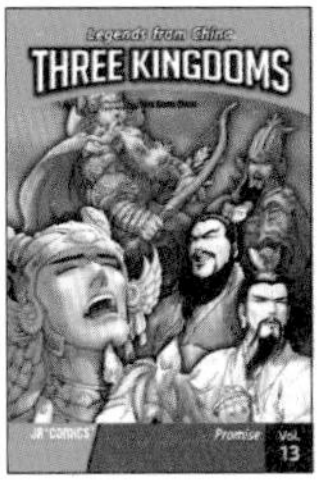
Legends from China
THREE KINGDOMS
JR COMICS
Promise
Vol. 13

Vol. 13

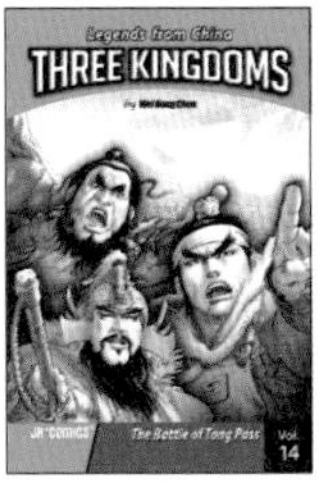
Legends from China
THREE KINGDOMS
JR COMICS
The Battle of Tong Pass
Vol. 14

Vol. 14

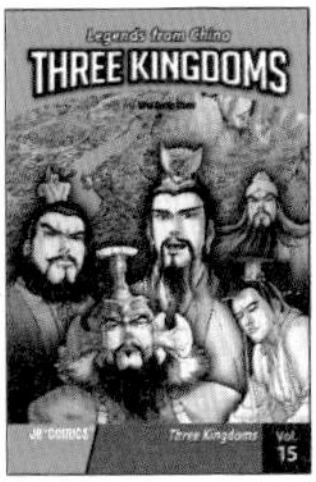
Legends from China
THREE KINGDOMS
JR COMICS
Three Kingdoms
Vol. 15

Vol. 15

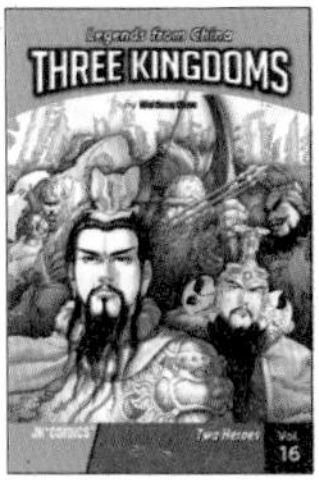
Legends from China
THREE KINGDOMS
JR COMICS
Two Heroes
Vol. 16

Vol. 16

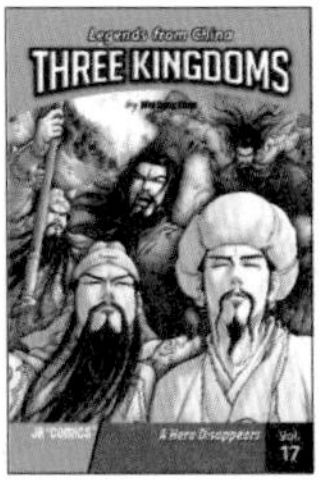
Legends from China
THREE KINGDOMS
JR COMICS
A Hero Disappears
Vol. 17

Vol. 17

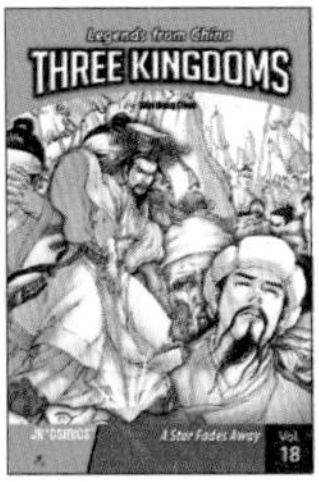
Legends from China
THREE KINGDOMS
JR COMICS
A Star Fades Away
Vol. 18

Vol. 18

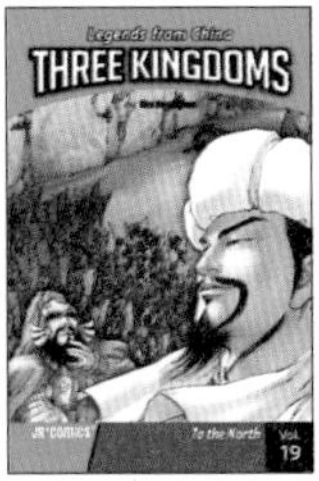
Legends from China
THREE KINGDOMS
JR COMICS
To the North
Vol. 19

Vol. 19

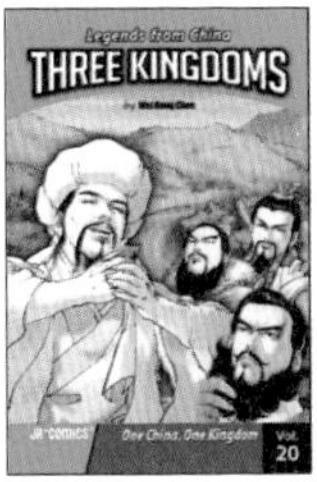
Legends from China
THREE KINGDOMS
JR COMICS
One China, One Kingdom
Vol. 20

Vol. 20